ROGUE ASCENSION

Book 1: A Progression LitRPG

Hunter Mythos

COVER

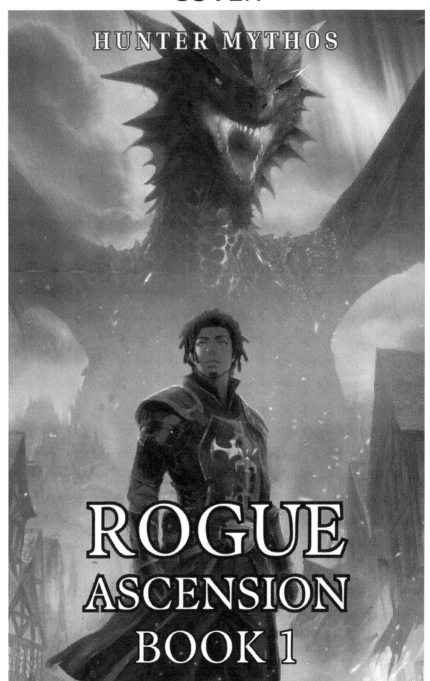

HUNTER MYTHOS

ROGUE ASCENSION BOOK 1

This one is dedicated to every action-adventure adrenaline junkie like me.

CONTENTS

1. WELCOME TO MULTIVERSE Z

[Adventurer or Commoner?]

Joey found himself alone in a stone room.

The walls were covered in strange runic letters that glowed multiple colors across the spectrum. He couldn't stare at them for long or his head would hurt.

The other things of note were the dark doorways, one to his left and right. And the blue system message floating in front of his face.

[Adventurer or Commoner?], asked the system message.

"This is a joke, right?" He chuckled. "Alright, it's time for me to wake up. Let's pinch my way out of this craziness."

Joey pinched himself. It hurt more than he expected. The lingering sting felt real.

"Uh."

He looked back at the floating system message. Then he examined his surroundings again.

For the first time, he noticed more system messages. Two, to be exact. Each floated over the doorways.

One said, [**Adventurer**].

The other said, [**Commoner**].

"Do I get more information than that?" Joey asked, waiting for someone to answer.

No response.

This was getting creepy for him.

I remember playing video games and getting drunk before ending up here, he thought.

He'd wanted a relaxing night to himself. His work at the shipping center was getting harder because of the holidays, but he needed the overtime. He could barely afford his rent even with two roommates.

"They spiked my drink, didn't they?" He palmed his face, feeling annoyed.

Life at eighteen years old with nobody to help him forced Joey to compromise.

Untrustworthy roommates?

Check.

Hard job with micromanaging managers?

Check.

Barely able to live because of rising inflation?

Check. Check. Check.

At least I only have myself to take care of. He sighed, wondering if he was going to play this straight or call out this nonsense. *Screw it. My curiosity is pulling toward the adventurer door. But let's not be hasty.*

Joey walked around to check his surroundings first.

He touched most of the walls. But not for long. Getting close to the runes gave him a weird tingly sensation and made his stomach quiver.

He was barefoot and dressed in black basketball shorts and a black tank top – his usual home outfit. So he stepped carefully wherever he went.

He'd hate to get something stuck in his foot and die of an infection.

If anyone was watching through a hidden camera, they would see a young man with dark skin searching every nook and cranny. As if he was in an escape room.

He was shorter than the average male. Young-looking while built lean with some athletic traits.

"Alright. So the drugs are strong as hell. Or my roommates know some rich people and set this all up to mess with me. Or I've been sold off, and I'm part of a strange game. Again, for rich people."

Either way, he was definitely not home anymore. And he couldn't find a trapdoor, a secret button, or any clues.

At least talking and thinking to himself helped him keep his cool.

When all other options are removed, make the best decision, he thought.

He faced the **[Adventurer]** door and carefully walked inside. Adventurer sounded more interesting to him.

Who would willingly choose the commoner door? Yeah, no.

The darkness transitioned into a gray light. When he

looked back, a stone slab closed off the last room.

There had been no noise.

He inhaled deeply and pressed forward. The tunnel led to another room. But the walls had less glowing runes compared to the last one.

Pale lights hovered in the air. No wires. No connections to the walls or ceilings.

He waved his hand around the pale lights. Each one was the size of his head.

They made him think of will-o'-wisps. He nearly touched one, but backed away.

"Nope."

He turned to assess the rest of the room. Two books waited for him on a stone podium.

[Greatness or Steadiness?]

One book had [Greatness] hovering over it. The other book had [Steadiness].

Joey sighed. "Oh, gods of trashy anime and web stories, why tempt me so? You know greatness is the only way."

He was leaning into the craziness now. But just to be on the safe side, he checked the entire room and found nothing suspicious.

The tunnel he'd come from was gone, too.

Back at the books, he touched the [Greatness] one.

The [Steadiness] book disappeared.

The [Greatness] book slid to the center of the podium. Joey stepped back and watched his chosen book do some funky things.

It flipped open by itself. The pages flew by. Then colorful runes floated into the air.

It hurt his eyes to look at them. Thankfully, a system message popped up between the floating runes and him.

[If you had an elemental aspect, what would it be? For example, fire, water, air, earth, or …?]

"Am I getting my celestial signs read here or something?" Joey rubbed the back of his neck, trying to play off his anxiety with jokes. "Oh, wait, did I get kidnapped by a rich stalker girl? Preferably one who wouldn't torture me and is actually kind of nice once you get past the crazy … side?"

He blinked.

"You know what, nevermind what I said. I'm a perfectly normal person, by the way." Hand to his chin, he refocused on the question. "Is lightning available?"

[Do you wish for the Lightning Aspect? *Turn yourself into a walking light show. Electrocute your enemies. Avoid the water or electrocute yourself. Maybe you'll smell as crispy as your victims.*]

Joey raised an eyebrow at the words for lightning. "Well, clearly that aspect has a dark connotation to it. And I'm a little unsure about messing with lightning. It's not really my go to element."

"Let's try something else. Fire Aspect?"

[Do you wish for the Fire Aspect? *Burn it all! The village. The villagers! The baby villagers! Burn, burn, burn!*]

"Bro, what is with these grim descriptions?!" Joey shouted. "That's not enticing at all. Why is it written this way?"

[Do you wish for the Writer Aspect? *Scribble down your* *hopes and dreams. Create unreal wonders from your thoughts. Keep yourself entertained even if nobody finds your writing in the dump.*]

Joey winced. That aspect description was the most brutal of all. But it showed the flexible range of the elemental aspects.

I'm wondering if the descriptions are there to warn of the follies.

If each aspect was given a negative description, it was a test of willpower to choose an aspect, anyway.

"Ah. So you really should go after the one you want regardless of the negatives." Joey nodded to himself. That felt right. "Is shade a thing?"

[**Do you wish for the Shade Aspect?** *Become a shadow of your former self. All your friends will be ghosts. In your house of darkness, you will be forever damned.*]

"Shadow. Ghosts. Darkness. Yup. That's the one."

He always found this elemental type interesting. He'd looked it up while imagining his own original character and story.

He'd never gotten around to writing it. Maybe that was a good thing. He would've been an edgy writer.

The shifting runes and system messages might lead to a fantasy come to life. Depending on how long the rich people running this simulation kept the charade going.

[**Shade Aspect selected**].

A new message overlaid the first.

[**If you had a spirit creature, what would it be? For example, monkey, ox, snake, rooster, or ...?**]

"Dragon," Joey said seriously.

[Do you wish for the Spirit Dragon? *Princess-hungry. Gold hoarders. Wretched terrors of the skies. Pride and greed flow through their veins. Nothing but death and destruction and treasures can satisfy them.*]

"I would be disappointed with myself to go with anything but a dragon," Joey said. *The other option would be the monkey, but I'm not feeling for the trickster angle right now.*

[Spirit Dragon selected].

A third message popped up over the last two. This one was different.

[Select a class: Rogue? Warrior? Archer? Tamer? Cleric? Mage? *The initial classes are your foundations, your guide. How you grow from here is up to chance and choice.*]

Joey stared openly at the selection. For some reason, this felt stranger than the last picks.

At the same time, he felt weirdly excited. There was only one class suitable for him.

"Rogue."

[Are you certain on selecting the Rogue Class? *Scoundrels. Backstabbers. Thieves. Daggers in the night! The only good rogue is a dead rogue. And if they aren't dead, then you better have enough coins to pay them off.*]

Joey chuckled. He liked the rogue description. Even with the negative angle, he had no doubts about his class choice.

It was his go-to class when he gamed, and rogues had great evolutions or powerful skills that made them heavy player-versus-player threats.

Joey imagined the rich people setting this up were

going to pit humans versus humans, so he might as well pick something that could help him fend against the deadliest animal alive: man.

"Yup, rogue." He smiled. "So what's next?"

[Compiling choices. Do you agree with this path: Shade Dragon Rogue?]

It combined the elemental aspect with the spirit creature and his class. That was an interesting system feature.

No doubt, Joey must've picked something unique. "That sounds like money."

[Creating a great adventurer profile for Joey Eclipse.

Preparing for the beginner challenge realm.]

The lights dimmed. Darkness surrounded Joey. Fear and excitement gripped him equally.

Then he noticed a new light somewhere in the distance. Like the light at the end of a tunnel.

Before he could take a step, a new message appeared.

[Congrats, Joey Eclipse. You've chosen the path of a great adventurer. You are on your way to becoming a Shade Dragon Rogue. But heed this message's words before heading to your beginner challenge.

If you happen to die in the beginner challenge realm, do not worry. Your first death will be covered by divine mercy, and you will be revived. However, you will fall from the path of a great adventurer.

And you will become a commoner.

With that said, you are allowed this one moment to back out of the path. You can become a steady adventurer instead.

Your elemental aspect and spirit creature choices will be removed. You will only be allowed a class choice. But you can die and retry in the beginner challenge realm as many times as you like without risking an instant reset into commoner.

Would you like to reverse your choices and go steady or continue being great? Or would you prefer to back out all the way and become a commoner now? As a commoner, you would receive a role, a decent way to live, and be at the mercy of those with greater powers than you.]

Joey shook his head at the longest system message he'd received. "Don't even play with me. I've already lived as a commoner, and that stinks. Steady won't be enough for me. I have to go for greatness all the way."

In most situations, Joey wouldn't care. He'd be happy with being average.

But this excited him more than most things in life. More than free running or playing video games.

Even if this was all fake, he was invested.

And being a Shade Dragon Rogue sounds too good to let go.

[Please walk forward, Shade Dragon Rogue.]

Joey did as instructed. With every step, he felt strange tingles inside and outside of him. It was as if he was being transformed.

[Initializing ...]

Joey stumbled slightly as bigger changes passed through his body. But he kept moving forward.

[Initialization complete.]

Joey reached the light at the end.

[Welcome to Multiverse Z.]

2. NEW REALM AND SPELL PICKS

It was like stepping into a fantasy. The night sky was covered in many moons. Behind the moons was a watercolor backdrop of a starry cosmos. Yellows, pinks, and purples swirled together up there. The artist Van Gogh came to mind.

Joey couldn't help but stare with his mouth hanging open.

Awestruck.

[You've entered the Tidal Moon Realm. Review your profile and prepare for a great adventure, Joey Eclipse of the Shade Dragon Rogue Path.]

Joey closed his mouth and squinted. *Again, I have two options. Call shenanigans or go full tilt.*

The decision wasn't too hard. It was better to believe what he saw and treat the danger of being a great adventurer seriously.

He didn't want to screw up and become a commoner if this was all real.

All in? He thought to himself.

All in! He nodded.

First, Joey observed the nearby area. Seeing was one thing. Feeling and hearing were another.

Right away, the rocky sensation under him caught his attention. He noticed the sound of flowing water next.

He was on a wooden platform in the middle of the water. Looking back, he saw more of the platform, water, and moon-heavy night.

The tunnel he'd come from was gone. It was as if it had never existed.

The platform was more like a steady raft. About thirty feet wide in both directions. No railings.

The rocking sensation under his feet was soft. Only calm waves, if anything.

The next notable thing was the wooden crate in front of him. It contained one book. It had a thick black cover and some runic writing on the surface. No glow.

Joey crouched and carefully picked the book up. He cracked it open.

Colorful runes leaped from the pages. They weren't uncomfortable to look at, thankfully.

A system message filled in the gap in his understanding.

[Congrats! You have the opportunity to learn the Analyze Skill!]

[Analyze (Basic): Some levels, qualities, creatures, text, languages, and signs can be analyzed through a system message. Your profile runes can be examined deeper. *Knowledge isn't always power. But it's nice to know which ancient dungeon pathway has a sign saying "safety is this way" and which* *one says "you're going to die if you go this way."*]

"I'm going to need that. But let me check my other options first."

Joey closed the book and snuffed out the colorful runes. The Analyze messages disappeared.

Looking around again, everything seemed fine, if only very odd.

The Tidal Moon Realm might not work based on the natural laws he'd known. He would check that out later after scanning his profile.

"Profile," Joey said, calling out on gut instinct. It worked. But not in the way he'd expected.

Runes floated out from his body and gathered in front of him. Without the system's extra help, he could read them. They were his runes.

Great Adventurer: Joey Eclipse

Race: Basic Human

Age: 18

Path: Shade Dragon Rogue lvl 1

Skills:

Spells: [Please select three spells].

Semblances:

Essence: 300/300 EP

Mind: 11 (+2 per a level)

Body: 12 (+2 per a level)

Spirit: 7 (+1 per a level)

Free: 3 (+3 per a level)

Joey blinked at his profile. He scanned up and down. His eyes stopped at the spell selection request.

He held back from selecting to get a better understanding of everything. The runes wouldn't explain themselves further.

Yup, getting the Analyze skill.

Joey cracked open the book again. Once the runes hovered out and the system message popped up, he willed to have the skill. The book faded away. The skill runes flew straight into his face, nearly shocking him.

[Congrats! You've learned the Analyze Skill!]

Joey looked back at his profile and noticed a difference. He started with the bottom five rows since stats were always important to understand right away.

[Essence: Your inner power source made from your Mind, Body, and Spirit stats. Used for fueling offensive, defensive, and utility based abilities. Might have extra uses for you to explore.]

"That's uniquely different." Joey sat with legs crossed in the middle of the raft. "So there's only one status bar to worry about. No Health, Stamina, or Mana. That puts an emphasis on managing your one resource."

Joey could see how that was both beneficial and detrimental. Bad resource management could wreck someone's magical fuel and leave them vulnerable. But all the stats poured into essence, so it would grow fast.

And is it safe to assume the abilities include everything on the profile?

Probably.

[Mind: This stat governs intellect, focus, perception,

and essence control.]

[Body: This stat governs toughness, strength, agility, and essence recovery.]

[Spirit: This stat governs willpower, fortune, alignment, and essence power.]

Joey frowned. All the stats were important, but it hurt to know his spirit was the lowest of the bunch. Thankfully, free points were a thing.

[Free: Use these points to raise any main stat.]

Before Joey inserted his free points, he scanned his profile quickly. He noticed a peculiar thing with his new Analyze skill.

[Analyze lvl 1 (Basic).]

It has levels. Joey figured that would be important to train up.

[Great Adventurer: This one is Joey Eclipse from a newly integrated universe with newly initiated people. He has potential and was given a chance to choose the path of adventurous greatness. Perhaps he will bear fruit.]

Joey stared at the part about the new universe and newly initiated people. That was too much for him to think about, so he moved on quickly.

He paid more attention to the next sentences about the path of adventurous greatness.

Was there a chance that I wouldn't have had a choice? Were there people with so little potential they couldn't choose to be a great adventurer? Or even a steady one?

Joey gulped.

[Basic Human: One of the most common racial

templates in Multiverse Z. Perhaps it could be improved in an interesting direction.]

[Age: This human has lived 18 years according to his former solar calendar. Thankfully, this almost matches the multiverse core calendar of 360 days a year, 30 days a month.]

[Shade Dragon Rogue: This path might be one of a kind. Shade grants shadowy, necromantic, and dark powers. Dragon grants incredible power at the cost of emboldened vices. Rogue improves on focus, agility, fortune while having an affinity for short blades, stealth, and dishonesty.]

Joey smiled. It would be interesting being one of a kind. And the potential power combinations filled him with excitement.

Shade Dragon Rogue for the win!

[Skills: These abilities can be learned from books, mentorship, or dedicated practice. They are subtle abilities that are general or specific to classes.]

[Spells: These are personal powers of your class or path. These are raised from within you or gained through special circumstances.]

[Semblances: You need not always face a battle alone. With good fortune, a semblance would arise from the death of an enemy creature.]

Joey's excitement peaked. This was an interesting RPG set up. And he was his own character. But there were a few issues.

He saw nothing else on the raft with him other than the empty crate. He was still in his comfy home clothes. And he had no more information.

"I'm a lone man on a raft." Joey looked up at the

watercolor night. He felt more whimsical than concerned.

I should be scared, but I'm not. I'm ... in a new universe that's part of a multiverse with new opportunities. If this is real, this could be everything I've dreamed of.

He glanced at the water and spotted something passing through the surface. It disappeared before he had a good look.

Ah, there goes the reason to be scared. Joey's heart sped up. He mentally shoved his free points into the spirit stat.

[You've raised your spirit from 7 to 10!]

Joey felt something inside him swell weirdly. It felt like inner strength. And determination. And more. He shook his head and dug into his spell selections.

[Select three spells: Dark Dash (Superior), Shade Dragon Tail (Epic), Shade Blade Extension (Superior), Phantom Phase (Superior), Spectral Hands (Superior), Shadow Clone Magic (Epic), Shade Dragon Claws (Superior), Dark Fists (Superior), Death Echo (Epic), Bigger Backstab (Basic), Cloaking (Basic), Simple Unlock (Basic).]

Joey gawked at the twelve spells to choose from. Nine out of the twelve sounded great to him. *Why can I only get three, dammit? This is unfair!*

Something bumped against the raft. Joey clenched his jaw to keep from shouting.

He rushed through the list of spells using Analyze.

[Dark Dash (Superior): Release darkness in a burst from your lower legs. Propel yourself like a projectile. The more darkness, the more potent. *Wait a minute. Isn't this fire dash but with darkness instead? Ah, whatever. Dark types are too busy brooding to dash around like crazies.***]**

[Shade Dragon Tail (Epic): A ghostly dragon tail

extends from your tailbone. Most won't notice it while it's passively there. Channel your essence to actively use its power, flexibility, and reach. Beware of the dragon price for power. *Have you ever been struck by a dragon's tail? Most don't see it coming. This version is so sinister the lords and ladies should ban it.*]

[Shade Blade Extension (Superior): Coat a blade in your hand with shade. While attacking, the shade will extend to attack the victim's essence directly. Slashed essence can sometimes fall out of a victim for collection. *This is why light, radiance, and other similar aspects exist. To beat back scary powers like these.*]

[Phantom Phase (Superior): Become like a ghost, intangible and translucent. Then phase through solid objects and physical attacks. Some magic may have a stronger effect during this phase. *Ah! Who goes there? Oh, it's you. Har. Har. Can you stop phasing through everything to spook me? I'm going to call a cleric sooner or later.*]

[Spectral Hands (Superior): Conjure multiple hands around you. These hands can manipulate half the weight you can. Spend more essence to make them invisible. *Well, we'll know who to turn to when we need extra hands. Just don't get too handsy, okay?*]

[Shadow Clone Magic (Epic): Conjure copies of yourself. They will have less of your potency but can use your abilities, copy some of your gear, and think independently and as a team. *Oh, goodness gracious, you really can't get enough of yourself, huh? Well, at least we know who will trigger the traps. You, yourself, and your reflection.*]

[You've leveled up Analyze from 1 to 2!]

Joey cut off the analysis after the system's level-up interruption. From the corner of his eye, he saw something dark and slimy rising beyond the edge of the raft. It had tentacles as thick as tree trunks, too.

Oh, no, no, no!

All around the raft, the water quavered and splashed with rising tentacles. Joey struggled to stay steady at the center of the raft. He forced his attention back to the spells he'd read.

Gut instincts took over. He willed for the three spells he figured would help him survive. The system responded to his wishes.

[Congrats! You've learned the Dark Dash Spell!]

[Congrats! You've learned the Shade Dragon Tail Spell!]

[Congrats! You've learned the Shadow Clone Magic Spell!]

Strange sensations shivered through Joey's body. He felt each spell go from a potential idea to an actuality.

He stumbled forward as a twenty-foot tail extended from behind him. It was ghostly and dark and thin. It ended with a sharp point. It made serpentine movements on its own until he willed it to the side and back.

The tail responded to his thoughts and the shifts of his body. He couldn't help but stare at it as it snaked around.

This was beyond freaky.

I barely feel the weight. It's like it's there and not there at the same time. Joey hoped he made the right choice with the tail.

"You better back off! Or I'll tail whip you! Hard!" Joey tried to sound as menacing as possible.

His new tail rose behind him like a viper. He had no idea what he was doing. He had no idea how to respond when the dark tentacle creature made weird flute-like noises.

The shrills had a melodic pattern to them. When he listened harder, a system message appeared.

[Help me! Help me! The snappers are hurting me!], translated the system.

Joey froze for a second before using Analyze on the big tentacle creature.

[Tidal Moon Denizen: Voyager Kraken: Trader lvl ?]

A denizen as in an alien? No, I'm the alien here! It's a local to the realm! And it's able to speak to me through the system.

Joey's panic mixed with confusion and amazement. He snapped out of it when the kraken kept making more flute noises.

[Please help! I will trade for assistance. I hate it when the snappers keep eating me], the kraken pleaded.

"You better not be lying to me!" Joey shouted as he stepped closer to the kraken's main body.

It was the size of an inflated air balloon. Each of its chaotic movements bumped the raft hard and nearly pitched Joey off his feet. His rogue class kept him upright, if barely.

[Not lying. There's more than usual. Three snappers. Three trades! Help me, adventurer,] the kraken begged.

"Try to lift one for me. I'll see what I can do!" Joey ordered before rethinking his decisions. *What can I do against a monster that can hurt a kraken?*

It was too late to back out now. The kraken did as ordered. One thick tentacle rose out of the water.

Under the bright moonlight, a greenish creature stood out against the dark skin of the kraken. It was humanoid and had a shell-like body. It reminded Joey of a man fused with an ugly turtle with a rabid appetite.

Joey analyzed.

[Tidal Moon Monster: Man Snapper: Grunt lvl 12.]

The snapper shook its head like a rabid dog and ripped a chunk of kraken flesh from the tentacle. Dark blood poured from the wound.

The snapper's attack was too small to endanger the kraken wholly. But Joey could recognize this was a painful assault.

"Move it closer."

The kraken shrilled. [Ow! Ow! It hurts!]

The tentacle with the snapper swung away. The raft jerked. Joey barely kept his feet on the wet wood floor.

"If you want help, get it together. Move it closer to me!" he yelled.

[Okay, okay!] The kraken shifted the tentacle with the snapper closer to Joey. Fifteen feet separated them.

Joey let his instincts take over. He thought of his essence and willed for it to push into his tail. He inhaled sharply when he felt the magic happen.

3. A GREAT ADVENTURER'S START

Turning Shade Dragon Tail from passive to active felt like real magic happening inside of Joey's body. Cool and ethereal sensations cycled through him.

The sensation – the essence – shifted the tail from ghost to solid. The tail blurred into view while whipping from Joey to the snapper in a wink.

The tail cracked louder than a bullwhip. It slashed open the snapper's face in a spray of blood.

The snapper's raspy scream filled the air and nearly drew all of Joey's attention. He barely noticed an eye from the monster splashing into the water.

The kraken shook its wounded tentacle and dropped the distracted snapper onto the raft. The floor under Joey tilted toward the snapper, and he nearly slipped. *Back away!*

His tail pushed lightly off the floor. It leveraged its length to help him stay upright.

Joey felt the magic feeding into his tail in a consistent flow, keeping it tangible. He also felt this was costly, too. He scrambled back quickly before attacking again.

The snapper raised an arm to block. The tail smacked the block aside and left a dark bruise on the snapper's scaly forearm.

Joey almost wanted to freeze, but kept attacking instead.

The Shade Dragon Tail lashed down from the top and struck the snapper's head. The creature's face hit the raft hard. Blood leaked from a nasty cut left on the head.

The snapper tried to push up. Joey's tail hit the head again and dropped the snapper once more.

Again, the monster struggled to stand. But Joey's tail kept dominating the monster with another headshot.

A feeling like an eggshell breaking vibrated down his tail. Multiple system messages popped up in the corner of his vision.

[You've slain a Man Snapper Grunt lvl 12! For slaying a monster over ten levels above you, bonus experience is awarded!]

[You've leveled up Shade Dragon Rogue from 1 to 3!]

[You've raised your mind from 11 to 15!]

[You've raised your body from 12 to 16!]

[You've raised your spirit from 10 to 12!]

[You've raised your free points from 0 to 6!]

Joey toggled Shade Dragon Tail back to passive to save his essence while his body shook from the sudden rush of added stats.

It felt like he was expanding and morphing. Yet, nothing

about his body changed physically.

It was all internal, beneath the skin. It felt incredible. And there was more where that came from.

He willed for his profile to insert free points into spirit and mind. The system responded instantly.

[You've raised your mind from 15 to 17!]

[You've raised your spirit from 12 to 16!]

Joey inhaled a sharp breath while feeling his brain tickle with snappy changes. His spirit swelled into something more firm.

He wanted to check on his essence, but the kraken thrashed suddenly. Harder than before. He barely kept his balance when another snapper hit the raft near him.

The monster stood tall. Joey had to crane his neck back to look at the monster's face. *Big.*

The creature's dark eyes glared at the lone human. It braced itself to lunge at Joey, but the spiky end of Joey's tail reappeared by the snapper's side.

The tail thrust into the snapper's neck. It didn't go all the way through, but the attack staggered the monster. When the tail pulled out, blood squirted out like a faucet.

The snapper staggered some more, surprised.

Joey's mouth fell open in surprise at seeing the blood spray.

Some of it splashed into his mouth. Joey gagged. He barely saw the snapper cocking back for a swing.

It moved fast for a hurt monster. Faster than Joey. The claws swung at his head while he willed for a spell to help him.

More essence circulated into his lower legs before

bursting with a small whoosh. Joey zipped backward and avoided the deadly head swipe.

Inky black lines streaked between where he'd been standing and his lower legs. *Dark Dash?* He wondered.

"Dark Dash!" Joey cheered, pumping his fists.

He landed outside the raft and submerged in cold wetness. Salty water invaded his throat and went down the wrong pipe. He panicked and thrashed, bumping into large and slimy shapes in the water.

Scared to death, Joey forced himself to think through the problem. He realized the shapes were tentacles. He grabbed one, hoping for the kraken's help.

His body felt heavy while rising. When he broke the surface, he coughed and hacked up whatever had gone down the wrong way. Holding onto the tentacle became his life mission while he recovered.

The kraken was communicating something. Joey was too busy recovering to listen. He then noticed the snappers had grown in numbers on the raft.

One was dead.

One was holding its bleeding neck.

And a third snapper glared at Joey.

Oh, we've flipped positions. Joey scrambled to get on top of the tentacle. He slipped backward.

He activated his tail – it had gone passive when he hit the water. His tail coiled smartly on the other side of the tentacle and leveraged Joey up to the top.

Then it wrapped around the tentacle and helped him stand.

Joey coughed and sputtered. He blinked through his tears before placing his shaky fists on his hips.

"Listen here, you ugly things! I'm the scariest guy you'll ever meet! And this kraken's working for me! So you better run off!"

Joey's shouting had no logic or planning involved. He taunted like he would against all the jerks he'd met in life.

The snappers glared while listening to him. *Maybe they're analyzing what I'm saying.*

That was fine. Because he was trying to give himself time and figure out a way to deal with them safely.

He had the high ground with the kraken's help. But the snappers could charge into the water and bite the kraken. Joey's high ground would become too shaky to hold.

The healthy snapper made hissy sounds and pointed. [Adventurer! We will eat your guts and give your head to our leader!]

Oh, great, they can taunt back!

That was nearly as disturbing as Joey's chances in this fight. Now the snapper's looked determined to make their threat a reality.

The healthy one led the way. The hurt one followed slowly. Joey was running out of time.

A wild thought came to mind. "Fools! You should've believed me! Suffer the wrath of my army!"

Joey thrust his hands forward. The snappers hesitated. Nothing happened.

They snarled and moved forward again. Joey smiled like a wild man and pushed his essence around to summon the calvary.

Inky blobs shot out of his torso one at a time. Essence circulated even faster inside of Joey with a frigid chill, like his veins were turning to ice.

He stopped at seven shadow clones.

Each one landed with a roll before standing in a circle around the snappers. The clones looked exactly like Joey – basketball shorts, tank top, bare feet – but with a tiny difference in hue.

They're slightly darker than me. The difference is so small they might as well be perfect copies.

But they moved slower than him. They were also weaker. But the monsters didn't notice right away while getting surrounded. The clones revealed more interesting quirks, such as taunting.

"Yo, yo, the gang's here!"

"Who are you gonna eat now, losers? Not us!"

"They're so ugly they were cut out of The Little Mermaid to keep it PG."

"Your warts got warts. You need some cream to take care of that."

"Hey! Hey! You're leaking out your neck. Someone, call this man a doctor."

They pestered the snappers while keeping out of reach. The monsters forgot about the original and looked at the copies warily.

Because of the distance and numbers, the snapper's threats and swings did nothing unless they fully committed to fighting the clones.

The shadow clones took advantage, leading the snappers around until the monsters gave their backs to Joey. But as the newest opportunity revealed itself, he could feel his insides freezing from the rapid essence expense. These spells weren't cheap.

I'm cutting this close!

Joey unraveled his tail from around the kraken's tentacle and jumped with leg power alone. Before he hit the raft, his tail struck a headshot on the healthy snapper from behind.

Joey landed in a crouch and rushed the monsters. His tail whipped back and forth as fast as the eye could blink.

He smacked the neck-bleeder in the face and staggered it aside. He landed another headshot on the other snapper – the one that taunted about eating Joey's guts.

When he turned back to the neck-bleeder, all his clones jumped in. They tackled the back of the monsters' knees and knocked them down.

Joey backed up for space and let his tail work some more. It moved lightning fast. It cracked like the heaviest bullwhip and struck headshot after headshot.

Eventually, two more skulls shattered like gory eggshells. System messages stacked up in the corner of his vision.

Joey dismissed his spells and collapsed on his hands and knees, breathing raggedly. He felt frigid in his veins and sick to his stomach.

He pulled up his essence.

[Essence: 226/690 EP]

Joey blinked. "Oh. That's not as bad as I thought."

The coldness was fading away at a good pace, too. Maybe the cold feeling was a stopgap measure.

It was like running at top speed and burning up stamina. Pouring out essence was the magical version of sprinting. Cold instead of hot.

Joey thought about the fight and realized it didn't last more than several minutes. It was hard to judge if he'd done well or not.

He'd spammed his spells in a panic. That turned out as a good thing for a quick fight.

And I survived.

Joey smiled for a few seconds. Then he stood to his shaky feet, stumbled to the edge furthest away from the gore, and vomited into the water.

He kept puking until he was empty. Even then, he still felt like gagging. He rubbed at his eyes before looking down at his shaky hands.

"Was that all real?" he asked.

He looked back. His Shade Dragon Tail slithered behind him while in its ghost form. It was twenty feet of deadliness and strength, waiting to be activated again.

Joey couldn't believe how an overpowered spell landed in his lap. And he could control it whenever he wanted.

With a whim, he had it move to the left. He had it move to the right.

The way it swayed to his command was creepy and eye-catching. It seemed like nobody could see it when it was in its passive ghost form. It was invisible to everyone but him until he was ready to activate it and strike.

Incredible.

I picked it out of pure instinct because it had epic in parentheses and sounded like the biggest weapon I could use while staying safe.

Joey shook his head in amazement.

Would I have picked it if I was under normal conditions? Without the stress? Getting a tail spell as one of your first doesn't come to mind under normal conditions.

That's like trying to pick the tail whip move at the start of a Pokemon game. Unless there's a more advanced version of that. I don't remember.

Joey hadn't even read all the spells when he made his choices under pressure.

Still, everything worked out. Despite the panic, horror, and blood, Joey survived. And he had more levels and stats.

[You've slain a Man Snapper Grunt lvl 14! For slaying a monster over ten levels above you, bonus experience is awarded!]

[You've slain a Man Snapper Grunt lvl 15! For slaying a monster over ten levels above you, bonus experience is awarded!]

[You've leveled up Shade Dragon Rogue from 3 to 7!]

[You've raised your mind from 17 to 25!]

[You've raised your body from 16 to 24!]

[You've raised your spirit from 16 to 20!]

[You've raised your free points from 0 to 12!]

Not only was he reeling from the fight, he was also dealing with the increase in stats. It happened in the background, nearly surprising him while he was getting past the blood and mayhem.

This was the most confusing and exciting dopamine and adrenaline cocktail Joey had ever experienced.

He almost wanted to cry, shout, cheer, and do cartwheels even though he was still exhausted from his first life-and-death fight.

Again, he felt stronger in mind, body, and spirit. And he had free points to use.

Before he did anything, he came to another realization. *Ah, I had more room in my essence because of my levels. But that's after killing the last two. I was sure I was running low before reaching level 7.*

Joey breathed deeply before he distributed his points based on what he needed. He braced himself for the changes.

They weren't so thrilling after the first couple of times, but he definitely felt different compared to when he first ended up on a raft. He felt less … pathetic. And he had a strategy on raising his stats based on his gaming experience.

[You've raised your mind from 25 to 27!]

[You've raised your body from 24 to 28!]

[You've raised your spirit from 20 to 26!]

While the main three stats should be raised relatively together, I feel like it's good to give body a little more. It has agility, which is important for a rogue. And it helps with essence recovery, which I'll need if spamming my spells is my strategy.

Now if only Joey knew how essence recovery worked. He wondered if it was passive or meditative.

He had a lot of questions, honestly. Too many.

He even had one more system message.

[Congrats! You have the opportunity to learn the Headhunter Skill!]

[Headhunter (Basic): Sharpen your aim and strike true. Your attacks to the head will hit a little harder as you grow more confident. *If you're going to kill a man. Do him a favor and aim for the head. I've died quite a few times, and I rather go instantly.*]

Joey still felt a little sick beyond the excitement from all the level ups and rising stats.

He knew this skill resulted from all the accurate headshots in the heat of his first battle. Probably the fastest way to learn a skill was to achieve it during a fight.

He needed the skill even if he felt uncomfortable.

It was one thing to play as a rogue from his gaming experience. It was another thing to actually do it and commit to it in real life.

However, Joey had to be practical. His Shade Dragon Tail was accurate against distracted targets.

But what if monsters could read him better and dodge? Having this skill would help against the monsters trying to get smart against him.

Joey took the skill.

[Congrats! You've learned the Headhunter Skill!]

The raft jerked and nearly pitched him back into the water. He scrambled from the edge.

Turning around, he saw the bulging black thing hadn't gone away. It took him a second to remember the reason for all of this.

At the same time, he realized his crate was gone. That

made him feel a smidge bad.

The crate had offered him his first ability in Multiverse Z.

Joey shook off the weird sentiment and refocused on what mattered. The kraken made flute noises.

Analyze translated: [Thank you, adventurer! There's no doubt our meeting was fortunate. You're not just any adventurer. You're a great one, aren't you?]

Joey stared at the giant octopus head. One of its dark eyes was larger than Joey's torso. All of its giant tentacles surrounded him while caressing the edges of the raft.

All in? He asked himself. *All in.*

With a sigh, he shifted from the edge. He was tired, wet, cold, and thirsty now.

The combat high was leaving him, and his growth in stats didn't make him superhuman.

Yet.

He still held his head high and pretended he hadn't panicked from start to finish like an amateur.

"Yeah, I'm great." Joey put on his best smile. "So, about those rewards. Is there room to negotiate? They had higher levels than me. It was a struggle even for a great adventurer."

[You're right! I don't mean to swindle you. My clan are the most honest traders in the Tidal Moon Realm, after all. Maybe in all the realms! How's two small rewards for every snapper?]

"So, only six small rewards in total?" Joey asked, feeling greedy for more. Really greedy, strangely.

[Haha! Don't forget your rewards from the snappers, too!]

"Say, what?"

Joey glanced down at the corpses. He struggled to look past the gore until he noticed pale runes circulating near each corpse.

The runes faded and left some objects clattering over the bodies.

Loot drops.

4. MAKING DEALS
WITH A KRAKEN

Joey was a little overwhelmed. So much happened in a short amount of time.

He had stats that were changing him, making him something new, something more. He was becoming different.

He had unbelievable powers because he was a great adventurer with a path called the Shade Dragon Rogue. His tail was swaying behind him while invisible to mostly everything except him.

Now the sight of coins shining under the bright moonlight while touching the blood of the monsters he'd just killed was exciting to him. He ran over and grabbed them, ignoring his exhaustion after the combat high, and ignoring the corpses of dead monsters.

Each coin was a little over an inch wide. They had weight to them, which kept them from getting swept away by the waves.

The first two kills provided coins. The third provided something different.

He picked up a smooth square tile with a bluish symbol on one side. It was a little wider than his palm.

A new system message popped up with added context.

[Congrats! You've looted 13 Tidal Moon Copper Coins and 1 Breath Glyph Tile (Basic).]

The kraken added some helpful context: [Fortune smiles upon you. As it should for a great rogue! The system has let all the monsters drop loot.]

"They usually don't?" he asked.

[It is usually a one out of four chance. Granted, since you seem to be new, the system is likely to be kinder at your level. And you are a rogue, so you are most fortunate.]

This is a responsive system if what the big octopus is saying is true. I need to get as much information as I can. Joey was also aware that information was part of trades. He wanted to make his rewards count.

Joey stood tall, or as tall as his short height could achieve. With everything calm, the raft felt stable.

He was more surefooted, too. At least slightly more than before. The increases in his body were apparent enough.

Moving away from the corpses, Joey used Analyze on his new loot.

[Tidal Moon Coins (13): Currency from the Tidal Moon Realms.]

[Breath Glyph Tile (Basic/1): Activate with essence. Gain a single lungful of breath.]

Joey noticed there was no extra commentary about these items. Maybe the system preferred to use extra commentary with skills and spells alone.

Who was the system using for those personalized messages? Or was the system making that up?

He could think about that later. There were more important matters, like knowing how the economy of this place would work, or better yet, how to get to safety.

At the very least, he was fortunate. Very fortunate.

Rogues have a buff in fortune. And fortune is covered by the spirit stat.

Another way to look at fortune was considering it the luck mechanic in games.

More fortune means more loot drops and lucky outcomes. Maybe the spirit stat should get more points.

If this was like previous games he'd played, he would make money easier here than in real life. He could make a better life for himself in this fantasy world.

I can live a life!

That was stunning to consider.

Joey shook his head to concentrate on the now. Wet wood under his bare feet. Water and moons everywhere. Dead monsters. A kraken trader.

Food. Water. Shelter. Tools. Information. These were his primary concerns. His survival needed the basics covered.

"What's your name?" Joey asked. "I'm Joey Eclipse."

The kraken made flute noises, sounding out the name. [Joey Eclipse. An interesting name. Back in my home tide, my clutch mother named me Curious because I was always curious. For short, Curi always works!]

Joey thought of curry. His stomach rumbled.

The kraken made noises the system didn't bother to

translate. Was that laughter? If Joey looked closely, the kraken's eyelids could give away emotive expressions, too.

[Would you like to make the first small trade? How does a fish called a tidal racer sound? When eaten, it will grant a slight agility buff for six hours.]

Even the food has magic to it?

Joey tried not to look too eager. At least he knew there was food with the kraken. And Joey loved fish.

But I need to cover all my bases.

"Curi, you're right that I'm new around here. I'll need help to survive." Joey hoped he wasn't sounding too eager. His words were spilling out messier than he liked. "Water would help. And a way to get to land where other humans are."

A tentacle rose out of the water. Joey watched it closely until the kraken tapped its squishy cranium.

[Oh, ho! I know how to help you. After all, it is interesting to find you on the Geala Tide. That's ... hm.] The kraken tapped its tentacle on its head again, thinking. [Where you need to go is ten days from here. And that's not including the land you'll have to cross to reach the closest human port. By my calculations, based on a Level 25 human body, you'll take six to eight more days to cross the land. A total of eighteen to twenty days if you remain fortunate.]

Joey read the translation while staying as calm as possible. Even with his growth in the mind stat, he felt overwhelmed trying to understand how the kraken knew all of this.

"I'll need to get to the land first," Joey muttered.

The kraken waved one tentacle around in the air. [Yes, indeed. So if you will allow this humble trader to assist in your situation, I can provide services. Food is one small trade. Water is another small trade. Taking you across the tides to the land will cost four small trades.]

Joey hesitated. This was too kind. Surely, there was a catch. Before he could think of what to say, the kraken continued.

[You'll also need a bag for your loot. And a weapon! A short sword with rust resistance is one of my best wares, in fact. You seem to lack information, too. I can provide that as we go along. These are costly trades, however. But if you are willing to fight monsters and provide half of their loot and bodies to me, I think this will be a worthwhile venture.]

Joey felt an irrational rush of greed. This deal was great for him!

The feeling only lasted so long once he noticed his shifty emotions. Then his uncertainty took over.

I don't know. This is too good to be true. Am I being scammed somehow? Did Curi purposely let the snappers attack him and to make itself seem weak and innocent? Is this a trick just to get a rogue on a leash?

Curi patiently waited for a response. At least he or she wasn't a pressuring salesperson.

"Random question."

[Why would a question be random?] Curi tilted its head.

"True, but here it is. Are you a girl or a boy?"

[Ah, this is an excellent question. I'll tell you if you tell me.]

Joey blinked. *It can't tell if I'm a boy or a girl?*

That was honestly a shock for him. And it shouldn't be.

Logically, a kraken's anatomy would be very different.

But Curi talked like a person. A person would usually recognize the gender of another person right away.

My home may all be underwater, but I'm really not in Miami anymore.

Joey calmed down. "I'm a male."

[And I'm a male, too. Does knowing another's gender build trust with human adventurers?]

"It has certain cultural and societal meanings from my ... old universe."

Knowing more about Curi helped Joey trust him. The same would've happened if Curi had said female or whatever.

Curi had a name, a gender, an occupation, and ...

[Tidal Moon Denizen: Voyager Kraken: Trader lvl ?]

"Another question. And sorry if this is unfair to our trades. Please, just humor me. How come I can't see your level?"

Curi laughed – or whatever Joey figured was laughter for a kraken. [I think this is valuable information to give for a trustworthy and profitable venture. You should have the Analyze skill. It's probably at a low level. Every level grants you the ability to see an extra ten levels higher. At your level, you'll need Analyze at Level 7.]

So, Curi's basically in the high Level 70s. But why would a kraken in the Level 70s let weaker monsters hurt him?

[We do not fight,] Curi said, reading the human better than Joey could read the kraken. [Some denizens can fight. Some do not have the capacity for violence. My kind is the latter. To act violently sickens us instantly. It is the price for the many benefits and abilities we have as voyager krakens. One of my abilities is healing the damage right now, so I will be healthy soon.]

"But you're okay with me being violent?"

[It's the best part of having an adventurer around. Especially a great one! They are so helpful against evil monsters and can lead to further profits. And I sense you are good, unlike the bad adventurers, so hopefully you won't swindle me.]

If that was all true, the future partnership made sense. Joey had no ill will against the kraken. He'd helped against the snappers without knowing Curi, after all.

Joey also thought back to Curi's prediction about a Level 25 adventurer crossing the land. *Is Curi assuming I'll get to level 25 before landfall?*

That also meant there would be more fighting ahead. More killing and gore.

But more opportunities for levels, abilities, and loot. A journey across the sea … or the tides … for ten days could turn a profit for both the human and kraken.

Joey looked up and noticed the night sky becoming brighter. On a distant horizon, a shining light slowly rose.

It was probably dawn breaking on a new day.

"Curi, my new friend, you got yourself a deal," he said, grinning at the sunrise.

[Excellent! While I provide you with some needed items. May I in turn ask a question?]

"Sure."

[Would you happen to have any strong desires on keeping the snapper bodies? I can use their parts for trades. And eat the meat.]

The kraken raised more tentacles, which rocked the raft a little. The massive and slimy limbs hovered over Joey. Suction cups puckered on the underside of each tentacle, as expected.

Joey cocked his head to the side as he took in every detail of the gargantuan creature. It took him a second to register the question.

"Oh, yeah, sure. You can have them. In fact, I'll trade my half of the bodies in the future for continued good will."

[You are a gracious one! Much appreciated, Joey Eclipse.]

Unexpectedly, the tentacle tips had foot-wide slits that peeled open and extended mini-tentacles. The mini-tentacles were as long as a forearm and as thin as fingers.

From out of nowhere, items popped into view within the mini-tentacles grasp: a half blue short sword, a sleek but long fish, and a pouch as big as Joey's head.

Joey felt like a kid in a magical amusement park and analyzed each item.

[Holding Bag (Basic/1): It's tougher than a mundane bag. It has rope binding, too.]

[Tidal Moon Beast: Small Fish: Racer.]

[Tidal Short Sword (Basic/1): An enchanted sword with the rust resistant glyph. It will last you long in and out of water.]

First, he placed his loot in the bag and tied the binding around his waist. It cinched well enough at the top of the bag, so Joey had no worries about losing his stuff.

Next was the sword.

The handle had a comfortable leather grip with a shell-shaped metal pommel. The guard was a simple metal bar. The blade was a little longer than a machete and triangular. Wide from the base and narrow at the top.

Both edges looked sharp while the tip was absolutely deadly.

Joey had never held a sword before. He'd once used a machete when he was younger, but that was it. The sword was mostly gray except for the bluish tint at the middle fading near the tip and the base.

In the middle of the blue tint was a pale symbol. Most likely a glyph. It seemed different compared to the system runes. He figured that was the source of the rust resistance.

"A magic sword." Joey could hardly believe he was holding one. "It's real. It's a magic sword."

Joey's inner nerd was throwing a party.

The spells were out of this world and amazing. But he'd rushed through their showcase. He wasn't in a rush with his first magic sword.

With a wave of his arm, he cut from shoulder height to outside his right leg.

He felt his body move naturally in sync with his arm. He listened to the metallic whoosh, the air and metal vibrating together in symphony. And he felt the *rightness* of the swing.

But wait, there was more. It was a good sword swing, especially for his first. But Joey sensed it could've been better.

From the edge of the raft, Curi laughed merrily. [A natural in the making. But I must wonder, do you have the Short Sword Proficiency skill?]

"No." Joey swung again. It felt right, but could be better. It was bordering on the line of good enough.

But I don't want to be good enough.

Joey swung some more.

[Allow me to strip the snappers and eat. I'll prepare the tidal fish for you, too. I hope you don't mind it being fresh. It'll still be healthy and good for your agility. Meanwhile, you can keep practicing until you have the skill. It shouldn't take too long for a rogue if you dedicate yourself.]

Swing. Swing. Swing.

The magic blade sang.

"That works for me. Thank you," Joey said while mostly distracted.

Swing. Swing. Swing.

Joey kept cutting at the air. These were good cuts thanks to his rogue class. His short blade affinity was helping him. But these sword cuts weren't good enough for him.

I know I can do better.

Swing. Swing. Swing.

The kraken shifted around to work. The raft rocked about. Joey staggered and nearly whacked his face with the sword.

He waited out the rocking and went back to swinging at the air. He didn't bother to tell the kraken to be more mindful.

Instead, he thought of the rocking as an extra difficulty setting while he swung the sword with one arm. When he grew tired with his right arm, he switched to his left and swung the sword some more.

Swing. Swing. Swing.

Joey had no idea why he was into swinging the sword so much in the first place. But he was enjoying himself.

There could be a skill reward. And he wanted to be more

than good enough with his first magic weapon.

So he practiced as the sun rose higher.

Sweat covered his body. He ignored the meal Curi had prepared for him. He even told the kraken to rock the raft a little more.

Joey adapted to the rocking as he cut, sliced, and thrust with one arm. Then he repeated the same actions with the other arm.

Before it became obvious that it was time to move on, a system message popped up.

[**Congrats! You have the opportunity to learn the Short Sword Finesse Skill!**]

[**Short Sword Finesse (Basic): Take your short sword proficiency a step further by attacking with grace and cunning. Spot gaps in your opponent's style and finesse your blade into openings with more ease.** *You think yourself a fancy swordsman, huh? Well, if you can swing as much as you can talk, you might have more steel to your skill than expected.*]

Joey finally stopped and reread his new skill. He explained it verbatim to Curi. The kraken sounded surprised.

[On the benevolence of the Tidal Moon Lord! I haven't heard of this version of a short sword skill. Thank you for sharing, Adventurer Eclipse. I must repay you for this fortune.]

"Curi, just call me Joey. And pay me back however you see fit." Joey willed for the system to give him the brand new skill.

[**Congrats! You've learned the Short Sword Finesse Skill!**]

5. INTRO TO A ROGUE'S VOYAGE

Joey was lying on his back, feeling full from eating the tidal racer. His sword was embedded into the wood deep enough to remain put. No thirst troubled him after Curi summoned a flask filled with fresh water for him to drink.

The young rogue was also sore from the nonstop sword practice. The raft was rocking back and forth, lulling him to sleep until a shallow wave washed against his side and woke him up.

He couldn't stay awake for long, however. He was getting used to the waves even though he should be on guard to protect Curi. He tried to stay awake by looking at his profile.

Great Adventurer: Joey Eclipse

Race: Basic Human

Age: 18

Path: Shade Dragon Rogue lvl 7

Singularities: Agility Buff (Basic/6 hour).

Skills: Analyze lvl 2 (Basic), Headhunter lvl 1 (Basic),

Short Sword Finesse lvl 1 (Basic).

Spells: Dark Dash lvl 1 (Superior), Shade Dragon Tail lvl 1 (Epic), Shadow Clone Magic lvl 1 (Epic).

Semblances:

Special Stuff: Holding Bag (Basic/1), Tidal Moon Copper Coins (13), Breath Glyph Stone (Basic/1), Tidal Short Sword (Basic/1).

Essence: 489/710 EP

Mind: 27 (+2 per a level)

Body: 28 (+2 per a level)

Spirit: 26 (+1 per a level)

Free: 0 (+3 per a level)

It was fortunate his essence refilled itself even while he'd practiced. He guessed around 1 EP every two minutes during his four hours spent practicing.

Now he was gaining more essence while he rested. About 2 EP a minute for the past hour. He wanted to ask if there were faster ways to recover his essence. But he could barely talk. He was too tired.

Eventually, he drifted to sleep under the bright daylight and to the sound of waves.

He felt good until he dreamed about drowning in a tide of holiday packages. The nightmare led to him receiving an eviction notice because the rent was overdue.

Joey snapped awake, his heart racing.

The sky was watercolor pink and orange. A mosaic of sunset colors. The moons were still plentiful.

He was still on a raft with the edges gripped by giant tentacles. Rolling waves passed underneath. The salty breeze blew by and left him a little cold, but awake.

Behind him, the large dark shape of Curi's head parted the water as the kraken swam with the raft in tow.

Joey combed through his tangled hair and smiled.

The nightmare wasn't real.

The fantasy world was real.

He checked his profile and saw his essence had refilled completely. Nice.

"Hey, Curi. Sorry for falling asleep. You weren't troubled were you?" Joey asked.

[No troubles, Joey! I avoided a patrolling snapper group an hour earlier by spraying ink on them. I can do that much to avoid attacks, and I didn't think it was worth waking you.]

I don't know about that. What if something went wrong and I could use the wake up sooner to respond?

Curi sensed the issue. [Do not fret. I'm good at knowing if trouble is unavoidable or not. I was caught by the snappers you've fought because I was resting for too long. I can move two days straight without rest. I'll need at least 8 hours of rest afterward.]

"Then I'll definitely stay sharp when you're resting."

Joey sat with legs crossed and rolled his shoulders around. Still sore, but not badly so. His body stat helped toughen him, even if only a little.

"Curi, I have so many questions. I honestly don't know where to start."

[Speak, and I'll answer to the best of my abilities. However, there's some information I know that requires more advanced trades. Such as skills and spells of certain great ones

I have met. Or areas of opportunity.]

Is he telling me that on purpose? Joey figured Curi was an honest salesman, but a smart one. *Man, if there were more good salespeople like him, they would make way more business for themselves.*

"Well, let's start with the biggest attention grabber." Joey pointed at the sunset. "How is there a sun we can see when all the moons are in the way?"

[That is the solar moon or sun as you say. It's the brightest moon of the realm. All other moons shift aside as the sun passes during one of its several arcs, which changes per the seasons. It is also one of the few moons that doesn't have a tide.]

"Okay, so if the sun is a moon, then is it magic that gives all the moons their light? And what do you mean it doesn't have a tide?"

[The magic belongs to the Tidal Moon Lord, the ruler of this realm. And most moons have a tide connected to them, which you will see exemplified once we exit the Gaela Tide the day after tomorrow. However, the sun and dark moons do not have tides. And you must be wary of the dark moons passing. Each one hovers above a devil marching across tidal floors.]

"Well, if you can spot a dark moon, that means you can avoid the devil, right?" Joey figured those had to be scary strong monsters.

He shivered, thinking about devils and dark moons. Then he noticed Curi's silence.

The silence lasted for a few beats too long. [You can't always spot the coming of the dark moons.]

Oh, that doesn't sound ominous. Not ominous at all. Joey shivered again.

Curi raised a tentacle out of the water and waved it. [I avoided one six days ago. Our journey is unlikely to be affected by devils since I passed that one so recently. We will have concerns with snappers, crushers, and maybe some effects from the Dread Whale, most likely.]

"Dread Whale?" Joey blinked.

[Indeed, Dread Whale. It is a creature from another realm that took to living here. Adventurers have failed to kill it because it is far above Level 100 and it flees when near final death.]

"Okay, so I can't lounge around. I need to practice some stuff. And be prepared." Joey stood to his feet. "Another question. Is there a way to recover essence quicker?"

[Hm. If you're at 30 body, you should receive 3 EP a minute when meditating. Meditation with your channels in mind will draw ambient essence faster. If you can get the skill for it, the levels in that skill will give you extra EP on top of your natural recovery. Though, it takes long hours of meditation to receive the skill unless you're a mage or cleric. Most denizens and adventurers prefer resting.]

"What do you prefer?" Joey asked.

[Ah, that is a costly question.]

Joey yanked his sword out of the wood and gave Curi a cheeky smile. "You have a nice ability taking care of that for you, don't you?"

The kraken didn't answer.

The rogue rolled his shoulders some more. He hopped around and noticed the loot jangling in his bag.

He ignored the loose loot earlier. But now he figured that would be a problem. He removed his tank top and stuffed it into his bag to fill the space.

There were more questions in mind, but Joey wanted to focus on things he could solve.

Curi provided more fish and water upon request without having to slow down. Then Joey tested his abilities and paid attention to his essence points, which were already down some.

Huh, that's strange.

Curious about his missing EP, Joey started using his skills and noticed all of them cost EP. It only happened with Analyze while using the system for analysis.

Every time Curi communicated and Joey analyzed, an EP was needed.

When the rogue concentrated on an imaginary head to strike with Headhunter, he lost 3 EP.

When he concentrated on using Short Sword Finesse, he also lost 3 EP.

Using Headhunter and Short Sword Finesse together cost exactly 6 EP.

There was a physical difference when using his skills, too. He felt his body move with almost machine-like precision to hit the imaginary head when using Headhunter.

When using Short Sword Finesse, his next strike came out fluidly and with deceptive grace. The skills weren't showy, but they definitely had a magical effect on his body.

He could spam them quickly, too. Four strikes aiming at an imaginary head while moving with grace and cunning cost exactly 24 EP.

I was wondering if the essence system was balanced, and it turns out it is. In fact, having more active skills running in a fight can hurt.

Joey saw the bigger picture of having a single resource pool. Everything connected to it.

He spent an EP asking Curi about skill costs and levels.

[The higher your abilities, the more they'll cost you unless they are special abilities that are passive or they help with recovery instead. Anything else is unheard of for me. But a majority of abilities will cost, and the costs will rarely go down, only up with skill levels,] the kraken explained. [It is wise of you to pay attention to your essence, Joey. This will serve you well as a great adventurer.]

If skills could end up being expensive, Joey feared what his spells would cost him.

He tried them out with his eye on the essence counter. The results hurt some.

Dark Dash cost 10 EP right off the bat, and each use had a one second cooldown afterward. Then Joey noticed he could charge it to a limit and throw himself farther. The highest charge cost 30 EP.

It was fun being able to zip around with each dash, but he could see how relying on this too much could burn through his EP quickly.

The base cost could send him flying over ten feet to the side or four feet up without using his legs. The upper limit gave him over 30 feet to the side – where he hit water and needed Curi to stop for him – and twelve feet up without jumping.

Shade Dragon Tail was 30 EP upon activation and 3 EP every second while active. Thankfully, all actions during activation had no costs.

Admittedly, the tail's power and flexibility made Joey want to keep it active longer. He could spring himself around with his tail. He could adjust himself midair with its help by swinging it around.

It responded fast to his will, sometimes faster than even he could expect. The cost was well worth having Shade Dragon Tail active for a time, especially when he could throw his sword and catch the handle with a flick and wrap of his tail.

Yeah, having a responsive ghost tail was an overpowered ability.

Then there was Shadow Clone Magic.

"Oh, this is going to be trouble," Joey said.

"But not for us," his clone replied with a cheeky grin.

A ghostly tail waved behind the clone's back. In its hand was a shadow version of Joey's short sword. And within the clone's own hidden profile were all of Joey's abilities.

A base model clone costs 20 EP to summon and 2 EP every ten seconds to maintain. But Joey had the option of loading his clones up with abilities.

Adding Analyze cost 1 EP extra.

Headhunter cost 2 EP extra.

Short Sword Finesse cost 2 EP extra.

When granted these skills at creation, the clones could use them once each. But Joey could also stack for repeated uses with equivalent costs.

If he wanted a clone to use Short Sword Finesse three times, he had to stack it upon creation and pay 6 EP extra.

Spells worked similarly. The spells were halved in costs when applied to a clone but had reduced effects.

Shade Dragon Tail clones cost 15 EP and 2 EP per a second when applied to a clone. The tail came out fifteen feet, while noticeably weaker and less responsive.

It was still useful for the clones depending on the situation.

Forming a short sword for a clone cost exactly 20 EP and 2 EP every ten seconds to maintain. Any effective items Joey had cost the same as a clone. It couldn't copy the breath glyph tile, though.

Specific magic items might be a no no with the system. Imagine if there are health potions and I can copy those infinitely?

The most challenging part with Shadow Clone Magic was Joey needing to pre-plan each clone's creation with abilities and the extra EP to run them. He also had to risk losing the essence if the clones failed their purposes.

"This isn't easy," Joey said, sitting on the edge closest to Curi.

Water splashed up with every cresting wave they passed. New dawn shone golden on the horizon behind them, which was the direction east. Westward was the land Joey needed to reach.

"At the simplest level of using my abilities, I could get by," Joey explained further. "But the highest level of my abilities are so complex I can't imagine how I'll master them. There's so much risk management if I want to outplay an enemy. And I have to leave room for failure. Is this the cost of having superior and epic abilities?"

[Yes, Joey. Your spells as a great adventurer give you a huge advantage over others at your level. But you must also account for the difficulty or high costs or both. And there are other concerns.]

That sounded ominous.

"What do you mean by other concerns, Curi?"

[You are an adventurer on the path to greatness. It should be welcomed, celebrated, and supported. Unfortunately, I've heard too many tales of what great adventurers faced among the steady adventurers.]

Joey put two and two together.

"They'll attack me, won't they?"

Curi let his silence answer the question.

Joey looked down at his sword resting in his lap. He didn't know how to feel about attacks on the greats.

Then he thought about his old realm.

Wasn't the situation similar to how lesser gamers would try to take down the top gamers?

Maybe here in Multiverse Z there were major rewards for killing great adventurers. Besides, he'd picked the rogue class because of its PVP potential.

Although, based on the rogue's natural abilities in Multiverse Z, it might not be as big a PVP powerhouse as he'd thought.

Joey imagined bounties and such submitted by some bad people. Monsters had intelligence, so they could want the deaths of great adventurers badly.

Would monsters and bad adventurers team up?

But will people go out of their way to take down a great just because they want to? Joey was a little unsure.

This was a new life with endless possibilities. He was doing things he'd never considered he was capable of. He was changing himself along the way, and for the better.

Wouldn't other people do the same and change for the better? Even if they were steady, wouldn't they appreciate people on the path to greatness?

Or was that asking for too much?

Joey tried to distract himself from the somber questions with a different question. "Curi, what is the path to greatness?"

[That question has many answers depending on which great one you ask. It is personal to you and your peers. I imagine it is a driving force that'll help you climb the many levels to the top.]

The kraken tapped his head thoughtfully.

[I, a denizen, am like a multiverse commoner. I have simple wants and wishes. I exist to support the adventurers and the lords and ladies, in a sense. But I imagine the path to greatness has a few desirable qualities most great adventurers want. I can name one of these qualities that most would likely agree upon.]

"What quality is that?"

[Power, Joey. Great ones share the quality of having power. Even now, I sense I am under your power. More so than you think. Perhaps you will fall from the path and then lose your great power forever. But if you don't fall. If you continue to rise. Well, please think fondly of me, Joey, for this humble trader hopes he's providing a good service to you.]

Joey chuckled, feeling his mood brighten.

"You are, Curi. You really are."

6. MORE CONFIDENT IN BATTLE

[You've leveled up Analyze from 2 to 3!]

[You've leveled up Headhunter from 1 to 2!]

[You've leveled up Short Sword Finesse from 1 to 3!]

Joey smiled at his skill gains.

The first one came easy because of Curi pointing out interesting creatures for Joey to examine. The Tidal Moon Realm lived up to being a high fantasy place.

Fish with mirror-like scales launched out of the water and shone in the sunlight. They liked to soar over the raft in an arc leading back to the water, giving Joey a fun show.

Fish with alien designs lurked underneath, which Curi helped Joey see by holding him underwater. Joey had to adapt to the slimy hold while they continued to move speedily toward their destination.

It was worth the effort.

Joey analyzed a fish with a star-shaped head that would flash light when threatened by predators. He analyzed fish that were like giant balloons underwater. He even saw jellyfish the size of skyscrapers that gave off creepy vibes even from a distance.

Other than sightseeing, Joey slept, took care of his needs, and trained mostly with the sword. Spell practice was limited to keep his essence points above sixty percent in case of emergencies.

It was during a sword session when he realized he didn't have to practice alone and could work on his most complicated spell. He formed two sword clones with stacks of Headhunter and Short Sword Finesse for 110 EP total.

He quickly realized each clone was at least three-fourth as potent as him. So two clones could pressure him and cover for each other very well.

They put Joey in constant danger, which helped him learn to stay calm under pressure. The rocking raft stayed a factor, too. Thankfully, Joey's agility buff from eating tidal racers benefited his mobility.

[Agility Buff (Basic/6 hours): You get a 10% bonus to your agility.]

To avoid injuries, the clones stopped short of touching him. Joey stopped short, too, to keep his training partners from dispersing.

The sessions weren't long. Only three minutes a round. But the difficulty made up for it and pushed Joey into losses he learned from quickly.

He won some rounds, too.

After every practice session, Joey sat with legs crossed and his sword laying on his lap. He closed his eyes and focused inward. Curi gave him tips on meditation, and Joey drilled it consistently.

He breathed and channeled. The essence channels were like extra veins in his body and gave him cool tingly sensations all over.

When he channeled, the ambient essence seeped into him from the outside. It was a little chilly. But Joey liked it.

No matter how long he channeled, his meditation didn't bore him. It helped with soreness and stamina. It lessened his need for sleep, too.

Six to seven hours were his usual. Meditation shortened that to five. Joey maximized the time he was up by sightseeing or training.

[You've leveled up Analyze from 3 to 4!]

[You've leveled up Headhunter from 2 to 3!]

[You've leveled up Short Sword Finesse from 3 to 4]!

No meditation skill yet. But Joey didn't feel bothered. It was only a matter of time.

More concerning was Curi's need for sleep. That was drawing closer. So was the edge of the Gaela Tide.

They discussed a plan. Before reaching the edge, Curi would rest. He had an ability to conceal him, too.

Snappers could still pose a danger. The monsters liked the tidal edges the most.

So as the kraken and human drew closer to a resting point, Curi slowed down. Part of the plan required Joey to gain a new skill for just-in-case purposes.

Joey jumped into the water with his sword and swam harder than ever before.

He was an okay swimmer on most occasions. He did better now when he was in the water on purpose.

He swam on the surface. He swam under the surface. He slowed down to strike at an imaginary foe with his sword.

He quickly learned thrusts worked best. Or close up slices.

He also practiced effective ways to use his spells while underwater. Each one was viable. But he tried not to rely on them for swimming.

He needed to teach his body to swim aggressively on its own merit. For now, at least.

The skill they were waiting for arrived. Joey broke the surface in front of the kraken and grinned.

[Congrats! You have the opportunity to learn the Combat Swimming Skill!]

[Combat Swimming (Basic): Attack and defend with more effectiveness while in the water. Your movements will feel less burdened. *Even a landlubber can fight the creatures of the deep if they have the aptitude for it.*]

Joey took the skill.

[Congrats! You've learned the Combat Swimming Skill!]

The time for Curi to rest came. The kraken boasted about his full trust in Joey. The rogue handled the boasts with humility and a little nervousness.

Curi used an ability to turn himself translucent. He rested off to the side, with one tentacle extended between him and the raft. A single lifeline.

Joey stayed near the middle and faced the sleeping kraken. The solar moon rose behind him. His sword rested in his lap. He tried to calm his nervousness and hone his focus like a disciplined guard.

He held watch over Curi with more attention than he'd ever given anything.

He spotted shapes lurking down below. Mostly wandering fish. Nothing happened for hours as the sun crossed the sky and shifted the moons aside.

The raft tilted oddly behind Joey.

He pretended not to notice while shifting his legs. Knees up. Feet planted down on the wet wood. The sword moved to the side.

The raft tilted a little more.

Joey charged trickles of darkness into his lower legs. Then, with a deep inhale, he looked over his shoulder.

Four snappers looked at him like he was a snack.

The two at the front had their hand claws digging into the wood, feet set on the edge and ready to sprint forward. The two at the back looked just as eager to get on the raft.

Everything became a blur of action, and Joey set the pace first.

Dark Dash launched Joey forward and over the edge of the raft. He twisted around and waved his sword arm at the monsters before hitting the water.

The two snappers at the front bolted forward. The two snappers at the back reversed into the water.

The front snappers spotted their target and dove onto him with claws forward and mouths opened wide.

They hit the shadow clone and dispersed it into nothing. The real Joey clambered up on the side while another shadow clone distracted the back snappers in the water.

The front snappers looked around in confusion and rose

to the surface. Shade Dragon Tail appeared from behind Joey and whipped down at them, Headhunter activated.

Joey scalped the first snapper he hit and left a little dent in its skull. The Level 13 snapper sank almost instantly and nearly slipped away, but the tail struck again with a headhunting thrust.

[You've slain a Man Snapper Grunt lvl 13! Experience awarded!]

The remaining front snapper exploded out of the water. It slashed down with both hands.

Joey dark-dashed backward only ten feet. His tail swung around to the monster's side. The snapper swiped at the tail and missed.

The tail kept wavering close as a feint before the snapper looked back at Joey again and took a sword thrust up the soft side of its jaw. The hit landed with his skills Headhunter and Short Sword Finesse activated.

The Level 15 creature barely survived and could only stand while Joey ripped the sword out. Eager to slay it with a second hit, he nearly missed the thumping footsteps behind him.

He turned instead of dashing. A snapper grabbed his tail and jerked him back. The fourth snapper charged with all of its weight for a tackle.

Joey deactivated his tail and used Dark Dash for a dangerous move. He launched into a backward flip over the tackle.

It worked. For a second. Then the tail-grabbing snapper twisted for a swing and clipped Joey's side.

Hot pain sliced along his ribs. It was a glancing blow, but a painful one. His blood mixed with the salt water splashing onto the raft.

He lost his concentration and landed with a stumble. The eager snapper with Joey's blood on its claws jumped at him.

He seemed vulnerable at that moment. But Joey clenched his jaw and held his ground, wanting to strike back.

Shade Dragon Tail came alive again while already in motion, spearing into the attacking snapper's eye.

A second later, Joey used Dark Dash and stabbed out the other eye with his sword. The double head penetration led to new system messages.

[You've slain a Man Snapper lvl 16! Experience awarded!]

[You've leveled up Shade Dragon Rogue from 7 to 8!]

[You've raised your mind from 27 to 29!]

[You've raised your body from 28 to 30!]

[You've raised your spirit from 26 to 27!]

[You've raised your free points from 0 to 3!]

The last unharmed snapper hesitated. Joey sidestepped the latest corpse as it collapsed. He willed his free points into spirit. More essence added to Joey's spell strength.

[You've raised your spirit from 27 to 30!]

New messages popped up when the snapper bleeding from the jaw thrust prior finally keeled over. It died on its own.

[You've slain a Man Snapper lvl 15! Experience awarded!]

[You've leveled up Shade Dragon Rogue from 8 to 9!]

[You've raised your mind from 29 to 31!]

[You've raised your body from 30 to 32!]

[You've raised your spirit from 30 to 31!]

[You've raised your free points from 0 to 3!]

The last snapper charged. Joey dumped free points into body and stepped backward. The monster closed the distance and swiped at Joey's head.

It missed by a fraction of an inch without Joey having to dash away. The next swipe came right after.

Joey fell all the way backward. His tail coiled like a spring under him and launched him to the side. He deactivated his tail before the snapper caught hold.

When the monster tried to stop and turn, Joey flew with inky black lines behind his feet. Sword in motion, he chopped the blade into the snapper's face with Headhunter and Short Sword Finesse activated.

Not a killing blow, but almost one. The snapper stumbled and gripped its ripped open and bloody head.

Joey had all the time to land feet first and hack behind the knee. The snapper fell over and rolled pathetically.

It struggled to rise while Joey raised his sword with the blade pointed down and thrust with his skills activated. He didn't need the skills for this last strike, but using them was good for levels.

He checked his messages.

[You've raised your body from 32 to 35!]

[You've slain a Man Snapper lvl 16! Experience awarded!]

Joey yanked his sword out and staggered back. He lifted his right arm and looked warily at the painful cuts on his side.

Not deep enough to kill him. But he would need stitches.

He came out fortunate, though.

The increase in body might give him enough hardiness to tough out the damage. He checked his essence and saw it was well off.

Should I meditate? Joey thought. He was unsure. *One snapper sank dead into the water. That's blood down there.*

More snappers might investigate.

I'll have to meditate with my eyes open.

Only two out of the three corpses dropped loot. Joey quickly collected and placed the loot in his bag.

[Congrats! You've looted 16 Tidal Moon Copper Coins.]

He glanced over at the translucent Curi. The kraken remained undisturbed.

Then Joey sat down and meditated with his eyes open. It felt weird until he got the hang of it. His recovery was now 3 EP a minute. Another interesting thing came up.

His wound felt cool. Less blood leaked out. Meditation promoted better health if not outright healing. If nothing else, at least he would have his first battle scars.

Joey had the benefit of an hour to recover before the next monster wave. Man snappers exploded out of the water from all sides, six in total.

They landed hard on the raft and raced to tackle Joey while he remained seated. The rogue shifted forward only a little.

Shade Dragon Tail came to life and coiled under him. It launched him straight up with a high-flying spring.

The snappers crashed into each other. One bounced off

another's back shell and pushed away from the group. It looked up and took a tail thrust to the face followed by the point of a sword from a diving Joey.

[You've slain a Man Snapper lvl 15! Experience awarded!]

As Joey jumped into the air again, a shadow clone dropped to the floor with a sword, Dark Dash, and three uses of finesse.

Airborne, Joey took the attention of two snappers rising faster out of the pile than the rest.

The clone dashed from below and hacked behind the legs of the two distracted snappers. Purpose served, the clone ran around to distract the other three snappers.

Joey fell like a dark dragon on the hurt two. His tail whipped one in the face. His sword struck the skull of the other before his feet touched the deck.

He landed more headshots with his tail to finish the two off. Then he turned and watched the last three snappers tear apart his clone.

[You've slain a Man Snapper lvl 14! Experience awarded!]

[You've slain a Man Snapper lvl 13! Experience awarded!]

Joey looked past a new level up message and willed his free points into spirit. He strode to the remaining snappers and whipped out a tail attack with every step.

A snapper's forehead burst open like a melon struck by a hammer. Another snapper raised its arms and had the flesh ripped off both. The third ducked low and took the blow to the shell before rushing for a tackle.

Joey dashed in, trailing darkness behind his feet. His sword pierced the skull all the way through.

The monster's momentum kept going, ripping the sword away from Joey as he hurdled over.

The corpse fell into the pile behind him. The last snapper lowered its ripped up forearms and glared down at Joey.

It hissed, and Analyze translated: [We've seen you from afar. My brethren will tell the others. They will hunt for you, dark tail human.]

"Ever heard how the hunters can become the hunted?" Joey asked before lobbing a base shadow clone to the side. "I guess it won't matter. You won't be telling your brethren."

"Look at me, fool!" shouted the clone while making a silly face.

The snapper looked.

Joey took an eye with his tail. The next hit scattered the snapper's skull across the water.

The sixth died before it fell over. The raft could barely handle the new weight, but it stayed afloat with nine turtle monster bodies and a lone rogue.

"Huh," Joey said. "I become a savage really quick."

Instead of looking at the dead monsters, he caught up on some system messages.

[You've leveled up Shade Dragon Rogue from 9 to 10!]

[You've raised your mind from 31 to 33!]

[You've raised your body from 35 to 37!]

[You've raised your spirit from 31 to 32!]

[You've raised your free points from 0 to 3!]

[You've raised your spirit from 32 to 35!]

[You've slain a Man Snapper lvl 17! Experience awarded!]

[You've slain a Man Snapper lvl 13! Experience awarded!]

[You've slain a Man Snapper lvl 19! Experience awarded!]

[You've leveled up Headhunter from lvl 3 to lvl 4!]

[You've leveled up Finesse from lvl 4 to lvl 5!]

Joey smiled at the skill gains. He still had more messages.

[You've leveled up Shade Dragon Rogue from 10 to 11!]

[You've raised your mind from 33 to 35!]

[You've raised your body from 37 to 39!]

[You've raised your spirit from 35 to 36!]

[You've raised your free points from 0 to 3!]

Joey spread his free points out.

[You've raised your mind from 35 to 36!]

[You've raised your body from 39 to 40!]

[You've raised your spirit from 36 to 37!]

But wait, there was more.

[Congrats! You have the opportunity to learn the Combat Acrobatics Skill!]

[Combat Acrobatics (Basic): Make aerial maneuvers in a fight more effective. Strike and dodge with more power and control. *I laughed myself unconscious when I heard some flippy man was entering a tournament. Then it turned out the stages had elevated platforms and different level beams. The flippy man stopped being a joke.*]

Joey took it without a second thought.

[Congrats! You've learned the Combat Acrobatics Skill!]

Three corpses dropped loot. Joey collected them quickly. Mostly coins with one new glyph tile.

[You've looted 15 Tidal Moon Copper Coins and 1 Beacon Glyph Tile.]

[Beacon Glyph Tile (Basic): Activate with essence. The tile will shine like a beacon for a minute.]

When Curi woke up in the afternoon, the kraken stared silently at the corpse laden raft. Joey had little room to sit on the wood if he wanted to avoid blood and gore. So a snapper's back shell at the top of the middle pile served as Joey's seat.

Legs crossed. Sword on his lap. Eyes half-lidded but observant. Joey meditated and recovered essence at 4 EP a minute. He stopped meditating when the kraken became visible.

"Good afternoon, Curi," Joey said with a smile.

[It is indeed a good afternoon.] The kraken blinked slowly. [You know, Joey. I've come to realize it'll be more beneficial if I take less of the loot and have at the bodies. How does that sound?]

"Ha. I like that." A greedy feeling rose inside of Joey. He shook his head and suppressed it. "Actually, are you sure that's okay with you?"

[Oh, I'm sure. Very, very sure.]

7. THE SCENIC DISCOVERER SKILL

Curi only took four coins, two for each day he'd ferried Joey across the Gaela Tide. Before they continued their journey, the kraken needed time to process the snapper bodies.

While Joey sat near the edge, having his tidal racer meal with fresh water, he watched over the kraken. Curi ate two of the snappers while stripping away all the shells.

The process was methodical, bloody, and quick. Plenty of fish swam nearby to snatch away snapper pierces from the bloody chum.

As Curi worked, he explained how snapper shells were good materials for crafters. Armor could be made from the shells. Or they could be used as part of potions. The kraken trader could also sell the meat. He had a spatial storage ability that could preserve them.

Joey was easily impressed. Spatial storage had to be the cream of the crop of utility magic.

While the kraken finished up his processing, economics came to Joey's mind.

He asked for examples on how far his coppers would take him. Curi knew a lot thanks to his curiosity.

At the lowest and dingiest tavern in the Tidal Moon Realm, Joey could expect to pay seven coppers a night. A meal with a full tankard of ale would cost two coppers at the same tavern.

"Huh. I'll need to work harder at killing things. I'm hoping for more spending room than that."

[Keep in mind those low end taverns will be in small towns or a village where locals will trade goods and favors instead of coins. So you might not always need to pay with your earnings if you can negotiate and use your good fortune. You can also earn a coin or a meal completing local quests. And lest not forget that you have glyph tiles! Those can sell from twenty coppers to almost an entire bronze coin depending on the rarity, your location, and how well you can bargain.]

"And a bronze coin is how much in copper coins?"

[One hundred copper coins is a bronze. If you somehow gain one hundred bronze coins, you'll have a whole silver coin. But that's harder to achieve in a lesser realm like this one. Especially since we're on the lower end of the lesser realms.]

"Huh, okay." Joey mulled over his next question, his greed flaring until he suppressed it. "And you're not going to ask for the tiles despite their worth?"

[I'm getting plenty from you already. Besides, our next days of voyage may see us profit even better than this!]

Oh, goodie, more crazy death fights with scary monsters!

Joey chuckled to himself.

The blood and gore had less of an effect on him than before. But once the adrenaline had gone away, he still felt a little squeamish with his new savage qualities.

If it wasn't for the system, there would be no way I could fight like that. No wonder being a great adventurer comes with so much risk. You get the overpowered start. But that has a price just like everything else so far.

Thinking about his spells led to another question swimming in the back of Joey's head. "Curi, my spells aren't leveling. What's up with that?"

The kraken finished processing the snappers. His tentacles gripped the raft before they set off toward Joey's first tidal floor crossing. [They're superior or above, aren't they?]

"Yeah."

[You'll need greater challenges to level those, Joey. Consider it a mercy at your low level. Can you imagine what they will cost you if the expense rose with the levels?]

Joey flinched at the thought of rising spell costs. His base essence was at 1130 EP now. He could fight for longer and try more complex maneuvers now. Shadow Clone Magic would benefit as long as the costs remained manageable.

And I can improve the spell power gradually if I invest in the spirit stat.

But he needed to keep his body up for faster recovery. His mind stat helped with his focus, which gave him a killer edge in fights.

That last battle had pushed his focus hard to keep track of his skills, spells, and tactics.

Okay, basically, I freaking need all my stats.

But was that true?

"Curi!"

[Ask away, and hopefully I can answer.]

"I can't decide on which stat to push ahead. They all help me a lot."

[Oh, ho, ho! This is a good struggle, and I'm glad you're discussing it. You could've fallen into a trap.]

"Really?"

[Yes! The trap is thinking you should focus on one or two specific stats and neglect the remaining. This may work for steady adventurers who have a team covering their weaknesses. But you are a great adventurer! You will need all of your stats for different situations.]

Joey wondered if he would ever have a team.

Technically, Curi and him were a team. But this was a partnership where they benefited differently without getting in each other's way.

What if Joey had to slow his growth because his teammates took potential kills away from him?

However, having a team could help Joey cover more ground and fight more enemies. They could help him take on bigger challenges and monsters with higher levels, too. Teammates who focus on certain stats could leverage their specialties even more.

But what Curi had advised focused on the great adventurers.

"There are less great adventurers than steady ones, huh?" Joey asked.

[The difference is quite large. For every ten thousand steady adventurers, you'll find one great adventurer. And then you have a difference between the great ones who will stall or fall and the great ones who are rising stars. You'll find one rising star out of ten thousand other great adventurers.]

"And adventurers are smaller in numbers compared to commoners and denizens, huh?"

[I honestly can't estimate the numbers. I've yet to meet someone who could tell it to me accurately. This realm, for example, is smaller than most, but I have yet to see much of it. And Multiverse Z is, well, a multiverse of realms! Let's say the adventurer pool is much smaller compared to everyone else.]

"Makes sense." Joey struggled to continue the conversation. Then, in a quiet voice, he asked, "Do you think I can be a rising star?"

[We shall see, won't we?] The kraken laughed.

Joey shook his head and laughed with him. Curi was right. They were about to see if he could be a rising star.

The next obstacle showed Joey how truly big, magical, and demanding Multiverse Z could be. The rogue could hardly believe his eyes even with Curi's explanations.

The water had a downward curve in front of them. The further the kraken led Joey's raft westward, the more pronounced the curve became.

Meanwhile, Joey noticed the dip between bodies of water further out. There was a gap of air separating Joey's current tide and the next tide.

At a certain point, when the downward curve sharpened even further, Joey saw the bottom of the next tide and the floor between. Then his view of the floor expanded more and more until Joey realized there were miles between the tides.

"Whoa, Curi, you weren't lying!" Joey exclaimed, stabbing his sword into the raft. He pushed down to the guard as his feet slipped from under him, leaving him to dangle.

The drop toward the tidal floor sharpened further and further under Joey's feet. They were still thousands of feet up in the air, too, while the kraken traveled with the curve and repositioned his tentacles to keep the raft from falling away.

If it wasn't for Joey's amazement and growing spirit stat, he'd suffer primal fear like most humans.

A majority of the water near Joey ignored gravity and kept the tidal wall together. Meanwhile, loosened water fell from the tide's magical hold. Endless cascades dropped along the tidal wall in great white sprays with Joey drenched in the middle of it all.

The waterfalls created thick mist clouds that hovered in the air near the tidal walls. Rainbow arcs bent through the mist clouds. And through a gap in the waterfalls, clouds, and rainbows, Joey spotted the solar moon on its late afternoon descent toward the western horizon.

Joey felt like a man out of his depths in an ultra fantasy painting. He had his sword. His raft. A kraken ferry. And an entire alien landscape that didn't care for the natural laws of his old world.

It was crazy. And he gained a skill from the experience.

[Congrats! You have the opportunity to learn the Scenic Discoverer Skill!]

[Scenic Discoverer (Basic): You'll passively sense areas of opportunity for a great scenic view. It could lead you to interesting locations. *Part of the fun with this adventuring business is the views. No matter how detailed the tales, seeing is believing.*]

"I'll take that!"

[Congrats! You've learned the Scenic Discoverer Skill!]

Joey burst into sudden laughter. He waved his free hand and shouted into the roaring waterfall and scenic views.

"Hello, Multiverse Z!" Joey yelled. "You better be ready to watch your favorite rogue pull off more crazy stunts!"

***

It was all business once they reached the tidal floor. Joey dislodged his sword from the raft and bounded to the closest twisted rock spire jutting out of the floor water.

The tidal floor was flooded. Some areas had a hundred feet of water between the surface and the bottom.

Curi explained plenty of how they could navigate so Joey wouldn't fall unaware. His best bet was staying above the flood.

The kraken pointed out rock spires, fossilized coral towers, and silt mounds along the floor for the rogue to use. It was Joey's job to scout ahead and persuade monsters to face an early end.

Curi would follow behind the rogue and pick up bodies. To Joey's constant amazement, the kraken could move well even in shallows.

Curi was a thick mass of rolling tentacles and a big head while out of the tide. His tentacles slithered at the front, reaching to grasp spires, ledges, or old coral.

Tentacles at the back helped propel him forward with strong pushes. Four tentacles held the raft on top of his head, keeping it safe as he moved like a wheelless locomotive.

It was while they transitioned from tidal wall to flooded floor when Joey grasped how fast the tides moved as a whole. Not fast at all, actually.

Joey could run along with the Gaela Tide as it moved

northward. Their next tide, the Siren Tide, moved in a similar speed and direction.

The craziest fun fact was how the moons matched the speed and direction of the specific tides they hovered over. The moons and tides redirected around other moons and tides and would avoid collisions most of the time.

Curi explained they were in luck because the Gaela Tide and Siren Tide would normally have more space between each other. They only had to cross twenty miles of the monster infested and flooded tidal floor instead of the usual distance of a hundred miles.

Knowing Curi's level, he could probably breeze through this section. He doesn't really need my help to avoid trouble.

Joey could ride on the raft while it was balanced on Curi's head, too. But there was more to this venture than traveling safely.

We're here to profit together. I need levels, stats, and loot. And Curi could use the bodies of my kills.

Joey had to reach level 25 before landfall, after all. He knew Curi was setting that level as a goal to help him. *I might need to be that level or higher to survive on my own.*

Balancing the need for safety and profits, Joey set off ahead of Curi with a pounding heart. Behind every spire or old coral tower, a monster could lurk in wait for unsuspecting prey.

Joey had to account for his bare feet, too, and avoid stepping the wrong way.

Hopping from spire to spire and running on the bends and cliffs of ancient coral towers gave Joey perspective on his class choice. The only other option was archer, but Joey preferred being a rogue for all of its up-close benefits.

Most things on the tidal floor were gray or black. Here and there bloomed colorful life where coral grew in disregard of its bleak surroundings. The livelier coral were distant from Joey, but the nearest one seemed to squirm with movement.

No, it's not squirming. Joey looked closer and noticed crab-like creatures scuttling all over the coral. *Man, from what I can see at this distance, those crabs have to be huge.*

They were too far for him to analyze. Shaking his head, Joey kept going. He limited his use of Dark Dash, hoping to acquire another movement skill.

Acrobatic Combat worked best in fights. It would be nice getting something else in the lull periods. But he soon realized his acrobatic skill would see its first use.

A monster scuttled into view.

[Tidal Moon Monster: Hull Crusher: Runt lvl 8.]

It was a crab the size of a large dog. Its shell was gray, and its eyes extended up on two stalks. It had two big claws and two mini claws.

When it looked up at Joey's aerial form, bubbles foamed and popped from its toothy mouth with a recognizable pattern.

[Adventurer human! Submit yourself to the mighty hull crushers and our leader, the Almighty Claw!]

Joey landed a downward thrust through the runt. The runt collapsed on a slab of rock above the flood.

[You've slain a Hull Crusher Runt lvl 8! Partial experience awarded.]

Yeah, I imagined weaker monsters would give less experience.

He waited to see if any loot would appear. None dropped. When Curi caught up, Joey stood with his sword slick with brownish blood. He pointed down at the slain monster.

[Eh, the runts aren't worth much. Try for hull crusher grunts. They're in the level 20s, in fact. However, be careful if they're in large groups. Hull Crusher Bruisers might accompany them, and those can range from mid 50s and up.]

"I'll stay alert." Joey continued onward. He reasoned he would still kill runts for the partial experience.

Unless the runts were too weak and gave no experience. He hadn't asked Curi about kills that gave no experience, but Joey figured he would find out on his own.

8. SOME DEADLY ROGUISH ACTION

A fourth hull crusher runt died from Joey's dive attack.

[You've slain a Hull Crusher Runt lvl 4!]

"Ah, there it is. No experience."

Being thorough, Joey waited for the loot to drop.

No loot appeared.

That was okay. He now had a good idea where the experience benefits cutoff from. *I won't get anything from a monster lower than five levels from me.*

Maybe it was possible to grind for loot on weak monsters. But Joey imagined the system would reduce chances for drops. If that was the case, the system was showing its flexibility and sense of balance.

The system might even be harder on great adventurers than steady adventurers. Joey could see the system pushing great adventurers to live up to their name. No easy handouts would be found from the system if that was the case. *There's a price for our power.*

Joey looked up from his position on a silt mound. The area here was elevated above the flooding. The ground slurped at his feet almost like quicksand when he moved. It was a workout to keep from getting stuck.

Leaving behind the runt, he continued his jog forward while searching for more monsters. His sweep across the silt mound found nothing out of the ordinary.

At first.

Then he noticed a bump in the silt ground ahead of him. It didn't seem too unordinary. And it was stationary. But the bump was twenty feet wide and noticeable enough. The hairs on the back of Joey's neck stood.

"Let me get a volunteer," Joey said, conjuring a shadow clone.

"Aw, man, does it have to be me?" the clone asked, showing a personality. How that worked, Joey had no idea, but it was interesting to see.

"You're the best man for the job." Joey shrugged.

The clone shrugged back before running half heartedly toward the bump. In an explosion of silt and water, a dark hole appeared and slammed down on the clone. The shadow dispersed, leaving the ambusher with nothing to eat and giving itself away to Joey's Analyze Skill.

[Tidal Moon Beast: Big Fish: Trap Door Springer lvl 41.]

"Yeah, no," Joey said.

He picked up the pace and ran around the floundering beast. It made a bubbling noise that Joey couldn't translate since it was a beast and had no intelligence.

He figured the big fish was angry at the missed meal, but that wasn't Joey's problem. It only became an issue when the tidal springer's wide and flat body floundered around and focused its gaze on Joey's back.

Then it began a chase that was both scary and laughable. It was like having a giant Magikarp chasing after him for a bite-size meal – him. It became scarier and less laughable when the beast gained on Joey steadily even when all it could do was flounder.

It had more levels and stats, after all.

Oh, hell no! I am not dying to a stupid beast like this!

Joey used his strongest version of Dark Dash and launched further ahead. But the tidal springer floundered even harder and sent its big body flying to cover the gap.

Its landing hurled silt everywhere without stopping. The gap was closer now than before. Joey tossed a look back and couldn't believe it as he ran away. *Seriously? This is what I have to deal as a great adventurer?*

If things didn't change, the flounder might land a meal in the end. But to Joey's fortune and misfortune, the situation changed drastically.

The rogue heard a loud, foamy hiss to his left. From out of the brackish flood rushed large scuttling shapes.

He stopped counting at a dozen when the mob moved with a strategic slant to cut off the rogue and his pursuer. He only had to analyze one to confirm the next wave of trouble.

[Tidal Moon Monster: Hull Crusher: Grunt lvl 21.]

The grunts looked more humanoid compared to the runts. But not by much. They had two body parts separated by a shell-covered waist. The bottom part of their body had six legs with fin-like protrusions extending from the sides.

The upper part was like a crab on its own, but with

more fins, a pair of giant pincers, and another pair of smaller pincers. Its mouth was wide enough to bite off Joey's head with room to spare.

The grunts had nothing more to say. They were all about the action. But their current course wouldn't reach Joey in time before the springer caught him.

Aw, man, I have to get crazy with this!

Joey veered to his left, toward the grunts. The springer slammed down behind him and prepared to pounce again.

The grunts noticed Joey's redirection and ran straight at him. The closer he drew, the more he appreciated their size. Each one was at least eight feet tall. Their big pinchers could reach around his entire waist and snip him in two.

The groups came to a head with a climactic collision filled with frantic movement. The springer landed a few feet short of Joey's back as he dashed with all his might, leaving streaks of black. Scuttling legs with sharp points missed him by a few inches.

Joey's tail whipped into view and caught a grunt's big arm at the elbow joint. Using the grunt as a swing, he jerked the monster to a stop while swinging away from reaching pincers. He deactivated the tail and flew away.

Grunts at the front fought against the tidal springer. Grunts at the back adjusted to Joey's short flight and shifted to intercept.

Dark Dash took Joey away from their reaching pincers and toward cover. He hit the silt heavily and activated his tail again to help him like a bendy walking stick.

It was an odd way to move, but he wound up moving faster instead of getting stuck in the quicksand-like silt.

Meanwhile, shadow clones peeled away and distracted

grunts from pursuing the real Joey. The monsters weren't as fast as the springer, so Joey reached the outcropping of tall rock spires and dead coral towers before they could catch up. Then the game changed from there as Joey disappeared from the grunt's sight.

[We will find you, adventurer human!] a grunt shouted. [The Almighty Claw will be pleased to have you. He will eat half of you. Then he will give the other half to the next generation.]

[For the Almighty Claw!] a grunt roared.

Other grunts roared the same.

There were seven of them searching for Joey while the others fought the springer. The rock spires and coral towers offered plenty of nooks, crannies, and cover. Joey was a slim guy. He could find lots of places to tuck into and hide.

However, the tidal floor was the home turf of the hull crushers. They moved around like experts over the obstacles and through the flooded portions. These monsters knew what they were doing. They had multiple advantages.

But Joey didn't care.

Joey's appearance showed up to the monsters left. Three grunts responded at once. Four grunts waited back. The clone distracted them for a bit before the real Joey launched down from a nook in a coral tower.

He struck with both tail and sword on the grunt furthest to the back. The tail sliced off an eye stalk. The sword cut off the other.

The monster hissed and reached with its pinchers. The rogue barely twisted out of the way, slammed shoulder first on top of the blind monster's shell, and rolled off. He touched his feet against the side of a spire instead of hitting water and dashed away with a dark burst. He barely slipped out of view when the other grunts responded to the attack.

Joey circled around. Without needing a clone, he attacked another grunt from behind. He weaved his tail around the big pincers twice to eliminate the monster's eyes. Just like that, a second grunt lost its vision.

The group roared angrily. Three grunts scuttled around in search, running into the last place they'd seen Joey. Two healthy grunts remained with their blinded brethren. Their attention was split in different directions.

Joey bounded from the top of a tower and fell in between. He took the eyes of one. While his third blinded victim panicked, he faced the fourth with a small rock mound under him.

The grunt rushed him, splashing brackish water. Joey jumped backward, and the monster's eyes followed. It missed the two clones remaining on the rock Joey had jumped from.

Both clones thrust up with copies of Joey's sword, headhunter, finesse, acrobatics, and dash. Together, the sword clones thrust deep into the grunt's mouth and into its cranium. It lurched to a stop while its pincers crashed down on the copies, dispersing them.

Injured, but alive, the monster sagged downward. Its eye stalks looked around weakly when a dark form fell from above.

Joey thrust down with all his weight behind his sword and pierced the shell halfway through. The grunt jerked. Its pincers spasmed while trying to reach for Joey.

But the rogue leaned away from the pincer grabs and lashed his tail around the area his sword entered. After three hammering tail blows, the shell broke from around his sword.

Joey grabbed the opening with his free hand, lifted his sword, and thrust down with great effort. All the way to the guard.

The grunt collapsed and became still.

[You've slain a Hull Crusher Grunt lvl 24! For slaying a monster ten levels above you, bonus experience is awarded!]

[You've leveled up Acrobatic Combat from 1 to 3!]

[You've leveled up Analyze from 3 to 4!]

[You've leveled up Headhunter from 4 to 5!]

[You've leveled up Shade Dragon Rogue from 11 to 12!]

[You've raised your mind from 36 to 38!]

[You've raised your body from 40 to 42!]

[You've raised your spirit from 37 to 38!]

[You've raised your free points from 0 to 3!]

It was tempting to stuff more points into spirit and body. But that could build a bad habit. *All my stats are important for different situations. In fact, right now I can use my focus to stay on top of my game.*

Joey inserted 2 free points into mind and 1 into spirit.

[You've raised your mind from 38 to 40!]

[You've raised your spirit from 38 to 39!]

The rogue had a determined look on his face. Three blinded grunts drifted toward him. The search party would be on their way, too.

He had his work cut out for him. But it wasn't bad. Joey could feel himself growing. A roguish smile appeared on the young man's face while surrounded by man-eating monsters.

***

From outside of Joey's fight against seven hull crusher grunts, the voyager kraken watched. If the young adventurer looked like he might face an early demise, Curi would dash in and whisk the rogue out of trouble.

The kraken held back because great adventurers needed space and strife to grow strong. But the kraken feared for the young human. Curi had helped great adventurers before.

And I've failed each one.

The kraken felt fear. What if this one took on more than he could handle? What if this one ignored Curi's advice and strayed away from balanced stats?

Maybe Curi should stop concerning himself with great adventurers and deliver the young human where he needed to go pronto. The kraken could move plenty fast at his level. There was no need to help grow a great one.

It was a lost cause, some would say.

Great adventurers were like shooting stars. They were as shiny as they were fleeting. No matter how much Curi hoped for the great adventurers he'd met to turn their potential sparks into an everlasting light, the task of guiding them always became a fool's errand.

But then there was Joey.

He was both eager and wary. Both curious and courageous. He wasn't too foolhardy. But he was just foolhardy enough to have great aspirations. He even had the most unique path Curi had ever seen in his sixty multiverse years.

A dark and serpentine tail reappeared and disappeared behind the rogue in the blink of an eye. Lines of darkness hurled him in any direction of his choosing. And when he needed help, he had his own dark reflections to bail him out.

His spells were by far the most multiversal Curi had seen. Joey's class as a rogue fitted his spells perfectly, too.

And the way the young human took to the short sword was marvelous.

Even while having the system and class to help them, many adventurers wouldn't push to master their abilities. They would settle with the bare minimum of effort.

Skills didn't happen automatically, after all. The system needed an adventurer to meet them halfway with impressive effort.

It still astounds me he discovered his own short sword skill and told me about it, Curi thought.

So watching Joey swoop, outflank, and plunge on top of his enemies like a dark-tailed dragon was a pleasure to witness for anyone who was a fan of the greats. Curi's insides quivered weakly while near all the violence, but he could still appreciate the artistry of a great adventurer reaching for excellence.

By the time the seventh hull crusher grunt fell, the rogue stood amid the corpses while looking up at the darkening sky. He seemed lost for thought. Neither happy nor sad. He wasn't a blood-lusting adventurer. But he was committed to the grim work.

Then a smile appeared on his face. It looked like Joey was okay with his work. He looked earnest and eager for the next action and adventure.

Maybe this one could be the one, Curi thought with cautious hope. The kraken crawled out from his hiding spot as if he'd just caught up to Joey.

The rogue looked back. His smile widened into a grin, happy to see Curi.

The kraken could recognize human facial expressions pretty well these days. Their genders were still a mystery to him, however.

He did his best to return the expression in a way a human could pick up on, and he spoke with an enthusiasm that whistled up from within.

[Well, well, now! Look at you. I shiver to think what would happen to me if I had the misfortune of ever being your foe!]

"Thankfully, that'll never happen," Joey said. "Who'll clean up the bodies I leave behind and turn them for a profit?"

Curi laughed, feeling joyful. Maybe he was more of a fool than a trader. But it was so much fun being around a great adventurer's journey. Curi couldn't stop himself from helping another on their path to greatness in the realms of Multiverse Z.

9. LEVELS, STATS, AND CHOICES

Joey and Curi took a rest stop at a cropping of dead coral towers. The kraken wedged the raft between the structures and squeezed into a gap in the water.

Joey found a small cove above the water. Moonlight filtered through the gaps while the rogue sat back, meditated, and tended to his wounds. He hadn't come out of his last fight unscathed.

Brushes with passing pincers left bleeding wounds all over his limbs and torso. He always managed to twist out of the way in the nick of time when the monsters had attacked, but he couldn't avoid everything perfectly.

But it's so bothersome when they touch me. I honestly hate getting hit.

[Would you like some healing algae ointment? I'll apply it on your wounds as you meditate.]

Joey thought about the cost. Curi was a step ahead of him.

[The hull crusher grunt bodies have you covered.]

"Thanks, Curi," Joey said.

The kraken summoned a green ball between his mini-tentacles.

[Tidal Algae Healing Ointment (Basic): It won't bring back an arm but it'll help with cuts and bruises.]

Joey found it funny how he completely trusted Curi to apply the ointment on him while he meditated. From an outsider's perspective, it would look like a young man was getting surrounded by dark and monstrous tentacles rising out of the tidal pool.

For Joey, each application of the ointment was a blessing. His wounds hurt less and felt cooler while he recovered his essence.

Joey also found it convenient that he could review his system messages while meditating. For this once, he waited until after the battle.

He could be more methodical with his free points this way. And the system readapted some messages for him, too.

[You've slain six Hull Crusher Grunts ranging from lvl 23 to 28! For slaying monsters ten levels above you, bonus experience is awarded!]

[You've leveled up Acrobatic Combat from 3 to 4!]

[You've leveled up Headhunter from 5 to 6!]

[You've leveled up Short Sword Finesse from 5 to 6!]

[You've leveled up Shade Dragon Rogue from 12 to 16!]

[You've raised your mind from 40 to 48!]

[You've raised your body from 42 to 50!]

[You've raised your spirit from 39 to 43!]

[You've raised your free points from 0 to 12!]

With little thought, Joey inserted two into mind and seven into spirit. He held back on the last three free points to think.

I'm going to lean more toward my spirit just a bit. It has a handicap, and I want more power for my spells.

Joey dumped the last three free points into spirit.

[You've raised your mind from 48 to 50!]

[You've raised your spirit from 43 to 53!]

If this was the end of his gains, Joey would've been proud. But he had another reason to smile. The entire situation from the springer to the defeat of his first hull crusher grunts was fortunate in other ways.

[Congrats! You have the opportunity to learn the Chaos Finder Skill!]

[Chaos Finder (Basic): You will passively notice weaknesses and exploits that can produce chaos for your enemies. The chaos will better your focus, too. *You have two types of adventurers. They're both a pain. But I deal better with the orderly ones. It's hard predicting the ones who thrive in chaos.*]

Joey nearly broke his meditation to pump his fists. But he held back since 5 EP a minute was worthwhile to keep going.

He took the skill and moved on. He had more to look at.

[Congrats! You've learned the Chaos Finder Skill!]

[Congrats! You have the opportunity to learn one of these two skills! The Armor Breaker Skill! The Armor Piercer Skill!]

Joey recovered 100 more EP before breaking his meditation. "Curi? Question."

The kraken made bubbly flute noises while under the water. The Analyze skill translated. [What's on your mind, young great?]

Joey chuckled. "I have this new thing from the system saying I can learn one of two skills."

[Ah, this can happen sometimes. It's the system's consistent effort in balancing. It's also an interesting mechanic for shaping your adventuring profile. Thirdly, it can be a test of knowing yourself and your potential so you can avoid making the wrong choice.]

"I can't get both skills?" Joey asked.

[It wouldn't be balanced if the system gave you everything. And from my knowledge, you've been picking up skills quickly. Quicker than most! Now the system is checking to see which way you lean toward with an opportune skill choice.]

"Thanks, Curi. The skill choices are Armor Breaker and Armor Piercer, by the way."

[My, my, that's interesting. Those are warrior spells! Having the skill versions of those will be less effective. But you'll have the skills of the warrior class in your back pocket.]

"Well, I'm more of a battle rogue than anything else right now," Joey admitted. "I haven't done any thieving or lying. Will that mean I'll suck at the other rogue abilities now?"

[You're still a rogue. And your path is still young. I think you have plenty of time to add more to your roguish ways later. But as of now, take advantage of this battle rogue growth you have. You'll surprise your enemies when you show them you can hold your own!]

"Good to hear. I'll read them now before I decide." One choice was more likely than the other. But reading new skills for the hidden lore could be fun.

[**Armor Breaker (Basic): Surge with power and strike a hammering blow with a weapon. It might take more than one hit, but those hits can break through with enough commitment.** *I never get along with those brutish oafs and their primitive murder sticks. Where I can cast wonders with my mind, they see a wonder and hit it until it breaks.*]

[**Armor Piercer (Basic): Thrust with power and pierce the obstacle in your way. Works best if you target a weak point unless you keep thrusting to make one.** *There was once a warrior who spoke proudly of his lance. He wielded a hammer, however, so I spoke to correct him. Consequently, he corrected me with a tale of how he had been stripped bare and had to best a female orc with his lance.*]

Joey gawked at the description to piercer before feeling his neck heat up. He glanced back at the breaker skill, shook his head solemnly, and picked the skill that would suit him best.

[**Congrats! You've learned the Armor Piercer Skill!**]

Last but not least, Joey checked his loot message.

[**You've looted 57 Tidal Moon Copper Coins and 1 Tough Glyph Tile!**]

[**Tough Glyph Tile (Basic): Activate with essence. Make your body 30% tougher for 30 minutes.**]

That was the end of the review. Joey focused on meditating for the next hour and a half. By then, his essence topped off and his wounds sealed. They were still tender, but the bleeding and swelling went away.

The recovery was miraculous, honestly. He even felt ready to go find more action and adventure.

Before he did anything, Joey checked his profile. It was a little stunning to see how far he'd come.

Great Adventurer: Joey Eclipse

Race: Basic Human

Age: 18

Path: Shade Dragon Rogue lvl 16

Singularities: Agility Buff (Basic/2 hours).

Skills: Analyze lvl 4 (Basic), Headhunter lvl 6 (Basic), Short Sword Finesse lvl 6 (Basic), Underwater Combat lvl 1 (Basic), Acrobatic Combat lvl 4 (Basic), Scenic Discover lvl 1 (Basic), Chaos Finder lvl 1 (Basic), Armor Piercer lvl 1 (Basic).

Spells: Dark Dash lvl 1 (Superior), Shade Dragon Tail lvl 1 (Epic), Shadow Clone Magic lvl 1 (Epic).

Semblances:

Special Stuff: Holding Bag (Basic/1), Tidal Moon Copper Coins (97), Breath Glyph Tile (Basic/1), Beacon Glyph Tile (Basic/1), Tough Glyph Tile (Basic/1), Tidal Short Sword (Basic/1).

Essence: 1530/1530 EP

Mind: 50 (+2 per a level)

Body: 50 (+2 per a level)

Spirit: 53 (+1 per a level)

Free: 0 (+3 per a level)

"Wow," Joey said. "I've grown."

[Really now?]

"I'm Level 16. I have a bunch of new skills. I can afford more than a week at a poor tavern. My essence is way higher than when I started. And I feel stronger." Joey smiled. "This is awesome."

The kraken laughed.

Joey continued, having more questions. "When will I get a new spell? And when will I get a semblance?"

[Ah, yes, the hunger of the great adventurer. Must have more and more!]

Joey felt embarrassed and proud. His greediness surfaced without being suppressed this time around. "Yeah, I do want more. It's scary to get it. I'm covered in new scars. But getting stronger and having more feels so good."

[As it should, Joey, as it should. You will be able to select a new spell at Level 25. And semblances are rare. And highly randomized. All I can tell you is that you'll need to defeat your foes directly and hope the semblance comes from something worthy.]

"Are you telling me I could get a semblance from a runt?"

[Yes. So don't hunt those too often. Semblances can grow in levels. But you will want a good semblance worth summoning.]

Another reason to fight creatures above my level, Joey thought. *I wonder if I can push further than ten levels above me. Can I beat something at twenty levels above?*

[Patience, Joey, patience.] The kraken either had a mind-reading ability or Joey was pretty easy to read. [You're doing great work. Now I must urge you to slow down for a bit. Perhaps for the next day.]

"Why?"

[As practice for controlling your eagerness. It's always a good idea to take a step back now and then.]

"When we make it to the Siren Tide, I'll take a step back. But while we're crossing, I want to push further." Joey waited a beat before saying, "Please."

He heard his heart pounding louder while waiting for the kraken's response. [Well, who am I to slow down a great adventurer? Fine then, fine then. Just be careful, okay?]

Joey sighed in relief. Curi handed over some water and a piece of tidal racer. Joey wished he could make a fire to enjoy the fish more, but at least it was edible. His agility buff returned to having a duration of six hours.

Ready to go, Joey crawled out from the cove and scouted the way ahead. Then he watched Curi slither out before seizing the raft from its lodging.

The rogue and kraken journeyed onward, Joey leading the way. Sometimes he had to take detours to avoid large bodies of tidal flooding with no solid footpaths.

He even diverted a little off course when he caught a small group of monsters. They were man snappers skulking about.

"This isn't your territory," Joey said while crouched on a coral ledge above the man snappers. The turtle monsters looked up at him in surprise.

[Tidal Moon Monster: Man Snapper: Grunt lvl 17.]

[Tidal Moon Monster: Man Snapper: Grunt lvl 16.]

[Tidal Moon Monster: Man Snapper: Grunt lvl 18.]

The Level 18 Grunt pointed up at the rogue. [All territories will belong to us! Just like your guts and your head, adventurer human!]

"Nah, I doubt that." Joey tilted his head to the side and pretended to listen to more of the monster's threats.

Three clones sneaked up on the distracted grunts like Navy Seals. They moved quietly in the flood, each having a sword copy along with the finesse, headhunter, swimming, piercer, and dash abilities. An expense of about 170 EP total.

When all his clones dashed and pierced the skulls of each unaware snapper, Joey figured the results were worth the expense. Especially since he gained some levels.

[**You've slain a Man Snapper Grunt lvl 16! Experience awarded!**]

[**You've slain a Man Snapper Grunt lvl 17! Experience awarded!**]

[**You've slain a Man Snapper Grunt lvl 18! Experience awarded!**]

[**You've leveled up Armor Piercer from 1 to 2!**]

[**You've leveled up Combat Swimming from 1 to 2!**]

[**You've leveled up Shade Dragon Rogue from 16 to 17!**]

Joey skipped past the next system messages and spread his free points evenly. The system messages readapted on the fly.

[**You've raised your mind from 50 to 53!**]

[**You've raised your body from 50 to 53!**]

[**You've raised your spirit from 53 to 55!**]

He figured he'd spread his points for Level 18 and Level 19 the same way. Then he'd dump his free points on spirit again at Level 20.

He waited for loot drops and saw none, which was fine. He was more eager to find greater challenges.

What if I hit Level 25 before we reach the Siren Tide? Joey smiled, feeling greedy and being okay with that. It felt good to let his greed out.

Once Curi hauled the snappers into his spatial storage,

the rogue ran off again. The smile on his face dimmed when he realized his positioning.

The Siren Tide's white misty wall wasn't far.

How did we get so close already? Joey stopped to think on the top of a dead coral tower. *Oh, of course. I'm faster than before. It's incremental with the individual points, but it feels like a bigger bump every ten points. With my body having 53 points, I'm probably way faster than a normal human.*

Realizing this, Joey would have to readapt his limited references to his growing capabilities. Twenty miles would seem daunting to him before Multiverse Z. But now it was more manageable to his current self.

He should be glad. But Joey felt anxious. He had more battle opportunities while crossing between the tides. That would drop after leaving the tidal floor.

Can I make it to Level 20 first?

Joey looked around before noticing a flash of light in the distance. He looked closer and saw humanoid figures darting through the shadows and moonlight.

Joey figured the flash had come from a magic power. The figures appeared to be in battle with a larger version of a hull crusher grunt. The figures weren't man snappers, though. And they looked to be holding weapons.

Spears? Could those be people?

If they were people, they were unaware of more hull crusher grunts grouping behind some rock cropping. It looked like an ambush getting ready to spring.

Joey was less than seven miles from the Siren Tide if he kept going that way. The situation with the spear people and hull crushers was one mile away.

Joey figured he should keep going and let things be. But he was hungry for more levels and growth. And he could make a new friend – and earn awards – helping some people out.

"Curi, major detour!" Joey shouted down and pointed his sword. "South! One mile!"

[I trust you! Just be careful!]

Joey hopped off the tall tower. He descended fast, the salty air whipping past him.

One Dark Dash turned his downward descent into forward movement and simple acrobatics. His feet lunged from a silt mound, to a boulder, to a ridge of dead coral, and beyond.

He ran and jumped harder than ever before. But he didn't reach the spear people in time to thwart an ambush at their flank.

A couple of things became more apparent as he drew closer. The fight might be out of his league based on the monsters' higher levels. The spear people weren't people people. And they were under leveled compared to the monsters.

[Tidal Moon Monster: Hull Crusher: Bruiser lvl 51.]

[Tidal Moon Monster: Hull Crusher: Grunt lvl 32.]

[Tidal Moon Denizen: War Siren: Seeker lvl 29.]

Hero time? Or scavenge at the end? Joey could go either way, but first, he had to get closer.

10. RAGE, YOUNG GREAT, RAGE!

Joey scaled the tallest rock spire in the area while near the battle. He wedged into a crevice large enough for him to fit, concealing himself while he surveyed things.

He only lost view of the sirens for a half a minute. Much hadn't changed from what he could see now. Things were still looking bad for the sirens.

The war sirens were all female based on their figures. They had two arms and two legs like humans. But their skin was covered in fishlike skin, silver in color. Their hair differed in colors, vibrant reds or blues. They had flipper-like feet and webbed hands. They wore tight body suits the color of seaweed.

Their weapons reminded Joey of double-sided pole arms. At one end was a harpoon's head. The other ended as a long spear.

Their strategy made sense when they had numbers. Some war sirens used their harpoon heads to pierce and lockdown a target. Other war sirens thrust in and out with the long spearhead and skewered the target to death.

This was a sound strategy, which amassed deaths among the grunts. But therein came the problem with using teamwork. The sirens needed to outnumber their targets.

In the time Joey took to get close and survey, one siren died in exchange for three dead grunts, leaving eleven sirens against twelve grunts and a bruiser. One of those elven sirens was holding off the bruiser by herself, and she could barely survive while being the strongest siren at Level 29.

The bruiser had four massive pincers and looked like an oversized grunt. Instead of standing eight feet tall, it stood twelve feet tall. Its crab legs dug deep into the rock. But when it touched silt, the flippers on the side of each leg flexed down and distributed the monster's weight.

This allowed the big monster to move in all terrains, in and out of the flood or across solid ground. It was not fast, thankfully. But it had a thick shell that could take a beating, and its attacks were constant and ferocious.

Only the Level 29 Siren could hold it off, and that was because of her magic. With a thrust of her polearm, she released a short range thunderbolt, frying a patch of the bruiser's shell.

The monster stumbled for a moment, stunned by the electrical attack. Then the bruiser shook off the damage and continued the chase with its four pincers attacking in a rapid sequence.

The siren fled, looking haggard and doomed. The other sirens were in the low 20s in level and had some helpful magic. They were barely holding their own against the grunts and could offer no help to the stronger siren.

All it would take for this to turn into a disaster was for another siren to fall. It could be a weaker siren, which would lead to a domino effect. Or it could be the Level 29 Siren, which would certainly lead to a wipe out.

Joey could imagine this because of previous times playing MMORPG games. He could let the party get wiped and pick off the monsters while they were distracted and weakened. To insert himself now would risk him getting killed in the chaos.

Shouldn't I take Curi's advice and stay safe? Or should I go anyway and see what I can do? Think of the levels, man. And the awards.

Joey's greed flared even more. He welcomed the feeling like it was his friend. And Chaos Finder was nudging him to thrive in the chaos.

With a self-deprecating chuckle, Joey crawled out of the crevice. He clutched a small crack in the rock and hung over the battle, waiting for an opportunity to enter and try some new ideas with Shadow Clone Magic.

A siren cried out from a pincer punch she barely blocked with her polearm. The weapon snapped, and she flew back into the muddy silt. She struggled to get up as a grunt scuttled close for the kill.

Joey dropped like a diving dragon, lines of darkness trailing behind him. A clone formed ahead of him before passing him its sword copy. The next split second had Joey crashing down on the grunt, piercing the shell with his original sword, a shadow sword, and his tail.

The grunt stumbled to a stop, stunned. Joey ripped his real sword and tail out from the wounds. He used the shadow sword as an anchor and thrust down multiple times fast and hard with his other weapons.

At the same time, the clone he'd formed dropped into the silt and grabbed the siren's arm, helping her stand. The siren took the offered aid and grabbed one half of her weapon before the grunt fell dead at the spot she'd been stuck in.

Joey entered the moonlit sky with a Dark Dash. He set his feet on a rock spire and jumped off. He hung in the air before using Dark Dash again to rise higher. His gaze settled down on an aggressive grunt split from the others.

As Joey plummeted, he tilted his body forward and down. Then he dashed in like a dark dragon, streaking the air black behind him. He hit below the upper body, skewering the waist connecting the bottom with the top.

He managed one good strike with his real sword. But his next move focused on fending off the smaller pincers reaching around to snip at him.

The arms were thin but flexible while connected to the smaller pincers. Joey had little foot room or space to work as the grunt moved in a frenzy.

The rogue jerked away from a snip at his face and hacked the arm with the shadow sword. His tail lashed wherever it could hit, cracking against the upper body shell or striking one of the legs. When his tail hit a leg joint, the crab scuttled in the opposite direction of the strike.

Joey repeated the same strike and nearly broke one of the grunt's six legs. The monster jumped to the side and crashed into another grunt. Joey nearly fell off, replacing his feet on the lower body while scrunching awkwardly into the gap.

His tail kept lashing around, striking the elbow joint of the big claw, getting another response. The grunt struck out to the side and hit the other grunt.

The other grunt replied by striking Joey's grunt in return. Grunt versus grunt violence shook up Joey's position and risked attacks from multiple pincers, the big ones included.

The rogue ditched his ride and dismissed his spells. He hit the flood and swam away until he reached silt.

A weary siren nodded at him before moving on to help a companion. The fight evened out for the weaker sirens while against the grunts. They would survive longer, at least.

But when Joey turned to the bruiser fight, his heart sank from a horrible sight. The Level 29 Siren was falling in pieces, her blood slicking the snapping claws of the victorious bruiser.

The big monster reached down for the torso. It shoved the head into its mouth and chewed with clear glee in its eyes.

Joey didn't know how he should feel. Even his greed was paling.

But he could describe one feeling that rose to the top. Anger.

Recognizing this feeling, Joey rushed forward to correct the problem in front of him.

It has to die!

He darted off to the side and rounded some dead coral. A winding path led up twenty feet onto a ledge.

Joey jumped, prepared to try the same aerial strategies on the bruiser. One of the eye stalks turned to look up at him, surprising the rogue.

Joey changed his plans on the fly.

A sacrificial clone came to life and offered its back for Joey to kick off. The clone fell into the snapping pincers of the monster. A second pincer reached around, but Joey had a fresh Dark Dash to use. He sped right by the attack and hacked into the bruiser's eye.

The armor around the eye was tough. His sword cleaved

halfway through and spilled blood.

The monster growled angrily. Another pincer swiped at Joey.

The rogue's tail appeared while wrapped around the other eye, jerking Joey out of his flight path and away from the third pincer. He swung up at the bloody mouth and gave the monster something to chew on, a sword thrust.

Joey pierced and drew more blood.

The monster stumbled in shock and pain, giving the rogue time to dismiss his tail and fall away. He hit the water and conjured his tail again. He used a strategy he only practiced a few times – tail swimming like a water snake.

Pincers crashed down after him, splashing heaps of water while Joey slithered through small gaps. It felt like being a fish trying to flee from a grasping hunter.

Going down turned out as his best option. Gaps in the dead coral allowed him to find crevices to slip into.

The bruiser continued its attack undeterred even if blindly. It smashed and smashed, hurling silt, chipping away at rocks, and breaking up fossilized coral.

Joey could hear his pounding heart in his ears. He had no oxygen in his lungs after the heavy exertion to get under cover. The impacts shook him hard, too.

I need air.

Joey panicked. Then he remembered what he had on him. He dug into his bag and felt over the tiles. But he couldn't see, so he didn't know which was which.

Activate them all!

He pushed essence just like Curi had told him. It was a mental effort to channel essence from his body to an object that was ready to receive it.

The tile in his hand responded by activating. The surrounding space became a bright light.

No!

Quickly, Joey formed a clone and passed the beacon tile to it. The clone had a dragon tail, too, and tried to swim away. It only managed ten feet before the bruiser grabbed the clone and crushed it.

The beacon fell to the bottom and shone close enough to illuminate Joey's position.

Activate the others!

Joey channeled his essence into another tile.

[You've received the Tough Buff Singularity for 30 minutes!]

[Tough Buff (Basic/30 minutes): You're 30% tougher for 30 minutes.]

Joey's lungs were burning. He reached down for a third time and activated the last tile.

He nearly opened his mouth to gasp, but held back when fresh oxygen filled his lungs. He immediately calmed down and reexamined his situation.

The bruiser had stopped attacking his position and moved over the beacon. It was digging through the silt in search of Joey.

The rogue swam in the opposite direction from the bruiser. He followed the turns and bends in the area before surfacing in a small cove for a breath.

All in? Joey asked himself. *All in.*

Half a minute later, six shadow clones with swords and

tails fell upon the bruiser. The monster reacted late.

Its pincers caught one and crushed it. The other five landed downward thrusts with their swords and tails, leaving streaks of darkness behind them. The monster screeched from the assault.

The attacks weren't deep, but monster blood leaked from ten new openings. The bruiser snatched and crushed more clones with its pincers, but not before the shadow clones added more damage with repeated sword thrusts and tail strikes.

Another shadow clone with no abilities appeared to the bruiser's left, peeking out from behind a rock spire. The monster turned to attack the clone when Joey flew in from behind with a second shadow clone.

This clone had its hands wrapped around Joey's hands. The two worked together and used all of their might to stab Joey's sword through the monster's waist.

The clone disappeared. Joey curled into the more spacious gap between the upper body and lower body of the bruiser.

The monster screamed. It kept screaming as Joey whipped his tail around and struck the leg joints.

Just like the grunt earlier, the monster scuttled away from the direction of the hits. A vicious smile crossed Joey's face as he whipped and rode the monster. He forced it toward the grunt versus siren fight.

Another clone was already there, shouting for the sirens to peel away. They followed the clone's orders pronto.

When the grunts tried to follow, Joey's hijacked bruiser crashed into its own brethren. With a tail whip to the pincer joint, the bruiser reached to the side and caught a grunt's arm and crushed it.

The grunt squealed before catching the bruiser's leg with its own pincer. The grunt damaged the leg. The bruiser tried to scuttle away.

Joey punished the bruiser for running with a tail whip to the opposite side. He kept punishing the monster and convincing it to fight its own brethren until the situation turned into a monstrous melee with hull crushers against hull crushers.

Things became dangerous for Joey, especially when he received some glancing hits by happenstance. The tough buff helped, but he hated the punishment. Finally, he wrenched his sword back and dashed out.

He hit the flood again and swam until he reached a silt shore with the remaining ten sirens. Joey was cold while the sirens looked haggard and beaten. They all nodded at him, then looked back at the monster bash.

Joey didn't question how easily they followed his orders and accepted him. He sat down with his sword on his lap and meditated to help recover from the huge exertion of his essence and stamina.

Half an hour passed before all the grunts fell to the bruiser. The big creature remained the last standing. But it had lost multiple legs, leaked from multiple wounds, and was barely fit to keep fighting.

[Adventurer, the kill is yours,] a siren said in a singsong language.

"It needs to be," Joey replied without thinking. He stood smoothly. "I'll be mad if I don't get it."

The sirens nodded at once. The rogue ran off. He jumped onto a mound of rock and stood in front of the bruiser. There were no tricks. No backstabs or aerial maneuvers. For now, at least.

The monster glared at him with its good eye before charging in for an attack. It struck down with its lowest right pincer.

Joey dodged back to another solid platform.

The monster twisted around and struck with its lowest left pincer.

Joey outmaneuvered the same.

Frustrated, the monster lunged and came crashing down with all of its pincers. It missed for the third time, but the rogue was moving forward instead of back this time.

Joey's feet trailed dark lines behind his dash. His tail whipped down fast and hit the healthy eye stalk.

Heavily blinded, the creature thrashed around in pain and delirium. When it stopped, Joey dove in with a tail thrust from above. It pierced through a previous wound and skewered deeper into the monster.

Then Joey faded back and let the creature thrash around more until another opening showed itself. Joey dove in and pierced the monster with his tail.

Again and again, the bruiser rampaged and suffered, getting punished in its futile attempts to fight. The rogue gave no mercy.

Eventually, it stopped rampaging and fell over.

Joey landed on its upper body and thrust down with his short sword a few more times until he was sure it was dead. He had stacks of system messages he'd ignored, so he had to check physically.

With the monster defeated under his feet, he stood and

looked around for more monsters. He spotted a few runts watching from a distance away.

The creatures saw him looking in their direction. They turned around and fled. Joey ignored the urge to chase them down.

A siren approached. [You risked much in helping us.]

"Honestly, I did it for the levels." Joey shrugged. "But I should've been faster. The siren fighting this bastard could've lived if I was faster. Sorry."

More sirens approached, huddling close to each other. They studied him with big reflective eyes and alien but beautiful faces. They were tall, too. At least half a foot above six feet.

They'd dwarfed him while he stood on their level. While on the bruiser's dead corpse, he stood above them.

The sirens glanced at each other. Then the speaker continued. [We must bring you back. Your assistance is needed in explaining our blunder.]

Joey eyed them carefully. "Why?"

[This was supposed to be our crowning hunt as new seekers of war. The seeker who died against the bruiser, Marytea, was the princess's favorite trainee. It would be helpful if you accompanied us while we explain to the princess how Marytea died.]

[Well,] Curi said, peeking out from behind some rock cropping with the raft on his head, [This can be problematic. Or this can be an opportunity. What will you do, young great? Turn away from these troubled sirens and continue our journey? Or go with them and face the War Princess?]

11. BIG GAINS, BIG DECISIONS

Joey felt out of his depth while facing new situations, which were becoming the norm. He held his silence and kept his expressions neutral in front of the war sirens.

He would prefer to keep going on his adventure to landfall. But he felt guilty about being selfish and couldn't admit that to the sirens. *I don't want to meet a princess and have her hate me, either.*

The sirens turned from him to Curi. The lead siren continued to act as the speaker.

[Blessed moon, kraken trader,] the siren greeted.

[And blessed moon to you, too, siren seeker,] Curi replied. He drew closer and stopped in a pool behind Joey. Having the kraken there and talking made the rogue feel better. [Before we make any major decisions, how about we focus on the here and now? Does that make sense, young great?]

"Yeah, yeah, that makes sense. We can focus on the levels. And the loot."

Joey looked down at the loot drop from the bruiser. Greediness sank its hooks deep into his spirit. He concentrated on suppressing it.

"I'm going to take the bruiser's loot. And loot from one grunt. The rest is yours."

The lead siren turned to the others. They whispered among themselves. Then the lead siren looked back at Joey.

[We would've died or been captured as sacrifices for their leader. And you are a great rogue, so there are more loot drops than usual. You should have all the loot.]

"No!" Joey shouted, making the sirens flinch back.

The rogue wrestled with his inner feelings, anger and greed clashing. He wanted to split the loot to remain objective and not feel bribed.

"I'll take what's mine. The rest is yours."

The lead siren slowly blinked her reflective eyes. Her gaze turned to the kraken. [We can only take so much from the hull crushers. But you are a kraken trader. You can take these bodies, can't you?]

[I can. But that depends on later decisions. Let's focus on levels and loot and our health. Give us a moment, please?] Curi sounded firm.

The lead siren nodded. Her fellow seekers nodded in unison behind her. They shuffled away, looking a little sad but ready for battle in case another found them.

Surprisingly, Joey felt wary of another battle. *I honestly would prefer a long break right now.*

He glanced at Curi and saw the kraken watching him closely. Joey grimaced, knowing Curi could sense the rogue's change of heart.

Okay, okay, you had a point. Joey sighed. *I can't jump at every opportunity for crazy stunts or I'll burn out.*

Joey collected his share of loot. He found a round rock to meditate on and recover the essence he'd spent.

From here, he could calmly look over his gains with the system rearranging everything for easier reviewing. His mood brightened at the wonderful sight of growth.

[You've slain a Hull Crusher Grunt lvl 30! Experience is reduced for having assistance. For slaying monsters over ten levels above you, bonus experience is awarded!]

[You've assisted in slaying four Hull Crusher Grunts ranging from lvl 30 to 33! Some experience is awarded!]

[You've slain a Hull Crusher Bruiser lvl 51! Experience is reduced for having assistance. For slaying a monster thirty levels above you, bonus experience is awarded!]

Joey luxuriated in the feeling of defeating a monster thirty levels above him. Regardless of having help, that felt impressive. More so than any major feat he'd done so far.

The fight with the bruiser felt like a blur in his memory now. It was incredible that he'd survived, so it was nice to soak in his success before moving on.

[You've leveled up Analyze from 4 to 5!]

[You've leveled up Headhunter from 6 to 7!]

[You've leveled up Short Sword Finesse from 6 to 7!]

[You've leveled up Combat Swimming from 2 to 4!]

[You've leveled up Combat Acrobatics from 4 to 5!]

[You've leveled up Chaos Finder from 1 to 3!]

[You've leveled up Armor Piercer from 2 to 5!]

I wonder why the growth is low for Headhunter and Short Sword Finesse. Did I hit a soft leveling cap even with the overpowered enemy? Or was I not headhunting and finessing enough?

His skills seemed harder to level up compared to his path. There could be extra requirements beyond using a skill repeatedly, too. Still, Joey was happy that most of his skills had gone up.

[You've leveled up Shade Dragon Rogue from 17 to 21!]

Joey willed the system to follow his stat spreading strategy with Level 21 having an even spread. The system moved to the end results for him.

[You've raised your mind from 53 to 64!]

[You've raised your body from 53 to 64!]

[You've raised your spirit from 55 to 65!]

Still pretty even. Joey looked his stats over a couple of times before moving onto the next system message. What he saw next knocked him out of meditation, which was a shame because recovering 6 EP a minute felt like a lot.

"Whoa!"

[What's wrong?] Curi asked.

Joey looked at the watchful sirens before covering his mouth and whispering. "Semblance."

Curi raised a tentacle and circled it around in celebration. Joey's mood was sky high as he examined the latest gain.

[You've gained the Semblance of a Hull Crusher Bruiser!]

[Adventurer Semblance: Hull Crusher: Bruiser lvl 51:

A rough and tumble semblance that would fight to the bitter end. Tough armor. Rapid pincer attacks. Fairly big and hulking at 12 feet tall. Not a fast mover, but it could move well on land or in water. Has one passive spell – Self Regenerate. Has one active spell – Molt Drive.]

[Self Regenerate (Basic): Heal injuries passively. Works better while resting. *What? You're already back on your feet? Lords and Ladies, answer my prayers and stop blessing these crazy masochists!*]

[Molt Drive (Basic): Molt your armor and move with a faster drive. The speed may be worth the reduced protection. *Hahaha! You may be armored, but you're too slow to catch... Oi, wait. What are you getting naked for?*]

[Do you wish for the Semblance of a Hull Crusher Bruiser to (1) transfer all experience to you, (2) split experience evenly, or (3) receive full experience for its own actions? You can only change this feature once a week.]

Joey gave a prayer of thanks to whoever created the system. Clearly, they had been gods who enjoyed challenge, fun, and efficiency.

He willed the system to give him option (1), the rogue receiving full experience from his semblance's actions.

[For the next seven days, you will earn full experience from the Semblance of a Hull Crusher Bruiser's actions.]

"That's a mouthful. You are now Al Bruce Crabton," Joey whispered. "We will be good friends."

[The Semblance of a Hull Crusher Bruiser will now be designated as Al Bruce Crabton.]

[Adventurer Semblance: Hull Crusher: Bruiser lvl 51 (Al Bruce Crabton).]

The system goes all out for this, huh?

Joey could hardly believe his luck. But he still had more to go before his review finished. No new skills, but his loot looked promising.

[You've looted 67 Tidal Moon Copper Coins, 1 Barrier Glyph Tile, and 1 Water Bolt Glyph Tile!]

Not as exciting as getting a strong semblance, but it'll replace some of the tiles I've spent.

Joey could see himself selling the water bolt glyph for more coins. The barrier glyph might come in handy in the future.

The descriptions of the glyph tiles matched the names and were only worth a quick skim. With his system review concluded, he knew it was time to face the elephant in the room.

He still had more essence to recover, and he still felt beat up from the fight. But he would hate to make the sirens wait.

It was time to figure out the next step forward.

Joey stood and waved for Curi to follow him. They stopped on a mound of silt some distance away but in view of the watchful sirens.

"What do you think?" Joey asked.

The kraken tapped the side of his head with a tentacle. [Consider your adventuring prospects, past and future.]

Joey furrowed his brow. "Well, I've grown really fast for a great adventurer the past few days and nights, right? We have more days ahead to reach land. Then I'll have to cross from there to make it to the port on the other side. I'll have more opportunities to grow during the trip."

[And then you'll be back among adventurers. Sharing resources. Competing for resources. Following the paths of others while searching for new discoveries that'll dwindle if they haven't faded completely.]

"Are you saying I'm in unexplored territory?" Joey asked, glancing at the war siren seekers.

[Not entirely unexplored. It has been eighteen years since the last arrival of new adventurers. Adventurers have been down this path before you. But that is history now. Enough of it for you to explore and find plenty of new adventures to call your own.]

"But doesn't the detour bother you?"

[Why should it? Am I in a rush? And it's a detour of two days, give or take.]

Joey rubbed the back of his neck. *Why am I trying to rush? First, I wanted to take advantage of level opportunities. Now I'm afraid of more detours.*

He would feel more stable on solid ground with other humans like him. Every step out here hurled him into incredible situations he'd never experienced before. Like a great adventurer. But even with all the gains, Joey could still feel weary from the constant newness.

It would be nice to sleep in a simple bed and have a roof over my head. Joey's temptation to stay the course grew stronger. But he hesitated from an outright decision because of Curi's subtle influence.

Joey knew the kraken wanted to go with the war sirens even though it could lead to trouble. But the kraken wouldn't say it outright. Why was that?

Curi would follow my decision even if it wasn't the best decision, Joey realized. *So what is the best decision?*

"More information," Joey mumbled. "I need that."

He returned to the war sirens. They'd been taking turns looting and looking over their own system messages and profiles.

He couldn't see their personal runes, but he could tell when they looked into space and mumbled to themselves. He found the lead speaker, the one with the most purple in her long hair.

"My name's Joey, by the way," he introduced.

[Mirashell,] she replied. [Will you accompany us?]

Damn, she's direct. Joey harrumphed as he looked up at the tall water woman. "I'm not sure if I will. But I'd like to hear more about your princess. What's her personality?"

Mirashell swayed her head from side to side. [Like a cliff standing against stormy surf. Nothing phases her. We can never know what she's thinking. But she would smile for Marytea sometimes.] Mirashell fell silent, looking down with a dark gaze.

Joey could feel a cloud of sadness and anxiety hanging over the seekers. He felt bad for them, but he didn't want that to weigh on his decision.

"Are your people okay with adventurers?" Joey hedged.

[Why wouldn't we? We welcome adventurers who can fight, especially great ones. In fact, it has been years since we've had another adventurer in our city.]

[Blessed moon, adventurer, we welcome you,] another siren said.

[Please, come to our city,] a third siren urged.

[And talk to the princess instead of us,] added a meeker siren.

Joey kept a neutral face before turning away and walking back to Curi. The rogue pondered, and the kraken waited on him.

"It doesn't seem like a bad thing for me to go," Joey said. "I'm sorry for their losses. But I don't want to get tangled up with an angry princess. If they're welcoming to adventurers and the war princess isn't going to slam me, I guess it'll be beneficial. They have a city, and I'll be the first adventurer to visit for a while. So, it'll be kind of special."

Joey glanced over to where a siren held mementos of their dead, which were shell-like jewelry attached to necklaces. It seemed like they were leaving the bodies behind. *Unless Curi carries everything back to their city.*

"You've been there?" Joey asked.

[I have,] Curi answered.

"Why are you making this my decision, then?"

[You dove into this situation and saved these ten young lives. It is up to you to let them go their own way or see things through on this detour of yours.]

Joey grimaced, sensing a strange but familiar feeling in his chest. He was unsure if he liked the feeling. But he didn't exactly hate it.

The rogue sighed, then spoke aloud, "Curi, can you pick up all the bodies of the hull crushers and fallen seekers? We'll take everything with us to the siren city."

When he glanced over at Mirashell, the thankful smile on her face emboldened the weird feeling inside of him. The best way to describe the feeling was having determination. He wanted to see the ending of something he'd started like a completionist gamer.

Curi collected the bodies and stored them away quickly. Joey still had more essence to recover, so he asked Curi if he could ride on the raft while he carried it. The kraken was fine with that.

Then Joey noticed a few of the sirens limping and looking hurt still. He asked Curi if it was okay to invite them all onto the raft. The kraken agreed.

After some urging from the charismatic Curi, all ten sirens sat in a huddle around Joey. It needed to be this way for balancing the weight.

But they are really close to me.

Joey tried to keep his focus on meditating and observing the way forward. Curi moved at a good speed even with the extra cargo. The sirens had lighter bodies compared to the man snappers, at least.

They were more lithe and graceful with toned muscles, like swimmers, while also having bodies ranging from girlish thin to full figured. They had subtle fishlike features that made them alien, but they still looked beautiful, almost bewitching. Like sirens of myth.

I swear, they're squeezing close to me on purpose.

An inch of space had disappeared in front of him. Then inches of space disappeared to his right and left. Mirashell hovered near his back, her breath on his neck.

A few minutes later, they were pressed in tight.

Worst yet, the sirens were mindful of their height. The ones in front of Joey leaned out of his way without having to ask. They would lie over each other and look forward like it was no big deal. Their militant silence added to the tension in the air.

Maybe this is a cultural thing. Close skin contact isn't a problem for them, so they're treating me the same.

Joey nodded slowly to himself.

I refuse to be the guy who pisses off an entire city of water amazons. I will not be known across the realms as a creep.

Joey hardened himself and stayed focused on meditation. The chilly circulation of new essence helped.

He was also distracted by the potential future for Al Bruce Crabton, Joey's first ever semblance. Thus, his meditating became easier, and the journey felt smoother.

They reached the white, foamy wall of the Siren Tide quicker than Joey had expected. Thousands of feet of magic-bound water and mist clouds loomed over them. Moonlight and vapors sparkled in the air while it rained.

Once again, Joey found himself as a man surrounded by an incredible situation before diving into another incredible situation. He then noticed Scenic Discoverer pulsing passively, too. The skill added enthusiasm to his new completionist feeling.

I guess I have more room for adventure, after all.

Finding other humans on land could wait a little longer.

12. GOING TO AQUA STAR CITY

[Have you ever scaled up the tidal wall before?] Mirashell asked from behind Joey. Her head was looking over his shoulder now.

It took the rogue a few seconds to stir from meditation and answer. "No. It seems like it'll be harder going up than down."

[We will disembark and escort you up. It's easier for us to swim.] All the sirens stood swiftly at once. They were already tall, so the view from Joey's seat added to their looming presence. [If we face resistance on the way up, would you want us to fight them all or allow some through?]

"Who would fight us on the climb up?" Joey asked.

It was Curi who answered this time. [Man Snappers are notorious for it. Though, I'll be surprised if they're being prevalent in siren territory.]

[That is a conversation best held with the princess and elders.]

"Well, I can take on some man snappers if it comes to it," Joey said.

Mirashell and the other sirens jumped off the raft. They landed gracefully even with their injuries.

Joey's essence was topped off now, so he moved to the edge and watched the ten seekers march side by side with militant grace.

Their figures looked tiny compared to the massive tidal wall, as if they were going to get crushed under the fall of an entire ocean. But they dove into the surface with confidence and disappeared from sight.

"Wow," Joey said. "Other than being afraid of their princess, they're pretty awesome."

Curi was happy to explain. [War sirens are taught from a young age to face all challenges with a calm and steely presence. They are some of the most skillful denizens in the Tidal Moon Realm. And these war sirens are the best of their territories, too. Aqua Star City is their home capital, mistress of most siren territories.]

"And we're about to meet a princess with the coldest personality they have?" Joey shook his head.

[Ah, yes, we'll be meeting the princess. Quite the honor, young great.]

Something about Curi's tone sounded off to Joey, which was telling since the kraken spoke by making flute noises that were translated by the system. Still, the way Curi spoke of the princess sounded troublesome for some reason. Hopefully, she was one of the lesser princesses if there were more than one.

At least I'm not meeting the queen, right? Joey figured a princess wouldn't bring him as much trouble as a queen would.

Before the rogue could ask further questions, the kraken reached the tidal wall's solid edge.

Joey thrust his sword down into the raft's wood. He lowered his head as pounding water struck all over, the floor tilting underneath him until his feet were dangling.

Curi merged with the tidal wall, using four tentacles to pull the raft up the surface. He skimmed through the water while the raft cut through resistance from the waterfall.

Joey endured as the ride upward became bumpier than the ride down. The kraken was also moving faster than before to shorten the not so pleasant experience for Joey.

The things I do for action and adventure, Joey thought with some humor.

He let out a sigh and tried to challenge himself by meditating despite his position. He was stronger now, so he felt more secure with his sword grip. It was still tricky to meditate like this, but he eventually got it.

Sometimes, the meditation slipped away when the ride became bumpier. But Joey went back to channeling essence and feeling cooler than the water.

Something thumped against the raft. A dark humanoid shape gripped the edge above Joey. He had to blink water out of his eyes to see clearly enough.

It was a man snapper, and it wasn't alone. Two more rode down with the waterfall until they struck the raft edge above Joey.

The first one started trash talking until Joey's tail appeared around its leg. The rogue braced his feet against the raft. His tail yanked the man snapper off the raft and hurled it into the open air.

The other snappers hissed in anger until Joey's tail whipped back at them and struck their legs. One had its knee shattered. The other dove off the raft and back into the tidal wall. The one with the broken knee fell toward Joey.

The rogue swung himself to the side of his sword and called up a shadow clone with a sword copy. The clone passed the sword to Joey before the rogue thrust the extra weapon into the snapper's throat as it fell by.

His aim was off by an inch, but the blade still tore away some of the neck. The snapper fell, gushing blood, and Joey dismissed his spells.

He also dismissed the system messages since the monsters were weaker than him. Partial experience only.

Joey shook his head and went back to hanging by his sword and meditating.

Eventually, the vertical water cliff turned into a slope. Then it turned into a leveled plain for Joey to sit and relax on the raft. The sirens raised their heads above the surface.

[All is well, Joey?] Mirashell asked.

"Yeah, I'm well. Just had some pesky snappers."

[Pesky indeed.] Mirashell nodded. [Let us continue. It'll take two nights and two days to get to our city.]

The journey to Aqua Star City was a peaceful one. Joey trained with his skills, tried some other unique ideas with Shadow Clone Magic, and meditated for long hours.

He even practiced spending essence with no specific directions. It turned out to be hard for some reason.

And uncomfortable. Like channeling in reverse.

At most, he could squeeze out 1 EP a minute when he released essence without a place for it to go.

Joey had no idea if there was a purpose for doing that. But it felt interesting. He asked Curi about it, and the kraken didn't have an answer for once.

The sirens stayed mostly in the water. But a few would climb onto the raft and offer to spar lightly with Joey.

Without spells, the rogue lost every spar, which made Joey realize how the sirens could survive against the higher leveled grunts.

They really are skillful!

The sirens moved with deceptive grace. Sometimes slow and methodical, but that would only last until they found a hole in Joey's guard to exploit.

Then they surged with speed, precision, and years of technique.

The spars changed drastically when Joey introduced his spells. They ended with his victory each time.

As long as he could fend off the first couple of polearm attacks, he could overwhelm them within the first fifteen to thirty seconds with his variety of shade dragon tactics.

[Denizens do not grow as quickly as adventurers do. And we do not earn our first true spell until we are level 25,] Mirashell explained while sitting and eating tidal racer with Joey on the second night. [Marytea was the fastest grower, however. You might've seen what she could do. That's one of the offensive options we have at level 25.]

"She was pretty awesome. I was hoping she could keep holding her own while I helped you guys. Then we could've teamed up on the bruiser."

Joey looked down, feeling ashamed. He ran in there for levels and his own greed. He'd gained much while the sirens paid a heavy toll.

[We didn't follow our instructions as we should've. We

rushed for the bruiser kill instead of scouting the entire area carefully. For that, we deserve the blame. Thank you for arriving as you did, and thank you for coming along to assist us.] Mirashell smiled, which looked radiant on her face as her hair blew to the side from the wind.

Joey nodded and looked away. *First adventurer in years. You're a rep of humanity. Keep it friendly, man.*

It was helpful having sirens around since they had plenty of tips on fighting in the water. They were experts in their craft.

During the hours when Curi was resting, Joey hit the water with the sirens. All ten swam around him with incredible grace. They barely left much evidence of their passing.

It was a little scary when they closed in on him, but he kept his cool. He practiced swimming and fending off the multiple hands smacking him around.

He did terribly without his spells. But things improved when he used his tail, enabling him to move like he'd done against the bruiser.

They even raced around a bit, which he made competitive even when losing in the end. The sirens looked a little bothered that a human rogue nearly won underwater races.

That was the advantage of having an epic spell like Shade Dragon Tail. It was growing to be his favorite, honestly. There were so many ways to exploit a semi-invisible ghost tail others could only see when it became active and solid.

Of course, if Joey truly wanted to win the underwater races, he would've injected Dark Dash more. But he accepted the personal handicap as more of a challenge for himself.

The way the sirens smiled and showed more of their personalities made him think he was going about things the right way.

[You've leveled up Combat Swimming from 4 to 5!]

By the time they neared the city, Joey's group met with two other siren patrols. One of those patrols had a strong war siren.

[Tidal Moon Denizen: War Siren: Specialist lvl 66.]

It was sunset hours, the solar moon painting the watercolor skies pink and orange, when the specialist climbed onto the raft. She wore armor made of shark teeth or whatever beast they'd hunted in the tidal depths.

A fish skull covered her head like an oceanic knight helm. She held the same weapon as the seekers, but she was bulkier and taller.

She gave off an intimidating presence, so Joey did his best to stand upright and hold a neutral expression. Deep down, he was nervous and unsure of what would happen next.

The singsong language came out as more girly and attractive than expected from the specialist. [The seekers told me you've come to their aid and slain the beast who took our Marytea.]

"I didn't act fast enough," Joey said. "And I was there for the levels."

[A great rogue, and an honest one at that. The Tidal Moon Lord has truly blessed us with your arrival.] The specialist dipped her head down at him before standing tall. [I will escort you the rest of the way to the princess. The seekers will head to their barracks and await orders there.]

"I'm thankful, but I'll feel more comfortable if I have a

face I know," Joey said quickly. "Marishell, for example."

[So be it.] The specialist dipped her head again before turning and walking off the raft.

Minutes later, the seekers Joey had saved waved at him before they departed.

Marishell climbed onto the raft to join him, and Curi followed the specialist and her patrol group of twenty war sirens.

[Wow, isn't this quite the escort? This treatment is a first for me, honestly.] Curi was a bundle of joy. [I think things are looking good. Unless the princess will be angry with us, then this will be a little painful. But still an experience!]

Joey stopped himself from berating Curi when he noticed Marishell gripping her polearm tensely. A few days of being around the sirens helped Joey notice more of their personalities or traits. That might be because of the improved focus inside of the mind stat.

She's nervous. Joey wondered if Marishell would rather not be here beside him. *My bad, but you wanted me to come along. So, we'll do this together.*

Around the raft, more siren patrols surfaced and gave short reports to the escort detail led by the specialist. Then the specialist stopped to talk to another specialist at a higher level.

They nodded at each other, coming to an accord, before the sirens guided Curi to a spot in the water that looked the same as everywhere else.

"What now?" Joey asked, looking around at the many sirens popping up.

[We go down.] Marishell stood rigid as the Level 66 Specialist climbed onto the raft again. [Enjoy.]

[Oh, he certainly will!] Curi added.

Before Joey could question them further, all the sirens sang in unison.

Joey swayed, feeling imbalanced and confused. The wordless song sounded like the choir of angels. Having so many reaching him at once made him feel weak and want to fall to his knees.

He resisted as best he could and stayed upright, even if the weakness didn't go away. He didn't feel exactly bad, though. And the singing was lovely. But it definitely left him vulnerable.

He searched his profile for a debuff but found none.

I don't think they're singing is for me.

This was confirmed with the actions of the Level 66 Specialist. She held her polearm up in one hand and outstretched the other. She was singing, too. At the same time, the surrounding water reacted strangely.

The raft sank down. Tendrils of water thrust upward, reaching higher and higher. Then the water tendrils bent in and touched at the top, the sides closing together.

The singing continued, and the raft continued to sink while in a water barrier one hundred feet wide, entrapping the air with the raft. The more Joey paid attention to the water magic, the better he felt.

What I'm feeling is a byproduct, which is crazy!

Joey wondered if the singing was to enhance the water manipulation. If so, then Joey could take a logical guess why.

He eased to the edge and looked down. Far below, deep in the depths of the Siren Tide, was a sight few men would ever see.

First were the gargantuan jelly fishes. Each one had bone-like structures built on their heads. Sirens looked out from the structures' windows as if they were living in fortresses made for underwater military activities.

Then, beyond those mobile underwater fortresses, was an even greater sight. Far below was a five-armed starfish. But from this distance, Joey was certain the starfish had to be miles wide.

It had to be alive, too. Joey could almost see the starfish was shifting in a single direction, even if slowly.

On top of the arms and the middle mass of the starfish were glass-like structures filled with activity. The middle had the biggest and most colorful dome of them all. The walls glowed with lights.

There was colorful coral rock at the base of the dome. Living coral, too, from what Joey could tell. The other structures had the same, but the big dome in the middle had more of the coral surrounding the base.

Joey wondered why the coral was there. Thankfully, he had Curi, who inserted himself as the ever helpful and knowledgeable kraken.

[If you don't know, and you probably don't, the domes are hollowed out pearls from the Mollusk Tide far south from here. Quite the feat of transportation and crafting, which are among the many talents of war sirens despite their mainly militant outlook. As for the coral, that's local, of course, and is responsive to enchantments. It's through the coral halls and doorways we'll enter the city center. Much of the inside is built with it, too. It'll be quite the view, especially on our way to the princess.]

The excitement in Curi's tone was palpable. Joey figured the kraken was having a new adventure right along with him.

[Oh, and if you hadn't figured it out yet, sirens have a special ability that allows their singing to enhance others, so this entire bubble we're riding is the work of one being supported by the many. Of course, they have other powers to go along with their vocal talents.]

Could those powers include charm magic? Joey stopped himself from shivering. *I don't think Marishell or the others used that on me. I'm sure of that. But now I'm really on the hook if the princess gets mad at me.*

Joey imagined the princess would have stronger charm magic. Hopefully, she wasn't the type to abuse it.

He would also count himself lucky if he could avoid their queen.

Charm magic or no charm magic, the view is awesome, Joey thought, focusing on the positives. *Giant jellyfish fortresses. A moving starfish the size of a city. And on the starfish's back are domes crafted out of giant pearls. Nobody would believe me unless I snap a pic.*

For the first time since getting here, Joey wished he had a phone and internet connection. Then again, he had little to no social media presence before arriving at the Tidal Moon Realm.

Nobody would miss him from the old world, which was sometimes sad to think about.

At least he was free to go wherever he wanted. Like taking a trip to the war sirens' capital to meet a princess.

True story.

[You've leveled up Scenic Discoverer from 1 to 2!]

13. MEET THE WAR PRINCESS

The singing didn't stop even when they reached the coral docks, even when the siren escorts themselves stopped singing. Joey swayed a little as the water barrier fell and new voices and songs swept over him.

But the effect was weaker than before because the new singers weren't as coordinated. They weren't enhancing each other. They were just singing for the sake of singing.

If that wasn't interesting enough for Joey's intro to Aqua Star City, the explosion of color was another feature of note. The coral shifted hues as easily as they shifted functions and forms.

After the escorts guided Joey and Curi down and up into an air pocket, Joey's raft bumped near the rising steps leading out of the water. The coral nearest to the water looked porous and spongy, but once Joey climbed onto a solid platform, the coral shifted into stone-like material without a break in between.

Different sirens and a bustle of activity surrounded the rogue. He wasn't the only one docking.

[Tidal Moon Denizen: War Siren: Specialist lvl 61.]

[Tidal Moon Denizen: War Siren: Seeker lvl 45.]

[Tidal Moon Denizen: War Siren: Guardian lvl 70.]

[Tidal Moon Denizen: War Siren: Laborer lvl 33.]

[Tidal Moon Denizen: War Siren: Laborer lvl 28.]

[Tidal Moon Denizen: Land Siren: Miner lvl 42.]

[Tidal Moon Denizen: Ice Siren: Hunter lvl 37.]

Joey might have to fear for his neck's health as he turned his head left and right rapidly. He noticed late that his mouth was hanging open.

He clenched his jaw as various sirens stared at him while doing their work or passing by.

There were plenty of war sirens. The female amazons of the water stood out as the tallest and most intimidating – the guardians wore even heavier armor than specialists. The armor might've come from a truly, truly terrifying beast of the deep.

Then Joey's eyes and Analyze skill feasted on the siren subgroups. Land sirens had a green hue to their skin and were the shortest of the sirens while also being wider. Ice Sirens had snow white skin, slim builds, and dark sinister eyes that glared daggers at everyone who passed.

Each siren subgroup worked around their particular vessels that looked like flat rowing ships vikings would use.

They would have to carry their own ship and cargo when crossing between tides. Joey's mouth fell open in surprise again. *Holy shit, how would they pull that off and defend themselves?*

[I know that look of curiosity on your face. And I can guess the question and give an answer.] Curi was waiting in a channel of water leading deeper into the dock. Right beside him was another voyager kraken he'd been interacting with moments ago. But like the knowledgeable kraken he was, Curi couldn't help but turn to Joey and give helpful info. [The answer is war sirens, Joey! They're all around you. The connective tissue of all siren societies.]

Joey took Curi's brief explanation and expanded on it by observing the war sirens themselves. Seekers and specialists hung around each subgroup of sirens.

Despite their differences, the sirens seemed very amicable toward each other.

All the singing wasn't just for fun. It was their natural way of communication with a hint of siren charm. And war sirens seemed to be heavily ingrained in it all.

Does this mean war sirens are sent everywhere where there are sirens?

It was like the American military having a presence in areas that interested the country and its allies. It would help to have war sirens around when crossing over tides or between them.

Are war sirens only used for sirens? Could there be other denizens who have war sirens around?

Glancing at the other voyager kraken, Joey noticed a small group of war sirens escorting that kraken in particular. That confirmed his question.

This also made Joey wonder what purpose did adventurers have if siren society had so much?

Are we just mercenaries? Extra muscle with special powers?

The questions floated around in his head, but not for long. The specialist escorting them finished reporting to a guardian and gestured with her head for Joey to follow.

They walked beside the waterway, which acted like a canal. The water also defied physics by being able to flow upward when they had to ascend.

They entered a vibrant coral tunnel where Joey was thankful to have Marishell close by. So many unfamiliar sirens brushed past him constantly. Each one looked down and stared at him until they couldn't stare any longer.

Ah, yup, this is what I needed, a reason to have my old friend anxiety make a visit. Yup, loving it!

Joey looked down at his sword hand and noticed the tenseness of his grip on the handle. He also noticed how ragged and bare he looked. His basketball shorts were shredded and barely much more than threads.

They're going to let me clean up before I meet the princess, right?

Before he could muster the courage to speak, they exited the tunnel and entered the city. Joey stumbled from the loud volume of singsong voices and the burst of colors and activities.

It was bigger inside the dome than he'd expected, and it was more lit up than he'd thought. The magic lights near the ceiling were like mini stars.

Joey felt like he was entering fantasy Manhattan with spires of coral rock reaching as high as skyscrapers. Sirens looked down from balconies and windows or talked to each other in the open.

The main street was straight and organized to follow a canal where sirens and other aquatic creatures could swim or walk beside. So there was a reason to think of the fantasy version of Venice, too.

Not all the buildings were tall spires. And not every

structure was solid coral stone. Some were spongy. Some structures were living creatures with waving fins and open chambers. Others were made of giant bones and skulls from leviathans long dead.

Joey could barely look at anything for long because another amazing sight would pop up right after another. Then came the royal castle that had been looming from the distance until they suddenly walked up to it without Joey feeling ready.

It had the tallest spires and a bulky and hard exterior that was all black and ready to weather a siege. It took up the most space at the center of the domed district.

Guardians patrolled all around its thirty-foot walls. The gate was made from the head of a huge sea beast with sharp teeth taller than Joey.

They stopped to be checked by the guardians with question marks hiding their levels. Curi had to climb out of the canal to get checked, too.

It was here when Joey noticed his raft had been left behind. Before he could think about that further, a guardian reached for his sword.

Don't swing! Joey yelled in his head.

His grip was tense around the sword handle. But the guardian didn't force the issue. She simply looked at him and waited.

Little by little, Joey released the weapon, feeling embarrassed for making a scene, even if it was a small one.

With the sword and raft gone, Joey felt more afraid than ever before. More afraid than his first brush with combat.

The sea beast gate opened up like an awaiting mouth. The group walked in and crossed the barren courtyard under the gaze of watchful guardians.

The front entrance stairs led them up into a grand foyer with materials Joey wouldn't expect in an underwater city.

[You've leveled up Scenic Discoverer from 2 to 3!]

Marble floors. Wood railings following double spiral staircases. He noticed rich tapestry and furniture, cabinets, rugs, and even paintings. They moved between the staircases and entered another room with a giant crystal chandelier up on a high ceiling.

"Wait here with my partner," a guardian said, leaving them and entering through the next door.

Joey blinked.

Joey blinked some more.

Joey opened and closed his mouth in doubt. Then he looked at Curi, who was looking with humor at Joey.

[Yes, that was English.]

Joey blinked a few more times.

[It's one of the more popular languages of the common human tongue. But you also have Spanish, Chinese, and the ultra elite tongue, Creole.]

The words Joey wanted to say kept failing him as his mind reconfigured around this new multiverse info.

There should be an eureka moment or a rush of even more questions flowing out. But truthfully, he was so overwhelmed by his situation, hearing English had fried his brain further.

Because of his nerve-wracking predicament, Joey barely noticed when Marishell was called into the next room. Then he felt a new onset of panic when Curi was called into the next room.

The kraken slithered by and squeezed through the double doors, his size being a nonissue. The doors shut right behind him.

Joey remained alone except for the original specialist and the guardian hovering over him. There were other guardians in the vicinity, but they weren't as close as the one taking up his space.

"Am I going to be okay?" Joey asked his guardian.

"I think you will be," the guardian answered – with English. "I've heard of what you've done. You will be awarded. Pray to the moon that it's merely monetary compensation or a few items."

"What other awards could there be?" Joey asked.

For some reason, even behind her thick skull helmet, the guardian seemed to give Joey a sad look. She didn't answer his question. But she did shift closer until her arm was against his shoulder.

The specialist shifted close to do the same. It was that close contact thing the sirens favored. Joey found it strangely comforting even though he didn't know the guardian or the specialist that well.

A different guardian poked her head out from between the doors. "Come forth, Adventurer Joey Eclipse."

Joey entered the next room and immediately felt his anxiety shoot up even higher. He recognized the place as a throne room from the media he'd consumed.

Big spacious hall. Important-looking people standing to the sides.

They even had male sirens!

[Tidal Moon Denizen: War Siren: Caretaker lvl 40.]

Joey had figured if there were male sirens, they would probably be diminutive and placed in reverse gender roles. That was not entirely the case.

The male sirens were taller than their female counterparts and absolutely shredded like professional bodybuilders. There were two dozen in the room, which Joey imagined was a total flex of power by having a bunch of rarely seen male sirens.

Before Joey even looked up at the most important person in the room, he knew for sure he wasn't dealing with a simple princess.

I've been set up!

Joey followed orders to stop at the center of the room. It was an even distance from the throne and the door he'd come through.

He thought of running. But with all he'd seen, he knew he wouldn't make it. And he couldn't leave behind Curi who was resting in a pool of water perfect for him. Marishell was off to the side, looking absolutely distraught.

Finally, Joey looked up at the person sitting on the throne.

"Why is there a little girl on the throne?" Joey mumbled without thinking.

She was human and couldn't be any older than fourteen.

On top of that, she looked plain with pale skin and dark hair that fell around her soft round face. But she did have on the seeker bodysuit.

"Analyze me," the girl said with a flat voice, ending the loudest bit of silence Joey heard since coming here.

[Multiverse Adventurer: Superior Human: Warrior

lvl ?]

[You've leveled up Analyze from 5 to 6!]

"You are a strong little girl," Joey blabbered, unable to control himself now that his anxiety had escaped containment. "The superior human part is interesting. Are you like a half siren or something?"

"I am," she said. "Is this your attempt to mock me for reasons I've yet to understand?"

"Mock you, no, no, no. You see, I'm a man who has no idea how he's gotten here. Or why I'm even here in the first place. I was literally getting drunk and playing video games before waking up and being asked to be a great adventurer or a commoner? I chose to be great, and ever since then, I've been bloody killing monsters like a psychopath and helping random nonhuman strangers while far from anything I recognize.

"And this is while I'm surrounded by water filled with dangerous beasts and monsters or crossing freaking magical gaps where more dangerous beasts and monsters lurk. And I've only been doing this for... six days? Has it only been six days? Wow. I can't even tell you if that's a short amount of time or a long time. I'm not even sure how I'm still alive in front of you right now."

Joey inhaled a deep breath. "By the way, I feel like I've been tricked. This isn't some meeting with a princess. You're the queen, aren't you?"

He glanced around as if waiting for someone to step in and punch him in the face. Nobody did a thing. The sirens stood perfectly still and emotionless, like statues.

Curi was doing all he could to not laugh while in his pool. The only person who spoke was the girl on the throne.

"There are no queens. Nor are there kings or emperors

or the likes. Beneath the Tidal Moon Lord, only princes, princesses, and lesser titles exist. This is a situation you'll find in most realms of Multiverse Z."

The little warrior girl slowly stood up.

"Do not worry about not knowing this. You are very new. It is impressive how you've adapted quickly. You've also done me a service by helping my war sirens and avenging Marytea's death. For this, I congratulate you. And I also thank you."

She walked down from her throne and stretched her hands to her right. A muscular female siren tossed two dull-looking swords and knives to her.

The girl caught them all without missing a step, her bare feet touching the marble stone and carrying her closer to Joey.

"Now let me introduce myself. My name is Maylolee Suzuki. I am seventeen years old. I am the daughter of a great adventurer and the previous war princess. I am the current war princess, the ruler of Aqua Star City and all the vassal territories of the war sirens. I am also the Lead Siren of all siren subgroups under my protection. Additionally, I'm also known as Chief War Instructor Suzuki. But you may refer to me as Instructor Suzuki."

She stopped in front of Joey and passed him a dull sword and dull knife. He figured they were well-used for training from all the nicks they had.

Looking from the training weapons to Instructor Suzuki, Joey found it refreshing to have someone shorter than him. Seventeen or not, she was tiny.

But why is she giving me these?

"Are we going to have a practice spar?" Joey asked.

"No." Instructor Suzuki rolled her shoulders around and shifted her hips left and right, warming up. "A practice spar is not enough. We are going to have you instructed for however long I see fit."

Joey blinked. "Instructed?"

"I suggest you start running. But do not worry, orders will spread to give you access to most places you wish to run to or you'll be redirected safely. But you won't be allowed to purchase food or drink or have a room with a bed. You'll have to steal all of that. And everyone will tell me where you go or where you're hiding."

Joey gawked at her, lost for words.

"Adventurer Eclipse, you're wasting time. I'm only giving you an hour before I chase you down. But do not worry. You will see me coming." Instructor Suzuki cocked her head to the side. "Congrats on acquiring this award. You will now have personal instructions from the strongest adventurer of your beginner challenge."

[**Congrats! You have the opportunity to learn the Stress Management Skill!**]

[**Stress Management (Basic): Instead of letting stressors dictate your emotions, placate them as best you can. This will not eliminate all stress, but help mitigate it.** *Best way to deal with stress is to stuff it down a hole and hope it never blows. Ever since I started doing that, I've been the most sane man who can claim to be sane!*]

[**Congrats! You've learned the Stress Management Skill!**]

14. BEAT THE WAR PRINCESS

Joey quickly learned war sirens were efficient with their waste processing. They had little to no trash. If it couldn't be tossed into the tide and broken down naturally, they recycled everything or fed it to tidal organisms that looked like sea anemones.

They placed those on different corners of their well-designed roads. The water parks had the most sea anemones, some of them standing as tall as the rogue.

Joey learned to tail whip pieces off the sea anemones and eat that. The taste reminded him of pork. If he had time to make a fire, sea anemone would be a great substitute for bacon.

[Run, the war princess is on her way!] shouted a laborer.

The bustling market corner next to the water park cleared of people fast. They knew where to hide and avoid instruction.

Joey's attempts to flee with them had been barred by high-level sirens. He'd watched enough coral doors shut in his face to get the hint.

They all knew he was the source of trouble when the war princess left her castle and prowled among her subjects.

Being Chief War Instructor gave her privileges to teach anyone, and they couldn't say no. She'd run drills for the entire city, locals and visitors alike, and everyone was left sore and bruised up afterward. These were things Joey had heard from locals who were willing to talk to him.

Now Joey hid behind a low wall with porous holes he could look through. Sometimes, hiding would have Instructor Suzuki move off his trail if she failed to locate him. He had to see what direction she went first, however.

Staying blind behind cover had led to bad outcomes, and Joey still felt those bruises. So he risked looking from behind the corner wall near the water park.

Instructor Suzuki's little form strode out from behind a low coral building. She stopped in the middle of the street and slowly looked in the opposite direction. Then her head snapped in Joey's direction.

He didn't allow himself to flinch. Spending essence on Stress Management was worth it.

Instructor Suzuki searched with her eyes in his direction. She looked away and walked toward the next street. Joey tried not to get his hopes up.

[He's behind the wall by the park!] shouted a siren up on a nearby balcony.

Joey jumped from behind cover with a burst of rage. "The next time I go hungry, I'm stealing all your food from your place!"

He was wasting time. But he needed to spend the anger now so he could concentrate on what came next.

Instructor Suzuki's dark eyes were on him now, showing no emotion. Her body rotated to face him before she sprinted with the most robotic form ever.

She was like a little T-800. She terminated the distance between them easily. But Joey's clones outnumbered her ten to one with swords in hand, at an expense of 400 EP.

He fled, not needing to see the results. The instructor would rip through his clones like they were wet tissue paper.

That was okay. They only needed to slow her down a little as he sprinted through the water park.

It wasn't a place with water slides like his old world. It was a park with pools of water and plant life that could live in both water and air.

Nothing tasty, unfortunately, but Joey used the twisty branches of water trees to reach a higher elevation.

It was always a good idea to get higher when Instructor Suzuki was chasing. Dashes and tail swings helped him get away as he left behind the park and reached the balcony of a tall coral spire.

Joey stopped on a ledge and saw the instructor leaving the park, her eyes locked on him. Her knife wasn't in her hand.

Joey dashed away in time to avoid the thrown knife. But the weapon itself wasn't his biggest concern. The issue was Instructor Suzuki locking her spell on the weapon.

He moved to another balcony. In the split second he was going to land, the instructor's sword flew past his face. Instructor Suzuki teleported with her knife and sword back in her hands. She landed on the balcony Joey had chosen.

They traded attacks, hard and fast. Joey swung his sword with finesse while balancing on the ledge. The instructor blocked or dodged with the most impassive face ever.

She barely took a breath before jumping through his guard and kicking him into the open air.

The most annoying part about Instructor Suzuki was how she delivered damage. It was enough to sting. Sometimes her hits would bruise. But it was never enough to give Joey a reason to lie flat.

It was like suffering a death of a thousand cuts, but with no end in sight.

Joey would keep flowing with the damage, doing his best to deflect them or make them land with less of a sting. When he would start to succeed, the Instructor would hit a little harder and force him to get even better at absorbing hits even though he hated getting hit.

In the case of getting kicked off a balcony, he was already dashing backward to lessen the pain. The air time didn't bother him until the instructor hurled her knife.

His tail whipped around to knock it away, but she teleported to the weapon a split second faster. Her sword deflected his tail while she stabbed her knife toward his belly.

All while mid fall.

Joey's knife skills sucked compared to the instructor. He twisted out of the way of the stab instead of deflecting and pushed his knife at the instructor's throat in return. She used her sword to whack his knife aside.

Joey took his chance to exit, dashing to the side a second before hitting the ground. He also left two shadow clones to gang tackle the instructor so she could suffer the fall fully.

She dismissed the clone tactic with a teleport upward – she had tossed her knife the moment she missed her stab. She completely ignored the clones destroying themselves with a crash and continued chasing Joey.

The two became a crazed aerial and magical dance of darkness and teleports. Through the streets. Up the tall spires. Amid bustling markets with denizens who hadn't the time to flee as Joey and Instructor Suzuki crashed through.

The opportunity to steal food and water presented itself, and something in Joey's head flipped like a switch.

He skidded to a stop during a backward retreat, braced himself, and sprinted at the instructor. Joey attacked first.

Sword thrust. Knife slash. The instructor blocked both attacks.

His tail whip swung in low. The instructor skipped over.

Joey flung his knife, and for a moment, he saw Instructor Suzuki's eyes squint with annoyance. She batted his knife aside in the direction he'd predicted she would.

A clone appeared and grabbed the knife while having a knife copy. The clone used both for a double stab at the instructor's left side.

At the same time, Joey thrust his tail at her right side. He also thrust his sword at her torso for the trifecta.

Instructor Suzuki's response?

She kicked off the ground to clear every attack and chop her sword at his head, which was good. The way forward was clear.

He dashed under her feet and beyond the sword chop. But he could feel what would come next. He left shadow clones behind as sacrificial pawns against the teleporting instructor.

He took a few seconds of reprieve to grab a melon-like fruit and bite into it ravenously. His mouth was full and covered in sweet sugar and watery goodness when he turned toward a flying knee aimed at his stomach.

Every part of Joey wanted to keep this succulent morsel of food inside of him. So he pushed himself to react within the narrow window.

He twisted his torso and tucked his elbow in the way of her knee. He moved his sword guard to cover his face and tilted his head toward the multiple impacts to come.

The flying knee made his elbow pulsate with pain. Her sword pommel crashed against his sword and smacked the guard into his face. Her knife came down last for his head. His tail deflected the head stab.

He swallowed his meal entirely. It was amazing and worth the effort.

A strong grip seized his sword wrist. Joey realized too late she'd dropped her sword to grab hold of him.

Here came the grappling while bashing and stabbing at each other like crazed killers. The instructor refused to let him go while on their feet or rolling across the ground.

For every successful pommel strike he landed with his sword she would land half a dozen knife strikes. Nothing big. All a bunch of small cuts and thrusts – again, a death by the thousand.

Joey kept rolling, scrapping, and learning her patterns as they tumbled across the ground like brawling cats.

Nine times out of ten, every flip pushed Joey's face into the hard floor. She landed on top, taking the front mount or his back. So he tried to buck and flip again even when the attempts would feel futile – with or without his tail.

She handled the fifth limb with more violence. She taught him the tail could transfer pain through the spell, a weakness of its solid form.

Joey would usually collapse in exhaustion and quit. Then Instructor Suzuki would find the nearest canal and toss him in the water. She'd give him a few hours to recover his essence or rest before they repeated this song and dance.

But something about fighting the instructor more aggressively and having one sweet bite gave Joey some extra vigor. So when physical exhaustion burned his muscles, and when essence exhaustion froze his channels, Joey clenched his jaw and pushed.

Then things changed.

Joey suddenly knew what to do to slip out of a bad grappling position and take her back. For a split second, Instructor Suzuki's neutral face broke with shock.

He moved his sword in front of her neck and grabbed the blade with his free hand before wrenching back.

She teleported away by dropping her knife. But Joey's tail whipped at her side before she fully braced herself. Her flawless technique faltered to deflect the tail whip.

When she looked at him, his sword was flying at her face. She moved her head aside and into the way of his palm thrust. His unarmed strike flew faster than any prior.

She spun her head out of the way.

The palm thrust glanced off her cheek.

She would've punished him for going unarmed, but he had clones grabbing his weapons and attacking her from behind. He kept snapping out palm thrusts at her head and torso. She retreated while fending off Joey and his clones.

Right when she swung a strong attack to kill his clones, they moved into the blow on purpose and passed Joey's weapons back to him.

She recovered a split second too late. He knocked her knife out of her hand and stabbed her in the eye.

"Ow." Instructor Suzuki stumbled back and rubbed her eye with the back of her hand.

Joey froze, feeling feral and ready to attack some more. But Instructor Suzuki's response was the most unexpected thing he'd faced yet.

What trick could this be? She was probably planning something devious.

A shame for Joey. He was familiarizing himself with her tactics. Now she was changing everything. Even her next words filled him with dreaded anticipation.

"Good job, Joey, you've beaten me."

She's trying to trick me! Why is this little girl so cruel? Joey growled like a wild animal, his weapons raised to fight.

Instructor Suzuki looked away from him – another trick! It was like she was baiting him to attack. More nonsense came out of her mouth.

"Yeah, I think seven days have been long enough. You must've gained some great abilities."

Joey attacked to test her new tricks. He moved only a single step before a song entered his ears and struck his brain.

The rogue nearly fell to his knees. It took more willpower than ever to keep from falling. But it felt like he didn't have enough willpower.

Right when he was about to kneel, something changed inside of him. He found extra grit and raised his head. He couldn't move more than that, but at least he wasn't down on his knees.

He remained standing!

The instructor stopped singing. Then something more shocking happened. A flicker of emotion showed on her face. A cute smile.

"You've gained something to defend yourself against charms. Good. That has been the downfall of many adventurers. Or poison. Make sure to get a poison resistance ability when you can."

"Why are you talking so much?" Joey asked, losing his edge.

"This version of instruction has ended, Joey. You've done well. Better than expected."

"Really?" Joey lowered his aching arms. Everything hurt around his body. His channels felt like thin veins of tundra ice.

He noticed a mirror in an abandoned stall. He suffered the horror of seeing himself.

He saw a beaten and haggard black guy with kinky black hair that was knotted from the lack of care. He was so scrawny he could count his ribs. And his basketball shorts were one rip away from showing the family jewels.

"Why am I doing this to myself?" Joey asked.

The instructor collected all the training weapons. She turned and held them out.

A war siren sprinted from around the corner and grabbed the training weapons before bolting back out of sight. Then the instructor stood by his side and looked him up and down.

"Do you want help to get back to the castle?" she asked.

Joey stared off to the side. Then he shook his head. "Just

lead me there, please. I'll walk."

She nodded and started walking. She was fine despite all the fighting.

Joey staggered behind her before straightening his posture and dismissing his weakness as best he could. He held his head up, looking proud even if he didn't feel it.

"To answer your previous question of why you're doing this, it's because you want to protect your greatness and become greater," she said. "My adviser was badgering me during your rest time, telling me I'm being too cruel. She told me I would end up breaking you and ruining the growth of a promising adventurer."

"Really?"

"Your kraken friend was especially worried. I had to bar him in a private room. No harm came to him, of course. And the room had plenty of space, water, and comforts a kraken enjoys. But he's hard to placate, and very talkative and smart. He also wants to tell you sorry for not preparing you before. Even my students have pleaded with me for mercy. Marishell thought I was getting revenge on you for Marytea's death. That is not the case."

"Why were you doing this if you're facing all this backlash?"

The war princess looked back. Her expression was hard to place. It was mostly impassive but had a hint of something more.

"I have my reasons. For myself. And for the good of my people. I won't ask forgiveness when instructing another great adventurer."

Damn, she is tough for seventeen. Has she always lived like this? Joey mulled over her words. "I haven't looked at my gains.

I'll let you know if you're forgiven based on the results."

After seven days of fighting a relentless war princess, Joey knew he'd gotten some amazing results. The suffering almost seemed like background noise.

He felt the euphoria of a kid about to open presents on Christmas. If only the princess stayed on topic when she spoke next.

"Pardon, do you have particular body preferences or personalities you prefer? They'll be ready to serve you at the spa if you can say it aloud for my attendant to hear. She's within listening distance. And this is no cost to you. Consider yourself my esteemed guest from now on."

The princess looked at him seriously.

"You can ask for up to twenty-four females. Of those twenty-four, you can have eight as seekers or trade those eight for a single specialist. Then you will have sixteen laborers under the specialist's command. I've been advised war sirens with battle experience are both assertive and likable for adventurers. But you can also switch from the female package to the male one. But you only get one male."

"Why am I being told this?" Joey asked, incredulous.

The princess blinked. "Your first award has more awards than what I led you to believe. And don't male adventurers love special attention, rich food, and good drinks? That's what I've been advised on."

15. WHEN THE ROGUE HAS CHARISMA

Joey woke up in comfort. There were tears falling from his eyes, but they fell out of happiness. He'd never slept so well in his entire life. He'd never slept in a nice bed, either.

The rogue slowly wiped away the tears. He pushed the comforter down before sitting up.

He winced in anticipation of pain. *There's no way I'm healthy after everything I've gone through.*

He felt no issues. None whatsoever.

While he'd chosen to go without the special packages, the rehabilitating spa was worth a visit for his wellbeing. The treatment from the superior green algae healing pool had Joey feeling like a new man.

He tossed aside the covers and looked himself over completely. No scars. No signs of all the strife and struggle he'd gone through. A clean bill of health.

The system and magic stuff are the most amazing things

ever if you can get past the hard work and danger.

The bed was bigger than an Alaskan King. The room dripped with classical luxury. Rich wood furnishing and furniture. Big wardrobe dresser in one corner. A shelf filled with books in another corner.

Set against the wall opposite of the bed was a big oak-like desk with a crystal ball at the center. Joey could barely recall the castle servant's instructions on how to operate the ball.

It's supposed to work like a magical phone or computer with a network attached. Fancy stuff.

He was still a pinch unclear about his health or if he should leave bed. Maybe he should sleep in longer. Who knew when he would have this luxury again.

But he hadn't looked at his gains yet. He was waiting to have a rested mind and a sitdown meal with Instructor Suzuki and Curi. He wanted them around while he looked at everything.

The instructor also had more tips and vital system information to give him. The theoretical knowledge to apply with the practical knowledge.

Joey scooted out of bed and stood on his feet. He rolled his shoulders around and twisted this way and that at the waist. He still felt nothing wrong.

He felt lighter. More capable. He knew he could jump across the room and move like a whirlwind compared to his pre-system, no-magic self.

Come on, let's not delay any further. Joey moved to the wardrobe. The servant had told him to check what was inside once he woke up.

He swung the doors wide and stared at three modified seeker suits. One black, one white, and one dark forest green with brown and black splotches.

Next to the outfits were an assortment of blades sheathed in brown scabbards on brown harnesses. Beneath those were two pairs of brown boots, lightweight and all-terrain. Joey hurried to put them on while using Analyze.

[??]

"Wait, what?" Joey paused. "What does it mean that I can't analyze them? The only way for that to happen is if it's way above my level. Or maybe there's a spell blocking me?"

Joey was a little nervous. He wouldn't know what he was wearing.

But Joey was greedy. He donned the first outfit he reached.

The white one.

"Damn, that's an accurate fit." Joey admired himself further in the mirror.

The bodysuits reached from his ankles and up to his neck. The sleeves cut off at the biceps. The opening at the front sealed on its own once he slipped into it. He had no idea how to take it off, but at least he was comfortable.

The suit felt breathable, too. They were probably designed with a human in mind, so they would dry quickly out of water.

Wearing the white one represented a fresh start. In some cultures, white represented death, too. Add on the brown from the harnesses and boots, and Joey had the look of a confident mercenary.

He summoned a few clones for their opinion.

"Uh oh! Nobody thought the shadow gang could look good in white!"

"Our haters gonna stay hating!"

"We don't have haters."

"No worries! When we show up for real. The haters will come!"

Joey chuckled at the reactions and tomfoolery of his silly clones. He dismissed them and looked back at the mirror with an eye for function now.

The weapon harnesses and belts were easy to manipulate. Joey counted two short blades and four knives. Then he noticed the knife handles ended in recognizable rings.

"No way."

Yes way. Kunais.

Joey shook his head, feeling unsure about the ninja knives. Yeah, he was a fan when watching anime or cartoons. But he wanted to be serious about his rogue weaponry.

Would Instructor Suzuki have these made as a joke?

No, she's not the joking type. She's probably serious about these.

He would have to ask for instruction on the reasons for the ninja knives. Until then, he played with the straps and rearranged the scabbards based on intuition.

He fixed a kunai behind the small of his back. He strapped one upside down on his chest. The last two went to the left hip and the side of his left boot – it had a friendly knife-holding design.

He then noticed his short swords came at different sizes. The shortest one could be drawn from over the right shoulder while on his back. The longer one stayed at his right hip. He practiced the hip draw and back draw to get a feel for them. He approved.

When he dug around the wardrobe, he found a traveling backpack with his old holding bag inside. All of his stuff was in it – except for his old tank top.

Joey had no issues with them tossing that out. The backpack had plenty of space for the extra gear.

He threw the pack on his shoulders and played with the straps and buckles until it was a perfect fit. Good to go.

These are fancy designs for a fantasy world. Joey imagined having a system and an entire multiverse filled with possibilities would transfer some modern ideas around.

"English is a primary language," Joey murmured to himself, sliding off the backpack and returning it to the wardrobe dresser. "That's got me curious. Honestly, lots of things have me curious."

Alarmed voices and shouts sounded from outside of Joey's door. He heard the squelching contact of something slimy and bulky moving over the polished floor and rug.

Joey walked over to his door and opened wide before Curi's tentacles knocked. The kraken's flute-like language whistled loudly with exclamations.

[On the grace of the Tidal Moon Lord, Joey, it's good to see you! And – oh my, look at you in white! I must say that is a dashing look you have. Forgive me for having a poor vision for your gender, but I can admire superior quality craft like no other.]

"Superior, huh? That's just like the description of a spell of mine. Is that next level stuff?"

[Indeed, it is. You probably can't analyze it yet unless you have the skill at level 10 or you get closer to level 100.]

Curi's large dark eyes studied Joey up and down, ignoring the servants and guardians standing behind him. Then the kraken began fidgeting again in obvious distress.

[Ah, what am I doing? I'm not here to admire! I'm here to apologize! I didn't know the war princess would do what she did. I'll admit I withheld information I knew you wouldn't know, but I thought it would be humorous and interesting for you to experience firsthand! But what I've heard of the young great war princess could've helped you!]

Joey rubbed the back of his head and stopped in surprise at how velvety it felt. The spa servant had treated his hair and twisted the strands into starter dreadlocks, too. Less of a hassle for the future.

Curi took his silence the wrong way. [I'm failing at this apology business aren't I? Well, I apologize and will completely understand if this is a break in our partnership. I'm undeserving of being a peer after the stunt I've pulled.]

Joey chuckled. "Curi, relax. What happened won't break what we got going on. But I will say this. It was terrible for my anxiety going in blind like that. It would've helped to get the information I needed."

[Ah, yes, you're right. You're absolutely right. Let this humble trader do all he can to make up for the blunder. I'm just happy you're okay. The past two days have been worrying since you've been so silent in your room.]

"Two days?"

Joey looked from the kraken to a servant. The war siren nodded in confirmation. *Huh, I guess I really needed the rest.*

"Well, I'm up now. And you caught me at the perfect time. Let's go find Instructor Suzuki and have a meal with her. We can go over my gains together."

Curi shifted his tentacles awkwardly. Joey picked up on the kraken's discomfort. With a smile, Joey stepped forward and placed a hand between Curi's eyes.

"Let's give her another chance, okay? I think what she did was her way of helping me."

The kraken let out a big musical sigh. [Fine. But once you're ready, let's leave. I'm going to feel terrible the longer we're here.]

"Hey, hey, now. When did the voyager kraken become the one to rush?" Joey teased, getting some satisfaction from Curi's embarrassment. "Just another interesting adventure to learn from, right? Always an experience."

[I'm being tormented by my own words! And it hurts!]

Joey walked past the kraken with a big laugh. A waiting servant nodded at him, and he nodded back with a smile.

She perked up and happily led them through the large and well-kept castle. They passed through a bunch of halls until they reached a banquet room.

Maylolee Suzuki – the War Princess, Lead Siren, and Chief War Instructor – sat with thick volumes of books on one side and a small platter of food on the other. Her chair was big, heavy, and made for a ruler regardless of her small figure.

In front of her was an extended table filled with an abundance of food and drink.

Joey saw a dozen types of dishes he could recognize. And a dozen he couldn't. Many of the dishes had types of fish that were new to him.

Servers stood waiting around the room. Hovering over the princess's shoulders were two elderly but graceful sirens.

[Tidal Moon Denizen: War Siren: Attendant lvl ?]

[Tidal Moon Denizen: War Siren: Adviser lvl ?]

The attendant and adviser looked like humanoid shackles. Maybe they didn't mean to be, but Joey's enthusiasm dimmed seeing them loom behind the princess, serving as the heavy and unbreakable bonds of her throne.

Or maybe he was looking too deeply into something that wasn't there and should mind his own business.

Let's go back to having my fun.

"If you can win games with how bored you look, you'll crush all challengers." Joey strode up and folded his arms on top of a high-back chair close by the princess. "By the way, do I still call you Instructor Suzuki? Or do I call you Princess when we're relaxed? Or maybe Maylolee? May? Lee? I think I like Maylolee as a whole. It has a fun ring to it."

As the princess examined him, Curi maneuvered over to an awaiting pool. There were multiple. He chose the one farthest from the princess.

The kraken glowered silently like a grumpy … octopus.

"It should be War Princess Maylolee," the attendant muttered.

"Let the war princess correct him," the advisor added.

"Maylolee," the princess said flatly. "Call me Maylolee, and I'll call you Joey."

"Works for me!" Joey cheered before yanking his chair back without the help of a servant. He sat down in a comfortable slouch.

"You're being extra showy," Maylolee said. "Why?"

"Are you kidding? Look at me! I'm dressed in white with the nicest fit I've ever worn. And I'm about to look at my system gains."

"You really waited." Some emotion flashed on Maylolee's face. "You don't have to tell me. Yes, I am helping you. But we are great adventurers. There could be a day when we're rivals."

The matronly sirens openly glared at Joey. But they couldn't dent his enthusiasm. He was brimming with it.

"I don't care if you know every part of my profile." Joey leaned forward, grinning widely. "If we fight fair and square, I'll still come out ahead."

There was silence.

Then there was tense silence.

The latter filled the room until the princess replied.

"Oh? You think you can beat me if you reach Level 100?" Maylolee leaned forward slightly. "Why?"

"Because I want to, so I'll make it happen." He pulled a plate of something that looked like scrambled eggs and salmon.

He took the nearest utensil and dug in. One scoop nearly hit the spot. He refrained from another bite to speak again.

"I bet it gets boring being at the top without a challenge, huh? You don't push people that hard unless you're looking for others to be right there with you. So not only will I forgive you, I'm going to surpass you so you can try running to keep up with me."

[Please don't torture him again! He doesn't even know how most things work in Multiverse Z! He's just a rambunctious and ambitious young great!] Curi waved his tentacles around in worry, forcing the servants trying to feed him to step back.

Joey tried to keep from laughing while having food in his

mouth. He swallowed, took a goblet freshly poured with melon juice to drink – ah, refreshing – and refocused on Maylolee.

Her attendant and advisor were dark clouds hanging over the princess. At first glance, Maylolee looked indifferent.

Joey noticed the quiver in the corner of her mouth. She was trying not to smile.

"Look at your first system message," Maylolee forced out. "You are too far beneath me to think you can match me. But maybe you'll get closer if the results are great."

Joey wondered what could be special about his first system message. He figured he wouldn't get any path levels since he killed nothing. He should only receive new skills and skill levels.

Taking her advice, he took a quick peek and noticed something vastly different. The system had more features he'd yet to explore.

[Congrats! You've accomplished a Hidden Quest: Beat the War Princess (Difficulty: Level 63)! *Adventurer Eclipse, since I am a ruler, I can serve as a limited quest giver. My instincts say you can handle this. I will adjust myself to be a hard but winnable challenge. I will chase, spar with you, and deny you adequate needs for however long it takes for you to truly quit. Please beat me convincingly instead of giving up.*

Conducting quest results evaluation!

Did you do poorly? No.

Did you do well? No.

Did you do great? … … Yes!

For accomplishing great results on a quest forty levels above you, double bonus experience is awarded!]

[You've leveled up Shade Dragon Rogue from 21 to 28!]

[Congrats! You have the opportunity to learn a new Spell! Please check your profile to select your Spell!]

Joey set aside the other messages. "Can I hug you?"

"I haven't been hugged in thirteen years," Maylolee said. "Maybe another time."

"I'll save it in the bank. The best hug I can ever give anyone. It'll be worth a lot."

Maylolee blinked at him. "Interesting."

Joey willed the system to bring up the profile. He dove into his spell selection. There were many familiar spells and a few new ones. It was stunning for him to decide on one. He was pulled from his hesitation when the princess spoke again.

"Marytea ... I've given her a similar quest adjusted for her. Rarely has anyone passed. A few have. Marytea was one. You are another. I hope this helps further your greatness."

"I'm sorry about Marytea. And thank you for your kindness. If there's any way I can help your people or further your greatness in return, let me know," Joey replied.

Maylolee nodded.

Joey nodded back before reevaluating his choices.

[Select one spell: Shade Blade Extension (Superior), Phantom Phase (Superior), Spectral Hands (Superior), Shade Dragon Claws (Superior), Dark Fists (Superior), Death Echo (Epic), Bigger Backstab (Basic), Cloaking (Basic), Simple Unlock (Basic), Smoke Bomb (Basic), Necrotic Touch (Superior), Shade Dragon Breath (Epic).]

16. SKILLS, MAGIC, KNIFE FIGHTS

Joey slammed his hands down on the armrests and hurled himself out of his chair. He backflipped onto the open floor and yelled, "Chief War Instructor Suzuki!" Then with a smile, he said, "This adventurer needs instructions."

Maylolee raised her hand and beckoned for the nearest servants. Four sirens ran to her and pulled her heavy throne from the table. Maylolee stood with a rigid posture and walked over to Joey. "Let's go to one of my training yards, Adventurer Eclipse."

The training yard was hard packed sand in a rectangular field. Blue fuzzy grass surrounded the perimeter. In the yard, young sirens clashed with practice polearms or performed drills under the watchful eye of their elders. They were working hard, showing little to no weakness, or they would suffer punishment.

A servant tried to run her fastest to warn the training group of the great adventurers coming. Joey and Maylolee moved faster, showing up on the edge before the servant.

The servant shook her head and left.

"Continue practicing on that half of the field," Maylolee ordered. "Consider the lack of space a new challenge."

The trainees and trainers nodded and packed it together on one half of the field. It clearly wasn't enough space, but they made it work.

Joey chuckled at the ease Maylolee had with ordering people around. He followed her to the middle of their space and sat with her, legs crossed while opposite of her.

"Adventurer Eclipse, what instructions are you seeking?" she asked.

"I don't think I'm a normal rogue," Joey said. "I'm going to check my skill gains, but I could already tell they're geared toward heavy combat. Maybe I should choose a spell to cover weaknesses or help me do more rogue stuff. Or I follow the trend of me doing what I like to do."

"What is it you like to do?" Maylolee asked seriously.

"Fighting with my shady powers," Joey answered.

"Review your messages and stop before selecting your spell." Maylolee raised a hand. "Do note that you are sharing vital information with me. It can be used against you one day. Even if it's in the distant future. Are you sure you're okay with that?"

"Yup," Joey said.

Maylolee nodded.

Joey dove into his messages, the system adapting to his will on the fly.

[You've leveled up Shade Dragon Rogue from 21 to 28!]

[You've raised your mind from 64 to 78!]

[You've raised your body from 64 to 78!]

[You've raised your spirit from 65 to 72!]

[You've raised your free points from 0 to 21!]

The temptation to dump his points into a specific stat arose. Joey looked up to see Curi swimming through a canal away from listening distance.

"Instructor Suzuki, do you prefer keeping balanced stats?" Joey asked.

"I had a few situations that required more points invested in one stat. But in the end, I needed all my stats raised together. It will help in the future."

"Do you get more than eight points on every level?" Joey asked.

"Everyone gets eight points a level. Adventurer, denizen, monster, beast. No more. No less."

Huh, so points aren't too big of a deciding factor. Then it might just come down to opportunities and personal abilities. And the system. Joey didn't see a reason to diverge from Curi's advice, especially when it's backed by the chief war instructor.

Eight points went to mind. Eight points went to the body. The rest entered his spirit. Joey smiled, feeling the growth from the inside while seeing the numbers rise.

[You've raised your mind from 78 to 82!]

[You've raised your body from 78 to 82!]

[You've raised your spirit from 72 to 85!]

Joey arranged for the skill gains to come up next. *It's hilarious how I was excited for my skills. But now they're the lead up to the big showy magic.*

[Congrats! You have the opportunity to learn the Roll With The Hits Skill!]

[You've learned the Roll With The Hits Skill!]

[Congrats! You have the opportunity to learn the Slick Knife Tricks Skill!]

[You've learned the Slick Knife Tricks Skill!]

[Congrats! You have the opportunity to learn the Fight Prediction Skill!]

[You've learned the Fight Prediction Skill!]

[Congrats! You have the opportunity to learn the Assassin Grappling Skill!]

[You've learned the Assassin Grappling Skill!]

[Congrats! You have the opportunity to learn the Hands of the Fade Skill!]

[You've learned the Hands of the Fade Skill!]

[Congrats! You've acquired the Dragon Pride Singularity!]

"Uh."

"What is the matter, Adventurer Eclipse?" Maylolee asked.

"I'm looking at my skills. I don't recall accepting any of them. But I've already learned them without reading them."

Her eyes sharpened. "Did any present choices between different skills?"

Joey shook his head.

"Good. The system selected them for you while you were distracted. If it's all to your liking, then be thankful. The system was being nice to you. But don't let that happen again."

Joey nodded.

Wow, that was dumb of me not to figure that out. I didn't make the connection that the skills were learned already. I was using them at the end when I started doing new things to beat the war princess, too.

They all sounded good based on the names.

Once he started reading, the skill descriptions had him smiling from ear to ear.

[Roll With The Hits (Basic): The attacks are coming. And you can't avoid them all. Endure what you can. Lessen the damages with deceptive movements. *I could've sworn I was hitting this guy with everything I have. But then my sword arm gets tired, and he attacks like he's never been hit!*]

[Slick Knife Tricks (Basic): In your hand, the knife is both an arsenal and a tool for showing off your dexterity. It only looks stupid if you fail. *I don't get people sometimes. Beasts have their claws and use them as they should. But give a person a knife, and it's now an arrow, a can opener, a boomerang, and everything else but a knife.*]

[Fight Prediction (Basic): Recognize patterns faster while fighting a single opponent. Hone in on their habits, good or bad, and design limited projections of their next moves. *I was talking to this one bloke, and he swears he knows everything I'll do because he watched how I fiddle with my fingers. I was going to stab him, but I left the tavern instead.*]

[Assassin Grappling (Basic): Get in and out of grappling situations intending to kill or severely harm a target. This works better while on the move, keeping your momentum. *I watched this big warrior attack this little man in rags. The little man became a blur of action and jumped the warrior, crawling all over. What I saw next still haunts me to this day.*]

[Hands of the Fade (Basic): Strike hard and fast when going from armed to unarmed. Palms and backhands work

best. *"Heh, heh, heh. We took away all of your weapons. And the room is bare, so no makeshift weapons. Now you're dead meat!" These were the last words of a villain before receiving a backhand that shattered his skull.*]

"I can kill with a pimp slap!" Joey laughed like a loon. "Please, system, don't give me any haters. They're really going to love to hate me."

"The skills are to your liking, then." Maylolee nodded. "You are fortunate."

"Very fortunate. Five new skills. They do exactly what I enjoy doing, helping me fight up close and personal. I even got this singularity, too."

"The one that helps you against charms like mine and my sirens," Maylolee said softly. "I'm glad you have that."

"Don't you want me feeble for you to trick later." He wriggled his fingers at her.

She stared at him blankly. "You need some resistance when we work together. I've yet to use my full power."

"True. True." Joey rubbed the back of his neck. "Let me finish up then get to the point."

Before touching on the singularity, Joey checked his skill levels. To his surprise, there were more than just the skills.

[You've leveled up Combat Acrobatics from 5 to 7!]

[You've leveled up Chaos Finder from 3 to 4!]

[You've leveled up Stress Management from 1 to 6!]

[You've leveled up Roll With The Hits from 1 to 5!]

[You've leveled up Slick Knife Tricks from 1 to 4!]

[You've leveled up Fight Prediction from 1 to 3!]

[You've leveled up Assassin Grappling from 1 to 2!]

[You've leveled up Hands of the Fade from 1 to 2!]

[You've leveled up Dark Dash from 1 to 2!]

"I leveled up one of my spells," Joey said, incredulous. "Granted, it was superior. I think fighting you helped improve it."

"Good. One level up from a superior spell is worth around six to seven levels in a basic."

Joey stroked his chin. "I didn't notice it at the time, but my dashes were moving me faster and harder. And they didn't cost more."

"I recall the change toward the end. And costs usually go up every five levels, so you don't have to worry about your essence supply there."

"I've noticed that with my skills. I keep track of my essence all the time."

Maylolee looked with a glint of approval. "Anything else?"

"Hold on."

[Dragon Pride (Superior): Your pride as a dragon refuses efforts to rule over you. Gain a 100% buff to your willpower when under unwanted influence.]

Huh, that's an actual buff. A permanent one at that. And it has no extra description.

"Superior," Joey said. "How did I get a permanent buff like that?"

Maylolee looked shocked for a split second before neutralizing her expression. "You'll become dangerous once you grow into your own."

"Uh oh. Does that mean you'll send a hit squad my way?

Woe is me."

"You are silly," Maylolee said, glancing away briefly before looking back. "Beware of getting more singularities that are permanent. You'll evolve from basic human to superior human. In this realm, that's a giveaway of being a great adventurer."

"Curi told me steady adventurers could get nasty with the great ones," Joey said.

"I've read of it and had secondhand sources tell me the same. Great ones such as us have been brought down by steady ones because of their numbers and tricks." Maylolee's face darkened. "I'm glad you're great. I can't help but see steady adventurers as pathetic or devious. They're best used as fodder."

Joey's good mood dimmed. He didn't like the reality of adventurers attacking each other. Even if Joey would revive after the death, that would end his great adventurer climb.

Then he would become a commoner.

It would feel like going back to the same old thing, being another nobody.

Looking back, Joey noticed Curi remained away from the training field. The kraken was giving them space but staying in the area to keep watch.

He's so petty and protective. It's like dealing with a cat with tentacles.

Joey stood, and Maylolee did the same. The two moved about and warmed up, looking at ease around each other. The princess became a little less rigid.

Maylolee called for training knives. Two flew over from the active side of the field. The great adventurers grabbed a knife each.

Without another word, they attacked each other.

Joey moved lightly on his feet while using his knife with deceptive slashes. Maylolee stayed tight and low with a disciplined guard, defending and advancing. She forced Joey to move backward, but Joey took advantage of his reach to keep her wary.

"I'm a battle rogue," Joey said. "I've got no skills for sneaking or stealing. And I've tried for a week to do just that. Sometimes it worked. Oftentimes, there was a guardian in the way, and I came out with empty hands."

"This is all known to me while you were assessed," Maylolee said. "You are not the usual rogue. Other than using your environment for outflanking and some cunning maneuvers, you are more direct than a normal rogue would be. You also pick up close combat well, incorporating it like a warrior with a rogue's cunning."

Joey flipped the knife in front of Maylolee. She smacked it out of the way, revealing her knife arm for him to grab and control.

She kept a strong grip on her knife to keep from being disarmed, but he was distracting her until he could grab his falling knife from the air. The moment she'd smacked it aside, he used Shade Dragon Tail to smack it up so it would fall where he needed it.

Maylolee used her fingers to flick her knife to the side. She teleported in the same direction, escaping his attack. Joey smiled as they continued exchanging knife attacks and bursts of tactical magic.

"Why do my skills slow down after level 5?" Joey asked, dodging a cut for his throat. "I have a few at level 7 that won't budge."

"Good, I was hoping you would ask. You've reached the brute force limit. Now you must actually become skillful." She blocked three rapid strikes, totally unfazed. "This is where essence control comes into play. It's the opposite of essence power. You need to concentrate on limiting your skills while using them in training or against opponents that present a fair challenge. The same concept can be applied to spells, which is vastly more difficult if they're above our levels in quality."

"So if I want my skill at level 7 to go up, I have to weaken it?"

"Think of it as controlling the magic surrounding the skill. Right now, you're using all magic and burning through essence. True skillfulness is maximizing the abilities you've learned from the system and doing so without heavy reliance on magic. If you want the fast track for your growth, you must limit yourself and attempt the same skills the hard way."

"Huh," Joey said, pivoting away from knife slashes and thrusts. "That might take some thinking on my part. But I guess you're the example. Is that what you're doing with me? Limiting everything you use?"

"Yes."

"Is it hard?"

"Very hard. You do not make anything easy. You have tricky abilities. If warriors at you level fight you unprepared, they'll die fast."

Joey smiled. "I guess that leads to my next question. Should I stay focused on the close combat battle rogue style? Or branch out with a spell that's different?"

"When making this decision, consider that you won't get your next spell until level 75. Then you'll get your last spell at level 100. Six spells in total."

"I didn't know that. Now the next decision matters even more."

"You're going to want a spell that will make the biggest difference for the next fifty levels. You can figure out the last two afterward. And if you improve your skills enough, you won't always need spells to match your main theme."

Their knives clashed. She shoved him back hard. Joey stumbled, feeling her raw strength.

He smiled as the princess attacked with more Level 100 power. She kept instructing, too.

"Spells can be enhancers while your skills do most of the fighting for you. So if you have a spell option that pushes your greatness faster and harder, then it'll be a good choice to choose that spell."

Maylolee smiled a little. "Besides, you're very versatile and creative. You can use anything and make it work."

Joey stopped.

Maylolee stopped her knife thrust from hitting his throat. She lowered her knife but remained close to him.

[You've leveled up Slick Knife Tricks from 4 to 5!]

[You've leveled up Fight Prediction from 3 to 4!]

"Thanks for that. I really needed to hear these instructions."

"I'm glad I can help a fellow great adventurer."

"Even if you think we'll be rivals for whatever reason."

"I have vast reservoirs of knowledge made available to me because of my position. Some of that knowledge is from beyond this beginner area and way above our levels. So I can say this with confidence. The climb is testing. Few can make it with friends intact."

Joey nodded. "I believe you."

Maylolee tilted her head. "Really?"

"I'm not going to scream at the heavens and pretend I'll fight anything to protect friendship. I have no idea what's out there. But I'll deal with it as it comes. And for now, I'm glad we got this thing going on."

"This thing?"

"Yeah." Joey grinned. "Let me decide on the spell. After that, you want to go out and show me your favorite spots in the city? I think today will be nice to see the sights before Curi and I leave for landfall."

Maylolee didn't say anything. Joey sat back down and focused on his spells. He skipped the basic ones for powerful spells.

[Shade Blade Extension (Superior): Coat a blade in your hand with shade. While attacking, the shade will extend to attack the victim's essence directly. Slashed essence can sometimes fall out of a victim for collection. *This is why light, radiance, and other similar aspects exist. To beat back scary powers like these.*]

[Phantom Phase (Superior): Become like a ghost, intangible and translucent. Then phase through solid objects and physical attacks. Some magic may have a stronger effect during this phase. *Ah! Who goes there? Oh, it's you. Har. Har. Can you stop phasing through everything to spook me? I'm going to call a cleric sooner or later.*]

[Spectral Hands (Superior): Conjure multiple hands around you. These hands can manipulate half the weight you can. Spend more essence to make them invisible. *Well, we'll know who to turn to when we need extra hands. Just don't get too handsy, okay?*]

[**Shade Dragon Claws (Superior): Shoot out ghostly dragon claws, tearing into the flesh and bone and more. The claws can phase through physical objects and armor, especially those that lacked the needed magic. Beware the dragon price.** *I thought I've seen the worst dragons imaginable. Then came this one terror that was as silent as a grave. I don't know why it left me alive. But I've stopped dragon hunting since then.*]

[**Dark Fists (Superior): Gather darkness into your fists. Emit pulses of heavy darkness upon impact. The weight and power of darkness grows in the dark.** *I thought the darko-types were too stuck in their books, brooding about darkness. Apparently, there are ones who brood and punch the lights out of people.*]

[**Death Echo (Epic): Kill an enemy and create an echo. The echo will perform the same death strike on the nearest enemy. If successful, the echo will repeat itself.** *"We have you surrounded! You can't kill all of us!" The last words of a victim before all his men died with him.*]

[**Necrotic Touch (Superior): Coat your hands or your weapons with a necrotic aura. The flesh of your victims will suffer painful rotting on contact.** *I have this thing against black-hearted villains. Can you blame me? They always leave examples that make the hardest men weak in the stomach.*]

[**Shade Dragon Breath (Epic): Inhale deeply to charge this power. The longer you charge it, the greater the power unleashed. Then exhale. Physical obstacles without magic are to be ignored. Magic and essence will attract your flame, but you will suffer the dragon price.** *It was eating me from the inside out. My essence was oil for its shadowy embers. Oh, lord, I still remember the pain to this day.*]

17. ROGUISH AND IRRESPONSIBLE

To Joey's surprise, five out of the eight advance spells were easy to eliminate. Spectral Hands was too focused on utility, which Shadow Clone Magic had covered. Shade Dragon Claws, Dark Fists, Death Echo, and Necrotic Touch were too focused on attack. They had few uses outside of being offensive.

Out of the last three, Joey eliminated Shade Blade Extension next. It was a useful ability, but he wanted to achieve essence sustain through a meditation skill. And he wanted spells with the most versatility and impact in any situation.

He liked Phantom Phase because of the many possibilities. Inside of combat, Joey would force enemies to rely solely on magic if they wanted to harm him. That would depend on knowing he was there, of course. He'd become like a ghost with this spell – better than a natural rogue.

Outside of combat, his exploration abilities would widen. Inaccessible areas with walls or obstacles without magic would become accessible to him. Powerful enemies he couldn't afford to fight would become easier to avoid.

However, Phantom Phase had weaknesses against magic, which would ruin its gimmick. He was sure there were specific counters to this ability, too. Maybe Phantom Phase would become a spell he'd go for at level 75 or level 100.

In the end, Shade Dragon Breath was the clear winner. Joey wanted the dragon breath spell the moment he'd seen it. Now he was viewing it under a different lens.

It was more than a flashy magic attack. It was a powerful anti-magic ability in a world that loved magic.

Joey was going to be a menace for mostly everyone even if they didn't rely on magic. He could attack a target's essence and make them hurt badly. That could impede skill and spell uses.

The shadow gang is going to love this, Joey thought, selecting Shade Dragon Breath. He grinned as he felt the spell become a part of him.

[Congrats! You've learned the Shade Dragon Breath Spell!]

His dragon greed intensified. Joey battled with it, feeling desires that were inappropriate.

He was more aware of his greed because of overt connections with dragons. His Dragon Pride singularity cinched it for his understanding, too.

Thankfully, the permanent buff had no downsides. It was his dragon spells forcing him to pay the dragon price – greed.

"You have the spell," Maylolee said. "Did you choose the one with the biggest impact?"

"Yes," Joey said, still wrestling with himself. "It's taking some time to adjust."

Maylolee scrutinized him. "My path is War Princess Warrior."

Joey looked at her in shock. His greed settled down, giving him room to breathe. "I wouldn't think a princess would count as a creature."

"I wanted to be like my mother."

Joey tip-toed around that emotional landmine. "My path is Shade Dragon Rogue."

"I see." She nodded. "Be careful. The dragon is popular since it is powerful. But there are many accounts of that path ending in self-destruction. Will you be able to overcome the dragon price, Joey?"

The rogue shivered. *Damn, she really is knowledgeable. I feel kind of naked right now.*

"I'm going to have to try," he said. "Or I'll turn away the other dragon options."

Maylolee nodded. An uneasy silence fell on them.

The clamor of trainees drilling on the other side of the field filled the air. It was obvious the sirens were eavesdropping on the two great adventurers. Be that one was their war princess, who could blame them.

The awkward silence became an invitation for Maylolee's attendant and adviser. The elderly sirens walked with rigid postures and even paced steps. They took the spots behind the princess's shoulders – Maylolee looked gloomier with her elders there.

"If the instructions have ended, we must be off," the attendant said. "War Princess Maylolee has important matters to attend."

"Please take a guardian and see the city with a more

relaxed eye while you're here," the adviser suggested. "Perhaps you may find this place suitable as a home. We can use a great adventurer as a retainer. Though your orders will come from others beside the princess. She can only spend so much of her time on one thing."

Joey looked from attendant to adviser and back. In his mind, this was another fight. *Conflict isn't always physical.*

They were challenging him for the princess when she hadn't made a decision. The dragon in Joey wanted to growl. The rogue used words instead.

"When was the last time Maylolee had a break?" Joey asked.

The older sirens looked at him with darker expressions.

Before they could speak again, the rogue stepped closer to the princess. "Hey, I get you're in an important seat of power. Lots of people are counting on you, no doubt. But having a day to kick back and have some fun is important, too. It'll help strengthen you in the end. You get me?"

"I don't," Maylolee said flatly. "I've spent too much time with you. I have to catch up on my duties."

Joey shook his head. "Come on, Maylolee. Just one day."

"I am War Princess, Lead Siren, and Chief War Instructor," she replied. "Enjoy your day in my city, Adventurer Eclipse."

"Good day, adventurer." The adviser placed a hand on the princess's shoulder and guided her away.

The attendant smirked while on her way out. "Don't forget the special spa packages are always available to our esteemed guests."

***

After calming his anger, Joey ended up going out alone. Curi needed time to sell and buy stuff since he'd been distracted with Joey trying to beat the War Princess. The rogue figured a guardian guide was unnecessary and left the castle to see the sights himself.

His Scenic Discoverer pulsed as he wandered from the city center and toward a coral tunnel. He'd seen most of the center while running around and battling the princess. He'd yet to see the other domes, so he chose an arm tunnel at random.

The guardians let him through without question. They knew to look out for him, and he heard them sending messages through a crystal ball.

[Adventurer Eclipse is traveling down Agriculture Arm Two.]

So, each arm has a purpose, Joey thought.

He picked up his pace and visited the domes down on the second agriculture arm. The further from the center, the more different the domes became.

Whole tanks and watery fields spread out amid farms in all directions. It was almost trippy to see the difference once Joey exited a tunnel and entered a new dome. Some domes focused on water plants. Others focused on creatures.

One dome was mostly filled with water, and Joey had to traverse through tunnels with see-through pearl windows. When he reached the last dome, he found a detachment of war siren specialists and seekers. They were a quick response team living in their own bubble that had everything they could want. From taverns to farms.

"Why does this area exist on the arm tip? Wouldn't you be far from all the other places?" Joey asked at a tavern with bluish coral decorations. A specialist had invited him to have a drink – all free.

[The distance allows us more freedom than other war siren units. We can respond to outer threats as we see fit and stay away from the mess the center can become during big issues,] the specialist responded. [And you want distance when we're guiding fortress jellies down for the heavy maintenance they need here.]

Joey imagined the maintenance for fortress jellies was a big endeavor. He was thankful for the information and had one drink with the siren and her friends.

Then he excused himself because he wanted to visit the other arms. That included every arm for agriculture. The rogue wanted to uncover as much as he could see.

On his way out, he overheard the sirens jostling the specialist he'd received answers from. [Darn the dark moon, Miyashore! If you weren't going in for the catch, you could've let me answer his questions. I would've –]

Joey stopped analyzing the conversation and went back down the tunnel. He visited each of the agriculture arms.

None of them deviated from each other, which was smart. If something happened to any agricultural arm, it would be less of a hassle if each arm had the same crops and livestock.

When he visited the war arm, he needed an escort to walk him through areas he was allowed to see. That didn't mean it was a boring trip. In fact, Joey saw more than he'd expected.

The war sirens had animals trained for war like sea horses the size of actual horses and bus-size sharks that worked as mounts and battle partners. They had magical constructs that could move underwater and serve as defensive armaments or siege weapons.

Joey watched as two specialists propped a harpoon down beside him. It was five times his height.

Each dome on the war arm had specific uses, from training war sirens to crafting new weapons. The domes here were hives of activity and had plenty of areas with thick coral walls he couldn't access.

He reached the end of the arm where another war siren detachment lived in isolated freedom. So far, he was four for four in having a drink at a tavern and letting the specialists flirt with him until he moved on.

The mercantile arm had domes jammed packed with heavy activity. Laborers worked in factory spires that touched the dome ceiling. The dome walls held more coral structures, too.

Aerial bridges connected most of the structures, suspending thousands of sirens above Joey's head. On the ground, vendors and their stalls lined the sides of most streets, if not all of them.

He saw other siren subgroups more often here. The streets could be filled with them. He also found other denizens.

[Tidal Moon Denizen: Voyager Kraken: Trader lvl 59.]

[Tidal Moon Denizen: Ship Dog: Sailor lvl 37.]

[Tidal Moon Denizen: Pilgrim Penguin: Monk lvl 40.]

[Tidal Moon Denizen: Water Naga: Mercenary lvl 57.]

He didn't see Curi anywhere, but finding other krakens slithering around was amusing. The other species was even more wondrous.

The ship dogs were walking seals that talked like sailors.

The pilgrim penguins had flat fingers at the end of their wings. They wanted him to join their strict religious order for worshiping the Tidal Moon Lord.

A water naga slithered around with a long and thick lower body tail that supported their muscular torso and arms. Its serpent's head and eyes were turned to Joey, the hands near the handles of its scimitars that were bound to the waist.

The rogue flashed a ferocious smile, revealing a kunai already in his hand and getting spun by the ring. The naga mercenary continued to stare while the two stood on a bustling street.

[Keep your head down, adventurer. The monster leaders have bounties,] the naga mercenary hissed.

"That's nice of them to send me gifts," Joey replied. "I'm always hungry for more levels."

[Enjoy the feast.] The naga made hiss-like laughter before slithering off.

Joey journeyed through more domes, seeing non stop hustle and bustle. When he reached the war siren detachment at the end, he stayed a little longer at their tavern and drank more.

At this point, his body couldn't toughen out the alcohol and keep it from affecting him any longer. The specialists kept leaning against him or brushing past him. Joey tried to listen to his greed for once.

It was dead silent. Uninterested.

With a sigh, he excused himself. He took a slow walk back to the city center.

While walking down a familiar street next to a water park, he glanced at the system message waiting for him.

[You've leveled up Scenic Discoverer from 3 to 7!]

"She was right," Joey said.

The entire time Joey ran up and down the arms, he had Scenic Discoverer under his control. He'd reduced the skill to a Level 1 power, which wasn't easy to manage.

The pulses felt weaker than they should and almost forgettable. Every time he felt it slipped out of his grip, he hardened his control.

The results spoke for themselves. Jumping from level 2 to 7 was impressive.

Once released, Joey felt powerful pulses of the skill wanting to guide him. He had to sit near the water park and get used to its new power until it was background noise.

What would happen if I get all of my skills higher than the brute force limit?

How crazy would his skills become past Level 10? Level 20?

That would take commitment. He'd need constant action and adventure to hone his skills. He'd need a nonstop grind.

I would get that once I reach landfall.

Joey felt an excited rush. It mingled with his greed. Letting the dragon stretch out felt great.

His attention drifted upward to a specific spire with a specific balcony. At the same time, his stomach growled, feeling hungry.

He narrowed his eyes. He remembered that balcony belonging to the siren who'd ratted him out to Maylolee two days ago.

Joey had promised revenge, didn't he? And he was just drunk enough to do it.

Minutes later, Joey and three clones dashed out of the home they'd raided. The clones laughed and shouted silly slogans as they fell onto the street and ran.

Joey had a smile only a dragon mom would love. Food spilled from his and the shadow gang's arms, which was okay. The whole point was for Joey to fulfill a promise. Eating was secondary.

"Adventurer Eclipse," called a guardian waiting around the street corner.

"Oh, damn, it's the po-po! Scram!" shouted a clone.

"This is why they don't let hoodlums around nice folks!"

"Shadow gang forever!"

Joey dismissed his silly clones and raised his hands. There was no point in trying to escape, since that would cause needless trouble and the guardian was way higher leveled than him.

The guardian took him to the brig where other troublemakers waited in cells.

He noticed half of them were non-siren denizens. A quarter of his fellow prisoners were siren subgroups.

The rest were seekers who had too much fun visiting the center while on rest and recovery.

Everybody was drunk, so things became even more rowdy and fun when the adventurer showed up. By the time morning arrived, everyone was trying to teach Joey to sing their favorite tidal songs.

Some denizens knew English, so they helped him learn

the words as they sang together through the enchanted bars of their cells.

The brig guardians watched in amusement.

One guardian turned and saw a little figure enter through the doorway. The guardian stood rigidly and shouted, "War Princess Maylolee!"

"Is this a good or bad situation, adventurer?" asked a sea dog sailor across from his cell.

"We're about to find out," Joey replied.

"On your knees," Maylolee growled.

All the guardians dropped as ordered, heads pressed to the floor. The seekers in their jail cell did the same. The subgroup sirens fell to their knees but kept their heads up.

The other denizens looked around and lowered enough to show respect. Joey stayed upright, but felt uncomfortable.

"Whose idea was it to jail a great adventurer for a petty issue?" Maylolee said. "Do note, jailing a great adventurer is nearly comparable to jailing me."

One guardian let out a sob of horror. They could barely speak since their faces were flattened against the floor.

"Hey, hey, Maylolee, let's show a little mercy, please?" Joey asked. "They were kind to me. And I did the crime, so it's my fault."

"If you're this self aware, why did you do it in the first place?" Maylolee asked.

"I was drunk and having fun. And I promised that one siren I would steal her food, remember?"

Maylolee stared at him with a complicated expression. In the next three minutes, Joey found himself free and walking out of the brig with the princess.

A siren yelled from down the street, warning everyone of the princess being out in public. Each street the great adventurers walked on cleared fast of denizens.

"You weren't bothered to be in the brig?" Maylolee asked.

"Are you kidding? That's a really nice jail, prison, brig, whatever. Everything's pretty nice here. I've only seen a few homeless people."

"We do our best to help the vagrant, especially those with mind debuffs. But not all can be helped. And some are willfully disobedient, so they are given supplies and sent to live elsewhere."

Joey snorted. "That's so damn fair. I'm honestly angry."

Maylolee stopped and showed a shred of worry. "Why?"

"Where I come from, I was homeless and pathetic at the age of fifteen. One time, bad guys attacked me because they didn't know me. The next day, my version of guardians attacked me because they'd mistaken me for a criminal. Every attacker hurt me. Badly. But I'm eighteen now, and I've done well to move on."

The memories of his past came and went. Joey didn't like to think about it much.

Joey waved around at the gorgeous underwater city. "But seeing everything you have under your rule and all this niceness has me so jealous I'm angry."

"Oh." Maylolee looked away, unable to meet his eyes.

Joey put aside his issues and changed the subject. "So what took you till morning?"

"I was asleep. But a situation like yours is serious for me." She shook her head. "Do not worry. I will deal with my attendant and adviser for withholding this. Everyone can be instructed no matter their position."

"Nice." Joey chuckled. "Thanks for coming to get me. It'll also mean a lot if you see me and Curi off."

"It'll mean a lot to me as well."

Joey tilted his head. "Oh, yeah?"

Maylolee sighed. "I need your help. Or I will die."

"Wow. That is an attention grabber. Can you tell me what can kill a great adventurer like you?"

"The Dread Whale."

Joey grimaced. *Whelp, time to be a responsible adult again.*

18. TO ACCEPT A GREAT QUEST

After one last visit to the spa for a luxuriating bath, Joey went to his room and changed into the forest color bodysuit. He secured his harnesses and weapons before tossing his pack onto his back.

The backpack was heavier than the last time he checked. The princess had left him more gifts. He would see what was inside on the way to landfall.

Joey met the princess at the front of the castle. Curi had gone ahead with an escort team. The kraken wanted to check on the new vessel the princess had prepared for them, leaving Joey and Maylolee to walk and talk between themselves. Denizens scrambled away and cleared the streets ahead of the rogue and princess.

"I can see why you're cool about secret stuff," Joey said.

Maylolee raised a glyph tile and activated it. The surrounding air shimmered, placing them in a bubble.

"Noise cancellation?" Joey asked.

"An interesting way to describe it, but yes."

"Magic can truly do it all," Joey said.

Maylolee gave him a questioning look before growing more serious. "For three hundred years, the Dread Whale existed and caused havoc around this area. The Siren Tide we're currently in was once a different tide. We renamed it when we had to move from our ancestral home. Because of the Dread Whale."

"How?"

"It's in the 300s while in a corner of the Tidal Moon Realm locked for mostly Level 100s. There are only a few beasts past Level 100, but they are within my range to kill. And I've done so quite fine. But a creature in the Level 300s is two leveling realms above us. Or the equivalent of an epic power."

Joey paled the more he listened about the dread whale. So many questions came to the forefront of his mind. He seized the best one. "What powers does it have?"

"Only six big ones, like most creatures. One: the closer you get to it, the more dread you will feel. Two: its physiology is believed to be a spell which would explain its huge size and alien anatomy. Three: it can levitate itself. Four: it shoots constant volleys of dread beams that are painful and can increase your dread. Five: it self regenerates. Six: if you get overtaken by too much dread, you will become a Dread Slave. Then the whale can control you and grant self regen."

"How am I supposed to help against that?" Joey shook his head slowly. "Princess, this sounds like you need an entire raid. Your city looks like it can do the job. The war sirens aren't enough?"

"I'll answer your second question first. It's simple. We are not enough. We've tried. We've failed. For hundreds of years. We've also called upon our sister sirens, other denizens, and adventurer teams. My mother and father created the biggest coalition they could muster thirteen years ago."

They entered a street where Joey and Maylolee had fought each other. That intense moment seemed distant now as he listened to more of the princess's explanation.

"Fifty adventurers who hadn't ascended joined this coalition. Three of them were great, including my father. It was said to be the most promising attempt ever. They never came back and our war power was so reduced, the monster population spread unchecked in result.

"We still haven't recovered. You might've seen man snappers acting brazenly on your way here. This is not only prevalent, but the monsters have mutated to include new variants because of our failure to cull."

"Alright, I'll keep that in mind about the man snappers. But let's get back to the reason we're having this conversation. How can I help? And let's add another question. Why are you doing this when it sounds futile?"

"Again, I will answer you out of order." Maylolee clenched her fists. "I want to ascend. I don't want to stay at Level 100. But I can't abdicate my throne until the Dread Whale is dealt with. I'm the most powerful person the war sirens and all siren societies have. I am their daughter and princess. I have a duty to fulfill before I can go."

Maylolee trembled.

Joey reached over and placed his hand on her shoulder. She relaxed after a while and stopped trembling.

"I've petitioned the Tidal Moon Lord," Maylolee said. "His response is vexing. He cannot remove it because of an issue on his side. But he will give support only when the time is right. The timing is coming up in eight months when the Dread Whale will be at its most tired and attempt to sleep. It does have a critical weakness we can reach when it slumbers. But we'll need to beat its Dread Slaves. This is where you come in."

They reached a heavily guarded tunnel. Maylolee dropped the noise cancellation bubble as the guardians stepped aside without checking them.

Joey tried to guess what Maylolee wanted from him. It could be anything. *But I think I have a clue after hearing all the context.*

Instead of saying it, Maylolee gestured at him. An urgent system message popped up.

[You have the opportunity to receive a Great Quest: Slay The Dread Whale! (Est. Difficulty Range: Between Level 90 and Level 400)! This quest has multiple parts. Part 1: Gather the adventurers. *Joey, I want to trust you. You are a reliable and determined rogue filled with great potential. If you decide to accept this quest, I'll need you to bring me 100 hundred steady adventurers and another 4 great adventurers. I need them to be over Level 75 but below Level 100. I've given you 50 bronze coins plus extra to help with bribery if necessary. I can't go in person since I'm needed here, and I won't choose less than a great adventurer for this quest. If you can do this for me in seven months' time, I'll be deep in your debt.*

Do you accept the quest?]

"What will you do if you can't get the adventurers you need?" Joey asked.

"I will go fight the Dread Whale with what I have."

"For three centuries, your people have failed. And you're going to just go and do it?"

They reached the private dock of the War Princess. It had an impressive size, despite being used less than the other docks.

Curi and other sirens were crowding around a boat,

finishing preparations. It was dark brown wood with a wide body. Two poles rested inside with some riggings and a folded sail.

The eye catching part were the thick ropes looped through heavy rings on the sides and front of the boat. Curi held ropes with his tentacles like a horse getting ready to pull a cart.

"Joey," Maylolee called.

"Yes?"

"I would rather die reaching for greatness than to continue living this way," she said.

"That's dramatic."

"This is what we are. There is no other way. Once you are on the great path, you must keep reaching." Maylolee looked at him fervently, as if she was going mad. "I hit Level 100 three years ago. And every day I don't see a new level or raise my stats feels like torture."

"And ascending allows you to keep leveling?" Joey asked, clearly new to the term.

"You go to a new realm with new challenges, allowing you to continue leveling. In this corner of the Tidal Moon Realm, it can only be done at Level 100 for adventurers." Maylolee grabbed his hands. "Imagine it, Joey! I've been looking at the ascension offer for three years! Stuck at the same level with the same stats. Imagine it!"

The activity around the boat died. A heavy silence filled the dock area. The war sirens looked down in shame.

Joey pried himself free when Maylolee's grip started to hurt. He looked around at all the ashamed war sirens.

It's like they know they're holding her back. But they can't wish her off. They need her to lead the fight against the Dread Whale. But they also have to suffer while she's losing her sanity.

This place was a city of shackles under the water. All because of some distant threat Joey hadn't seen yet.

Now that he was seeing the big picture, Joey reflected on hints of the problems he'd glossed over yesterday.

Everything was nice. But everything was being forced to be nice. Constantly. The hustle and bustle and niceness kept the war sirens on edge.

If the princess had to suffer being on the throne, then the tradeoff was suffering from her tyranny.

So why would I say yes? Joey asked himself.

Ignoring that he'd vowed to repay the princess for her kindness, there were obvious benefits. His dragon greed was burning up inside of him right now, in fact. His greed loved the idea of having a princess in his debt, especially if he was the key factor in defeating her people's ancestral enemy.

But what was in it for Joey as a man?

It would be an achievement that would make his path all the brighter. There would be significant awards for bringing down a terrible creature like that. Lots of coins. Singularities. Skills. New powers. A ridiculous amount of levels and stats, for sure.

That's the surface stuff, though. Joey looked up. *There's a deeper reason. A quest like this can do a lot for everyone even if I gain the most.*

"I wonder what it would look like," Joey said, "if we can bring together a raid team with a bunch of adventurers fighting together. Steady. Great. All of us working as one with your war sirens and allies."

Scenic Discovery pulsed inside of him sweetly. His greed roared with agreement. Joey gave the princess a roguish smile. "I want to see my first major raid and be in the thick of it."

[You've accepted the Great Quest: Slay The Dread Whale! Part 1: Gather the Adventurers!]

"Thank you, Joey," Maylolee said, looking faint.

"You owe me so much."

"I know."

"I will come to collect. But first … what's with the sirens on my new boat?" Joey pointed.

[I can explain that!] Curi waved his tentacle, sounding friendly and light. He was helping transition them from a serious mood to a more lighthearted one.

Joey appreciated the effort.

A specialist and four seekers would accompany them to landfall. Once Joey split off from Curi, the war siren unit would guard Curi during his travels before returning to Aqua Star City in six months.

Curi would return with them, hauling goods for the princess. Joey would get to reunite with Curi once he completed part one of the great quest.

Maylolee took over by explaining there was a means to contact her in Joey's backpack. She also left him some freshly written books with information from her libraries.

It would bring him up to speed on the things steady adventurers would know, since they had an easier start in major port towns.

The books would break down how the inner stats within the main stats work, talk about the strengths and weaknesses of each class, and explain some of the unique features of adventurer hub towns – dedicated adventurer guilds, stores attached to the wider multiverse system, and others.

She also left him manuals on his gear, so he wouldn't be clueless about the superior quality magic they had.

"Why the ninja knives?" Joey asked.

"Ninja knives? You mean the kunai blades?" Maylolee looked at him blankly. "They're multiversal tools. You can dig, insert them into walls to help climb, attach rope to make them into grappling hooks, and more. When I was working with my crafter, I wanted the kunai because they suit your flexibility."

Joey rubbed the back of his neck. "You've put a lot of thought into helping me."

Maylolee gave him a cute smile. "It was fun. I've been the only great adventurer for so long until you showed up. I hope it all helps you."

"It will," Joey said seriously.

They traded farewells, which felt more emotional than Joey preferred. His greed wanted something outrageous, which was a little distracting.

It didn't go unnoticed he was more fixated on the princess compared to all the other women. Maybe it was because she was a princess. Or maybe it was because she was a harder nut to crack.

Nonetheless, they'd only had a short time together, and Joey was getting ready to set off yet again. With a team, too.

The specialist was a Level 90, and her name was Mollysea. Her seekers were in the high Level 40s, and their names were Muragale, Mormelt, Mavolts, and Milhiss. They would become specialists or guardians once they returned to the city.

For now, the seekers performed their song and enhanced the specialist's water manipulation spell. They only needed thirty feet for the bubble to wrap around the party, although it was a tight fit with the kraken and his big tentacles.

Joey had a thoughtful expression on his face while Aqua Star City and the fortress jellies fell away. He barely felt the side effect of the sirens singing because of Dragon Pride.

He was not the young man he'd been entering the city. He was different by a large degree.

I'm always becoming different. How much more different do I need to be to succeed in part one of my quest?

[I can't predict what you're thinking,] Curi said.

"I'm thinking about how different I'm becoming," Joey said.

[Ah, yes, that is quite the thought. Is it a difference that feels right with you? Are you becoming something you never thought you would? I, for one, feel afraid and thrilled from all of this difference!]

Joey closed his eyes and listened to himself. They hit the surface. Joey opened his eyes and checked his profile.

Great Adventurer: Joey Eclipse

Race: Basic Human

Age: 18

Path: Shade Dragon Rogue lvl 28

Singularities: Dragon Pride (Superior), Slay The Dread Whale (Great Quest/Part 1).

Skills: Analyze lvl 6 (Basic), Headhunter lvl 7 (Basic), Short Sword Finesse lvl 7 (Basic), Combat Swimming lvl 5 (Basic), Combat Acrobatics lvl 7 (Basic), Scenic Discoverer

lvl 7 (Basic), Chaos Finder lvl 3 (Basic), Armor Piercer lvl 5 (Basic), Stress Management lvl 6 (Basic), Roll With The Hits lvl 5 (Basic), Slick Knife Tricks lvl 5 (Basic), Fight Prediction lvl 3 (Basic), Assassin Grappling lvl 2 (Basic), Hands of the Fade lvl 2 (Basic).

Spells: Dark Dash lvl 2 (Superior), Shade Dragon Tail lvl 1 (Epic), Shadow Clone Magic lvl 1 (Epic), Shade Dragon Breath lvl 1 (Epic).

Semblances: Hull Crusher Bruiser lvl 51 (Al Bruce Crabton).

Special Stuff: (??), (??), (??), (??), (??), (??), (??), Beginner Adventurer Study Books (3), Tidal Moon Bronze Coins (50), Tidal Moon Copper Coins (500), Health Potion (Basic/10), Stamina Potion (Basic/10), Essence Potion (Basic/10), Barrier Glyph Tile (Basic/5), Water Bolt Glyph Tile (Basic/5), Breath Glyph Tile (Basic/5), Camouflage Glyph Tile (Basic/5), Silence Glyph Tile (Basic/5), Unlock Glyph Tile (Basic/5), Healthy Fish Meals (Basic/10), Fresh Water Refill Flask (Basic/1), Adventurer Contact Plate (Maylolee Suzuki) ...

Essence: 2488/2490 EP

Mind: 82 (+2 per a level)

Body: 82 (+2 per a level)

Spirit: 85 (+1 per a level)

Free: 0 (+3 per a level)

Joey nodded at his profile before looking at Curi with Analyze.

[Tidal Moon Denizen: Voyager Kraken: Trader lvl 80.]

I'm not the only one who has changed. You were in the high level 70s, but you've leveled up to 80 now. Congrats.

Joey had learned denizens leveled up through

accomplishments dealing with their roles. The greater their accomplishments, the better their experience gains.

It was still slow compared to adventurers unless they were in the company of an adventurer. Curi's gains came with bonuses because of Joey's presence.

Joey smiled. "I feel okay with the differences. I just need to adjust once I get solid earth under me. How soon can we make it to landfall?"

It was the specialist, Mollysea, who answered. "With the voyager kraken pulling the reins, we can get to landfall in five days. Leaving Siren Tide will take two days at his top speed. But it's the Storm Tides that'll be a bother. They're smaller, but come together as three. The entire area around them is treacherous. Inside the tides and between the tidal gaps."

[Originally, I was planning to skim around the edges of the Storm Tides, but having a war siren attachment makes me feel safer.]

"Monsters?" Joey asked as Curi swam forward until the ropes became taut. Joey sensed the kraken speeding up and sat on a bench.

The sirens sat on benches in front of him, Mollysea in the middle while wearing her hulking monster teeth armor for specialists.

"Higher leveled hull crushers. Man snapper variants. The man snappers will be more annoying."

"How so?"

"Thundershells. At level 25, they fly. If we face a level 50 one, prepare for their lightning blitz attack. You'll need to avoid them until I handle them all."

Joey chuckled darkly.

"You laugh, adventurer? You are only Level 28. Great or not, the Level 50s are a danger to you."

The rogue inhaled a slow and deep breath. After two seconds, a shadowy glow emitted from the back of his throat.

Dark sparks shot out from the corners of his mouth.

Then Joey closed his mouth and dismissed the spell. The glow disappeared, denied its release. For now.

All the war sirens stared at him like he'd turned into a dragon. Joey chuckled. "They may be stronger, but I will hurt them. Badly."

19. SHADE DRAGON BREATH GO!

After two days of tidal voyage, Joey and his escorts reached the western edge of Siren Tide. Curi took a break to sleep and prepare himself for a three-day marathon.

The moons and watercolor cosmos shone above as the rogue stood and stretched. He'd read all the books while the boat was in motion. Now was the perfect chance to move his body and train.

Joey requested the sirens to join him in the water and help him level up Combat Swimming. He stayed in the water until his stamina burned out.

He recovered fast by meditating on the boat. Then he jumped back into the water and continued getting thrashed.

He kept Combat Swimming under control no matter how tempting it felt to unleash it. He knew his hard work and frustration would reap incredible results.

By the time the kraken awakened, Joey hit a new soft limit. Then he released the full power of Combat Swimming and surprised the sirens, getting revenge on them after all of his watery torment.

He made himself more dangerous to fight. He kept the sirens pressured and confused until they readjusted to his new competency.

Practice ended after Joey forced the sirens to take him seriously in the water.

[You've leveled up Combat Swimming from 5 to 13!]

"I wish you weren't claimed by the princess," the specialist said as the sirens and Joey climbed back into the boat

"What do you mean by that, specialist?" Joey asked.

He knew her name. But he also noticed they were a touch flirty when going by names. Saying their roles instead of their names helped keep the social distance.

"Our children would be powerful." The specialist turned to her seekers. "If the moons are merciful, maybe we'll run into adventurers like this one."

The seekers nodded at once.

Joey blinked, keeping silent instead of responding. Then he turned to Curi. "Ready to go all in, Curi?"

[No! We're going straight into danger with lightning and thunder.] The kraken shivered. [But I'll do it, anyway.]

Curi summoned a round red ball that looked like dough. Tilting back, he revealed the beak hidden behind all of his tentacles and fed on the doughy ball.

"What's that?"

[A dry energy potion. The immediate effects aren't too bad. You will see me become a – oh, oh, there it is! Time to go, go, go!]

The kraken launched like a torpedo. Joey nearly flew out of the boat as it zoomed across the water and jumped high over waves.

Joey allowed the specialist to hold his hand and keep him secured. Then he hollered at the wind and enjoyed the high-speed ride.

On the horizon, he saw dark clouds and lightning bolts looming between him and landfall.

Thundershells made themselves known while Joey and his party began their descent along the Siren Tide wall. Thankfully, other specialists and seekers made themselves known as well.

All around Joey's boat was a raging battle between man snappers and war sirens. And all he could do was hang on to the ropes while Curi held the boat upside down. The gear was secured with more rope, keeping everything bound to the boat.

Loose water poured over the bottom while Joey stayed mostly dry. Until he poked his head out to look around.

His siren escorts were in the water with Curi, keeping a close watch. One of the seekers had air magic. She could jump to his aid at any time.

He would get to see if she was being honest as four monsters drew closer to Joey.

[Tidal Moon Monster: Man Snapper: Thundershell lvl 44.]

[Tidal Moon Monster: Man Snapper: Thundershell lvl 47.]

[Tidal Moon Monster: Man Snapper: Thundershell lvl 49.]

[Tidal Moon Monster: Man Snapper: Thundershell lvl 63.]

The monsters were dark blue compared to the dark

green of the original grunts. Dark cloudy mists surrounded their shells, carrying them through the air like bumbling bees.

The Level 63 thundershell had little lightning bolts zipping out of its version of the cloudy mist.

With their eyes set on Joey as if he was a dangling snack, the man snappers left themselves open to the air seeker.

She flew like an arrow and struck the Level 49 thundershell with the harpoon end of her polearm. They plummeted together while the seeker stabbed with a knife as monster blood mingled with the waterfall.

Two powerful water torrents struck the Level 63 and the Level 47 thundershells. The torrents drilled holes through both monsters and dropped them.

Before a third torrent could strike, the weakest man snapper dipped down into a loop aimed at Joey.

The Level 44 monster looked eager to eat the Level 28 rogue.

It received a five second Shade Dragon Breath to test its appetite.

All at once, 200 EP disappeared. But the shadow torrent came out as a hissing stream twenty feet long.

It flared at the end when the man snapper ran into it. The flames phased through flesh and ignited the essence and magic cloud.

Distinct popping sounds like bubble wraps bursting could be heard under the man snapper's flesh. It stopped moving, giving Joey enough time to coat the entire creature with his dragon breath before the spell petered out.

The monster screamed and screamed, its flesh popping and blackening as its essence burned.

It crashed into the tidal wall, but Joey could tell the dark flames continued to burn from within the monster. No natural water could put it out.

Then a system message told him of the results. His greed flared, and Joey beamed a wide smile.

[You've slain a Man Snapper Thundershell lvl 44! For slaying monsters over ten levels above you, bonus experience is awarded!]

[You've leveled up Shade Dragon Rogue from 28 to 29!]

He invested a free point in each main stat.

[You've raised your mind from 82 to 85!]

[You've raised your body from 82 to 85!]

[You've raised your spirit from 85 to 87!]

For the next level, I might choose one for the immediate ninety milestone bump.

Choosing his spirit was tempting for the sake of more essence power. But losing 200 EP for five seconds of Shade Dragon Breath made him hesitant.

He would need to recover essence faster the more he used that spell.

I have too many costly spells. Recovery is the better choice. But damn, it would be nice to have more spirit.

Joey's siren escorts handled individual man snappers wandering near his boat. Other war sirens showed up to attack man snappers, covering for Joey and his group. They reached the bottom and entered the tidal gap.

It looked different from the last one. Less dead coral. More silt mounds and floods.

Hull crushers scuttled around, tearing into man snapper

corpses that rained down with the waterfall. They also had war siren corpses to feast on, too.

The temptation to fight every monster in sight nearly overwhelmed Joey. He grabbed the edges of the boat with a shaky grip, Curi holding it over his head as he propelled forward between hull crusher groups.

The war sirens stayed in the boat with Joey, aiming with their polearms like enchanted rifles. They cast spells through their weapons and released volleys of magical torrents.

Air, acid, lightning, steam, and water streamed out in flashy and powerful elemental attacks. After reading the beginner adventurer books, Joey was more impressed with the war sirens than ever.

They weren't merely warriors. Their roles were more comparable to battle mages. The mage class in Multiverse Z was different from what Joey knew from MMORPGs.

The air and acid seekers worked together on individual hull crushers. The lightning and steam seekers worked together just the same.

The Level 90 specialist killed two hull crushers for every one hull crusher a pair of seekers brought down. They killed quickly. But there was still a gap in their defense, and hull crushers tried to jump at it – the rear.

Joey meditated until he saw the problem. He stopped, summoned a clone, then continued to meditate.

"Let them know I went out like a rogue!" the clone shouted before taking a deep breath.

Six seconds later, the clone jumped from the back of the boat and breathed shady dragon flames on three hull crushers – an expense of 150 EP.

Less than a minute later, system messages popped up

with results. They were so shocking, Joey flinched out of meditation.

Apparently, touching monsters with his shady dragon flames could be a death sentence. Even while weakened through the use of a clone.

[You've slain a Hull Crusher Grunt lvl 39! For slaying monsters over ten levels above you, bonus experience is awarded!]

[You've slain a Hull Crusher Grunt lvl 44! For slaying monsters over ten levels above you, bonus experience is awarded!]

[You've slain a Hull Crusher Grunt lvl 49! For slaying monsters over ten levels above you, bonus experience is awarded!]

[You've leveled up Shade Dragon Rogue from 29 to 31!]

Well, nevermind, I'll hit 90 with all my main stats! Joey spread his points while favoring his spirit.

[You've raised your mind from 85 to 90!]

[You've raised your body from 85 to 90!]

[You've raised your spirit from 87 to 93!]

Wait a minute, something is dawning on me big time.

Joey thought back to the princess and her grief. Never had he seen Maylolee so open with her emotions.

It was so shocking, Joey had completely blanked that part out. Now that he was getting to revel in his newfound power, he realized he could understand the true depths of Princess Maylolee's suffering.

She couldn't watch the numbers go up for her path and main stats. She couldn't grow and feel that spike of pleasure that came with the process.

For three years, she was stuck like that.

Of course, she could pick up skills and continuously improve those. But that was a mere distraction from the true joy of seeing her path grow greater.

I'm sorry, Maylolee. I completely ignored your suffering and thought of myself first.

Joey felt horrible. Nobody should go through three years of having their great path stalled.

Then I'll have to find a way to make her patience worth it.

His dragon greed agreed. Nothing but the best would do.

Newfound determination wiped the smile off Joey's face. He returned to meditating.

***

He's an absolute monster, and I have to stay disciplined! Mollysea screamed in her head each time she glimpsed the great rogue displaying his dark power.

She was an older war siren with a fairly clean record except for getting caught flirting on duty years ago. She'd learned from that mistake quickly. Good timing, too.

The young princess made such mistakes more frightful to commit since the punishments were brutal. Mollysea refused to break her good streak. Especially with the male the princess had shown emotion toward.

But Mollysea could see her seekers were struggling. Because the rogue summoned a clone and had it jump off the boat like a suicidal hero.

Then three hull crushers burned, screaming to death under a coat of vicious dark flames that refused to go out. The way the monsters screamed – Mollysea would dream of it with horror and pleasure for years.

Like any good war siren, she controlled her emotions and kept them inside. Too much emotion could leak out with charm and distract the rogue.

The gap between Siren Tide and the first of the Storm Tides, Whirlpool Storm Tide, was a long stretch.

Flood lakes pooled around the open space between silt mounds. Rivers and deltas broke up the dark landscape even further.

Beasts appeared from shallow waters or under the silt floor. They eyed the group to see if they were potential prey or predators.

Mollysea shot water torrents to dissuade some beasts. Fights with Hull Crushers petered out in the open space, which made things more dangerous. A bruiser, or worse, could show itself with an ambush.

The veteran war siren put her eyes on the mounds and dark waters in front of her. She gave the voyager kraken orders to veer around suspicious spots.

"You guys are awesome," Adventurer Eclipse said.

Mollysea and her seekers kept their mouths shut. If the adventurer was Level 90 like the specialist, he would make them all look pitiful. It was hard to take the compliment with grace.

"You are a monster," Mollysea said. "I am glad you're helping us."

"Don't be glad, yet." He gave her a hard glare, which made the Level 90 specialist shiver for multiple reasons. "I'm literally holding the life of your princess and people in my hands. You might curse my name if I fail."

Mollysea was unsure if she would. She would've felt crushed if she was given such a mission. She half expected for him to fail. She wouldn't blame him.

"Do your best," she said before returning her attention to finding hidden threats. Their journey to Whirlpool Storm Tide found a long stretch of peace until an ambush appeared.

Fifteen bruisers and a hundred grunts rose out of the mounds and tried to cut them off. By concentrating all volleys on the bruisers, the sirens could slow the big monsters down while the kraken swerved around the ambush. The grunts moved faster, but Mollysea left them to the rogue.

He didn't move from his meditative seat.

But he did summon four clones.

"Haters, beware! The shadow gang has dragons on the loose!"

The clones took positions between each war siren. They drew in a deadly breath together. Mollysea counted the seconds to see how long this would charge for.

The hull crusher grunts drew closer.

The specialist worried.

The clones jumped at the monsters after seven seconds of charging. Mollysea and her subordinates faltered as the front of the ambush became a crackling and screaming sea of dark flames.

Not all the clones released their full breath. Some hit the ground and fell under step to a hull crusher.

But they did enough to spread fire over twenty grunts and three bruisers. The entire hull crusher ambush halted. The ones free from the dark flames ran away.

The screaming was the most nightmarish and amazing thing Mollysea had ever heard. She lost her discipline and laughed, her seekers laughing with her.

They should be better than this. They shouldn't lose their emotions or they would mistakenly charm the rogue.

But Adventurer Eclipse remained undisturbed, so Mollysea let herself shed some emotion she'd held in for a while. Once she calmed down, she looked over and stared at the rogue's levels rising sharply as hull crushers died in droves.

"I don't want him to leave us," whispered a seeker.

Mollysea nodded solemnly and leaned her shoulder against her fellow siren.

The specialist would do her best to find adventurers who were half as monstrous as the rogue. The war princesses, past and present, always knew how to pick the fun ones.

20. STORM TIDE ADVENTURES

Joey shivered from expending 700 EP in a short time frame. That was a fourth of his essence supply. The expense felt like freezing his channels solid from rapid overuse.

He nodded at the results of the shadow gang dragon breath dive and ignored the laughing sirens. He continued meditating to defrost his channels.

There was no doubt of the deadliness of his newest spell. As long as a creature had essence, the flames would continuously burn once it touched the target. Joey imagined certain abilities were needed to cleanse the shady flames without feeding it more fuel.

He also wondered if there was a natural way to cleanse the ability. Or snuff it. If there were such tactics, monsters would have a poor chance of removing the flames. They didn't seem smart enough to use creativity to save their lives.

Then again, the monsters that could regenerate and sacrifice their essence might outlast the flame damage and choke out its fuel.

Note to self, do not trust Shade Dragon Breath to kill anyone who self regenerates quickly. Works best as a painful distraction against those types.

Now, onto the results of slaying a bunch of monsters. Joey could only deny the messages so long with his greed rampaging impatiently.

After all, they weren't going back for the loot – which vexed Joey – but he had larger goals to work toward. And he could soothe himself with new levels and stats.

[You've slain nineteen Hull Crusher Grunts ranging from lvl 42 to lvl 48! For slaying monsters over ten levels above you, bonus experience is awarded!]

Unfortunately, Shade Dragon Breath had a limit. Toughness was a factor. Any monster above level 50 would have the toughness to endure and regenerate.

The bruisers had all the toughness needed to survive. But that took little from Joey's incredible results.

[You've leveled up Chaos Finder from 3 to 5!]

[You've leveled up Shade Dragon Rogue from 31 to 36!]

[You've raised your mind from 90 to 100!]

[You've raised your body from 90 to 100!]

[You've raised your spirit from 93 to 98!]

[You've raised your free points from 0 to 15!]

Joey inserted two points into his spirit and tracked the power bump. It was as significant as the past ten-point milestones.

Hitting three digits didn't raise the power any further, however. This seemed like a cautious design by the system to avoid power creep.

Too late for that. You let me have Shade Dragon Breath.

But in return, he had to be wary of more dragon spells. He wouldn't want to self-destruct.

For the sake of letting his spirit get ahead for once, and because of greed, he dumped the remaining points in spirit for more essence power and Shade Dragon Breath domination. The other stats would catch up soon if he kept going at this pace.

[You've raised your spirit from 98 to 113!]

They didn't run into any more ambushes from the hull crushers. The Whirlpool Storm Tide appeared before them. It was a different entity compared to the last tides.

Huge lightning bolts twisted in and out of black thunderclouds that covered the watercolor sky. Darkness engulfed Joey's group as they drew closer.

Directly ahead, Joey noticed the waterfall was thinner. He could see the tidal wall itself. It had twisting currents winding diagonally under the wall's surface.

"We're going to travel straight over this?" Joey asked doubtfully.

"No, we stay on the wall and ride it around. The kraken will move in the same direction," the specialist explained. "That's the fastest way to get past the Whirlpool Storm Tide and avoid getting devoured by the giant whirlpool."

The rogue laughed. "I don't know what's more fun. The constant new things this realm offers or burning monsters from the inside out!"

The specialist laughed, showing more of her emotions. The seekers joined in. They gave Joey a few tingles of their siren charm.

It's kind of fun having a bunch of water amazons be cool

with me, Joey thought.

The flirting was a bit much for him. But he let it roll off his back. He had big goals and quick levels at the forefront of his mind.

Curi kept steamrolling ahead. The kraken was concentrated on staying in motion and following orders. He wasn't up for much conversation.

He's definitely going to sleep for a whole day when we reach land, Joey thought humorously.

The rogue smiled up at the massive whirlpool wall and its hungry depths. The man Joey had been before the Shade Dragon Rogue path would've pissed himself.

Now he let out a whoop as Curi slapped his tentacles down and launched into the air. The kraken switched grips. His thick tentacles swung between the war sirens and the rogue to refasten his hold on the entire boat.

Curi splashed into the wall while holding the boat away from the surface. Joey had a better grip on the sides this time and didn't need the specialist's help to keep from flying overboard.

Curi took a second to readjust. Then he torpedoed with the whirlpool's current and at an upward angle. They rose until they were a hundred feet off the ground.

Joey watched the tidal floor rush by under him, which was a trippy view from a kraken-held boat. Then he looked up as the specialist cast some water magic. Loose water fell to the side instead of into their boat, keeping it from getting flooded.

Two seekers kicked back and used the tentacles as headrests. The other two stayed alert along with the specialist.

"Are you staying up for the whole trip?" Joey asked the specialist.

"Yes."

"Should I rest?"

"I'll wake you when we need you."

Joey nodded, trusting the professional.

He found a nook between the seat rest and under Curi's tentacle. It was times like these Joey was glad he was short. He could slip into smaller spaces easier, which could be important for a rogue.

His backpack worked as a headrest. His Stress Management helped him catch some rest. The thunder and rushing water of the Whirlpool Storm Tide became background noise.

Sometime later, Joey stirred awake at the sound of fighting. Since he woke up on his own, he trusted the war sirens had a handle on things.

I'll take a look just in case.

Joey lifted out of his nook with a war siren directly above him – the air seeker. She shot thin torrents of air and sliced through the torso of a thundershell trying to lightning blitz the boat. That stopped one among many.

"Ah, you're awake," the specialist said from the middle, shooting down multiple thundershells with piercing water. "We're going to use our charm. The worst of it will be directed at the thundershells. I just want you to be informed that you may feel it."

"Go for it," Joey said.

The war sirens started singing in unison. Joey felt the immediate urge to stand and hug the sirens. He wanted to hug the specialist especially and do whatever she requested of him.

Something inside of him raged pridefully and knocked the siren's charm out of him.

Joey shook his head, feeling angry, disturbed, and freaked out. He'd barely taken back control of himself, and this was without the siren song being directed at him.

He glanced over the edge and saw two dozen thundershells draw closer with lost looks on their faces. Each one had a goofy puppy dog face, but the monstrous turtle version.

The sirens kept singing while channeling their magic and blasting each thundershell as they flew to their death. They nearly wiped out all the thundershells, but a few snapped free and fled away.

The seekers dropped into their seats, looking weary. The specialist remained standing, holding herself up out of pride and experience. She was every part of being a Level 90 powerhouse.

From what Joey could tell, using their charm offensively sapped a lot of essence. But they could slaughter enemies wholesale without retaliation. That was a deadly power to have against their enemies.

It wouldn't work well for them if they had to outlast a large enemy force.

Joey could see the problem arising from failing to cull the monsters. They had the war sirens outnumbered at a ridiculous degree.

"Don't worry," the specialist said. "We can recover and fight just about anything. You won't have to help again."

"I don't mind helping." He wanted more levels, after all.

"You're going to make us look bad and hurt our feelings,"

the specialist replied with some humor. "No more of that."

Joey let out a little growl. "I do what I want. And you know you like it."

That last part came out unexpectedly, which annoyed Joey a little.

The war sirens chuckled. An hour later, they reached the other end of Whirlpool Storm Tide and descended its wall. Day one had come and gone.

Day two had little light without the thunderous clouds. Twisting lightning bolts flashed from above, illuminating most of the way between the Whirlpool Storm Tide and the Lightning Storm Tide.

This gap is a little scarier than the last ones.

Dark waters rushed back and forth in unpredictable currents, revealing little to no landmasses. It was all waves, rip currents, and splashing chaos.

There were fewer monsters. But scarier things rose out of the rushing water and acted like walking towers.

[Tidal Moon Beast: Big Fish: Floorwalker lvl ??]

The floorwalker stood like a hundred foot man with a fish head. It lumbered through the chaotic tidal gap undisturbed.

Its big glossy eyes stared at the lightning bolts twisting above. Its mouth opened and closed, revealing huge teeth and a maw that could swallow men whole.

"That's disturbing and fascinating all at once," Joey said.

"Let's hope it doesn't pay us much attention," the specialist said. "They're slow, but they have a strong range attack."

"Maybe when you become strong enough, you can kill it," said the lightning seeker.

"That'll be a sight," added the steam seeker.

"What's making you say that when your specialist would rather avoid that big thing?" Joey asked.

The specialist pointed her polearm at the distant floorwalker. "The princess hunts them when she's bored. Are you not able to?"

"Say no more. I'm going to hunt that thing when I'm Level 100." Or before then.

The war sirens giggled. Joey knew they'd provoked him on purpose, but he was okay with that this time around.

The princess drew a long shadow. Joey was living in it just like everyone else connected to Maylolee. But Joey figured that could only last so long.

It would be fun to have her in my shadow.

They saw more floorwalkers from a distance. Joey even got to see their long range spell.

Bright blue hydro beams lanced through the darkness from their mouths. Their targets were mainly hull crushers. Each beam blasted the monsters out into the open.

Most hull crushers died on impact. Then the floorwalkers took their time to grab the mangled monsters with their finned hands and feast.

The acid seeker explained how their jellyfish fortresses helped against floorwalkers. The big fish would sometimes gather and try to mob Aqua Star City. The jellyfish would use strong shielding spells and other tricks to fend against those attacks.

It was strange to Joey that floorwalkers counted as beasts instead of monsters. But the general census was that only monsters dropped loot.

Killing anything else didn't grant extra awards other than Experience.

They reached the Lightning Storm Tide, scaled up the wall, and proceeded straight across its stormy top.

Joey was unsure why they would present themselves to open air on the Lightning Storm Tide. Then he noticed six distinct towers of lightning withering in different directions far away.

"The lightning surges consistently at six spots for hours," the specialist explained. "You only need to be lucky a few times and not be where the lightning surges switch to. If you're not lucky, you're dead."

Joey thought about it. He kept his mouth sealed and went back to resting.

He got little sleep and would raise his head to watch the war sirens fight off thundershell patrols. One particular trio of thundershells gave the specialist a few problems.

The trio were in the high 80s and had a discharge ability that disrupted projectile attacks. The specialist growled in frustration as all three thundershells worked together to thwart her Level 90 power.

Joey thought about this issue before turning to the air siren. "Can you launch something up for me?"

"Okay."

A few moments later, a shadow clone soared through the air. The thundershells rushed toward the offered pawn, not seeing the true threat.

Dark flames splashed over all three. The monsters screamed in pain even though they weren't receiving too much damage.

All that mattered was the distraction of being burned inside-out. The specialist took care of each thundershell with her strongest magic water blasts.

[**You've assisted in the slaying of a Man Snapper Thundershell lvl 87! Some experience is awarded!**]

[**You've assisted in the slaying of a Man Snapper Thundershell lvl 88! Some experience is awarded!**]

[**You've assisted in the slaying of a Man Snapper Thundershell lvl 89! Some experience is awarded!**]

[**You've leveled up Shade Dragon Rogue from 36 to 37!**]

Joey smiled and distributed the points pronto.

[**You've raised your mind from 100 to 103!**]

[**You've raised your body from 100 to 103!**]

[**You've raised your spirit from 113 to 115!**]

Joey figured it would take twelve more levels before all his stats were balanced again. If he kept spreading his free points evenly.

I should really avoid the dump mentality. I'm going to need essence control and essence recovery for training up my skills quickly, after all.

But Joey couldn't deny the results of having more essence power. The higher level thundershells would've survived against Joey alone. But the Shade Dragon Breath did its job as a painful distraction.

Too bad Joey didn't get the satisfaction of helping again. The war sirens handled the next threats without needing him.

He mostly sat, ate fish meals, and drank from his self-refilling flask – one of the most nifty magic items he'd seen yet.

He also trained the skills he could use while doing nothing but sightseeing if he wasn't sleeping. His kunai saw some action getting whirled around from hand to hand.

He nicked himself a couple of times, but the levels soothed the pain.

[You've leveled up Analyze from 6 to 7!]

[You've leveled up Scenic Discoverer from 7 to 10!]

[You've leveled up Slick Knife Tricks from 5 to 8!]

They exited the Lightning Storm Tide by the next day. No lightning surges had struck close enough to worry them.

"You were leaning on my roguish fortune, weren't you?" Joey asked.

"What better use for a rogue than luck?" the specialist said.

They were crossing another tidal gap now. Before them were large ice blocks and frigid water. The ground was hard where the ice and water didn't reach.

Curi's speed was lagging now, but the kraken kept going no matter what. He slithered between ice blocks and across barren rock floors that stretched for miles.

A new variant of the man snappers appeared. And so did a new variant of the hull crushers.

[Tidal Moon Monster: Man Snapper: Iceshell lvl 76.]

[Tidal Moon Monster: Hull Crusher: Breaker lvl 80.]

The monsters shared the coloration of their location. More icy blue and white in hue compared to the past versions.

The man snapper iceshells moved over the ground alone. They weren't very fast.

The breakers were bigger than the bruisers. Their pincers were thick and heavy hammers they used to smash aside ice blocks.

The man snapper iceshells looked pathetic in comparison until they opened their mouths and shot out chunks of ice. The projectiles flew hard enough to dent breaker shells.

The monsters fought in territorial skirmishes against each other. This made things easier for Joey's group to slither around and head for the Hail Storm Tide.

"What's the trick for this tide?" Joey asked.

The specialist was beginning to answer when she turned rigid. After four days of traveling with the same war sirens, Joey picked up on most of their habits.

The specialist would squeeze her grip on her polearm when worried. She would always restrain herself to avoid breaking her weapon.

Now?

The polearm nearly snapped into splinters. A seeker shook the specialist out of her frightened daze, saving the weapon from further damage.

Even now, the specialist couldn't talk. She pointed behind them.

Joey looked back and noticed a weird spherical object in the air miles away. It was round and dark. When lightning flashed above, the light seemed to get sucked into the sphere. On top of that, it was moving gradually toward them.

Something under the sphere was making a mess of

things. It smashed through ice blocks and monster skirmishes in its way. Joey took a few seconds to realize what frightened the specialist so badly.

The round object in the air was a dark moon.

They had a devil on their tail.

21. PROMISE, ONE KILL AT TIME

Joey's time at the war siren taverns had been informative in more ways than one. He'd let the war sirens flirt with him as long as they could answer questions. He'd asked the same questions at different taverns to cross reference.

Every conversation veering toward devils and dark moons had killed the mood for the war sirens. Not for long. And not with lots of ale in their bodies.

The somber answers Joey had received weren't nice. Every specialist had horror stories from a run in with a devil.

Devils didn't care about monsters or beasts.

Devils chased after denizens, commoners, and adventurers alike.

Their appearance disturbed the other tides. Sometimes pushing them out of their natural movement patterns.

And all devils were unbeatable. Nothing worked against their bodies. Any attacks on the low altitude dark moon suffered heavier counter attacks from devils.

War princesses of the past had waged futile battles with

devils. They'd brought death to themselves and the many war sirens following them.

The only way to live was to escape.

Now Joey was going to see for himself.

"We're too far from the Hail Storm Tide," said the air seeker – Muragale.

"Specialist Mollysea is out of it. She's got the dark moon in her head." The acid seeker – Mormelt – snapped her fingers in front of the specialist, but Mollysea was unresponsive.

The lightning seeker – Mavolts – shook her head. She moved next to the steam seeker – Milhiss – at the back of the boat, forcing Joey to sit next to the specialist.

"I'll use all of my clones with my dragon breath," Joey said. "Maybe that'll slow it down."

"It won't," Muragale said. "We need to speed up."

"Specialist Mollysea needs to go the instructor's path permanently." Mormelt shook her head. "The old siren took on too many tours. Seen too many dark moons. She must've lied to the healer about being debuffed in the head."

A part of Joey wanted to laugh. It was crazy to hear the term 'debuffed' used for PTSD.

Then again, negative singularities were a thing just like how his dragon spells had negative effects on him. He knew that. But it was still trippy to hear while in a serious situation.

[You've leveled up Stress Management from 6 to 7!]

Joey held back a snarl, his mood flipping. He stood to his feet and kept his balance under him while Curi rushed around glacial obstacles and monster skirmishes.

The situation became so dire the kraken stopped giving

space to the monsters.

A man snapper nearly landed an ice shot on Muragale's head. A hull crusher swung close to the boat with its heavy hammer pincer.

The monsters were bigger threats to Curi. One or two hits could slow their mount and turn their dire situation into a deadly one.

"I have to try," Joey said. "Six with a six second breath each."

He stacked dark dashes on the clones, too. They departed from the back of the boat with a serious air they'd rarely shown. They hit the rocky ground and ran toward the incoming devil.

Soon as Joey watched them move as a group, he realized the problem. They were too weak and slow in this higher level area. Even with the dark dashes.

Hull crushers and man snappers tore the clones apart before they reached the devil. The monster of the dark moon drew ever closer.

Joey thought about using his semblance, but after reading the beginner adventurer books, he knew Al Bruce Crabton could hinder more than help right now.

"I can try again once it's right behind us," Joey said.

"No, we need to get you to Hail Storm Tide," Muragale said, meeting the anger in Joey's eyes with a determined look. "Your mission is greater than this battle."

"Trader Curi, how many can you carry?" Mormelt asked.

What is that supposed to mean? Joey glared at the seekers. "He's carrying all of us!"

[Two. No armor, please.]

"Tight fit. Take this." Muragale grabbed Joey's backpack.

The rogue stopped himself from jumping on it. Muragale tossed the bag toward an awaiting tentacle. Curi used storage magic to hold Joey's bag for him.

"All of us help with this debuffed head," Mormelt said. "Not you, Adventurer. You will get your share of helping her later."

All the seekers crowded around Mollysea and tore off her armor. Each piece flew away without a care until she was stripped down to a tight bodysuit.

They guided Joey to the front of the boat. He watched in confusion as they placed the bigger specialist in his arms. Then one by one they passed him their necklaces.

The rogue wanted to deny what he was seeing. But as the seekers tossed aside their polearms, he slowly but painfully accepted the reality of what was to come.

He put on a smile and let his greed guide him. He moved the specialist to the side, stood on the rocky platform that was their boat, and gave each war siren a hug.

"I don't know how. I don't know when. But I will hurt that devil and kill it." Joey looked them all in the eyes. "I can't accept this without promising revenge."

None of the war sirens could reply. They were still bewitched by the open affection Joey had given them.

A crackling sound of the devil smashing through another glacial mound woke them up. Then all the war sirens smiled with courage, ready to make the ultimate sacrifices in the line of duty.

Joey would like to think he could come up with something to stop all of this. Just like in the stories he'd consumed growing up.

Heroes would always beat impossible odds. Heroes would save everyone from dying gruesome deaths.

But then he lay eyes upon the devil. He saw why such a creature could leave mental debuffs on hardened battle veterans.

It was not very tall for a monster. Maybe only eight feet. It was not muscular or anything spectacular.

It was shaped like a man with longer limbs than what was natural for its proportions. The skin was pale like a corpse, but that didn't bother Joey much.

The way it swaggered after them like it was fast-walking and showing off was so bizarre it touched on the uncanny valley. And the way it grinned showing perfect white teeth and a smile that reached up to its ears was grotesque.

Worst of all was the look in its eyes. They were human eyes. But in the zaniest and most thrilled sense.

The devil was having fun. Like a toddler, chasing after bugs.

They were on barren rock now with the Hail Storm Tide feeling distant still. The devil picked up speed, lengthening its stride with lunges.

Hail Storm Tide seemed to move further away, disturbed by the coming of the dark moon.

"We have to make it," Joey said, looking at Hail Storm Tide. "We have to." He looked back at the seekers.

They were gone from the boat.

Muragale and Milhiss helped each other fly through the sky with air and steam magic. Mormelt and Mavolts sprinted across the ground and ran straight at the devil. They dodged monsters along the way with too many close calls.

Joey lost his coolness and started tossing shadow clones out fast. He stopped at twenty to keep his channels from freezing. The clones couldn't hope to catch up to the seekers, but they distracted the monsters. A few of the clones had two seconds of dragon breath.

Half of the clones survived the first brush with the monsters. Five made it further than the rest and had a clear stretch between them and the seekers' backs.

Milhiss took a dark beam to the chest.

She fell from the sky like a shot bird.

Muragale used her air magic to dodge around another beam and started singing. Mavolts and Mormelt split off in opposite directions while singing over their shoulders.

The devil slowed down.

Joey felt the pull of their charm magic even from a distance. He heard the happiness, glory, and duty in their songs. He could see the charm having an effect on the enemy.

The distance between him and the devil was growing. He had to wonder if they could distract the devil and escape on their own somehow.

His hope vanished when their voices disappeared one by one. Dark beams shot from the end of the devil's finger and silenced each siren, ending their songs. Forever.

The clones were getting closer to the devil now. Joey thought of dismissing the spell but shook his head. He focused to see if he could have an effect.

Four clones died one by one from dark beams shot straight to their chests. The last clone breathed a quick shady flame at the devil.

Nothing happened. Shade Dragon Breath had no effect. The devil kicked the clone away and kept chasing.

"They've made their sacrifices," Joey said, placing their shell necklaces around his neck. "But they didn't slow it for long."

Curi let out tired tooting noises. [They've lightened the load, young great.]

"That's a messed up thing to say, Curi."

[I know. I wish I had better words, but I don't. So please bear with me. The next part will be uncomfortable.]

The devil gained on them. Its deadly finger bobbed up and down as it honed its aim on the survivors.

It took one shot and missed a few feet to the right. It took a second shot and missed a few feet to the left.

Every part of Joey hated the devil. Hated the smile on its face. Hated the fun it was having.

It didn't belong here. It was a walking mistake. And it was having fun knowing what it was. The happy look in its eyes said it all.

Joey used Analyze now that it was close enough.

[Devil: Devil: Devil lvl 75.]

How can it cause so much damage and be a level 75? Joey was angered by the audacity of the devil.

"I will make you hurt before I kill you," Joey promised the devil

The devil, even when outside of listening distance, smiled wider. It heard the promise and openly mocked Joey with a bigger grin.

Joey held the devil's stare even when Curi's tentacles

wrapped him and Mollysea together. The boat fell away, clattering across the rocky ground. The devil trampled over it.

Then Joey felt a cold gust wash over him and saw darkness creeping around the edges. Even then, Joey kept looking the devil in the eye.

He didn't break eye contact until Curi ate him and Mollysea whole, engulfing them in slimy darkness with a pocket of air.

***

Joey hit the sand in a spray of itchy vomit. Mollysea landed on top of him, knocking out the fresh air he was inhaling into his burning lungs.

He shoved the war siren back. He scrambled away from Curi's body while the kraken sprawled across the sand and water.

Air! Sweet, open air! Joey couldn't get enough of it. Things had nearly gone bad inside of Curi.

The only way the rogue had survived was because of meditation and the skill he'd gained. He looked back at the messages that had saved and damned him both.

[Congrats! You have the opportunity to learn the Meditative Stasis Skill!]

[Congrats! You've learned the Meditative Stasis Skill!]

He hadn't even read the description. He took it right away to survive the lack of air.

His breath glyph tiles were in the pack inside of Curi's storage. Joey should've placed some on his person, but he hadn't thought to do it.

Stupid! That was a stupid mistake!

Joey paced side to side in front of the nonresponsive siren and unconscious kraken. He stopped and looked around.

They were on an actual beach. Water flowed through a river where he could see the other side. The water exited into what looked like ocean water, so they might've reached the river mouth recently.

On each side of the river mouth were green jungles. Palm trees. Big leafy fronds covering the ground. Colorful but spiky flowers. It was all wild while grown from the land. Permanently.

They'd made it to landfall. He'd finally reached a place where he could find more humans like him.

Joey fell to his knees. He grabbed sand in both fists and held them up, letting the grains fall from between his fingers.

His horror. His disgust. His anger. These emotions remained. But through it all, the joy of being on land sang the sweetest. It was a bliss like no other. But it wouldn't last.

Happiness was fleeting.

"Focus, Joey, focus," he told himself. "You're already all in. The great quest is on your shoulders."

The necklaces of Muragale, Mormelt, Mavolts, and Milhiss weighed heavily on his neck. The shells clattered against his chest when he moved. He'd have to bind them with something and quiet the clattering.

He could still hear the memory of their songs as they fought like true warriors. It was horrible. And it was beautiful.

Joey's greed took every piece of that memory. Since there was no running from it, he feasted on the experience instead. He consumed the pain and glory of what he'd gone through.

He felt like a scavenger trying to grow into something

bigger and deadlier by eating these strong experiences. Even if the growth was internal, his path required changes. He had to grow fast to survive the present and future challenges.

And thrive.

"Yeah, I have a great quest to complete. But I have to make it worthwhile. Make it big. And I can't let nothing stop me from doing that." Joey flashed a hungry smile. "The devil will pay his due. Sooner or later. But the great quest comes first. Just gotta take it one step at a time. One kill at a time."

A bird made a strident noise, almost like a warning. Monkey hollers followed right after before the jungle became silent.

"One kill at a time," Joey repeated, standing to his feet. He drew a short sword from his hip. "One kill at a time, one kill at a time, one kill at a time."

Hungry eyes looked out from the jungle brush. The eyes of a predator scanned the defenseless denizens behind Joey. Then the eyes examined the rogue's worth as an obstacle. And as a meal.

The rogue's smile became fiercer. "Come on. Let me see what you got. It's kill or be killed, right? So what makes you think you can kill me?"

The predator beast lunged out, hurling leaves into the air. It flew like a black blur, all muscles, claws, and teeth.

[Tidal Moon Beast: Big Cat: Shadowstalker lvl 40.]

The rogue dashed faster than the feline could run. Dark lines and spraying sand followed behind Joey as he thrust his sword. The big cat tried to cancel its charge and redirect midrun.

Too late.

Joey pierced its shoulder all the way to the sword's guard. The shoulder joint snapped. The foreleg bent like a wet noodle.

Joey vaulted over the beast while it hit the sand face first and tumbled behind him. The rogue reengaged faster than the beast could get up on three legs.

A palm strike to the nose backed the monster up onto its rear paws. Joey drew his other sword from his back and slashed the exposed belly three times before the cat could attack.

He pivoted away from a flailing claw strike and slashed twice more on the side. Blood and intestines splashed the sand. The beast howled in pain and frustration.

It tried to hobble away fast.

But the rogue moved faster.

Joey's tail phased into a solid form and pierced the other shoulder from behind. The tail spike ran through easily before phasing back to its ghost form.

The cat fell onto its face, scrambling with its back paws to get away. But there was no escape. The rogue had no mercy. He stalked from behind and thrust his sword through its skull.

[You've slain a Big Cat Shadowstalker lvl 40! Experience awarded!]

"Oh, too weak, oh, too weak. You're going to have to try harder." Joey surveyed the jungle. Nothing moved or made a sound. "Look at my neck. The necklaces are heavy. The weight will crush me if I don't get stronger. You'll help me get stronger, right?"

The jungle remained silent. It was as if the environment was afraid of the rogue who had gone mad with rage and hunger.

Joey looked back at the nonresponsive denizens. The specialist was breathing and awake, but stuck in her head. Curi needed time to recover. Maybe two days. Joey couldn't even ask for his backpack while the kraken was unconscious.

The rogue cleaned the blood off his swords with the cat's fur. He returned the shorter one to the scabbard on his back. Then he sat on Curi's big body and waited. Minutes went by before he glanced at his new skill.

[Meditative Stasis (Basic): Enter a stasis that reduces your bodily needs, clears clutter from your mind, and incrementally increases overall recovery. Even when time seems to flow faster, you can exit stasis instantly. *Monks told me I need to slow things down. Get in touch with myself to be my better self. I've tried it out. Now time seems weirdly liquid. It's a little freaky, but I can't stop doing it.*]

[You've leveled up Meditative Stasis from 1 to 5!]

It's an all rounder, Joey thought. He knew this would end his wishes for a good essence recovery skill. If it hadn't been for the situation with Curi, Joey would've refused the skill and kept aiming for the essence version.

I'll have to make the most of it. But not while on guard. I can't test this thing while lives are at stake.

At the very least, the skill lived up to its description. Joey's time inside of Curi hadn't felt like an entire day.

The skill had kept his mind from becoming utter chaos, too. He knew what needed to happen from here to the adventurer port.

He needed to become his own monster by grinding up his skills the hard way. He needed to become the greatest adventurer around.

22. DESERTERS
AND FAREWELLS

Thirst nearly broke Joey's focus. The temptation to use his stasis skill grew. But movement on the peripherals snapped him out of his stupor.

It came from the river. A first glance suggested a rough log. A big one. Two hungry eyes blinking at the front of the log revealed the truth.

Joey dove into the river and faced another beast that was trying to snack on the denizens. Analyze gave him a brief description: **[Tidal Moon Beast: Small Reptile: Croc lvl 38]**.

It was big for a small reptile – thirty feet long. But it was only a level above Joey.

Combat swimming and Shade Dragon Tail turned Joey into a deadly threat in the water. He slipped under the croc's lunging bite and drew his kunai knives from his harnesses.

He stabbed the underbelly three times before dipping under a tail swipe. He came around again as the monster turned and went for a double stab to the eyes, piercing deep.

Blinded, the croc thrashed and snapped its jaws in a

frenzy. Joey used Dark Dash to reverse out of the way, waiting for the beast to stop.

Then a realization struck Joey. *Don't I have something that can end this faster?*

This was not the time to test himself in water combat. He had his denizens to protect.

He resurfaced, breathed deep for three seconds, then dove back down. He exhaled shady flames onto the croc's face and over some of its torso.

Joey swam back to Curi's body as the croc boiled to death from the inside out. He gave the latest system message a glance before dismissing it, confirming the slaying of the croc.

The experience awarded gave him no new levels. That was fine. He was better off with his path staying at Level 37 when infiltrating the adventurer hub. Though, if he wanted to control his semblance, he needed to be Level 41.

A combination of personal power and essence control was required when dealing with semblances. Al Bruce Crabton was Level 51, which was out of Joey's range. It was a good thing he hadn't summoned the hull crusher bruiser or something bad could've happened.

I'll deal with my semblance later, the skill levels matter way more. This was true, but Joey couldn't concentrate on training until his pair of denizens woke up.

Once the adrenaline died down, Joey's thirst returned with ferocity. His tongue felt heavy and his throat ached. With all of his stuff stored away in Curi's spatial power, Joey had no way to drink fresh water.

I can't wait anymore. Joey knelt on the sand beside Mollysea and shook her by the shoulders.

"Mollysea. Specialist. Specialist Mollysea. Wake up. You

have to snap out of it. I need your help." Joey shook and shook, but he received no response from the traumatized siren.

Weakness entered his mind. His heart quivered. For a moment, he considered quitting. But the dragon in him raged with pride, so Joey hardened himself.

"Dammit, Mollysea, wake up!" he shouted.

Her hand snatched Joey by the throat. Her grip was crushing, and it took a lot to keep from gouging her eyes out with his knives.

Instead, he smacked her face with his open hand. Five fingers to the cheek, and he struck hard enough for his own hand to sting.

He kept hitting her until she woke up for real and let him go.

"Oh, no." Mollysea scrambled away as Joey curled on the ground and struggled to breathe.

The war siren gripped her head, looked at the jungle as if planning to flee, then dropped back down next to Joey. She helped him sit up and guided him to tilt his head back to draw in air easier.

"Meditate," she said.

Joey shot her a distrustful look.

"I'll take whatever punishment I deserve later. Let me take over for you here, at least."

Joey didn't want to trust leaving her by herself. But he wanted to improve his recovery. He entered stasis and immediately felt better.

He cleared his mind. Time flowed by, but he didn't miss much of anything. True to her words, Mollysea took over and handled the crafting of a simple camp for them.

Joey watched while both curious and detached as Mollysea moved like she was in a time lapsed video.

She gave Joey water conjured from her hands. Then she made a campfire, crafted a spear, and sprayed water on Curi to keep the beached part of the kraken from drying out.

In between each major action, Mollysea went back to dripping water into Joey's mouth as he meditated. He was already healed, but being in stasis felt nice. It made things easier for Joey while waiting on Curi. The kraken didn't stir until late in the morning the next day.

[Well, that was certainly one of the worst run-ins with a devil imaginable,] Curi shrilled, his tentacles moving lazily on the beach and in the water.

Joey jumped out of stasis and to his feet. "Curi, are you okay? Did you suffer any damage?"

[Lost a tentacle, but it'll grow back. Don't worry too much about old Curi, young great. It's more important that you are healthy and sound.]

"Well, don't worry about me. I'll get the great quest done pronto. I'm going to make everything worth it." Joey put on his brightest smile.

Curi made a sound like he was sighing. [Apologies, Joey, but I will worry about you, anyway. Gender differences withstanding, I can recognize a few things with you humans. But first, let me speak with the specialist.]

Mollysea stood to the side like an awkwardly placed statue. She looked anywhere else but at their eyes.

[My dear, look at me.]

The specialist grimaced and looked into one of the kraken's eyes. "Nothing I can say can correct the wrong I've done. But yet, I must apologize. I am sorry."

[The apology is misplaced. Perhaps, if you were of sound mind, you could've helped slow the devil further. You would've most likely died. All of you war sirens tend to go out together.]

"Four times," the specialist said. "I've always locked up when a devil engages. I've always survived. But it's been years since the last. The healer … we've talked it out. I'm one of the best specialists. But I'm sunk in the head for sure."

[Well, it's been twice in one month I've dealt with devils! Hm, perhaps I'm the problem here.]

"I'm going to hurt it and kill it," Joey said, mood dimming. Then he brightened. "But that's later. We have work to do, don't we?"

[Wait, wait, hold on. Let's slow down a bit.]

Joey didn't want to slow down. He wanted to sprint around and kill things and train himself into becoming a monster.

But Curi had done a lot to make landfall possible, so Joey kept his feet put instead of rushing off to the next objective.

The kraken made a bobbing tentacle gesture, showing that he was pleased with Joey's patience. Then Curi refocused on the war siren. [I can't take you with me, Specialist Mollysea. Between speed and protection, I'll choose speed. And if another devil happens, I would hate to compromise my safety with my morals once more.]

The war siren wore a long face. She slowly nodded before looking at Joey. "We are not allowed direct contact with new adventurers for one hundred fifty days unless we cross paths out in the open tides or tidal gaps. This is an order from the War Princess down to all professionals in service."

"It's been fifty-one days, right?" Joey said.

Mollysea nodded.

Joey's entrance was twenty-one days ago. In the books Maylolee had given him, he learned steady adventurers get a month-long head start ahead of great adventurers who were newly initiated.

It was almost ridiculous how much support steady adventurers received compared to Joey. However, the steady adventurers had their own weaknesses. Joey's start was the more favorable position as long as he survived.

Knowing what he knew, he could reason why war sirens shouldn't make direct contact for a length of time. It could lead to a Level 90 war siren playing around as a miniature goddess without supervision. Yet Joey might have to burn that bridge as he crossed it.

"You can't go with Curi," Joey said.

"Indeed, I can't. I am a liability outside of the protection of the Zambwi Land." The war siren pointed up at the moon hovering above the land.

Devils and their dark moons were repelled by it. Higher above, the solar moon shone bright in the moon heavy and watercolor sky.

"So, what now?" Joey asked.

Mollysea looked at the necklaces on Joey's neck. The rogue felt the inkling of giving them to her.

No, they're mine.

Joey refused to give up the mementos of Muragale, Mormelt, Mavolts, and Milhiss. They were a part of him now. He'd internalized the glory and the pain, changing and challenging himself.

The war siren saw the look in his eyes and glanced away.

"Then there's only one choice. I desert my duty."

Joey barely caught the pale runes appearing and disappearing around Mollysea.

The war siren looked woozy before walking over to a log seat and dropping hard. Elbows on knees, face in her hands, she sat like a beaten woman.

As her silver skin turned into a rusty orange hue, Joey used Analyze.

[Tidal Moon Denizen: War Siren: Deserter lvl 90.]

"Want me to lie and tell you I'm sorry and everything will be okay?" Joey asked.

Mollysea laughed with a self-deprecating tone that unnerved Joey a little. Then she shifted forward and fell on her knees, her head touching the sand. "Please allow this unworthy deserter to be of service, great adventurer."

Joey wanted to play it off and act uncomfortable. He looked hard at the siren's level and knew he wouldn't say no. But he had some questions.

"What's the difference between your old self and your new role?" Joey asked.

"My siren charm," Mollysea answered, head still down. "It'll weaken a target's magic and make others uncomfortable. It could anger some and outright scare others. As if I'm a hideous monster. Other than that, my water spells remain the same as with the rest of my power."

"Still have the dark moon debuff?"

"Yes."

"I'll keep that in mind if we're moving away from the land moon and crossing between tides." Joey thought about how the princess acted and decided to copy her by straightening his posture and appearing self-important.

[Congrats! You have the opportunity to learn the Machiavellian Agent Skill!]

No!

[Congrats! You've dismissed the Machiavellian Agent Skill!]

He had enough skills to take care of already. Anymore could hamper the growth of the others.

If there were going to be new skills, they had to be worth his precious time. Machiavellian agent sounded like a distraction to Joey, and he was also wary of what he would lose by choosing certain skills.

"Will you take me then?" Mollysea asked, head still down.

"Anything I should know before I do?"

"Ah, yes, I nearly forgot. Other war sirens will try to kill me unless you can explain the situation to them. Even then, they may want me dead."

Joey looked down at the necklaces on his chest. "They can want, but they can't have what's mine."

"Am I yours then?"

"Yeah, you're part of the Joey Eclipse cruise for greatness. It's haunted, damaged, and on a crash course for glorified hell. Enjoy your Bloody Mary with every trauma we give you."

"Adventurer references?" Mollysea rose to a seat on her heels and used water magic to wash her face of sand. "I will learn them if you're willing to explain."

"Honestly, the fact that English is a dominant language

makes it easier to do references. But that's beside the point."

Joey turned to his kraken friend. Softening his stance, he walked over and placed a hand in the middle of Curi's big eyes. "You're a damn hero, Curi."

[I don't want to be a hero. I want to be a profitable kraken with loads of tales to feed my curiosity. And safety. Lots of safety.]

"And yet you're going to leave me to do work for the princess. I don't get you Curi. You try to act like a coward, but you always do your best to be reliable," Joey said.

The kraken tapped the side of his head. [I get it now. I should learn to be less reliable. That's the answer to my misfortune!]

Joey howled with laughter before throwing his arms wide and hugging Curi's face. The kraken embraced him in return with his tentacles.

Before arriving at the Tidal Moon Realm, Joey wouldn't have ever dreamed of a situation like this. But here he was, making the most of his first friendship in Multiverse Z.

After the embrace, Curi pulled out Joey's backpack from storage. He also gave a bag and some supplies to the new siren deserter. Examining her again, it was interesting how a role change could affect a denizen so radically.

Then again, there were circumstances that could radically affect adventurers. Joey was one more permanent buff away from evolving from basic human to superior human, after all.

They spent the rest of the day relaxing together. Mollysea hunted. She also cooked. It looked like she would handle most of the survival and caretaking duties, which had Joey realize he'd received a Level 90 battle maid.

He kept that to himself, not because he feared Mollysea would get angry hearing that. He feared Mollysea would become delighted.

Then again, it looked like the deserter was keeping busy for the sake of keeping busy.

Joey didn't blame her.

The time spent with Curi was more lighthearted. Joey talked openly about his plans and Curi chimed in with his thoughts, concerns, and advice.

The biggest takeaway was for Joey to train up his skills and stay under the radar until he figured out how to accomplish his great quest without risk of assassination. Joey and Curi debated a little.

Joey wanted to go big and draw as much attention as possible as quickly as possible. Curi cautioned against big movements and pushed for steadiness.

"But I'm a great adventurer," Joey said, sitting back against one of Curi's tentacles. "Isn't going big what I'm supposed to do?"

[You'll be around steady adventurers. When among the steady, learn to have steadiness, too.]

"May I speak?" Mollysea asked while off to the side, alone.

"Never said you couldn't," Joey said.

"Find who are the power players. The strongest. Learn how they tick. Learn their weaknesses. Compare yourself and the great quest to them. Fifty-one days is enough time for them to establish themselves and their rule, and that might tell you what needs to be done."

"That bothers me," Joey said.

[Please speak further on why.]

"I'm not sure why yet. But I can tell it irks me when you speak about power players being established. And in rule."

"It's your instincts. You'll learn why soon," Mollysea said before lifting food from the fire. "Now, here. I've cooked fish for you, Adventurer Eclipse."

Yup, I've got myself a Level 90 battle maid.

Joey took the offered food. It was bland without the seasoning, but the preparation and cooking were great. Looking at the constantly busy war siren, a thought came to mind.

"If it came down to fighting them, would you be okay with that?" Joey asked.

The deserter stopped. She flashed a toothy smile that was a little disturbing. "You might've noticed I'm swimming crooked in more ways than one. I would love to work with adventurers if they're worthwhile."

Mollysea's wicked smile grew greater. "But I've killed my fair share, too. There's something more thrilling when fighting adventurers. They're smarter. Harder. But they die with more flair."

[Tidal Moon Lord, hear my plea and help these two,] Curi said.

Joey chuckled and kept eating fish, hiding how he was still unsure about fighting humans. And killing them.

It would be like player versus player matches, right? Right? I've done plenty of those.

Joey focused on finishing his meal. Without him needing to ask, Mollysea came over and dripped water from her hand and into his mouth. She really was good at serving for battle and convenience.

Her actions begged Joey to wonder something. *Has she worked as part of the extra spa package?*

Joey could honestly see her doing that.

He almost invited her to sit with him, but decided against it. He was still a little cross with her for nearly snapping his neck. She needed to work a little more to enter his good grace fully.

The night went by. They had a small ceremony throwing water up at the moons to honor their dead, an old war siren tradition Curi knew that was forgotten by present war sirens.

Mollysea cried off to the side by herself. Joey put aside his annoyance from earlier and sat with her.

He endured her disturbing charm until she recomposed herself. They said nothing about it and moved on.

The morning arrived. Joey stood on the river shore and watched Curi wave his tentacles in farewell before exiting the estuary.

Receiving a farewell from Princess Maylolee had left an effect on Joey. But parting ways from Curi hurt even more.

Joey lowered his head, his shoulders sagging. Mollysea stood beside him, motionless like a statue. She was big, imposing, and ready to serve.

"Alright, it's time to put me through hell," Joey said, raising his head. "I need your help for me to become a skillful monster, Deserter Mollysea."

"As you command, Adventurer Eclipse." Mollysea's smile could scare the undead back into their graves. "A monster, I will make you."

23. TO KILL YOUR FIRST HUMAN

Nine days came around. One by one, fifteen skills reached Level 15 or a little further. No new skills cropped up.

The system took the hint that Joey was focused on skill quality. But the system might also be angry with him turning down the last skill without looking. That was probably a little rash on his part.

Mollysea showed Joey new levels of training hell. Sometimes for the sake of his skills. Other times for the sake of training him like a war siren.

She gave him a comprehensive crash course on warfare in theory and practice for different situations. She knew plenty about the current location, for example, and how to handle urban setting combat he might experience in the port city.

She also trained him for the sake of her own sadistic fun and to test his dragon willpower. Joey quickly realized Princess Maylolee didn't know all the tricks that could make trainees hate their instructors with a burning passion.

The princess was young, after all, and Mollysea was experienced.

Joey learned he could push himself farther than humanly possible, which was scary. His determination was tied to his greedy need for improvement and power.

For once, this had nothing to do with path levels and main stats. Most of his combat training dealt with beasts close to his level, so he didn't gain much experience.

But Mollysea always knew how to make things harder, as Joey learned his skills the hard way.

She threw him in every environment in the area. The green jungles, the brackish rivers, the tidal ocean, and the mountain over yonder.

He faced many beasts contained in each area while handicapped with limited skills and little to no spells allowed. And he faced a lot of beasts.

Gorillas? Check.

Crocs? Check.

Snakes? Check.

Eels? Check.

Spiders? Check.

Hawks? Check.

Giant man-eating frogs? Check.

Giant man-eating worms? Check.

Creepy crawlers filled with magic? Check, check, check.

During the last days of training hell, the distance between Joey and the steady adventurer hub shrank. This was hard to believe for Joey. He couldn't imagine seeing other bonafide humans.

Then on the sixtieth day of the steady start ...

Which was the thirtieth day of the great start …

Which was the fifteenth day of Joey's great quest …

The rogue spotted other adventurers. And they were alive, which was incredible!

They were doing adventurer things while on a 'steady' adventure.

This was fascinating for Joey. It was like watching a different subspecies of humans interact. And they were unaware of the dangerous creatures above them, a Level 40 great rogue and his Level 90 battle maid (he'd let it slip during a conversation, and she wouldn't let it go. Now it was her unofficial role).

Mollysea tapped Joey's shoulder with her free hand. She pointed down and gestured for him to track as close as possible.

Joey nodded. He quietly descended from the treetops and touched the jungle floor. He followed behind four adventurers, his heart hammering.

Then he dialed down his stress. He became cold and calm while feeding his curiosity.

[Multiverse Adventurer: Basic Human: Archer lvl 30.]

[Multiverse Adventurer: Basic Human: Cleric lvl 29.]

[Multiverse Adventurer: Basic Human: Mage lvl 30.]

[Multiverse Adventurer: Basic Human: Warrior lvl 39.]

Joey judged which ones he would kill first and which ones he would wear down at his leisure. The killer instincts wouldn't fade even while standing behind fellow humans.

Fifteen feet separated him from their backs. He could smell their sweat. The wind blew at their faces, so his scent was masked. They would die without knowing how or why if he attacked.

Mollysea was right. Bathing him in enough blood, pain, and violence had turned him into another monster. But a controlled one.

I'm a little disturbed, but not entirely disturbed.

He was also bothered by the archer's lack of awareness. The archer class had improved perception in their mind stat. The cleric class had improved perception, too, but their perception targeted spiritual stuff.

The archer was failing his adventurers by not searching hard enough. But there was a bigger issue than the archer's failure.

The warrior was toxic.

"Shut your traps and follow what I say," the warrior said.

"Dude, how many times do you have to say that? We get it, you're the big bad warrior," the archer muttered.

"If you can snipe with your arrows like you can snipe with your mouth, I wouldn't have to be." The warrior aimed his big two-handed sword at the archer.

The archer had more to argue, but the cleric and mage hurried to calm him down. It looked like the archer, cleric, and mage knew each other.

The archer was a blue-eyed man in his late twenties with straw-colored hair and a Californian accent. He was the stereotypical example of a surfer bro looking for his next break as an actor.

The cleric looked like the usual officer worker in his mid forties. He was balding up top, a bit timid, and had a round belly. He had the features of someone who was easy to forget –

the background guy.

Joey monitored him instead of dismissing him.

The mage was a curious sight since she was elderly but spry, spinning her staff around her. She had a latina flair to her, but Joey couldn't place her origins based on the accent. Her hair was proudly maintained in a silver braid.

Joey sensed she was the most adventurous of them all. She also looked around the area more than the archer. Mages had improved intellect inside their mind stat, so it looked like she was trying to overcompensate for the group.

The warrior was some bruiser of a guy. He wore a permanent mean mug. He wore his armor like he wanted to show off his bare arms and all his prison-shaped muscles. Everything about the warrior was an act of intimidation and control.

While homeless, Joey had seen these types of men before. They'd preyed on him one too many times.

The archer looked like he wanted to fight the warrior, but didn't have the guts to pull the trigger. The cleric was scared. The mage was a little harder to predict. She kept a pleasant smile on her face, nothing seeming to faze her – she was the one to be wary of.

But the warrior has the highest level. Significantly higher than the predicted average, Joey thought, referring to the knowledge learned from his books and Mollysea herself.

At day sixty, the steady ones would range between Level 20 to 30. The best would get close to level 50. The weakest ones would be in the teens or below level 10.

Why the disparity?

Being able to adapt to magical violence, make strong connections, and gain access to the best quests were all factors.

And the crazy part is, it's not the high fliers I might need in the end. Joey looked at the average adventurers.

The three in the back had a strong bond. The rude warrior was a weak link even while being higher in level.

"Where the hell is it?" the warrior grunted. "Damn quest said a shadowstalker was around here."

Whoops, I killed that one already. Joey held in a chuckle.

"We can't go back and get another poor quest rating, man," the archer said. "Why don't we set a trap and wait for it?"

"I told you to shut it, didn't I?" The warrior grunted. "And waiting around is how you stay weak, like you three. You want to get ahead? You support me while I kill the damn thing instead of being hillbilly hunters."

He's not exactly wrong, but he's still wrong.

Joey was getting tired of the warrior being toxic. Maybe Joey should help.

He knew of a shadowstalker further north. He had let the big cat run away to hunt it another day.

The archer and warrior fussed at each other some more. Joey held in a sigh and sneaked away. He found Mollysea waiting outside of the adventurers' listening distance.

"Kill the warrior," she said.

Joey thought about it. "Without exposing myself?"

"Yes, but how will you make it interesting and progress our studies?" she asked.

Joey swayed his head from side to side as he thought about the issue. Then a brilliant smile crossed his face.

Mollysea nodded, looking pleased. She probably knew what he was thinking.

Half an hour later, Joey chased a Level 45 shadowstalker from its territory. Every time it turned to attack him, he smacked its rear with his dragon tail and kept the cat running where he wanted it to go.

The warrior and the archer were yelling and pointing weapons at each other. The archer looked the most scared while under the intimidating influence of the warrior.

The warrior's back was facing the oncoming threat, completely unaware. Joey split off before anyone could see him. He let everything unfold on its own.

"Shadowstalker behind you!" the archer shouted.

"I wasn't born yesterday you – ah!"

The shadowstalker ducked the arrow from the archer and crashed into the warrior's back. Large, dagger-like claws sliced through the harnesses holding the breastplate and dug into the flesh underneath. Big teeth clamped on the back of the neck and bit down until the warrior was nearly beheaded from the primal force.

The warrior died. But he might not die alone.

The mage whirled her staff to action. She launched four magic bolts that curved in a volley up before falling down.

The cleric aimed his mace. He planted a magic zone, capturing the cat within six clear walls.

The only way out was up, but the beast might not notice right away. Not when four magic bolts and a quick-fired arrow hit their mark.

The arrow hit the chest first. The bolts popped like mini bombs on contact, laying on concussive damage over the shadowstalker.

The beast cried in pain. It tried to jump away, but it

crashed into a wall, its escape blocked.

Another arrow sunk into the beast's side. Then two more in rapid session.

The mage sprinted forward, showing agility regardless of her age. She thrust with her enchanted staff and conjured a magic spearhead. She pierced the beast's hindleg before backflipping away from a swipe.

The cleric's focus was on maintaining the magic walls. He channeled consistently to lockdown the shadowstalker.

The next arrow shot came out slower, but it hit with more oomph. Gore blasted free from the shadowstalker's midsection.

The beast fell onto its side and thrashed in its death throes. But it still had some fight left in it.

"Dude, drop the walls and get the kill," the archer said.

"Thank you," the cleric dismissed his spell. Mace raised, he channeled a spell into the weapon. Then he jumped into the jaws of danger.

Clerics have tough bodies, so he soaked a paw strike on his pauldron well enough and traded with a blasting mace strike. The beast's head crumpled with a crunch and splatter.

The cleric rolled away smartly even while it was a slow maneuver. He rested on his knee. "I got the kill. Cover me while I heal."

"We'll cover you, friend," the mage said, moving to the cleric's flank. "I swear, there's something out there. Watching. It was too quiet until the shadowstalker jumped out. Animals will warn or get quiet when something dangerous is around."

"Could've been the kitty. Or us. Maybe it was us," the archer said, moving to the other side as the cleric used a healing spell on himself. "No lie, I'm glad it's the doofus over there who's dead."

"I don't know. Something is off. The shadowstalker came out running wrong. It was in a rush. But I've only fought these creatures recently, so I could be wrong." The mage looked around with a curious gaze.

Joey stayed in his hiding spot, letting the mage look past him. He knew the mage would fail to see him, but her intellectual mind was impressive.

"Should we take his stuff and sell it?" the mage asked.

"The revival hall is backed up for five days," the cleric said. "We're within the rules if we do. Though it's a little scary, we're having so many deaths."

"It's not enough to adventure around the starter areas these days," the archer said. "We either push north past the mountain or we take the ferry to other areas across the tides. But I bet most of our deaths are coming from the first adventurers branching out."

The archer confirmed the cleric was healed before putting his bow and arrow away. He pulled out a knife.

They had medium-sized backpacks with straps on the outside. They hooked the warrior's gear to their packs after spreading it among them. Then the archer took what remained of the beast's head.

"I'm finally Level 30," the cleric said. "Thanks for letting me get the last hit, Liam."

"No problemo, Nate." The archer – Liam – pulled out a burlap bag and dumped the head inside it. "So, can we finally agree on just the three of us? Hm, Emelia?"

The mage – Emelia – tilted her head thoughtfully. "I say we give it one more go. Maybe take on a rogue. If Nate can take the front, the rogue can help scout ahead."

The cleric – Nate – looked doubtful. "The dead guy was a reject from Domer's company, but at least he was willing to tank. It's bloody hell tanking. Cleric toughness, healing, pain tolerance, sure, I have that. But I can only tank so much."

"If the revival halls weren't so backed up, maybe we could risk things more," Liam said, patting Nate's pauldron. "But I get you, man. That's why I went with the archer class so I can stay back." Liam nodded at Emelia. "Maybe you should've been a warrior. You always enjoy being close to the action."

Emelia laughed. "I go where I'm needed. And as a correction, warriors have strong bodies, not tough bodies. The warrior seemed tough because of his level, but he was not truly. Anyway, I'm just happy there's us. Or it would be Domer and his crooks I'll have to work under."

"Ah, forget those guys. They're no fun," Liam said.

"Fun or not, they have a lot of organization with their company," Nate added. "We could get stronger faster if we get their support."

"And have to deal with their bull?" Liam pointed an arrow at the dead warrior. "There's more of that with those guys."

"I don't want to talk about this anymore. So, what will we eat at the tavern?" Emelia asked, switching the topic with a smart edge.

Joey watched the steady adventurers leave while being amicable with each other. They were also improving their awareness – the archer paid more attention to what was above and behind him after the mage reminded him.

Joey stayed back to avoid getting caught by Emelia and Liam. He saw enough, anyway.

Emelia is dangerous. Are all mages like her, or is she an exception among the steady mages? Also, Liam is a nice guy for letting Nate get the last hit. And Nate is braver than he seems and quick to respond.

As for my initial observation of them, I will grade them as decent. They meet the standards the steady ones should have. But they need a fourth. And they need to face more action.

Having four adventurers was the minimum. Having six with all the classes could be perfect depending on compatibility and how much action they needed to level up everyone.

But from what Joey could see, there wasn't enough action for large groups close to their starting point. Not for levels beyond 25.

They might need organization for more dangerous adventures. That sounded like an issue taken over by this Domer guy.

Could Domer be a great one? Or was he a steady adventurer taking advantage of a problem?

Still, it was interesting seeing the proper group setup. Joey could imagine how they would undo him if he let steady adventurers catch him unaware.

They would lock him down. They would attack him from multiple angles. They would overpower him with simple but useful spells. And they would outnumber him.

Numbers were their best weapon against great adventurers.

He could see himself dying just like the shadowstalker. If he allowed this to happen.

"Thoughts?" Mollysea asked, walking up behind him.

"Many thoughts. But first things first, I'm not bothered by the warrior's death," Joey said, cocking his head to the side. He left behind his hiding spot and stood next to the mess of two violently killed corpses. "I don't feel anything even without my skills."

"Shame. I enjoyed his death. It was like watching a story play out," Mollysea said with a smile.

"Eh, I guess I have an easier time with their deaths since they can revive." Joey shook his head. "But if I let myself die like that, there goes my greatness."

Joey frowned, having more to say. "They're too careless. They act like they don't have anything to lose. There's more than just the pain and lost gear."

Mollysea walked around him. "They don't pay the price for seeking greatness. You do. And all it takes is one mistake to end your path. One death. Then their class levels will continue beyond you as you live and die a commoner."

The bitterness Joey felt grew. He inhaled deep and tried to calm himself down without his skills. He switched his mind frame and focused on what he needed to do.

"I'm integrating into their society for a little while, Mollysea."

The war siren frowned.

Joey rolled his eyes. "Battle Maid Mollysea, I'll need you to wait for me at our hideout. I'll be among the steady ones, learning what I can to prepare for my takeover."

Mollysea smiled before nodding in the direction the adventurers went. "And you have an opportunity to join a group and get a deeper view of the steady ones."

Joey was unsure, but it did sound like an opportunity. He

could take advantage of it right away, too.

He'd found a dead adventurer yesterday. The corpses would remain until revival. The gear was up for grabs. Joey had stripped the dead adventurer of everything before cleaning the gear and then dirtying and ripping it on purpose.

Now Joey was wearing a black and dark brown top and trousers with simple boots that appeared to have seen long wear and tear. On his belt were roguish items: a short sword, a dagger, a grappling hook, some rope, and a potion pouch.

He also had a bag on his belt holding a hundred coppers, some glyph tiles, dry food, watery fruit, and other essentials.

Joey felt a trace of nervousness. Instead of crushing it, he turned it over for his study.

"I'm worried. What if I mess this up? What if I fail?" he asked.

"You are worth thousands of them, so if you're going to fail, make them remember you," Mollysea nodded and touched each of the necklaces she wore. She was being trusted with the four belonging to him.

Joey nodded back and departed for the adventurer hub. It was time to embed himself into adventurer society. It was time to be a steady rogue.

For now.

24. A STRANGER AMONG THEM

Joey had thought about different approaches for integrating with human society. Now that he was doing it, he needed some help from Stress Management to keep calm.

He was as ready as he was going to be, but his anxiety said otherwise. He needed to convince himself further. Joey figured his best approach was to break the ice and make an imperfect introduction.

Having this in mind, Joey caught up with the steady adventurers and simply walked behind them. He held his hands behind his head, fingers interlaced. His steps were careless on purpose, snapping a twig to alert them.

The archer spun around, arrow drawn back. The mage positioned her staff, with the end facing the perceived threat. The cleric followed his friends' example while looking around and shifting to the front.

Joey stood still, his hands behind his head. Then he slowly moved his hands until they were up and visible. He waved one. "Yo."

Liam eased the tension on his bowstring, but not by

much. He kept his eyes on Joey while Emelia looked around. Nate looked around the same.

Good, good, they're looking for ambushes. I am a rogue, so exposing myself will feel like a setup. Joey's opinion of them rose a notch.

Liam waited for a gesture from Emelia before he spoke. "What's the game, kid?"

"Been out in the wilds for a while. Saw you guys deal with a shadowstalker. I figured I'll catch up and walk with you."

Joey shrugged and slowly lowered his arms. Liam paid close attention to the rogue's hand placement.

"Where's your group?" Emelia asked, still looking around.

"I mostly do fights I can handle alone," Joey answered. "I'm a rogue who can solo."

"No way," Liam said. "What are you, a ninja?"

"You only know I'm here because I allowed it, Liam," Joey said with nonchalance. "You should pay more attention to your surroundings and not have Emelia cover for you."

The steady adventurers became dead silent. Nate blinked and pointed at himself.

"Barney the Dinosaur," Joey said. "No, man, I'm joking. You're Nate."

Nate lowered his hand.

Emelia took a gamble and stepped forward. Either she trusted her abilities or she was thinking ahead. Liam and Nate looked nervous as she placed herself in front of Joey.

"You've been out here on your own, child?" Emelia

asked.

"I'm eighteen," Joey said.

She continued to look at him like a caring grandma would. Joey felt uncomfortable and looked away, which was not a bad thing. He didn't want to come across as too sure of himself.

"Look, I could've killed you guys. I didn't. Can I walk with you or should I kick rocks?" Joey asked. "I can walk up front if you want. And no worries. Anything up to Level 50 is in my range."

"Okay, this is bull," Liam said. "Emelia, back away. You know how they try to sucker you in with kids. This is a con."

"No, this is a different case," Emelia said. "He should've ambushed us from behind. Or wait up ahead to have us stop. To expose himself when he has the advantage is telling."

Okay, good, she can be smart for me. Joey held in a sigh of relief.

He was glad he was telling the truth while being dishonest. Between Emelia having an intellectual mind and Nate having an affinity for truth, the rogue was placing himself in a dangerous position to build up his alibi.

Joey's gaze slid over to Nate for one last confirmation. Would the cleric expose the most important detail?

"He checks out with me," Nate said, failing to sense the most shady part about Joey – his tail.

Clerics had perceptive minds and spiritual affinity. Joey's best bet in hiding his Shade Dragon Tail was tucking it inside of his body while it was passive and ghostly.

Doing so felt weird and constricting. But it was the only way to hide the tail from clerics.

And it worked!

Joey had to know now before approaching human society. *And if it had failed, then I'd have to go in with guns blazing.*

Emelia backed off carefully. The three talked it out in front of Joey, not hiding their conversation while still searching for an ambush. Then Liam took over with a hard look.

"What's your name?"

"Joey."

"So why go from solo to groupo?"

Joey blinked at him. "I don't feel like being alone right now. Emelia said she wants a rogue. Nate said he hates tanking. So I'll do you guys a favor and be a dodge tank for a bit."

The three seemed disturbed by how much Joey had heard. Liam looked angry, but his frustrations would have to point back at himself.

The three talked about it some more. Then they agreed to have Joey join them on the way back to the city.

The rogue nodded before linking his hands behind his head again. He walked to the front of the group.

"Eh, don't shoot me in the back, please," Joey said.

"That'll be a crappy thing to do," Liam muttered.

"It would. But if you do betray me and fail to kill me, I'll make you all die painfully," Joey said. "Just saying."

That set the tone for most of the trip. Joey strode forward, being relaxed. He didn't do any of the sneaking and scouting a normal rogue would do. He could, but there was no point.

He wanted to sell himself as a unique rogue to give him wriggle room for later. This also checked if Nate could spot Shade Dragon Tail from the back. And the answer was no. The cleric remained ignorant.

There was little to no conversation. Joey could feel the tension behind him. The rogue was a stranger to them, and they were all in hostile territory.

Green jungles. High humidity. Squeeks, squawks, hollers, and howls rang out around them. Large insects buzzed from everywhere.

Daytime rain appeared and cleared up multiple times. The area was teeming with life and jungle magic. More beasts showed up soon enough.

[Tidal Moon Beast: Small Reptile: Frilly Leaper lvl 36.]

[Tidal Moon Beast: Small Reptile: Frilly Leaper lvl 35.]

[Tidal Moon Beast: Small Reptile: Frilly Leaper lvl 34.]

There were fifteen up the mud trail, blocking off a clearing the group was about to reach. The green reptiles had frills around their necks and could stand on their hind legs, reaching five feet in height. Their saliva carried venom, and their teeth could cut through basic leather with a single chomp.

The steady adventurers prepared for a fight. But they kept an eye on Joey to see what he would do.

The rogue continued to act nonchalant, drawing his sword and stepping forward casually. The nice thing with frilly leapers was their hierarchical tactics. The strongest charged first, with only a few at a time.

Three at Level 36 sprinted on their hindlegs and attacked Joey. The rogue stared them down and cocked his sword arm back.

He threw the sword straight into the chest of the middle one. Its blood squirted past his shoulder as he stepped aside to the left.

He backhanded the eye of the leftmost leaper, blinding and dazing the creature. Then Joey reclaimed his bloody sword from the middle leaper, ducked a chomp for his head, and hacked the legs off the last two standing.

"Kill them. They aren't worth anything to me." Joey stuck his thumb over his shoulder. "Go for the one with the chest wound first."

"Thank you," Emelia said quickly.

The steady adventurers mopped up behind Joey.

Meanwhile, another round of frilly leapers dashed at the rogue. These were Level 35s this time. They ran into the same sword throw, the beasts unable to learn from the demise of their fallen.

Joey moved the same way as the last exchange. He looked like a game fighter character performing the perfect sequence to defeat a specific enemy type. Efficient. Brutal. A true workman.

The frilly leapers ran away after the third round. Their Level 34s had fallen to the rogue just like the others. The steady adventurers continued to mop up behind him, taking turns to earn their kills safely.

It wasn't much. Joey dismissed the system messages without needing to look.

His earnings were barely anything, if nothing at all. The steady adventurers would've been able to handle things well enough without him.

But ...

"That was the easiest time I've had with those jerks," Liam said, sounding amazed. "I can shoot them pretty fast while Nate locks them down. But once you stop the first charge, another charge starts up and moves around to our side."

"Wow! You were really serious about being a dodge tank!" Nate walked up to Joey with a broad smile. "I wish I had moves like yours."

Emelia held her silence, frowning while deep in thought. Joey waited for her. He needed the mage to accept his abilities within reason. Or he'd have to ditch this plan.

"Strong," Emelia said. "And you are pretty unique. How did you cultivate your spells?"

"I wanted to be like an anime hero," Joey said. "Less backstabber and more finesse. And I have passive magic helping me."

Which is not a lie. I have passive abilities, but I'll need you to assume I meant my spells. Joey waited.

Emelia smiled kindly. "Maybe our luck is turning up. You're a scary child, but you seem very earnest."

"I've survived some bad stuff. I'm giving you guys a try. Don't disappoint me." Joey nodded before looking up the trail to play guard for the group.

Liam rushed to gather frills. Emelia gathered a few venom sacs with her own knife. Nate stood beside Joey like they were going to be best buds. The rogue remained impassive.

He couldn't let them get too close. They might want him dead if they realized the truth. He was here to infiltrate and learn about the state of things with steady adventurers, and then shake things up in his favor. These people could be his enemies if they caught on.

Thankfully, they had more skirmishes with jungle beasts where Joey could show his value. He held his ground, dodging and crippling beast after beast with swift counterattacks.

As he danced in the face of danger, he kept the heat off the others. Nate and Liam's spirits were soaring from how easier their fights became because of Joey leading the way. Emelia didn't say much, but she held no obvious suspicions.

He was glad his act as a dodge tank with a rough personality was building him a usable alibi. Dishonesty worked best when others created half the story for the deceiver.

***

Joey and his group exited the jungle treeline and stepped on a hard dirt road. His nerves grew taut, both thrilled and anxious.

The sight of more and more humans appearing around him was almost too much for his senses. Stress Management did some heavy lifting.

He spotted a few more adventurers. But their numbers paled compared to the majority. All the adventurers were among a massive herd of commoners returning from their assignment.

Even with all his preparation, it was still a surprising sight for Joey.

[Multiverse Commoner: Basic Human: Gatherer lvl 12.]

[Multiverse Commoner: Basic Human: Gatherer lvl 11.]

Multiverse Commoner: Basic Human: Gatherer lvl 10.]

They're so weak! Like runts, but with no defenses, Joey thought, holding in his shock.

He tried not to gawk at the commoners, staying impassive. He definitely observed them with side glances.

Some commoners had wary expressions. They feared the jungle even though they were leaving most of it behind. Others talked merrily with each other, not caring for the danger. The ones who smiled seemed to enjoy their work.

Wary or merry, they all had baskets strapped to their backs. Each basket carried a hefty haul.

Joey had to find a few people as short as him to take a peek at the goods. Lots of fruit produce, nuts, vegetables, eggs, and all sorts provided by the jungles of the Zambwi Land.

Some of it looked heavy, but none of the gatherers struggled. No doubt, they favored the body stat with their points. They marched quicker than mundane humans would. So, even with their low levels, they could enjoy the benefits of the system.

The road for adventurers and commoners took a curve around a bend and faced west. The reddish sunset shone on them while the watercolor and moon heavy cosmos glowed behind them.

The jungle thinned more the further they went. The commoners became livelier as the wilds gradually disappeared. Then they reached a small incline, climbed to the crest of the hill, and started their descent on a barely noticeable decline.

Before them was an entire city sprawled across the lands of a wide and gentle basin. The city nestled against an ocean linked to the land, which faced the opposite direction from where Joey had come from. The water looked like glowing crimson and stretched far without a break in the body, like an endless ocean.

Joey stopped to take in the view of it all. Great big walls facing the jungle. High towers spaced along the walls. Then many more towers with few purposes other than sheltering the new humans of Multiverse Z.

From here, Joey could see dynamic human life, nonstop activities, and considerable stability. He could hear the clamor and shouts of human existence thriving behind the walls. And as he stayed still, the herd of commoners sped by him. They were excited to be back with their fellow humans.

For them, this was a daily blessing.

For Joey, this was a death trap.

"Ah, civilization!" Nate cheered, turning to the rogue. "Isn't it great, Joey?"

Joey couldn't say so. He chose silence as his answer.

"You alright, man? You looked wiped out." Liam glanced from the port city to Joey. Emelia hovered nearby, always watching with her intellectual mind at work.

"No," Joey said. "Nervous."

"Why?" Nate looked confused.

"Ah, I get it." Liam reached over before realizing that it might be a bad idea to touch a rogue with a rough personality. He retracted his hand. "It's been a while, huh? Things have changed. The commoners got some smart people. They've renovated the mess it had been when we all got here. Everyone is working together to make a better life here in New Zam City."

Joey nodded, keeping his silence.

"How did you live out there for so long?" Nate asked.

"One kill at a time."

Liam and Nate shared an uneasy look. "Hey," they both said before stopping. The men gestured at each other for someone to talk to Joey. After some prodding from Liam, Nate led the next topic, which was coincidently the right move.

Clerics had improved alignment in their spirit stat. It basically made them more persuasive. Knowing this didn't necessarily make Joey immune.

"After we visit the guild, we're getting food at the tavern. That place hasn't changed much. You must've seen it."

"No, I have not," Joey said.

"Oh, then, hey, let's invite you over. Sounds swell, right, guys?" Nate asked the others.

"You're edgy and hardcore, dude, but maybe there's a good guy behind all of that. Come over to the tavern with us." Liam flashed him a Hollywood smile.

"I'm in agreement." Emelia nodded.

"We're in. So come join us," Nate said, smiling.

Joey felt the compulsion to say yes. Nate most likely had an imbalance with his stats, favoring his spirit more than he should or Joey wouldn't feel much of anything.

Still, Joey had enough willpower and awareness to shrug it off. He also had Dragon Pride getting ready to stomp on the compulsion.

"Okay," Joey said. He had no reason to say no. But he kept a note of Nate's habits when the cleric used his alignment.

Nate had a friendly salesman style, too. It was inferior to Curi's approach, but still noteworthy.

Joey's group and other adventurers followed the

cheerful commoners. Now everyone was becoming livelier.

Adventurers manning the walls watched closely. There were more archers and mages on the wall than anything else. The front gate had mostly warriors and tamers with a few clerics.

Good, Al Bruce Crabton is strong for a semblance.

Joey nodded at the ghostly beasts that the tamers claimed as their semblances. The tamer class had an easier time picking up multiple semblances, but there was a price for having extra help.

Still, it was quite impressive looking up at an elephant-like beast with six tusks. Or seeing a tamer sitting on a shadowstalker.

No rogues in sight. They're most likely hiding and watching.

Joey wished he could guide the system to give him a good sensory skill. His back itched with having so many people right behind him or to his flanks.

He felt stares from all over without knowing where they were coming from. Mollysea had touched on this being a possible hole in his defense. She had done all she could to build into him a sense of danger without magic.

Magic would obviously help a lot. But just like wielding a sharpened weapon, magic was only as good as the user. Since he had all the classes around him, Joey quickly ran through a list of their capabilities in his head.

It came to him automatically just like everything else he drilled by himself or with Mollysea's help:

1 - Rogue - focused mind, agile body, fortunate spirit with affinities for short blades, stealth, and dishonesty. Comments: *Pretty much the classic rogue design you'll find in most video games. However, I'm proof that there can be exceptions*

... granted, I have a whole path, so maybe I'm not a fair comparison.

2 - Warrior - focused mind, strong body, willful spirit with affinities for heavy weapons, endurance, and intimidation. Comments: *This is Princess Maylolee's class, and it fits her perfectly while also showing how dangerous warriors could be with the added magic. I can see a lot of adventurers choosing the warrior class, so I might fight these more often than not if it came down to it. None of them would compare to the princess, however.*

3 - Mage - intellectual mind, agile body, willful spirit with affinities for sticks, acrobatics, and magic. Comments: *It's an interesting design for the mages to be more agile than the common design from games. They seem more wushu while still capable of weaving wonders. They're also the only intellectual class, but that doesn't mean it's all good. Apparently, a dumb mage can use their intellectual mind to find dumb solutions faster. They're also the class you can distract the easiest if you give their mind something to chew on.*

4 - Cleric - perceptive mind, tough body, aligned spirit with affinities for support, truth, and spirituality. Comments: *This class diverges from common game designs by not needing a deity right away. They are more like shamans, honestly, but they have the option of gaining the favor of a deity or a major spirit later. Every group should have a cleric since they're the only ones with the heal spell from the start. And they're the only class with an aligned spirit, so they're all naturally persuasive.*

5 - Archer - perceptive mind, strong body, fortunate spirit with affinities for range, dexterity, and teamwork. Comments: *This class surprised me. I wouldn't have thought of archers having strong bodies until I put aside gamer logic and looked at historical facts. Archery requires strength, especially if the bow has a heavy draw. They also can kill the easiest between having a ranged weapon and a fortunate spirit, which makes their teamwork affinity an interesting factor.*

6 - Tamer - perceptive mind, tough body, willful spirit with affinities for grappling, hunting, and semblance. Comments: *This class is a mixed bag. They're the only ones who can get semblances fast. But they also have other tricks. They can get spells shifting them from human to beast, like a druid. Their grappling affinity gives them a boost in strength to go along with having tough bodies, so don't ever let a tamer grab you by surprise. Honestly, tamers would be the most geared toward being 'solo' if it wasn't for the heavy price when using semblances. Say bye-bye to 20% of your essence for every active semblance.*

Joey nodded at himself, feeling proud that he could remember the facts and his opinions of each class almost instantly. He'd prepared long and hard for his arrival at New Zam City.

"Who are you?" A Level 44 tamer guided his shadowstalker semblance into Joey's path in front of the gate. Another shadowstalker circled behind Joey. The second one belonged to the same tamer.

The ghostly creatures stared hungrily at Joey, and each one was Level 44. This was okay with Joey. The beasts had no idea how many of their kind the rogue had killed by himself.

"Well?" the tamer grunted, eyebrows furrowing. "Tell me who you are, kid. Or else."

25. ADVENTURE, ACHIEVE, YEAH!

"Yo, tamer bro, let us through," Liam said with a smile. "He's a new friend we picked up. He's been out for a while."

"He's Level 40," the tamer said, pointing down at Joey. "And I don't know him. That needs to be brought up with Domer."

This was Nate's time to shine, but the cleric faded into the background instead. For someone with his stats favoring spirit, he struggled to use it.

Thankfully, mages had willful spirits, and Emelia knew how to use it with her intellectual mind.

"He's human. He has no reasons to be withheld by you. No taxes are being collected at the gates, either, unless you want to get on the wrong side with the denizens." Emelia pointed her staff at the tamer. "You're holding up everyone trying to contribute to New Zam City. So what's it going to be?"

The tamer looked angrily down at Emelia. "I could crush you like a bug, old lady."

"Not while on the job, you can't. Again, do you want to

get on the wrong side of the multiverse denizens?"

"Move through. And watch it. I'm not always on guard duty." The tamer spat in front of Joey before his shadowstalkers moved aside.

Liam gave the tamer a rude gesture to his back, ignoring all the other guards.

Joey kept watch of everything he could, more concerned by what could be hidden than a mere tamer on a power trip.

Joey and his group moved through the entrance and entered what felt like a new alien environment for the rogue. But instead of being surrounded by fantasy creatures, Joey was surrounded by humankind.

There were too many of them. Joey wanted to run. But he managed his stress and moved with his group.

He made note of the structures. Sturdy. Simple. But there was a touch of green to everything. Vines, plants, flowers, life. Every structure was mostly wooden while bursting on the sides or rooftops with flora jungle themes.

Balconies and awnings had plank bridges connecting them. People used the bridges to walk above the ground, getting around to visit other homes or businesses set within the jungle towers.

The aerial bridge designs reminded Joey of the mercantile arm of Aqua Star City, which might mean humans adopted these designs from sirens long ago. Or the sirens had adopted these designs from humans.

If the city's remnants had been here when the new Multiverse Z initiates arrived, then all they had to do was use what was available and renovate. Joey could already see humanity's new influence all over.

Plenty of open-door shops. People worked on crafting

projects together in garage-style interiors. Street performers took up corners with little baskets for copper coins. There were even people selling newspapers, each page having a green tint with fresh ink.

When Joey thought he saw electric lights illuminating building interiors, he soon realized it could still be magic but funneled with a scientific design. Could they use glyphs to make explosives? Could they recreate guns? Could they take magic and recreate sci-fi effects? Magitek armor?

So many questions whirled through Joey's head about what humans could do with magic. He felt overwhelmed. The surrounding activity was nonstop. And it felt more claustrophobic and crowded compared to Aqua Star City.

In Aqua Star City, denizens had given him some space or purposefully brushed by him because he was a male adventurer and they wanted to seek his attention.

In New Zam City, he felt lost, squeezed in, and alone with everyone pushing by without a care. Just when he thought he could find his bearings, another incredible circumstance made itself known at a busy market square.

"Hello, hello, hello to our brand spanking new multiverse humans!"

An excited voice cheered from a giant crystal ball. It was propped on a tall stone column in the square's middle, easy for everyone to view.

Joey's impassive facade fell. He gaped at the elven girl speaking through the crystal ball. Despite the curvature, she was easy to view, displaying her high fantasy elven beauty.

"We're reaching the end of your sixtieth day, and every one of your multiverse denizens wants to tell you congrats on doing your best to adapt! It can be a little hard being in a new place while under new rules, but we hope you can take advantage of this fresh start!"

The elf performed a little dance. People laughed.

"Also, also! Let's be thankful to the Tidal Moon Lord for being a devoted host to your beginner challenge area! And let's give a round of applause to all our adventurers who are doing their best out there! You guys may be steady going, but you all rock!"

Commoners all around New Zam City cheered.

Joey felt like he was in the twilight zone.

He completely ignored his group while they were trying to urge him onward.

He ignored Emelia's observations of him.

"With that said, the multiverse denizens at the adventurer guild want to urge our dear, dear adventurers to remember something important. Don't forget to keep hunting for the High Moon Achievement List!"

A bunch of people moaned or booed.

"Oh, come on, don't be that way! Getting the high moon achieved is important! There's a face-to-face with the Tidal Moon Lord on the line. He could, you know …"

The elven girl looked left, looked right, and whispered aloud, "He could make you one of those infamous, rare, and crazy dangerous great adventurers! Then again, you might just become one if you accomplish one of the achievements on our list!"

"Dude, you okay?" Liam asked.

"No," Joey said. "I'm overwhelmed."

Nate and Liam tried to ask more questions. Joey ignored them, completely focused on what the elven girl would say next.

"High Moon Achievement List! Woo! If you get all seven done, you'll meet the Tidal Moon Lord and get some cool perks!"

As the elf spoke of each achievement, the crystal ball displayed the information like a system message.

[#1 – Get 10 great results on quests!]

[#2 – Slay 500 monsters that give experience!]

[#3 – Defeat a level 75+ dungeon!]

[#4 – Slay the Dread Whale!]

[#5 – Slay 100 steady adventurers above your level!]

[#6 – Reach level 100!]

[#7 – Slay 1 great adventurer!]

"Come on, everyone, let's root for our adventurers! You know what to say. Adventure, achieve, yeah!" The elf pumped her fist.

A city filled with people cheered with the crystal ball commentator. They roared so loud it stressed him out even with his skill helping.

The commentator kept chatting, shifting the subject to positive news focused on New Zam City and other human settlements across the western tides.

She gave warnings, updates, anecdotes, and shout outs to individual adventurers or groups for accomplishing great results on their quests. Her upbeat attitude had most people smiling.

Joey frowned.

[#7] was burned into the forefront of his mind.

The feeling that people were watching him, figuring him out, laying traps for him increased. Maybe he was being paranoid. Or maybe they already knew he was great and were setting him up.

"We won't kill you for a stupid achievement," Emelia said, snapping Joey out of his head. "We've heard the horror stories. Adventurers betraying each other for [#5]. Ugh, even mentioning that invites the weird system magic in my voice."

She was right. Hearing her say [#5] had a slight magical tone to it.

Joey could feel it in his head, too. It was stamped into his brain, giving him a perfect memory of each achievement. Out of a whim, he checked his profile singularities.

Singularities: Dragon Pride (Superior), Slay The Dread Whale! (Great Quest/Part 1), High Moon Achievement List (Great Quest/0 Complete).

There it is. And I have zero complete. Joey grimaced.

"So, let's finish our quest and go to the tavern, okay?" Emelia smiled, brushing past the rogue's worsened mood.

Joey nodded. He walked with his group and noticed how they surrounded him. It wasn't out of malice. He could tell they were trying to protect him.

How ironic.

Joey was not a target for being a great adventurer. He was a target for being higher level. The irony could only deepen from there.

I can see why the warrior was being toxic with his intimidation affinity. People would want to betray him for the sake of the list.

If only Joey's greed could ignore the list. But that was

impossible. There was [**#4 – Slay the Dread Whale!**] on the list.

This emboldened his greed. Somehow, someway, he would accomplish the other achievements along with his great quest.

Damn the dragon price! I'm not better than any other achievement hunter!

Joey sighed glumly in a city that wanted him dead twice over. A city he needed to rock and tilt in his favor.

His hand touched where the necklaces should hang. He felt a hunger in him. Determination.

It was necessary to feel concerned, but Joey refused to feel like a wimp. So he held his head up and prepared to fight anything or anyone.

The feeling of having eyes on him dimmed. He was the opposite of an easy mark. The rogue was a dragon in sheep's clothing, and he needed to act like it.

***

The adventurer guild looked like a grand jungle temple. Massive trees towered on the four corners outside the structure. Tree branches interconnected over the guild's rooftop and held tree houses with bridges and ladders. Somehow, there was not a speck of detritus on the curved rooftop.

The grounds were a curious sight, too. Instead of stone or gravel, everyone visiting the guild had to walk over thousands of roots, small and large. The front of the guild used roots like stair steps to reach the first floor.

With the red light of the setting sun, Joey's first visit to the adventurer guild felt like entering a brand new MMORPG with ultra immersive graphic settings.

Red sunlight and shadows intermingled and highlighted the guild's superstructure. Adventurers in their medieval gear chatted and moved about all around Joey.

So far, this was the most amazing sight he experienced from New Zam City.

But Joey kept a very strict expression to hide his newness. It was one thing to admit he never visited the adventurer tavern before. It was another thing to admit never having business at the adventurer guild until now.

He pretended he was bored instead, living vicariously through Liam and Nate as the two grown men acted like kids. They waved at other adventurers they knew and threw around lighthearted jokes, having lots of fun.

Lucky them.

Emelia had a pleasant smile on her face as she openly watched Joey.

She's not going to stop observing me, is she? Joey sighed internally. *I guess I'll be her intellectual puzzle until something else takes her attention.*

They walked up the root-made stairs and crossed through the grand open entrance.

Joey felt a weird tingle and a strange distortion in view. Then everything was normal once he set his feet inside fully.

But from what he could see, the proportions inside were way bigger than they should be. The guild receptionist area was massive.

Even with hundreds of adventurers filling the space, the area could take in way more. Thousands if necessary. It was like a stadium.

Joey followed behind his group as they visited a

station to their right. The station took parts from beasts or valuable plants. The vendor was another elven girl like the commentator and worked behind an enclosed box with a window.

Joey used Analyze.

[Multiverse Denizen: Superior Elf: Guild Worker lvl 166.]

Emelia was busy haggling for her group, so Joey allowed himself to show shock for a brief moment. *It's a good thing I trained my Analyze up to level 15 after all.*

The training for it had been tricky. He'd reduced its level until it was almost useless and guessed the level of a creature he was fighting. Guessing right led to Analyze's skill growth. Now he could see the descriptions of his superior gear and get a sense of higher power levels.

If an adventurer thinks they can hassle or threaten the elves, they'll get their heads ripped off. Joey found that a little funny.

No wonder Emelia had used the threat of a denizen. Although, there could be more to it than their high power level.

Joey made sure his impassive facade was up as his group received some coins before moving on.

He noticed how all the elves were the pretty and classical types. Elven ears, pale skin, long silverish hair, and unblemished youth. They were on the shorter side, so they almost seemed like teens.

Basically, they were Joey's people, all baby faces except for a few that had a mature air to them. While the group received their quest results for the shadowstalker, Joey's attention turned to the biggest and gaudiest display.

There was a massive building inside of the temple with

shiny wood finishes and a big golden plate over the doorway.

The plate said 'Great Adventurer Management Office' in bold. When the group moved for the exit, Joey looked through the great entrance.

All the way in the back, with the magic lights dimmed, a man sat behind a heavy desk. He was also an elf, but he appeared to be more mature than the others. Joey was close enough to use Analyze through the doorway, so he tried to take a peek.

[Multiverse Denizen: Epic Elf: Guild Manager lvl ???]

The epic elf looked up and gazed deeply at Joey. The elf's stare was piercing, nearly breaking Joey's impassive facade.

Before the rogue slipped out of view, the guild manager waved and beamed a teasing smile.

The manager knew.

He knows what I am! Joey suppressed his stress all the way and thought rationally. *Even if he knows, I don't think it's good for their game to oust me. Clearly, the difference between great ones and steady ones is all part of the beginner challenge. It'll ruin the game to expose me, won't it?*

But the manager definitely knew. Joey was sure of that.

What did that mean? What benefits could he get if he walked into the great office and met with the guild manager? It was tempting. Too tempting.

"I've always wondered what it's like to walk in there," Emelia said, standing right next to Joey.

"Anyone tried?" Joey asked as the group descended the root staircase.

"A few doofuses have tried," Liam said over his shoulder, leading the way with an extra perk to his step. "Nothing happens other than the entrance rejecting them. They get shoved back like it has an invisible barrier."

"Nobody great has walked in, though," Nate said. "It's one of the most talked about topics. When will a great adventurer show? Everyone's wondering about it. Heck, there's a job from Domer to sit in the guild and watch the management. All to see if they can spot a great one trying to go in. It's only for rogues, though."

"Boring," Joey said.

"Ha! That's right." Liam had his hand ready to pat Joey's shoulder. But once again, he backed off.

"To the tavern?" Emelia asked.

"To the tavern!" Liam and Nate cheered.

"Tavern," Joey said dully, following the group down a bunch of streets.

The tavern had a cozier draw than Joey expected. After seeing the grandness of the adventurer guild, he'd expected something just as big.

The tavern was indeed big, and it had a unique design of looking like a giant barrel placed on its side.

Joey felt a homey energy inviting him to enter.

The group walked through an entrance on the side. Again, he felt that shifty distortion until his feet settled inside.

Just like the guild, the tavern was more massive on the inside compared to the outside. But instead of elves, Joey saw other famous fantasy creatures. Two of them, to be exact.

Dwarves and gnomes!

[Multiverse Denizens: Superior Dwarf: Tavern Worker lvl 146.]

[Multiverse Denizens: Superior Gnome: Bank Worker lvl 152.]

The gnomes were on break from their actual job at the bank. So they had a booth to themselves.

Each one was around four feet tall and had wiry builds and a shock of hair that ran long from the front to the back. They had shrewd eyes and playful smiles as they spoke in hushed tones with each other.

The dwarves, male and female, dominated every lane they walked through. They were shorter than Joey, but he wouldn't want to stand in the way of their broad bodies as they zipped around to serve their patrons.

The males had long beards woven with bronze metal bands. The females had long hair that were also braided with bronze bands.

"Evening, adventurers, where would ya like to sit?" asked a female dwarf with freckles and arms bigger than Joey's thighs.

"Any balcony views available?" Liam asked.

"Yes, sir! Follow along." The tavern worker slowed herself down so the low level adventurers could follow her.

Knowing her level, Joey could spot the patience she needed to lead them to a staircase, take them all the way up, and then use a walkway that led to balcony seating.

The sun was gone, and the sky was heavy with moons and a swirling cosmos of colors. They found a good table near the corner.

"Sit there, Joey. Take in the view." Liam pointed at the seat closest to the wooden railing. The rogue did as instructed and leaned against the railing to look over.

"Huh," Joey said. "It looks nicer from here."

"It can be overwhelming on the streets, but this view makes it worth it," Liam said, sitting opposite of him. "First drink is on me, dude. Can I recommend their special?"

Joey blinked at the archer. "Sure." Joey looked back at New Zam City.

Magic lights. Nonstop humanity. Lots of noise. But from here, it was less chaotic and more like a strange symphony of progress. Not rapid progress. Not great. But steady, consistent, and positive.

It felt like most people were happy here.

And far east of this place, in a city under the surface of their tide, a tyrant weighed heavily on her people while her people weighed heavily on her. It would be interesting to see Princess Maylolee reacting to New Zam City.

Joey could see how being a steady adventurer with decent success was a nice enough gig. But he knew right away he couldn't get used to this.

He had to disturb this niceness. Maybe not entirely. But in some parts, he would make changes that forced steady adventurers to advance further and harder.

If he was going to challenge something as monstrous as the Dread Whale, he needed to build a large and strong raid party.

"Whatever is on your mind must be heavy," Emelia said, as the drinks arrived in large mugs frothing at the top.

The ale smelled heavy and thick.

I'm only taking sips. You won't loosen my lips easily. Joey kept his silence as Liam led the group into a toast, celebrating another day of adventuring.

Their mugs clashed, froth spilled over the top, and they took their first drink. It was fizzy and sweet. An enjoyable drink.

Liam and Nate drank heavily, ready to cut loose for the night. Emelia matched Joey's drinking pace, taking small sips.

"So, Joey, who were you before New Zam City?" Nate asked. Liam and Emelia looked very interested. What would Joey say?

26. FIGHT ME. OR KICK ROCKS.

"I was a nobody at a warehouse job in Miami," Joey answered. "Now I'm somebody who can use magic to make a difference."

"Amen to that," Nate said. "I have the usual story. Grew up and stayed in Connecticut. Divorced. The kids and dogs went with the ex-wife. My call center job of nearly two decades fired me to meet their bottom line. The usual."

Emelia reached over and patted Nate's hand.

"I was a teacher in L.A.," Liam said. "Terrible choice. I got through it with weekend surfs at Malibu and bad relationships you'll see in a rom-com. Hint, hint, they're not that funny to be in. So heed my words of advice even if you aren't looking, Joey. Make sure you're with someone who actually shares your passions."

"Yup," Nate added.

"I was a receptionist for a businessman in Columbia," Emelia admitted. "I never thought I'd be so adventurous, but I chose the option, anyway. It's like another chance to do things differently. It suits me well."

"Oh, trust me, I'm the happiest guy around when I'm not in constant danger," Nate said after another chug. "Which, by the way, is reduced thanks to you, Joey. I can't wait to tell people we have our own tank, but he's a dodge tank!"

"You're a tank, too, Nate." Liam elbowed Nate in the side. The two elbowed each other, which had Liam winning since he was stronger.

Joey couldn't stop himself from chuckling at the grown men being silly. Even beyond his own group, he could see plenty of adventurers having fun with their people.

Dwarves zipped around with drink and food. Their dwarf waitress came to give them the rundown on what food they were serving. Then she was gone with their orders.

The conversations shifted as the mood took them. Liam, Nate, and Emelia argued about what could've happened to their old world that led them into being initiated into Multiverse Z.

Nate argued they were chosen by the Multiverse Z System to have a new chance at life. Liam argued the apocalypse came for their old world and tossed humanity into Multiverse Z. Emelia argued they'd died and were resurrected, and that everyone was wrong about heaven.

From what Joey could tell, these three had argued this point multiple times. Even Nate would get animated trying to prove his point, which swayed Liam sometimes, but not Emelia.

Nobody knew the real reason for their relocation here. It was a large topic because New Zam City was made of different people from different corners of their old world.

But many of the people here had few connections from the old world and were older than eighteen. It was as if

Multiverse Z – or the Tidal Moon Realm – had taken all the adult loners or people who wouldn't be missed.

The multiverse denizens wouldn't provide answers to questions dealing with the wider multiverse. All that mattered was leveling up and getting those achievements.

Despite all the wonders and questions and inner differences, all the initiates could understand each other because of the Analyze skill, adventurers and commoners alike. Joey tested it when he eavesdropped on an entire adventurer group who spoke only Spanish.

The craziest part was when a dwarf waiter spoke Spanish with that group. It sounded fluent, which made the Hispanic adventurers happy. The dwarf came away with better tips, that was for sure.

Food arrived, which was tasty stuff. Ribs, steaks, fish, grilled veggies, fruit salad delights, and loads more.

Conversations died down as Joey and the others enjoyed the feast. But once they slowed down on eating, the socializing resumed.

Liam had stories for days, from back in Cali and from here in New Zam City. He'd gotten in trouble with a female tamer he was seeing.

Nate chimed in with jokes, showing more of his personality. And Emelia seemed distant but happy, gracing them with a comment that playfully denounced the men for being men.

Joey remained mostly silent, enjoying himself, but also feeling restless. He couldn't let this steady happiness last. The dragon in him had goals to conquer and awards to earn.

"Give me ten days," Joey said.

The group fell silent. Emelia took the bait, curious. "For

"To make you Level 40 like me," Joey said. "And to receive ten great quest results."

"No way," Liam said.

"That's a lot of work, Joey," Nate added.

"Why would you want to do that for us?" Emelia asked.

"I want to see if you can keep up. And it'll make a difference, won't it?" Joey looked across New Zam City. "It's nice here. But Multiverse Z is only nice for so long. Then it'll show you its ugly side when you least expect it. You need power for when that happens."

And I need to test how fast steady adventurers could level up when pushed, Joey thought to himself. *I also want to see how efficient we can be when we're in groups instead of alone.*

The group fell into heavy silence around Joey. Nate looked down. Liam looked frustrated. Emelia had a thoughtful expression.

"It's dangerous," Nate said. "Yeah, you have the revival hall. But you'll be five days gone if you die out there. And all your gear could be gone if your group gets wiped out."

"I don't know, man. Do we have to level up that fast?" Liam asked. "Things are pretty nice as it is. You can be our fourth. The levels and stuff would come with time."

"I'm more concerned with [#5] and Domer. No, I'm more concerned with Domer. You saw what happened at the gate. If we level up too fast, he'll want to push on us to join his company." Emelia sighed.

When Joey raised an eyebrow, Emelia continued.

"He's supposedly the strongest man in New Zam City. A cleric in the high 50s. And his managers are in the high

Level 40s. He has hundreds of adventurers working with him, too. All ranging from Level 30s to 40s. Organized. Strong. And wicked. They can't do much in New Zam City, but out there, they'll track you down and rough you up if you're not careful."

"Didn't you just paint a target on your back, Emelia?" Joey asked. "You stood up for a Level 40 rogue. Nobody knows me either."

"I don't think one case like that would bother Domer," Nate said. "Right, guys?"

"Not right," Emelia said. "A man like him will look into the smallest issue."

Liam looked hard at Emelia. "Did you know Domer would get pissed when you stood up to the tamer?"

"Yes," Emelia admitted.

"Why would you do it in the first place?" Nate asked.

Emelia looked away from the men and stared straight at Joey. "I have a hunch it'll be worth it. So I think we should take Joey's offer but push for more. We need to get close to Level 50 if we want to defend ourselves."

Joey tried not to grin. Emelia impressed him. However, he was not going to push for Level 50 right away or [#5] would become unattainable.

He felt confident about the course of things, so he gestured for everyone to get closer. He kept gesturing until they were rubbing shoulders together.

"I'll deal with Domer's men. All of you prepare for ten days in the wilds. We'll leave the day after tomorrow." His instructions were ironclad. They could hear it in his voice. Ten days, ten levels.

The trio slowly spread back around their table. They

finished their food and drink in silence. Nate piped up first. "Can we decide in the morning?"

"No," Joey said.

"I want to do it," Emelia said.

"Find, sure, I'm in," Liam said.

"Ugh, this is going to get bad quickly. I'll do it." Nate shook his head. "I guess we're officially a group now. Should we have a group name?"

"Let's decide when you all reach Level 40 first," Joey said. "And please no silly names. I'll be angry if you vote for something silly."

The older adults looked around instead of meeting Joey's eyes.

They're going to name the group something silly, aren't they? Joey sighed. *Freaking old people. Why do they act like kids more than me?*

Before they left the tavern, Joey ensured his new group would stay silent about what they'd discussed and watch their backs. He wasn't convinced that the 'anti-PVP' rules would protect them in New Zam City. Maybe Domer's guys could get around that.

When the group asked about Joey's location for the night, the rogue told them not to worry. They would link up at the guild when it was time for them to go.

Nate, Liam, and Emelia split the tab between them and didn't let Joey pay since he hadn't taken any payment from their loot.

Granted, Joey was probably the richest adventurer in New Zam City with his fifty bronze coins, but nobody needed to know that.

The group split off.

Joey let himself wander a bit, getting lost in the nightlife crowd. There were so many streets and alleyways, New Zam City could feel like a maze.

He asked some commoners about cheap places to stay. He asked passing adventurers about places where pvp-killing was allowed.

He found a location that bridged his needs. It was the far corner of New Zam City with the least amount of lights.

The Southside Zam District.

He saw fewer people while going in that direction. Fewer stores. More shadows and suspicious characters.

Adventurers became rare sights. Commoners moved shiftily while looking over their shoulders. The moment a commoner saw him, they ran away fast.

Joey didn't blame them. They were below Level 10 here. They went as far down as Level 1 for one man laying drunkenly in an alley.

Joey reached his first location of the night. A courtyard with a big gnarled tree in the corner.

Cobblestones and roots covered the ground. He looked over to the side and saw a red flag fluttering next to a dilapidated wall. Looking down, he saw faded red lines all around the perimeter of the courtyard.

"Well, here's our chance to talk," Joey said. "If it's talking you want."

Joey glanced over his shoulder. There was nothing but shadows and shifty commoners.

A cloud crawled across the sky above and blocked out

some light from the moons. Then the cloud cover cleared. Six darkly dressed men and women stood on the street.

[Multiverse Adventurer: Basic Human: Rogue lvl 42.]

[Multiverse Adventurer: Basic Human: Rogue lvl 44.]

[Multiverse Adventurer: Basic Human: Rogue lvl 43.]

[Multiverse Adventurer: Basic Human: Rogue lvl 44.]

[Multiverse Adventurer: Basic Human: Rogue lvl 38.]

[Multiverse Adventurer: Basic Human: Rogue lvl 49.]

"Domer wants to have a talk with you," the Level 49 said.

Joey swayed his head from side to side. He crossed the red line and walked to the middle of the pvp area.

"I don't care." Joey held his hands behind his head. "Fight me. Or kick rocks."

***

What is with these kids thinking they're comic book heroes? Robert held back from groaning.

Robert always wondered why people made things hard. Domer was a fair guy. Heavy-handed, yeah. But Multiverse Z was a place of danger, death, and gods dictating the livelihoods of mortals.

Robert understood what Domer was trying to do, so Robert played his part. But people wanted to make things difficult. Especially kids who thought having woo-woo magic made them invincible.

"I got this. He's a little boy, after all," Luciana said.

She was only Level 38 because she wasn't a fast killer. But her magic was the deadliest. She picked up a charm ability, and even Robert found that scary.

Luciana sauntered over to the kid. "Now, now, let's play nice. Who knows, you might get lucky."

She removed her head covering and showed off her wavy blonde hair and movie actress face.

Robert could feel the charm magic at work and hid his discomfort. The other rogues struggled not to get caught in Luciana's web since they were weaker than Robert.

There's no hope for that kid now, Robert thought.

The renegade rogue moved like a launched arrow. His feet left the ground, one knee rising. A loud and wet crunch resounded across the area.

Luciana stumbled back. Her teeth clattered across the stones and roots. She let out a scream before falling silent suddenly.

The renegade had a dagger in his hand that hadn't been there before. Luciana fell over, clutching her neck. The blood looked black in the dark.

"Go," Robert breathed out.

PVP rings had no rules against numbers. Anyone inside could get jumped at any time. Robert's remaining rogues – Tom, Bill, Sarah, and Gilbert – dashed in with short swords out.

The next sequence played out like an Asian action movie on fast forward. The renegade's arm blurred out of focus. A dagger appeared in Tom's forehead with a meaty thunk.

Bill sped up with magic and swung hard, but he hit only air. He took a backhand that broke his jaw and sent him spinning around.

Gilbert and Sarah attacked at once from different angles. They missed their swings, and then Sarah – somehow – ended up with a sword in her head.

It was just lodged in there, and neither Robert nor Sarah had seen how it got there. Sarah blinked in confusion before her eyes rolled back. She fell over dramatically, like she was in a play.

Gilbert screamed and popped his Smoke Bomb spell. He tried to escape the pvp ring.

The renegade flew through the smoke and was on Gilbert's back like a spider monkey. There was a grappling hook in his hand.

Gilbert reached a step from freedom when the hook dug into his chest. Loops of rope wrapped around the poor man's neck.

Robert stood outside of the pvp ring and smoke screen. He watched Gilbert fall short and get yanked backward like a horror movie victim.

The smoke cleared enough for Robert to see Gilbert's flailing body flip over the renegade's back and crash into Bill.

The two collapsed over each other. Gilbert struggled to unhook himself and remove the rope from around his neck. Bill tried and failed to shove Gilbert off as the two panicked.

Meanwhile, the renegade drew his own sword that he hadn't touched this whole time. Robert realized the sword in Sarah's head had come from Bill.

The renegade walked over to the struggling two. He was taking his time while surrounded by smoke and shadows.

"Wait, stop, please," Robert pleaded. "Please!"

"No," the renegade said, thrusting the sword through Gilbert's back and into Bill's gut. Gilbert died, and Bill screamed like a dying animal, still alive.

The renegade bent down and hit Bill with another

backhand. Bill whimpered through his broken face. The renegade yanked the sword out and sliced Bill's neck, ending the poor man.

Right now, the renegade's back was exposed to Robert. His trusty Backstab spell could land a quick killshot if he entered the pvp ring and used the remaining smoke as cover.

But Robert knew a trap when he saw one. He did the most reasonable thing a rogue in his position could do. He turned and ran.

***

[You've slain a Basic Human Rogue lvl 38! Partial experience awarded.]

[You've slain a Basic Human Rogue lvl 44! Experience awarded.]

[You've slain a Basic Human Rogue lvl 44! Experience awarded.]

[You've slain a Basic Human Rogue lvl 43! Experience awarded.]

[You've slain a Basic Human Rogue lvl 42! Experience awarded.]

Joey looked over his shoulder and watched the last rogue run away. *He didn't try to take my back.*

Unfortunately, Joey couldn't chase the man down. The Level 49 would avoid pvp rings and move faster than Joey. *Without Dark Dash, I'm not winning any races.*

Honestly, they all had better stats because of their higher levels. They likely had their stats placed heavily in body and spirit, too.

Unfortunately for them, Joey had higher skill levels.

Skills: Analyze lvl 15 (Basic), Headhunter lvl 16 (Basic), Short Sword Finesse lvl 16 (Basic), Combat Swimming lvl 15 (Basic), Combat Acrobatics lvl 16 (Basic), Scenic Discover lvl 15 (Basic), Chaos Finder lvl 15 (Basic), Armor Piercer lvl 16 (Basic), Stress Management lvl 15 (Basic), Roll With The Hits lvl 16 (Basic), Slick Knife Tricks lvl 16 (Basic), Fight Prediction lvl 16 (Basic), Assassin Grappling lvl 16 (Basic), Hands of the Fade lvl 16 (Basic), Meditative Stasis lvl 17 (Basic).

Roll With The Hits worked so fast I was already rolling away before their attacks got close.

Not only was the magic in his skills powerful, but he embodied his skills deeper than most adventurers. After all, he had thorough training from the War Princess and a veteran siren, two of the best fighters around. It felt like he'd grown twice over because of the system and his own determination.

Joey was a monster compared to everyone who lacked higher level magic and refinement. And he hadn't used any spells while the rogues tried to use their spells on him.

So, at long last, Joey had his moment to measure up. But here was the kicker. Joey was unsure how he should feel.

He still felt the rush of battle. He still felt the incredible ease of taking human life. Yes, he even felt unstoppable, and that thrilled him.

But in the end, he stood amid the human corpses he'd created with his own hands. The adrenaline was going away, and he was unsure what he should feel in the aftermath.

He was unsure if he should feel anything. He'd done well on his first human killing spree, and he could predict what would happen from here.

"Not bad," Joey said, nodding to himself. "But I still have

concerns."

The concerns could wait. His greed demanded a check. He pulled up an achievement.

[#5 – Slay 100 steady adventurers above your level! 4/100.]

It might be a good thing that Level 49 ran away. I need more fodder that's above me without leveling up too fast. Joey frowned. *What a tricky balancing act. Pretty annoying, too.*

With his greed satisfied, Joey picked through the pouches and pockets of the dead rouges. He used rope to bind the swords together.

He tossed extra daggers into a bag. He scooped up a smattering of copper coins and came out of the pvp ring with a nice haul.

[You've looted 256 Tidal Moon Copper Coins, 5 Short Swords (Basic), 5 Daggers (Basic), 1 Caltrop Glyph Tile (Basic)!]

Joey walked three streets down to a busted inn. He entered through the front entrance where a crusty old man waited behind a desk.

[Multiverse Commoner: Basic Human: Innkeeper lvl 12.]

"I don't want trouble," the innkeeper said.

"One room," Joey replied.

"Twenty coppers."

"Make it ten."

The innkeeper licked his chapped lips. "Fifteen, and that's the final offer."

"No, it is not." Joey stared into the innkeeper's eyes.

"Thirteen," the innkeeper squeaked.

"Now that is final," Joey said, smiling internally. *Thanks for giving me a decent sense of economics, Curi.*

"Breakfast?" Joey asked.

"Three coppers. And that's not for negotiation."

"Fine." Joey paid up.

The innkeeper prepared a glyph tile that worked as a temp key. The room was up on the second floor, down the hallway to the right.

Joey found it and entered.

He could hear the patter of little paws in the ceiling. Straw poked out of the bedding and pillows. The comforter had seen better days. And the space was small. But it had a window view of the water. Good view, but everything else was terrible.

That was fine with Joey.

Depending on how things go for the next two days, he wouldn't want to ruin a nice place. He set his loot aside and looked around further.

No crystal ball.

Ah, yeah, I'll probably have to access one at a better inn. Or maybe the guild might have one usable by the public.

He should send a message to Princess Maylolee soon. He didn't want her to think he'd failed. He also had to figure out how to explain the seeker deaths and Mollysea's desertion.

Outside of that, I kind of want to chat with her and tell her about my experiences. I wonder what she'll think about my fight against the steady ones and what I felt.

He needed to get to a crystal ball with a network connection. But before any of that, Joey placed his stuff in the corner.

He grabbed up the money, sat with legs crossed, and placed down fifty coins. After some hard thinking, he placed down another twenty-five.

Seventy-five total.

"System," Joey called softly, "I need a good perception skill. Please hear my call and let me trade Fight Prediction for something that can help me against multiple people waiting in ambush."

Sensing the rogues hadn't been hard. They'd wanted him to notice them.

Now they were going to do everything to hide and set ambushes. Joey needed more help against their numeral advantage.

Before Curi had left on his voyage, he'd told Joey of this system trick. It was old and unreliable. Like something out of a fairy tale. But Curi figured if there was something Joey needed badly enough, he should try making offers directly to the system.

It was one big magical entity that affected nearly everything. Why couldn't someone make offers to the system? So Joey tried.

No response.

Joey nodded. He placed down more coins.

One hundred coppers now. This was equal to a bronze coin, a large sum of money. But the skill he needed would be worth it.

The other option was for him to go to the Multiverse Spell Store and try to purchase a spell. It would be hyper expensive. And he couldn't access the spell selections again until level 75.

There were no stores for skills, however. And skill books were coveted, too. The one time use items would be stored away, hidden.

Joey needed a skill to cover a weakness. And it had to be now.

Yet, the system remained silent.

Joey placed down more. The offer went up to two hundred copper coins.

Still nothing.

Joey offered three hundred copper coins.

Nada.

Sighing, Joey turned toward his own pouch. He was willing to sacrifice everything.

A system message popped up, stopping him. Joey glanced at where the coins should be. All three hundred were gone.

The system had agreed to the transaction.

[Congrats! You have the opportunity to trade the Fight Prediction Skill for the Danger Sense Skill!]

27. DANGEROUS AND DOMINANT

[Congrats! You have the opportunity to trade the Fight Prediction Skill for the Danger Sense Skill!]

[Fight Prediction (Basic): Recognize patterns faster while fighting a single opponent. Hone in on their habits, good or bad, and design limited projections of their next moves. *I was talking to this one bloke, and he swears he knows everything I'll do because he watched how I fiddle with my fingers. I was going to stab him, but I left the tavern instead.*]

Joey didn't want to sacrifice Fight Prediction, but he knew it was the best trade he could provide. He needed to trade it because it was within the perception sphere.

The system likes balance, so it won't give me what I truly need if I have a skill like Fight Prediction in the way. And Fight Prediction had the weakness of focusing on a single opponent.

Predicting one hard opponent was great when up against a relentless and skilled princess. But it was not useful to Joey's current situation.

The current enemy had a large manpower advantage. All they needed was to catch Joey slipping up. *I'm powerful, but I don't think I'm unbeatable. I have a lot to lose. This new skill might be the answer to my main problem.*

[Danger Sense (Basic): Use all six senses to notice any strange things happening around you. These can be threats. Or it can be your paranoia acting up. Figure it out quickly, and feel better prepared. *He's gone paranoid, mate. I'm telling you, he keeps thinking people are out to get him. Yes, yes, he survived thirteen assassination attempts, but surely he can relax a little.*]

Joey nodded at the description for Danger Sense. *I like that it touches on the sixth sense, the supernatural one. But the paranoia part could be annoying.*

Joey was unsure if this skill would clash or work with Stress Management. Maybe it would be a give or take relationship between the two. He would find out.

[Congrats! You've traded the Fight Prediction Skill for the Danger Sense Skill!]

Joey expected a big power loss when dumping a Level 16 skill. There was none, however. *I would probably feel it when I'm trying to predict a single opponent.*

Though, he might be okay without it. He'd embodied enough of fight prediction to use it without the magic.

Danger Sense, however, was worth having with magic.

Joey used Danger Sense actively.

He paid closer attention to the rats scuttling around in the ceiling. He sniffed the air to make sure nobody was gassing him with poison.

He looked outside and watched suspicious characters loiter around. He felt around his mattress, searching for any needles. In case of poison.

He found no needles. But he triple checked just in case.

[You've leveled up Danger Sense from 1 to 2!]

It's a good thing this is an active skill rather than a passive skill. Or he would have its constant influence just like Scenic Discoverer and Chaos Finder. Passive skills could get annoying until Joey adjusted to their magic.

Feeling satisfied, he roughed up his bedding and placed the pillow under the covers. Then he sat in the dark corner on the side where the door would swing.

Joey activated Meditative Stasis. Time became liquid but observable. With his mind cleared of clutter, Joey could track any strange changes to his room and exit stasis instantly.

He liked being in stasis. He felt calmer. His bodily needs were reduced a lot. He wouldn't need to sleep for days because of this skill.

Sleep was still necessary, but Meditative Stasis could hold it off.

This allowed him to practice the reverse channeling trick he'd started a while ago.

He pushed essence out with nowhere specific to go. It fizzled in the air without a purpose. Now he could lose 2 EP a minute doing this.

Because of his recovery increasing with time, he couldn't lose EP fast enough before filling his essence all the way. He tried harder, feeling a hint of difficulty.

By the time morning came, Joey felt a breakthrough. He managed to push out 4 EP a minute.

For what purpose?

He had no idea.

It was an interesting exercise. No new skill came from it, but Joey didn't mind.

Activating Danger Sense, Joey checked his immediate area. All was quiet. He looked outside and noticed a gathering of commoners.

They looked rough and suspicious. They were all in their mid teens in level, too. More appeared from down an alley. Fifty in all.

Very suspicious. Joey backed away from the window and gathered his stuff.

He pushed open his door carefully and looked around the seams. No strings. No traps.

He used a sword to push the door open all the way. Nothing. He visited the bathroom to do his business, then carefully went down the hall and took the stairs to the ground floor.

Breakfast was being served in a small room. The innkeeper was there with a nervous smile.

"Here, I cooked this up for you. And got fresh milk early. Sit and enjoy." The innkeeper offered a platter of oatmeal, sausages, and eggs. There was a mug of fresh cold milk to go with it.

Joey used his free hand to take the platter and sit at a table. There was nobody else having breakfast. The innkeeper continued to smile at Joey.

"What's the rule about killing commoners?" Joey asked.

"Uh, what? The rule is you can't!" The innkeeper paled. "We have to pay in advance to be revived. Unlike adventurers."

"What's the rule about commoners killing adventurers?"

"Well, you see, that's highly unlikely. You're an adventurer with better magic than us commoners. Surely, we can't harm you." The innkeeper licked his lips. "I used to be a rich man. A powerful man. I was good, too. I gave to lots of charities, you hear me?"

"Uh, huh?" The food remained untouched.

The innkeeper talked faster. "So I ended up in a stone room covered in those glowing scripts. And the only option I had was the commoner door. Why?"

"Why what?"

"Why was my only option a common start? After all, I've done?" The innkeeper shook with rage before remembering who he was addressing. "It's just not fair, is all. I could've been a great adventurer if I had the chance."

Joey had his doubts. He didn't know the innkeeper from before Multiverse Z. The man could be lying.

But he knew something suspicious was happening thanks to his new skill.

"Is the food poisoned?" Joey asked, his tone warning against dishonesty.

"They told me I'll be part of their group. Domer would give me power to lead the other commoners. It's just not fair that I didn't get a choice. I had to do it. These are powerful men, you hear me. I had to."

"I want my money back." Joey cocked his head to the side. "Plus extra for the terrible service."

The innkeeper hurried to provide Joey coins plus extra.

"This isn't enough," Joey said.

The innkeeper gave more, with a pained look on his face.

[You've looted 64 Tidal Moon Copper Coins!]

"Good enough." Joey stood and upturned the meal. It fell with a sloppy clatter before he moved for the exit.

"You're not better than me!" the innkeeper shouted at his back. "You'll be humbled by Domer! I'll tell you! You'll be humbled just like everyone else!"

If only the shadow gang can come out and enjoy the hate energy. But the time for that isn't right. Joey was still pretending to be a steady adventurer, after all. Using any of his spells would oust him.

Still, it was a little funny to have someone yelling at him about being humbled.

Joey smiled internally before putting aside all distractions and needless emotions. He exited through the front of the inn, his haul of weapons held by rope and slung on one shoulder.

The commoners had doubled in numbers. Joey gave them another analyzing sweep and saw something interesting.

[Multiverse Commoner: Basic Human: Thug lvl 28.]

Most of the commoners had job-like roles: gatherer, fisherman, builder, cleaner, hunter. But at least twenty men had the thug role and were in the mid to late 20s in level. It was obvious the thugs controlled the other commoners.

"Clever," Joey said. "The system isn't going to stop crime. But it will funnel it through obvious criminals. I don't envy you."

"Different world, same rules, little boy." A bald man with large muscles stood in front of the commoners. He had a club in his hand. So did the others around him.

"I agree and disagree," Joey said, swaying his head from side to side. "I think the rules are different. But I also think power decides who's at the top or not. And that can create an even bigger difference."

"Well, Domer's the one at the top." The thug leader sneered. "And if I were you, I'll take the walk with us and play nice. Domer's people are interested in you, but they'll take you out if you keep playing hard to get."

Joey scanned the entire group from left to right. He set his gaze on the thug leader before dropping his extra swords and daggers.

He rolled his shoulders and his neck. Then he bounced from foot to foot, warming up. "Do not worry. I won't use weapons, nor will I use my hands to strike you. They can be deadly, and I'm unsure if I'm allowed to kill you while defending myself."

The thug leader looked in disbelief. "There's a hundred of us!"

Joey blinked. "You should've brought more."

***

Liam felt horrible. He stood beside a frustrated Emelia and a scared Nate while Domer's people debated in front of them.

Liam and his friends had left the dwarven inn ten minutes ago. Ten warriors and tamers had surrounded them on the next street over. It was obvious Domer's people had been waiting for this.

Liam had thought the worst would happen. *I thought they were going to threaten Emelia.*

That hadn't been the case. But they'd gotten info out of Liam, anyway.

The warriors were in the Level 40s, so their intimidation affinity had real power to it. Emelia had improved willpower, and Nate had his spirit stat raised up. The warriors had caught Liam lacking.

I'm sorry, Joey! Liam felt like a crummy man for giving info about a kid. Now Liam had to suffer the indignity of Domer's people speaking about Joey within earshot, not caring about the weaklings listening in.

"He has passive spells that make him like a warrior," one tamer said. "But he's not a warrior. He's one or two hits away from falling flat like any rogue."

"But I can see why our rogues failed. You can't send rogues to do a warrior's job. The renegade caught them off guard," one warrior said. "Since he's reliant on dodging, we can set a trap. Once we pin him with warriors and semblances, he will feel intimidated and make a mistake."

"Can we get an archer or two to help just in case?" asked a female tamer with a giant hawk semblance. "I don't like how his moves were described. He sounds deadly when you close in on him. He wants people to fight him upfront. We might need a cleric, too."

"We can't pull any archers right now," a different warrior admitted. "They're up on the wall most of the time with the mages. And the clerics aren't worth risking for this."

"I still don't like it," the hawk tamer responded. "But maybe our street guys will take care of the renegade."

"They better take care of the renegade. Or we will," a warrior said before turning to look at Liam's group. "We might have more questions for you later. Make yourselves available in the city today. Or else."

"He's one child!" Emelia shouted, before Liam and Nate

moved in front of her.

"He's a renegade," responded the warrior. "All we had were some questions. Things could've been simple. But now we have to come down hard on this."

Domer's people walked away, leaving Liam and his group alone. For now. But Liam could tell he was going to regret being a snitch for a long while.

Emelia's anger switched from Domer's people to him. She lay into Liam with angry Spanish. He didn't bother to translate.

It took Nate's soothing words to calm Emelia down (for now) and get them going. They were going to use the plans for a ten day outing as an excuse to distract themselves.

But in truth, they were going through the motions to keep from worrying about Joey and feeling useless. It was times like these Liam saw why power mattered a lot in Multiverse Z.

"I'm so sorry, Joey," Liam muttered while looking through a market for dry foods. "I owe you a bunch."

"You think he'll be okay?" Nate asked while examining glyph tiles for more support options. "He's a tough kid for someone as earnest as him."

"They're using their street team," Emelia grunted. "With enough commoners, any adventurer could get beaten down and captured. They're going to maul the child and nobody will do a thing because it's commoners."

Emelia crushed the fruit she was holding before looking at it in surprise. Liam couldn't toss coins at the fruit vendor fast enough.

Emelia glowered at him before giving him her back, shunning him.

Liam sighed.

***

Anthony always considered himself a survivor. And part of surviving was knowing who had the most power and working for them.

He entered Multiverse Z as a builder. But after showing his talents for 'enforcement' to Domer's people, the system offered him a role switch with a change of skills and spells.

He became one of the first thugs in New Zam City. He took pride in his role and the magic that came with it. He rose faster than most commoners and had enough power to make adventurers afraid of him.

When Anthony heard about a new renegade and the damage done to the rogues last night, he knew this was a big opportunity. Success here could have him rising as a bigshot for years.

He brought a hundred men with him, the most he'd ever gathered for the street team. Anthony was confident that enough men would have the renegade under control.

It started with ten men attacking the renegade at once.

Then everything fell apart from there.

What am I looking at? Anthony gaped as the renegade lunged from man to man and left them broken.

A man fell over with his leg bent in the wrong direction. Another man dropped screaming with his arm hanging loose. Another man fell, holding his crotch, and couldn't make a sound.

In less than ten seconds, ten men lay on the ground in pain, their clubs dropped, unused. The renegade stood in the middle of the crying men, hands behind his head.

He had a bored expression on his face that angered Anthony. As if he was unimpressed. That was the pure arrogance of an adventurer who looked down on hardworking men like Anthony.

I'll be the one looking down on you, brat! Anthony waved both arms forward.

Everyone rushed forward, yelling at the top of their lungs. A few hunters shot arrows ahead of the charge. Anthony sneered, telling himself the renegade would have to fall now.

The renegade's arm blurred from behind his head while he swayed out of the way of raining arrows. Something flashed at the feet of the charge. Little lights spilled wide from the flash before turning solid into spiky items.

Men cried in pain and fell over, tripping each other. Things fell apart even more while Anthony tried to spot what the renegade had used – the items were caltrops.

Oh, no. Anthony's eyes widened as the renegade bolted through the gap in the charge.

He used fallen men like stepping stones and dashed past Anthony. The hunters cried out one at a time. The renegade was hopping up to the rooftops to reach them all.

"Over here, over here!" Anthony yelled, pointing with his club. The men slowed down and changed directions. "Don't let him run away!"

"I'm not running away," the renegade said from behind Anthony.

The thug leader spun and swung, using his Big Hit spell. His club hit nothing but air.

A foot landed on his bald head before pushing off, forcing Anthony into a stumble without causing much damage. *Did he seriously use me as a launchpad?*

Anthony shook his head and refocused on the fight. His jaw slacked as the renegade kicked and flipped from man to man. He caught Anthony's men faster than they could swing their clubs.

"Get down here or we'll bat you for the home run!" shouted a young thug, using the Threat spell.

"Here I am," the renegade said, landing and striking first. He kicked the young thug into others. They fell over like bowling pins.

Anthony saw the advantage his men had in numbers disappearing the longer the conflict went. There were more gaps now. The men hesitated when attacking.

Coordination with each other stalled. Men cried painfully on the ground or lay out unconscious, tripping up the others.

The worse things got for the street team, the stronger the renegade became. The chaos didn't slow him. It was as if he thrived in chaos.

Anthony wondered if he'd met the one adventurer who was a literal one-man army. Like an 80s action icon.

Then the action suddenly stopped, and Anthony's survival instincts yelled louder than ever. He was too late to leave. Everything had happened so fast. Too fast.

Now the renegade stood across from Anthony. Squirming or unconscious men covered the ground all over.

Anthony stared in disbelief. *He took down one hundred of us. One hundred! And I didn't even see him use a damn spell!*

The renegade hadn't punched anyone or used his weapons just like he'd said. Then Anthony thought about the caltrops and realized the rogue had lied.

"Those are weapons!" the thug pointed.

"Yes, caltrops are weapons," the renegade said. "And rogues are dishonest."

Oh no.

The renegade moved like a blur. The last thing Anthony saw was a backhand.

Did he just ... pimp slap me? Anthony fell unconscious.

***

[Congrats! You have the opportunity to learn the Dominator Skill!]

Joey used the thug leader's shirt to wipe blood and slobber off his hand. He was trying to play off feeling tired from the stamina he'd burned through. Fighting a hundred men without killing or using spells hadn't been easy.

He was unsure about the new skill offer. But he was careful not to dismiss it. The system might get angry with him if he turned it down without looking.

But it makes me think of a dominatrix. Does that make me a male dominatrix?

Weird.

But there was another concern Joey had. Something had distracted him during the street fight.

He looked at a corner of a closed down store with Danger Sense active. He felt a powerful and deadly presence hiding there.

[You've leveled up Danger Sense from 2 to 5!]

Joey sighed. "Did I stay within the rules?"

A boyish figure peeked out from around the corner. He had long platinum blond hair and sharp ears.

[Multiverse Denizen: Superior Elf: Overseer lvl 187.]

The overseer glanced at all the commoners laying on the ground. He gave Joey a thumbs up. Then he gestured for Joey to leave the area.

"Cool, thanks," Joey said, picking his stuff up from the inn's entrance. Before he left, he checked each thug for something to take.

The overseer didn't stop him. But Joey didn't linger for long. He took the street to Main Zam, with new pouches on his belt.

[You've looted 2 Tidal Moon Bronze Coins and 566 Tidal Moon Copper Coins!]

28. ROGUE UPDATE, NEW TOYS

Joey was looking through an interesting shop when he heard the nearest crystal ball turning on. He walked out and entered a small square with a garden and some colorful flowers. Commoners enjoying their day stopped and looked up, Joey doing the same.

The crystal ball stood on a tall column in the middle. It projected the nameless elf from before.

"Hello, hello, hello to our brand new humans of Multiverse Z!" the elf girl cheered. "I know this isn't the usual time for our update, but Multiverse Z can throw anything at you at any time. Right now, word's getting out about some crazy action from Southside Zam."

Joey used Stress Management and Danger Sense at the same time. The combination felt weird and lucid.

He kept calm and logical while using all his senses to search for danger. Nothing stood out, but he kept his guard up.

The commentator continued with her endless enthusiasm. "Want to know what action can get me on the crystal ball this early? Well, it's worth mentioning there was a massacre between one rogue versus five rogues in a sanctioned pvp area. The solo rogue won! And if that isn't crazy already, the same solo rogue beat up one hundred thugs without killing a single one! This morning!"

If the commoners hadn't been roused already, now they were becoming more animated. Joey kept his face impassive as people wondered aloud about the identity of the rogue, what spells they were using, and their class level.

Nobody said a thing about the rogue being a great adventurer, as if Joey's path was a myth.

I'm a little bothered that people think this is the work of a steady one, Joey said, feeling confused by his own internal reaction.

I guess this is for the best. But I wonder what the multiverse denizens are really making of this. They must know I'm a great adventurer since the guild manager knows, right? And they are lying about the thugs since there were only twenty of the hundred.

But it sounded better to say one hundred thugs.

"Now, now, everyone! I'm getting some excellent crystal ball messages sent by our beloved viewers," the commentator said. "Don't forget you can always send us a message from your nearest crystal ball with a multiverse connection. Maybe you can tell us what you've seen about this one-man army of a rogue. Though, there's some information we can't give out to the public. I bet the rogue who's on a hot streak is listening right now and would like to stay hush hush. You know how it is with rogues! Cloaks, daggers, edge, edge, edge!"

People laughed.

Joey shrugged. *Let me have my edginess. Just do me a favor, commentator lady, and don't expose too much of me.*

"But there are some things I can say! It seems like this

particular rogue is unusual. He's more aggressive and warrior-like. Some may even say he has a subtle magic that'll make it dangerous to fight him up close. Looks like our warriors have no chance against a rogue who can get in their faces! Uh oh!"

You're instigating right now, aren't you? Joey sighed internally. *You're totally instigating.*

"So, now that we all know there's an unstoppable rogue out there, watch out! We always prefer to keep New Zam City mostly pvp free. But we always have the immunity clause. We can activate that for conflicts that need settling no matter what. If that's active, our awesome multiverse denizens will corral the danger and keep the bystanders as safe as possible! As for our renegade rogue ... keep up the good work! It's so fun having a rising star around."

Joey clenched his jaw.

"Don't forget everyone. Adventure, achieve, yeah!" The commentator and people all around the city cheered together. The crystal ball shut off the projection and left Joey questioning his current plans.

I might need to get the group and leave today. Joey refused to regret his actions. In the end, he needed to stir things up and see reactions from the power players in New Zam City.

But his Danger Sense left an impression that time was not on his side. He needed to move faster and be bolder.

All in? The corner of Joey's mouth quivered, wanting to smile. *Maybe half in. For now.*

Joey returned to the crafter's shop with a brighter expression on his face – it was halfway between his usual personality and his standoffish facade.

"Sir, is this what I think this is?" Joey pointed at a particular item that caught his attention.

"Of course, this is, of course!" A happy man with a big white beard laughed as he adjusted his spectacles. He was a Level 32 crafter. Based on his level, he'd done well for himself in his commoner role. "This, sir, is what your eyes are seeing and may not believe because of our new environment. But trust me, I'm certain what lies before you is real and functional. Go ahead and touch it."

He was confident that Joey wouldn't steal it. And he should be. There were two overseers standing close to the crafter's shop.

Joey reached into the open glass box and gently picked up what his eyes weren't believing. Until he touched it and used Analyze.

[Glyphlock Pistol (Basic): Activate with essence and pull the trigger. You have a 95% chance of shooting the ball successfully. One shot.]

It looked like a flintlock pistol crafted from wood, metal, and pale crystal. The handle fitted well in Joey's grip.

His finger touched the trigger by mistake before going straight. He remembered watching war movies and videos on how guns had rules everyone should follow.

He'd never used one before.

"How?" Joey asked.

"I was a gunsmith in my last life. Why change now?" The man chuckled. "I used magic to study the glyph principles closer. Then I combined glyph working and gunsmithing ideas together. I failed a bunch. Then the system finally gave me a win and things led to creating these first products way faster than before."

"But?" Joey asked, turning the pistol over to admire it further.

"They work like glyph tiles. One use. But, but! You have to admit there's something awesome – and effective – about pointing and shooting a magic pistol with an enchanted ball. And you're a rogue, so they're going to work really damn well for you. Think of all the flippy magic folks you can surprise with one between the eyes?"

Joey nodded. "Is it possible for me to learn crafting? Through skills?"

"Hah! Sure, why not? I have spells that help me a lot. But skills are all about the subtle stuff, right? Why can't they help you with glyph crafting? It'll take time, though. And, well, a fee for my time, too."

"Can't do it now. But I gotta admit this is way awesome." Joey smiled a little. "Price?"

"Alright, don't bite my head off. It's up there. Three hundred coppers a piece."

Joey's smile tensed a little. The air around Joey became domineering. The gun crafter froze as he felt the pressure of Joey's new skill.

[Congrats! You've learned the Dominator Skill!]

[Dominator (Basic): Exude a dominating air with your expressions, words, and actions. The more dominant you are, the greater the effect. You may notice your willpower and alignment improving a little. *I was facing this immense and scary black knight. I thought I was going to die. But then the hero arrives. In a pink dress. Me and the black knight started acting like wimps. I still have nightmares of that pink dress.*]

"How's two-fifty?" the crafter offered.

[You've leveled up Dominator from 1 to 2!]

Joey relented. He didn't want to push a potential teacher

too hard. "I'll take two. And that coat on the rack back there."

The crafter brightened. He moved with gusto and offered to package the pistols. Joey turned that down and wanted to walk out with the pistols worn under the coat.

Five minutes later, Joey left the glyphlock shop feeling good and dangerous. He now had on a black coat with silver shoulder pads.

Under his coat were two pistols, his sword, a dagger, and other personal items. He'd sold off the extra stuff from the rogues last night, so he had coins to spare.

Joey was halfway down the street when he realized he was ignorant about guns and shooting. Knowing stuff from war movies and videos wasn't enough.

Joey scampered back to the glyphlock crafter and told him the truth. The man laughed.

Joey held in his irritation as he took shooting lessons and little jokes from the crafter. Since each pistol was a small fortune, Joey trained with duds and learned the basic principles quickly.

**

"You're lucky you've never shot before. You have no bad habits to slow your aim. Glyphlocks have very, very little kickback even with the magic emission. Just point, aim, shoot, which can be hard for us old gunslingers to adapt to. Also, the enchantment on the ball shot absorbs a part of your essence power, so it scales up with your spirit stat."

Wow. Joey blinked. *This feels way too perfect for me.*

"It's weird when you make it seem that simple and strong," Joey said honestly. "It feels like it should be harder to work with in a fantasy setting."

The crafter leaned close to whisper. "Well, the tricky part is getting the max damage possible. You need to always aim for the head. Think critical hits if you're into games. If it isn't a headshot, it'll do so-so damage."

Joey glanced at one of his skill descriptions.

[Headhunter (Basic): Sharpen your aim and strike true. Your attacks to the head will hit a little harder as you grow more confident. *If you're going to kill a man. Do him a favor and aim for the head. I've died quite a few times, and I rather go instantly.*]

Headhunter was level 16.

There was his other skill that could thrust through toughened enemies. Maybe it could stack.

[Armor Piercer (Basic): Thrust with power and pierce the obstacle in your way. Works best if you target a weak point unless you keep thrusting to make one. *There was once a warrior who spoke proudly of his lance. He wielded a hammer, however, so I spoke to correct him. Consequently, he corrected me with a tale of how he had been stripped bare and had to best a female orc with his lance.*]

Armor Piercer was at level 16.

Would the system let me get away with a shot counting as a thrust? Is it possible for me to stack all of this with my spirit for multi-crits?

Was it possible to make copies for his clones? He'd tried with glyph tiles. Those failed automatically. But glyphlocks were solid weapons until fired.

Once he used a pistol, regardless of its success or failure, the pistol would disintegrate. He could see why people would avoid glyphlocks and prefer magic blasts.

The latter were cheap, predictable, and easy.

But super multi-crits might make a huge difference.

The point, aim, shoot part was also appealing for anything outside of twenty feet. He would certainly need a range skill to help with his aim.

Before Joey left the shop again, he flipped one of his pistols around and grabbed it by the barrel. He swung it around and tapped the handle against his palm, feeling out its impacts. The crafter explained the pistols were as solid as any basic club until fired.

"Good to know. Thanks." Joey paid the man thirty coppers for his time.

The crafter smiled and wished him to come back anytime. He called himself Glyphlock Kristoff, an easy way to remember him.

Overall, Joey's expense at the glyphlock shop came up to five hundred thirty copper coins. The new coat and holsters came free. He liked the feel of his new wardrobe and the enchantment.

[Black Raider Coat (Basic): It won't slow your movements and is made to last.]

Joey straightened the high collar and watched the billowy sleeves open and keep his forearms bare. A button at the front closed the coat and helped conceal the pistols and his dagger.

He had a pleasant smile and an extra perk to his step, moving around throngs of people coming and going around him. He passed under lines of people moving on the plank walkways above.

He kept track of people squinting at him, using Analyze

to see his 'class' and level before giving him a questioning look.

Am I the rogue the city is going abuzz about? Joey pretended he was ignorant of the watchful and gossiping crowd. *Nah, it can't be me. I look like a kid, don't I? I'm not using Dominator to make myself stand out. And I'm smiling like a nice and perfectly sane guy.*

Then again, he was walking out in the open instead of stalking through the shadows like most rogues. So his openness and nonchalance could play against him.

So far, he sensed people giving him fifty-fifty odds of being the solo rogue. Then Joey realized a stupid thing he was doing.

He had no idea where he was going and kept forgetting to ask for help. He'd stopped at the glyphlock shop because his Scenic Discoverer skill led him there. Then he'd gotten distracted by the shiny magic guns.

"Can someone tell me what street to take for the adventurer guild?" Joey asked.

All at once, he felt people give him zero odds of being the infamous renegade. Oh, well.

A friendly commoner and his girlfriend gave Joey directions to a big road. He only had to turn left and follow it to reach the guild.

The directions were solid. Joey followed the path and enjoyed the activity and crowds better than he did yesterday.

He even spent a few coins for street food from different vendors. Fruits, barbecue, and sweet water. He hadn't had a barbecue in a while. It was an enjoyable treat along with everything else.

Flash rain came and went over New Zam City before Joey reached the guild. The humidity rose a notch while the solar moon reached its apex above.

Joey shrugged off the rain and heat. He was Miami-bred, after all. Florida had trained him for showers and sunshine.

The guild's big, intercrossed tree branches offered plenty of shade. He found adventurers hanging out and having picnics.

And his group was here, too!

Joey waved with a smile.

"Joey!" Liam flew at him for a hug. Joey sidestepped the flying archer and walked up to Emelia and Nate.

"Joey!" his group shouted at the same time.

"Yeah, that's my name. What's up?"

Emelia looked him over. Nate's hand glowed with healing magic. Liam came around from behind and had a guilty look on his face.

"Ah, I get it. Did Domer's guys give you all a hard time?" Joey glanced at Liam. "It's okay. I expected you'd tell them about me. And remember? I told you I'll handle Domer's people."

His group stared at him. Before they could question him further, Joey waved at them to follow.

They fell in step as he moved with springy steps up to the guild's entrance. The group had a bunch of questions, but they couldn't get it out or figure out what to say.

Joey would prefer to get the next parts out of the way quickly. Emelia started to ask something when the rogue waved his hand to cut her off.

"I need to take care of some things," Joey said. "Then we have to leave right after. I'll answer more questions when we put distance between us and New Zam City."

Emelia looked frustrated. Nate shrugged, willing to roll with things. Liam raised a hand.

"Yes, Liam?"

"I just wanted to say that is a nice coat. Fits you well, dude."

Joey beamed a brighter smile. "Thanks!"

The group looked at him strangely. Joey turned away and walked over to a station where crystal balls were available for public use.

He overlooked them last time, but now he was determined to get a message out to Princess Maylolee. He had her contact plate to make things easier.

He placed his hand on the crystal ball's side and watched it project options similar to a system message. He selected the option to send a message. It asked for a contact plate, which was a finger long metal with glyphs identifying an individual.

The guild could create some for him. He could give them to others just like Maylolee had given hers to him. The ball accepted the contact plate, disintegrating the item and storing its glyph info on his account. Then the ball displayed Maylolee and her impassive face.

Yup, that's her.

The ball asked him to think intently of the message he wanted to send. This was a great feature. His group was hanging nearby, and he wanted this message to be private.

[Hey, Maylolee, it's your favorite rogue, and he's still alive! Though, I probably should put the cheer aside and get to the heavy news first. I'm only alive because of others making sacrifices for me. I've taken Muragale, Mormelt,

Mavolts, and Milhiss's necklaces when we had a devil chase us.

They gave the rest of us time to escape. I promise I'll hurt and kill that devil. I promise. But other than that, Curi parted ways after dropping me off on land. I reached New Zam City, as you will know once you read this message. I've done some training. I've grown. I've changed.

I've fought and killed other humans. Steady ones, but still, I didn't feel bad about it. I still don't. I'm pretty strong compared to everyone here, but they don't know I'm a great one. Yet.

I'm about to leave the city and take three steady ones out into the wilds to level them up. I'm going to test how far they can push themselves and use that info for the rest of part one.

Also, there's this guy named Domer who is the most powerful steady adventurer here. He acts like he's the big boss. I haven't met him yet, but adventurers and commoners alike listen to him like he's a king. Er, prince.

They even tried to send a hundred thugs at me. I beat them all without killing them. It was pretty hard, especially since I'm not using my spells. It was a good workout, though.

Everyone thinks of me as an unusual warrior-like rogue. They even talked about me on the city-wide crystal ball update with the commentator lady. She is an elf, by the way! They have gnomes and dwarves here. Multiverse denizens! And they have all these rules and reactions that make it feel like a big fantasy game here.

Oh! I got these interesting things called glyphlock pistols! They're magic guns. Do you know what guns are? Have they been created before? They work best for me as a rogue because of my fortunate spirit. I think I can use them to my advantage with my abilities. If it works out like I hope, I'll be even deadlier.

Please don't assassinate me. That would be no fun.

Ugh. Man, this is becoming a long message. I'm just throwing everything at you right now. I'm in a rush, but I want to say everything I can.

How are you? Are you still training your people hard and being bored all the time?

I'm going to come back with an army of adventurers and make you take a day off, okay? I'll probably bring you new headaches, too. But I feel like in the short time we've known each other you can tell I'll be trouble.

So, yeah, tell me what's been up with you. I'll read it when I get back in the next ten days. Chances are I'll have other crazy stuff to share.

Also, sorry for the text wall. And I'm sorry about the deaths. I'll end this message now for real. Until next time.]

Joey winced at the cringy writing. *Ugh, I've always sucked at these.*

He let himself feel awkward. Then he sighed and sent the message as it was.

Immediately, he felt like a doofus, regretted his decision, and forced himself to let it go in the end.

Joey turned to the most available guild worker. He completely ignored the guild manager watching from his great management office.

It was time to pick up ten quests to get great results on. And escape the city with his steady ones.

29. THE UNSTOPPABLE RENEGADE

"Joey, we need to talk," Emelia said firmly.

Uh oh. I don't think she'll let me slide by this time. Joey slowly nodded before looking around.

The guild had sections for loot, giving out quests, using crystal balls, having meetings, and more. He found the hall with private rooms and checked with an ear to the doors until he found an empty one. His group entered after him, nobody taking a seat.

It was a nice room. Jungle theme, like most of the guild. But Joey could tell nobody cared about the decor while he looked around to distract himself.

Finally, he let out a sigh and looked into Emelia's eyes.

"Ask away."

"Are you okay?" Emelia asked, catching him off guard.

Of course, I'm okay! Joey took a few seconds to put that

into words. "Yes. Why wouldn't I be?"

"You've been attacked in the city multiple times," Emelia said. "I'm assuming the city update was about you, right?"

"Yup."

Emelia shook her head like she was dealing with a troublesome grandchild. "Domer's people are going to go all out now. But I have to wonder if this is something you want to happen. This has me feeling, Joey, that you are more of a stranger than I initially thought and that I've misjudged you."

"Well, to be honest, it's only been a day since we've met him," Liam said.

"And he's doing well, isn't he?" Nate asked desperately. "Please, let's not lose our dodge tank."

Emelia ignored the men.

Joey looked at each of the older adults with long gazes. "Yes."

"Yes?" Emelia raised her eyebrow.

"I want Domer's people to go all out. So I can beat them. I'll get [#5] easier that way." Joey tilted his head slightly. "I don't like his people. They are too rude and pushy. So I'll fight them. Each and everyone. I'll fight Domer, too."

"Would you fight and slay us?" Emelia asked harshly. "Is that why you want us to level up? For the achievement."

"No," Joey said. "You're not my enemies. I just want to see if you can level up fast if push comes to shove. Besides, you can't stay in the city. Domer's going to come after you while I keep beating his people."

"Everything he's saying is the truth," Nate admitted.

"You can deceive others using the truth," Emelia said.

"Joey, I know there's something dishonest about you. How can I trust you? What if you're worse than Domer?"

"Okay, hold up, time out." Liam stepped in. "This is spiraling into some bad territory. Let me have a chat with Joey for a bit." Emelia and Nate were going to protest, but Liam cut them off quickly. "Just give me this one, okay? I wasn't the only one caught by Domer's people, unable to do anything. You two were right there with me as I snitched. Are you saying you would've done better? No? Then back off for a bit."

Liam hooked an arm around the rogue – and Joey allowed it. They exited the room and went to another private room.

"Emelia's going to curse your whole family tree," Joey said.

"Eh, let her. I don't have much on the family front," Liam said, sitting against the table. "So, what's up, Joey? What are you really?"

Hm, this is interesting. Liam isn't intellectual, willful, or aligned. He's the only one who can't pressure me even a little.

Joey looked the former L.A. teacher up and down. He glanced back at the door, knowing Emelia and Nate were outside in the hallway.

"I'm really someone who enjoys fighting," Joey said. "I love the powers I have. I'm greedy as hell. And getting new levels, stats, and achievements is fun. I just want to share that while accomplishing some big goals. I know I'm being vague, but I don't feel comfortable explaining things while inside the city. It's out there I can show you who I really am."

Liam looked at him without saying anything for a while. The man nodded slowly before readjusting the large bow he carried across his torso. "I believe you. And, honestly, we really do need to leave or Domer's people will have their boots on our necks. Trust me, that's no fun."

"I would break their necks in return," Joey said.

"Whew. Man. You are intense." Liam sighed. "So, ten days out? That'll be plenty of time for two quests."

"Ten."

"Yeah, I said ten days."

"Ten quests."

"Ten quests? We can't take on ten quests."

In the next few minutes, Joey let Liam convince Emelia to calm down and roll with things. Nate helped Liam get past Emelia's willful spirit.

Both men wanted to take a gamble on Joey. That took a lot of trust or desperation since they only knew Joey for a day. But the situation with Domer added enough pressure for the older adults to make rash decisions.

Thanks, Domer! Joey smiled a little as he walked up to an available guild worker. The male elf wore a stylish suit, merging modern designs with fantasy concepts. He gave Joey a welcoming smile.

"How may I serve you, adventurer?"

[Multiverse Denizen: Superior Elf: Quest Giver lvl 157.]

"Answer me this, did you apply for this job or were you chosen?" Joey asked.

The elf laughed. "Sorry, personal questions can't be answered except for certain conditions. And no, I can't tell you what those conditions are."

"Fine, fine. I'm in a rush, anyway. So, let me have ten quests ranging from Level 45 to 55 in difficulty. It'll be for me, Joey, and those three behind me, Emelia, Liam, and Nate."

"Unfortunately, Joey, we aren't allowed to give more than two quests," the elf replied. "And you must succeed on one quest first before we can trust you with two at the same time."

Joey could feel his group looking at him hard. The rogue readjusted the high collar on his new coat. "No exceptions?"

The elf looked up in thought. "I can send a message to the manager for you."

Joey tried to keep a neutral expression on his face. Was this part of the guild manager's plan? Was the quest giver in on it or did the guild manager keep his great knowledge to himself?

The elf waited patiently with an innocent look on his face. But Joey figured a Level 157 superior elf could play pretend easily.

"Yeah, give the manager a message. Tell him it'll be worth it." Joey watched the elf turn to handle a crystal ball that was out of sight.

"You haven't completed a quest here?" Emelia asked accusingly.

"It doesn't matter," Joey said, not sure if that was true or not. This was the first test of how far his great status could push things in New Zam City.

I'll look like a fool if the manager says no.

The quest giver looked up with a smile. "Well, the manager is being especially nice today. He's making an exception and allowing you to take on ten quests."

Emelia lunged against the desk. "Has that ever happened before?"

The elf blinked. "No. Not during this beginner challenge."

Emelia turned her head shakily and looked down at Joey. Her eyes widened as the pieces fell in place inside of her head. The men looked confused, still slow on the upkeep.

"Emelia," Joey said softly. "No more questions until we're far away from New Zam City."

"Yes, Joey," Emelia said quickly.

"And remember, I'm trusting you as much as you're trusting me." Joey smiled at her. "Please don't make me regret this."

Emelia looked down like she was a young girl being scolded. Liam and Nate stared at the interaction with open shock.

The quest giver added ten quests to everyone's singularities. Joey ensured each quest was a beast hunt that took them further away from New Zam City. The biggest problem was carrying all the proof required to receive their quest results.

"We have quest crystals that can do the work for you. But they come at a notable expense," the elf admitted.

"Can we get another exception?" Joey asked.

The elf messaged the manager. Once he received a reply, he turned and smiled.

"Yes, you can have another exception. All the crystals are empty. But once you use them, they'll key in to a quest if you focus on the singularity. That way, you don't have to carry proof. You just have to aim the crystal at the kills to record your progress and bring them back."

Interesting design, but why would the system create extra steps for people to earn their awards when the system itself can keep track? I can only think of the system doing this to create extra hassle. Just to make things harder. Maybe to create further challenges.

As Joey thought about the system's unique designs, he felt Emelia staring at him like he was an alien from another planet. Liam and Nate hadn't made the full logical leap just yet, but the men seemed to know something was off.

Joey let them be while collecting all the crystals into a pouch.

Quests and crystals acquired, Joey turned to look over his group. They all had packs and pouches stuffed with provisions and gear. They looked more ready for the outing than Joey.

Nobody was challenging him anymore. Emelia couldn't even look him in the face.

Huh, maybe we might make it out alright if things can stay with me in control, Joey thought, nodding to himself.

The big crystal ball in the lobby room turned on. Instead of the commentator lady getting projected, an alarm sounded with flashing red lights.

The words **[Immunity Clause Activated!]** crawled across the projection. Then more words followed: **[16 from Domer's People versus 4 from The Unstoppable Renegades. Everyone beware of the city-wide pvp action and find your nearest shelter or multiverse denizen for protection!]**

***

Congrats, Domer, you're going to force me to use one of my spells. Joey sighed, feeling a little frustrated.

He felt annoyed with Domer's people targeting his group for a slaughter fest. And he couldn't allow himself to play around with the lives of his group.

Even if they could revive in five days' time, that slowed his plans. It also bothered him since he had the power to even the playing field. But he didn't want to reveal too much in the city.

I have to give up something. Acting like an unusual battle rogue won't be enough if they have a solid team composition with warriors, tamers, and archers. If they have one mage or cleric in there, that can make things even harder. And I'm going to be distracted by the danger my group will be in.

Joey looked at his fretting group. The older adults had their weapons out while looking around the lobby area for an attack that could spring at any moment.

Joey was the only one who remained impassive and unarmed.

After all, he was Level 40 with overpowered abilities. The others were Level 30 with average abilities. The older adults were completely outmatched.

Glancing to the side, Joey saw the guild manager standing at the entrance of his great office. The epic elf smiled intently at Joey.

They both knew what this conflict was all about. Could Joey rise to the occasion and hold the manager's attention?

A test, huh? Joey rolled his shoulders. *I have to succeed now. This can decide how much I can leverage later.*

Dominator activated, Joey leered at his group. "I told you I'll handle Domer's people. Stick together. Protect yourselves. Fight if you have to. But leave the rest for me."

"We're dead, Joey!" Nate blubbered.

"I'll shoot whoever I can," Liam said with little conviction.

"You'll need more than what you've shown so far," Emelia said softly. "They'll know everything except for what you haven't shown."

Joey grinned fiercely, letting his dominant energy spread around his group. A blob of shadow flew out of him and hit the ground at their feet.

The older adults backed away.

A clone stood with a smile and two glyphlock pistols in hand.

"Call me Two Guns!" The clone laughed like a maniac.

Another clone appeared with two pistols. "Oh, man, I can taste the hate energy in the air. Hell yes."

A third clone formed with the same weapons. "Haters, beware! The shadow gang is strapped with g-locks! We are ain't playing in these streets!"

"What is happening?" Nate asked, completely out of the loop.

"I really need to hear the full story now," Liam said.

Emelia nodded as Joey and his clones strode out of the guild. The group lingered in the back while Joey checked for danger from the top of the stairs.

He received a heads up of an incoming arrow. The fight started earnestly from there.

Joey ducked out of the way, his clones scrambling in different directions.

He caught sight of four aggressive adventurers and four semblances pressing him. Two archers aimed and fired from the far corners of the guild courtyard.

Joey ran and rolled, avoiding deadly shots while using

Analyze.

[Multiverse Adventurer: Basic Human: Archer lvl 44.]

[Multiverse Adventurer: Basic Human: Archer lvl 49.]

[Multiverse Adventurer: Basic Human: Warrior lvl 45.]

[Multiverse Adventurer: Basic Human: Warrior lvl 47.]

[Multiverse Adventurer: Basic Human: Tamer lvl 46.]

[Multiverse Adventurer: Basic Human: Tamer lvl 42.]

[Adventurer Semblance: Small Beast: Jungle Boar lvl 45.]

[Adventurer Semblance: Small Bird: Snatch Hawk lvl 47.]

[Adventurer Semblance: Small Reptile: Croc lvl 48.]

[Adventurer Semblance: Small Reptile: Frilly Leaper lvl 43.]

Weaker ones first!

Joey shifted directions fast and ran straight at the charging semblances and adventurers. He ducked under another arrow aimed at his head and rolled under a red crescent wave swung from the two-handed sword of a warrior.

The pale leaper semblance reached him first, teeth glistening with poison.

A shadow clone formed beside Joey and aimed both pistols, triggers pulled. One failed, a dud. The other thrust a ball through the leaper's head and turned the semblance into sparkles.

[You've slain the Semblance of a Small Reptile Frilly Leaper lvl 43! Experience awarded!]

Before the adventurers could fully understand what

they saw, Joey pushed hard against them to leverage their confusion. He formed six more clones and dove into the chaos.

He sidestepped a crashing poleaxe that hit the ground loudly. He vaulted over a tamer trying to tackle him with her hands formed into talons. The big sword warrior swung too late to catch him while Joey soared by.

The jungle boar ran to his side while the croc lunged to bite him out of the air. Joey twisted his body around like a genius acrobat, kicking off the boar's head before tucking into a roll down the croc's back.

"Archers, what are you doing?" shouted a tamer with a wolf-like face.

[You've slain a Basic Human Archer lvl 44! Experience awarded!]

The other archer was busy in a shootout with two of Joey's clones. The archer was winning, but his attention was taken by the clones while the other archer lay dead.

"Should you pay attention to the archers or me?" Joey asked as a bunch of magic guns popped off all at once.

[You've slain the Semblance of a Small Beast Jungle Boar lvl 45! Experience awarded!]

[You've slain the Semblance of a Small Reptile Croc lvl 48! Experience awarded!]

Joey dismissed the clones that unleashed bullet hell on the semblances. He hadn't planned to aim for them first, but something shifted inside of him when he killed the frilly leaper semblance.

The hawk was outside of his range, unfortunately.

An explosive arrow struck the hawk's wing and dropped it closer. A clone jumped off the back of another and fired both pistols into the hawk's face.

[You've slain the Semblance of a Small Bird Snatch Hawk lvl 47! Experience is reduced for having assistance.]

[You've leveled up Shade Dragon Rogue from 40 to 41!]

It was bound to happen! Joey spread his free points.

[You've raised your mind from 112 to 115!]

[You've raised your body from 112 to 115!]

[You've raised your spirit from 121 to 123!]

"Dammit, he's getting stronger!" The female tamer with the talons pointed.

"Can't trust tamers for anything," the poleaxe warrior muttered. The big sword warrior backed him up as they closed the distance on Joey.

The wolf tamer dodged shots at his face and rip the last clone apart. The remaining archer, the Level 49 one, had fled from the scene after winning the shootout with Joey's clones.

Four on one. An ideal situation. But Joey wasn't alone.

His group sprung their attack. Nate locked the wolf tamer in a walled zone. Emelia rained down magic bolts from above. Liam struck an arrow on the man's leg, hobbling him as the concussive blasts beat him down.

Tamers had tough bodies, so he'd survive. Joey pressed the other tamer to keep her pressured, knowing the warriors would chase him.

The big sword warrior shouted with an aggro-attracting spell. It failed against Joey's pride and dominance.

The poleaxe warrior sped up with magic and prepared to attack Joey's back. A clone appeared in the way while aiming pistols at the poleaxe warrior's face.

The man canceled his attack and covered his face, blocking one bullet while the other came out as a dud. The bullet pierced the armor and left some serious damage, but the poleaxe warrior pushed through the pain to defend himself from the clone's palm strikes.

Given some time with the female tamer, Joey drew his sword and carved into her. She tried to claw and grab him, but he moved with finesse and kept laying the blade on her tough body, ripping her apart. Blood poured from her wounds as she tried to fight Joey off.

A clone formed behind her and aimed two pistols at her head. Both executed just fine, leaving a big hole in the back of her skull.

[You've slain a Basic Human Tamer lvl 42! Experience awarded!]

The warriors killed his clone and faced the original.

"Don't look down on us!" shouted the big sword warrior. He swung from overhead, swept across at chest height, and finished with a thrust.

Joey stepped and rolled out of the way of each strike, creating space. He formed another clone in front of the poleaxe warrior and switched weapons with it.

The clone grabbed his sword.

Joey grabbed shadow copies of the glyphlocks. The sword warrior lunged with a shoulder ram, trying to hide his face behind his big pauldron.

The rogue spun behind the warrior's back. The desperate man turned and swung with all his might and magic.

Joey hopped over the super blade swing. He set his feet on the warrior's pauldrons and pressed the barrels into the man's face. One glyphlock fired, creating a cavity in the warrior's head. Good enough.

[You've slain a Basic Human Warrior lvl 45! Experience awarded!]

"No!" shouted the poleaxe warrior, shoving the distracting clone away. When the warrior looked back, he found Joey flying at him fast.

No weapons. Only the back of his hand. The rogue struck, and the warrior tumbled backward.

Joey walked off the landing and received his sword from his clone before dismissing it. The poleaxe warrior shook off the hit faster than expected, his eyes glowing with magic.

He lunged at Joey with harder and faster attacks, forcing the rogue backward. The poleaxe head chopped down and thrust forward with blurring speed. It even sliced Joey's side, cutting open his coat and flesh, drawing blood.

The poleaxe warrior gave the rogue a mean grin.

Joey reached under his coat.

The warrior raised his vambraces to cover his face.

He cried out when a dagger hit his thigh with a bloody thunk. A sword up the jaw silenced his cry, the tip bursting from the top of the skull and spraying a fountain of blood.

[You've slain a Basic Human Warrior lvl 47! Experience awarded!]

Joey turned and looked over at the beaten down wolf tamer. He was still alive while kept in a magic cage. The level 30 adventurers had done well and remained unharmed.

"Want the kill?" Liam asked.

"Yes, please." Joey took his dagger from the poleaxe

warrior and threw it at the wolf-face tamer.

Headshot.

[You've slain a Basic Human Tamer lvl 46! Experience is reduced for having assistance.]

Five adventurer kills. Eleven more to go. And the system numbers were going up.

[You've leveled up Shade Dragon Rogue from 41 to 42!]

...

[You've raised your mind from 115 to 118!]

[You've raised your body from 115 to 118!]

[You've raised your spirit from 123 to 125!]

[You've leveled up Danger Sense from 5 to 6!]

[You've leveled up Dominator from 2 to 5!]

Joey checked the achievement list, hoping his hunch was right. He'd felt a radical change there.

[#5 – Slay 100 steady adventurers above your level! 13/100.]

Well, well, well. Joey smiled. *Semblances count!*

Joey's greed pulsed with hunger. The tamers were now an endangered species.

30. ROGUE OF THE MULTIVERSE

Joey looted from the corpses quickly, ignoring his injury and his frigid channels. He didn't trust anyone to respect the sacredness of loot going to the killer, especially when it was him.

In the meantime, all the adventurers and denizens watching from the guild entrance or around the courtyard were going crazy like esport fans. The adventurers were the most excited, which was clear by their comments:

"Bro! Did you see him double-up on the tamer girl and put two to the back of her head?"

"Yeah, I saw that! It was a straight up execution!"

"He summoned his own firing squad and laid waste to all the semblances like they were nothing!"

"There is no freaking way they can let him run a build like that. The system needs to nerf it."

"Are those really magic flintlocks? Is that a new rogue spell? And he can copy himself, too. That's a strong strategy."

"He's overpowered!"

"The guy with the poleaxe got it dirty. Knife to the leg. Then a sword up the head. Wow."

"Maybe leg armor and a helmet are worth it."

"Screw that. Where's the full-on tower shields?"

"If rogues can pop off like that, then get the spears, too. We need a whole phalanx out there. The meta is shifting fast."

"Ban him! Ban his spells! To hell with it, ban the whole rogue class!"

The denizens spoke with hush tones, showing their excitement with thumbs up and claps. Half the staff had come out to watch while the others had to continue working. The guild manager watched from behind his subordinates, smiling intensely at Joey.

"No pistol skill yet," Joey said to himself. "But things worked out better than expected."

Other than the firing success dropping from 95% to 70%, the magic guns worked well enough when copied by his clones. They stacked hardcore with his Headhunter and Armor Piercer skills.

Even with the pistols having reduced damage from being shadow copies, the multi-crits made up for it, anyway.

The five hundred thirty coppers paid to Glyphlock Kristoff had been well worth it. And Joey was making back his investment quickly.

[You've looted 378 Tidal Moon Copper coins, 1 Health Potion (Basic), 2 Stamina Potions (Basic), 1 Essence Potion (Basic), 3 Stun Glyph Tiles (Basic).]

I didn't give them time to use the stun glyph tiles, Joey thought. *I better watch out for the tricky tiles they might use. That can change an entire fight.*

"Hey, Joey, want me to heal that?" Nate pointed at the bleeding gash on Joey's side.

"Yes, please, and thank you." Joey looked around the courtyard and didn't sense anymore danger.

He relaxed a little as Nate healed the gash. The magic felt pleasant even if it took a minute.

"How much essence did you spend?" Emelia asked, as she and Liam approached carefully.

"Over 1100 EP," Joey answered. "I was feeling the big chill while up against the poleaxe warrior. That's why he got me."

"Dude, what the heck? That's a lot!" Liam shook his head in amazement. "How are you not a popsicle right now?"

Good question. Joey was unsure how he'd pushed his essence so hard without the deep freeze. That fight had gone by fast, too.

He had to press Domer's people hard to keep them in a constant state of chaos. That had kept them from adapting properly.

I can still feel Chaos Finder's influence. I have the advantage as long as I keep pushing before Domer's people can figure things out.

Joey checked with Danger Sense. The skill had a unique view of situations depending on what was likely the biggest threat.

Waiting felt dangerous.

Aggression felt safer.

Joey popped a bottle open and drained the essence potion.

[You've recovered 500 EP. But you're now immune to essence potions for the next hour.]

Joey smiled as he felt his channels warm up and refill. It didn't thaw him out completely. But that was okay. Movement would help warm up his channels. It was time to hustle.

"We need to find the rest of them," Joey said.

"Couldn't we take the option to run?" Nate asked, finished with healing Joey.

"No running. I agree we need to attack," Emelia said, tapping the end of her staff on a root. "It will make them think twice before chasing us in the wilds. But let's be honest. We're reliant on you, Joey."

"Fine by me."

"We'll need a tamer to hunt the archer who ran," Liam said. "Or use my tracker skill. It's not that good, though."

"Every skill can be useful if trained enough," Joey said.

He was fine with relying on Liam's skill, but a powerful presence revealed himself nearby. It was the boyish elf from before. The overseer.

"Hey, can we get help from you?" Joey asked.

The overseer nodded.

"Can you tell us where they are exactly?"

He shrugged.

"Can you lead us?"

The overseer turned and jogged out of the courtyard. Joey's group followed close behind, Emelia running with a quizzical look on her face.

"Can I ask about this?" Emelia pointed at the overseer's

back.

"I met him when I beat up those one hundred thugs. He was pretty chill with me, so it's cool he's helping me out." Joey smiled. "I bet the denizens want this conflict handled so the city can go back to normal. So, yeah, they're going to lead us straight to the fights."

"And keep innocent people safe, right?" Nate asked.

"Honestly, I think the denizens are more interested in the fights than protecting everyone," Liam said. "They give that vibe."

Emelia had a thoughtful look, hesitating to speak her mind. Then she blurted out, "Will you show more of yourself?"

Joey thought about it. "Maybe. It'll make things faster if I do. But I'll try to hold off as long as possible."

The streets of New Zam City looked like they were abandoned during an apocalypse. Lots of stuff had been dropped to the floor while commoners took shelter.

Faces looked out with scared or excited expressions from windows and doorways. It really felt like the entire city had been manipulated for two groups to get into a slaughter fest with each other.

Empty squares. Empty lots. Empty gardens and parks.

The only souls walking outside were adventurers who didn't fear the conflict, confident of their abilities. It would be easy to get lulled into a sense of tranquility while moving from one fight to another. But Joey's danger senses were tingling.

Joey activated one of the stun tiles and threw it behind him. He also pointed and shouted, "Nate, zone right there!"

The cleric reacted fast even while fearing for his life. His zoning spell walled the area around the bursting stun tile. The blast knocked a camouflaged man into open view.

The rogue shouted in surprise before sprinting hard to get away. He slammed into one of Nate's walls and stunning himself some more. The cleric grunted since he was locking down a Level 49 rogue.

"Liam," Joey said.

"Say no more." An arrow struck the rogue in the leg before he could jump away.

"Emelia, watch our backs." Joey took over from there, grappling hook and rope in hand.

Before the rogue could finally reorientate himself, the rope coiled around him and sunk the hook into his stomach. The man screamed while Joey yanked him back.

"Get over here," Joey said.

Nate dropped the walls. The enemy rogue hit the ground in front of Joey. The man didn't stay down for long. His body released a burst of magic and unraveled the rope and threw off the hook.

"An escape spell!" Emelia warned.

"A quick backhand." Joey struck the rogue before he could run, staggering him. "How about another sample?" Joey smacked the rogue back to the ground.

The man twisted around to crawl away. Stalking from behind, Joey grabbed his rope and wrapped multiple loops around the enemy rogue's neck. Then Joey stomped on the rogue's back and yanked hard – snap!

[You've slain a Basic Human Rogue lvl 49! Experience is reduced for having assistance.]

"I leveled up from that," Nate admitted.

"Same," Liam said.

"I leveled up from the tamer," Emelia said.

"Good," Joey growled. "Keep helping me as I clear them. That'll reduce the experience I gain."

The group stared at him.

"He really wants [#5]," Nate said.

Emelia shook her head and muttered in Spanish.

Liam chuckled. "I have to give it to you, Joey. You got that dog in you."

"Not a dog." Joey looted the rogue.

[You've looted 1 Tidal Moon Bronze Coin, 189 Tidal Moon Copper Coins, 1 Poison Gas Glyph Tile, 1 Poison Antidote.]

Joey flashed a feral smile at his steady ones. "I have a dragon in me."

***

The overseer led them to a five story building in a decent business district. Joey assessed the structure from the shade, gave his group a simple game plan, and jumped from a nearby rooftop to get the drop on the semblances guarding the front door. The shadowstalker looked up, ready to bat him out of the air with a big paw.

An arrow to the shoulder distracted the semblance and gave Joey his window of opportunity. He slid his sword through the semblance's skull.

[You've slain the Semblance of a Big Cat Shadowstalker lvl 44! Experience is reduced for having assistance.]

Joey stepped back, tossing active glyph tiles in front of him. The entire first floor of the tower had semblances ready to rush out and tear apart intruders.

The other front door guard was a feral monkey. From the door rushed a feathered snake, a giant praying mantis, a man-sized spider, a big-mouthed lizard, a raptor-like bird, another shadowstalker, and a second monkey.

Nate's zone spell had no hope of holding a menagerie of ghost beasts in the level 40s. But he still used it for one purpose: to slow them down. The walls held long enough for the eruption of two stun tiles and the poison gas tile.

The seven semblances cried out in surprise and anger. They were disorientated so badly they struck at each other.

Liam landed an arrow on each one. Emelia made it rain volleys of magic bolts. And Joey walked into the poison cloud, the antidote in his body, and finished each semblance with a sword thrust to their heads.

Eight different slain messages came up. Joey skipped past them for the most important message.

[You've leveled up Shade Dragon Rogue from 42 to 43!]

...

[You've raised your mind from 118 to 121!]

[You've raised your body from 118 to 121!]

[You've raised your spirit from 125 to 127!]

Joey gestured for his group to wait. He used Danger Sense to check for traps before entering through the front.

The first floor was a simple lobby with couches and a desk. The staircase was to the left of the front door.

Glowing glyph tiles flew down the staircase. Joey jumped behind the farthest couch as the tiles erupted into firebombs. The poison burned up fast, and so did the air. Joey felt the heat but avoided serious damage.

He formed a clone and took its shadow glyphlocks. Joey nodded at the clone before his copy ran out from behind the couch and shouted nonsense. A magic beam struck the clone, destroying it.

"Yee haw! I smoked the varmint up and got him! I told you I knew what I was doing!"

Joey stood from behind the couch and fired true with one of the glyphlocks. The other was a dud. No problem.

[You've slain the Basic Human Mage lvl 45! Experience awarded!]

"Dammit! I knew we shouldn't let the mage go down. He's as dumb as the smartest rock!" shouted a man up on the second floor. Then the same man spoke to Joey. "Watch it, renegade! We're loaded up here. Glyph tiles and all!"

"Don't be so scared," Joey said with a domineering voice. "Come down and fight me."

The man said nothing back.

A specific bird call sounded from out the front. Joey moved carefully to the door while facing the staircase. He slipped out and found Emelia beckoning him from the corner of the building.

Sprinting around, Joey followed her to a hanging rope. Up top, the hook was latched to the fourth-floor window. Nate was there to keep watch of their climb.

Emelia went up first. Joey went up like a squirrel.

"All down below us," Liam whispered while guarding the staircase. A glyph tile was active at his feet, dampening the noise in a circle around them. Smart move.

"Emelia, got a glyph ritual for us?" Joey asked.

One of Emelia's spells dealt with inscribing and casting glyph rituals with her fingers. It took time, but the group crouched by the stairs patiently as Emelia wrote glyphs on the floor.

She finished. The pale scriptures flashed with a slight blue light. The magic sunk into each group member.

[You've received the Essence Power Buff Singularity for 10 minutes!]

[Essence Power Buff (Basic/10 minutes): A buff from Emelia. Your magic is 25% more powerful for 10 minutes.]

"Follow me. Just like our first time together." Joey led the way down.

The stairs were stacked over each other. He sneaked low enough to peek around the railing.

He spotted the cleric at the top of the next stairs below. The archer was with him, looking down with a grim expression.

Joey leaned back and considered his next move. He decided to go with the dynamic entry option.

One clone later, Joey jumped over the railing and fell sideways, aiming two pistols at two targets. He lucked out and shot true for both.

[You've slain the Basic Human Archer lvl 49! Experience is reduced for having assistance.]

The cleric survived with the top of his head missing a chunk. But it was still some good shooting.

[Congrats! You have the opportunity to learn the Glyphlock Hitman Skill!]

[Congrats! You've learned the Glyphlock Hitman Skill!]

The cleric collapsed down the stairs. Shouts rang out from below. Hard footsteps crashed up the stairs, bringing the fight up to Joey.

Good.

Two tamers reached the third floor and crashed into a zone, Nate grunting from the exertion. Emelia lunged with a magic spearhead extending from her staff. She hamstrung one tamer while Liam fired over her head and pinned arrows into the other tamer.

Joey pierced the skull of the arrow-damaged tamer with his sword. He let go of the handle and ducked a mantis scythe from the other tamer.

A palm strike to the jaw staggered the mantis man and forced him to brace against the stair railing – he had the leg injury from Emelia slowing him. More arrows and another magic spear thrust tore the tamer apart.

Joey wrenched his sword from one tamer's head and thrust it into the other's chest. A dagger to the eye worked as the finisher. Too bad the mantis tamer dropped away with Joey's blades and fell on top of a spying warrior.

[You've slain a Basic Human Tamer lvl 44! Experience is reduced for having assistance.]

[You've slain a Basic Human Tamer lvl 49! Experience is reduced for having assistance.]

"Run, we have to run!" the warrior yelled, shoving the body off him with a shield. "Activate all the tiles and blow this place!"

Joey used Danger Sense and received a big warning. Not just for himself, either. His entire group was in serious danger now.

Joey felt a rush of anger.

"Okay, no more mister nice rogue," Joey grunted before taking a deep breath.

As Joey inhaled, the back of his throat emitted a dark light. Shady sparks flew out of the corner of his mouth. A dark furnace burned greatly inside him.

He waved his group back up to the fourth floor.

Once they fled up safely, Joey dashed down to the second floor and dropped amid the remaining enemies.

Lines of darkness faded from behind Joey as he looked around. Three warriors. Two tamers. And a dying cleric.

One warrior was holding a glyph tile next to a stack of them wrapped in magic bands. Joey zeroed in on that warrior as if he was preparing a bomb.

Joey stepped around a sword strike. A shield's rim rushed at his head. He ducked below while rolling past the grasping tamers. The warrior with the tile panicked and threw it away.

His comrades shouted in alarm and dove to the side. The tile sparkled as it landed on the dying cleric.

My kill. Joey's tail unrolled from inside of him, flickering in and out of view. It punctured the cleric's head before the tile burst into a mini pyre, consuming the body with red fire.

[You've slain a Basic Human Cleric lvl 50! Experience is reduced for having assistance.]

"We have him surrounded! Attack!" The last five enemies charged at once.

Joey roared, breathing dark flames in a circle around him. They phased through furniture, walls, and mundane materials, hungering for essence and magic. All five stopped their gang attack and screamed, the shady embers coating them with no mercy.

Shade Dragon Breath feasted on their essence. It burned greater, torching the humans from the inside out.

Their flesh bubbled and smoldered. Their screams became animalistic before their vocal cords snapped.

The warriors had the good fortune of dying first. The tamers took a little longer to cook, thrashing on the floor in a futile attempt to snuff out the inner dark flames. They eventually died.

The danger of the tower being burned down disappeared as the glyph tiles disintegrated without activating. Once all the essence and magic materials were eaten up, the shady flames died out. All that remained were black skeletons and ash piles.

With the battle won, Joey checked the slain messages.

[You've slain a Basic Human Warrior lvl 47! Experience is reduced for having assistance.]

[You've slain a Basic Human Warrior lvl 48! Experience is reduced for having assistance.]

[You've slain a Basic Human Warrior lvl 43! Experience is reduced for having assistance.]

[You've slain a Basic Human Tamer lvl 46! Experience is reduced for having assistance.]

[You've slain a Basic Human Tamer lvl 47! Experience is reduced for having assistance.]

Joey checked the achievement list.

[#5 – Slay 100 steady adventurers above your level! 31/100.]

Darn it. That one warrior at level 43 didn't count or I would have thirty-two. But other than him, I made a serious dent in this achievement.

Joey felt satisfied with his progress. But he'd have to be careful with his levels until he could complete **[#5]** or find steady adversaries at higher levels.

He hoped people would keep wanting to fight him despite his new arsenals and powers. Glyphlock Hitman might scare potential prey ... steady ones ... away.

[Glyphlock Hitman: Within 8 feet, your success rate when firing glyphlock guns becomes 16% higher. Within 24 feet, your aim and reaction will be admirable while having room for improvement. And don't forget, you can always pistol whip. *Why are there magic flintlocks? What are we now? Pirates traversing the Caribbean? At least, these things are more likely to fail or miss a shot than do any good. They're faulty things, really. A trap for newbies.*]

Joey chuckled. Now his original glyphlock pistols could always fire true at max power. The shadow glyphlocks would have an 82% success rate within six feet of a target.

The clones might pistol whip more often, too. The only bad thing was the max effective range at twenty-four feet for himself, eighteen feet for his clones.

That wasn't much further than his tail's max range, which was twenty feet for himself and fifteen feet for his clones. Joey had long noticed skills didn't change ranges, but added more power or control with levels.

I am a rogue. It wouldn't be fair to archers if I can shoot like a sniper. It also makes it less of a cheat power and more of a combat option. Now I can attack with my tail, short swords, knives, empty hands, pistols, a dragon breath, and anything else I can use for Assassin Grappling. Oh, and glyph tiles are always an option, too.

These were all close range options, but his options were plentiful. In other words, Joey was making himself the most dangerous person to have in a room.

**

Feeling ready to move on, Joey walked up two floors and found his group huddled in the corner. They looked at him with complete and utter fear. Joey's attention was mostly on their levels.

[Multiverse Adventurer: Basic Human: Cleric lvl 34.]

[Multiverse Adventurer: Basic Human: Archer lvl 34.]

[Multiverse Adventurer: Basic Human: Mage lvl 35.]

"Nice. You've all gained some solid levels from this," Joey said, smiling.

Nate was pointing with a shaky finger, his stutters making it difficult to understand him. Then he finally blurted out, "Tail. Ghost tail."

The twenty foot Shade Dragon Tail swayed behind the rogue. It felt nice letting it out after trapping it for so long. Joey smiled, as if having a ghost tail was perfectly normal.

He noticed Liam glancing up at the ceiling, struggling to split his attention from the rogue and the thing he was sensing above. Joey felt no danger coming from up there. What could it be?

"It's a voice," Liam said, pointing up.

"Are we safe?" Emelia asked Joey.

"I won't hurt you, if that's what has you worried," Joey said. "So, yes, we're safe. I've ended it. No more threats."

"Let's go see what's above us," Emelia suggested, approaching Joey bravely. Liam and Nate followed behind her, giving Joey furtive glances.

The group went up to the next floor. It was furnished well and looked like the business office for a manager. There was a safe, too.

"Finally, I can use this," Joey said with the simple unlock glyph tile in hand. It flashed, but the safe emitted a red glow around the surface.

"Unlock magic negation," Emelia explained. "You'll need to get past–"

Joey breathed out a stream of shady fire. The dark embers ate the unlock magic negation, leaving the safe undamaged.

Joey used another unlock tile. The safe spun and clicked, the door popping ajar.

Joey smiled and looted what was inside. His belt grew a little too heavy, barely able to handle more.

[You've looted 16 Tidal Moon Bronze Coins, 50 Tidal Moon Copper Coins, 1 Journal Transcript of Devil Observations, 1 Copy of Northern Zambwi Temple Directions, 1 Copy of the Tidal Moon Scriptures.]

"Interesting," Joey grunted. His greed felt fat, but always hungry. It was a gluttonous thing, so it took Joey time to consider his group.

He convinced himself that his steady ones were part of his … hoard. They were the living part of it. They needed nurturing to become more worthwhile.

"Payment." Joey split the bronze coins evenly. "For you. Take."

The steady ones looked at him carefully. Joey growled. "Take."

They collected their share. *Good, good. Become more valuable.*

Joey's attention shifted to the last item of note. A crystal ball broadcasting a voice and a man's face.

He'd been studying Joey and his group the whole time. They couldn't use Analyze on each other, but it didn't matter much.

Joey's great status would stop being a secret once Domer's people put their heads together. Unless Domer figured it out right now.

"You the head guy?" Joey asked.

"I think of myself as a servant of the people." Domer didn't look like a villain. He wasn't muscular. He wasn't bald. He wasn't nefariously old.

He was a middle-aged man who looked decently well kept. He looked fit, had an evenly groomed beard, and had the eyes of a thoughtful man.

"You really do look young," Domer said.

"I'm eighteen," Joey said.

"Have you done your taxes before?" Domer asked.

"No, but that's beside the point." Joey held up a booklet. "What's with the journal transcript on devils?"

"Something that should've been better protected, but not all of my people are the best." Domer sighed. "I cannot speak about that without knowing you better. I'm sure you know my name. Can I have yours?"

"Joey, but you should know that after your people intimidated my group."

"I just wanted to confirm. And I'm going to assume

you've beaten the people I've left in Zam."

"Not alone, I did," Joey said, glancing at his group. "We did."

Nate was about to speak, but an elbow from Liam quieted him. Emelia stood back, watching intently.

"No, no, I can tell where the talent extends from. And you're that talent, Joey." Domer's eyes shone with resolve. "Let's stop this. All I wanted was a quick checkup with you. An unknown rogue walks into New Zam City, is up to Level 40, and I haven't gotten the chance to pitch him? That was all I wanted. A chance for us to help each other."

"Things worked out well the way it did." Joey swayed his head from side to side. "I gained, and so did my group. But if you want to stop harassing us and stay in your lane, that'll work, too."

"Let me ask you something, Joey."

"Until I destroy this crystal ball, I'm going to assume you're going to ask stuff, anyway."

"What do you think of our situation? Of our entire existence placed in the hands of foreign powers? Powers we didn't choose, we didn't believe in, we didn't get to voice our opinions to. Don't you find that cruel and unjust?"

"You're asking me a lot, Domer," Joey said. "My violent and greedy brain is getting bored. But I'll get straight to the point and say this: I love it."

Domer shook his head in disbelief. "What?"

"You're deaf now? I said I love it." Joey waved the devil journal around. "No doubt, there's stuff that makes me angry. I hate it when others take what's mine from me, whether it is loot or people. So I have to have my revenge, no matter how long it takes. But even that gives me more passion and existence than my life before Multiverse Z."

"We are being used as slaves for their entertainment!" Domer shouted. "The only way to be free is to break the system and remake it to represent us first."

"Okay, I've heard enough." Joey waved his group back. "Let's skip to the end. We're going to be enemies. So if I see you in person, I'll fight you, I'll fight your people, I'll even fight your pet cat."

"I'm in the 60s, Joey! I have plenty of men and women in their 50s now! And we have scarier creatures than shadowstalkers." Domer glared. "You're just one boy getting toyed with by the so-called gods. Either I will end you, or Multiverse Z will."

"I don't care, Domer. I will survive you all. Nothing will stop me from doing what I love, and I love being a rogue of the multiverse."

Joey destroyed the crystal ball with Shade Dragon Breath. It shattered and melted into a black soup. The heat from its destruction burned the desk and lit it on fire – the normal kind.

Satisfied, Joey turned to his group. His tail curled around them with friendliness.

He was happy with the results after being outnumbered by a bigger group. His steady ones showed the potential he scouted yesterday, even if they didn't seem like much to others right now.

Nate struggled to split his attention between Joey and the tail. Liam was wiped out from a chaotic day of fighting above his weight. Emelia wanted answers to all the questions filling her head, but treated Joey as an unpredictable monster.

This was all fine.

They would have time to settle down and learn more about him in the wilds. Battle Maid Mollysea would be there to help, too. Surely, they would become fast friends with her since they were all older.

And there was lots of killing and sadistic training to do! Oh joy!

"My steady ones," Joey called proudly. "Let's go."

They exited the building and found overseers waiting. Elves, dwarves, and gnomes. The overseers walked silently with the renegade group and escorted them safely out of New Zam City.

Then Joey and his steady ones were left alone in the jungle, which was great. Joey could finally shed his sheep's clothing and go back to being his authentic Shade Dragon Rogue self.

Pretending to be someone he wasn't for a whole day was hard!

31. I AM A GREAT ADVENTURER

"Hey, look." Joey turned to his group. He held up two pouches filled with different coins. Before the overseers left his group in the wilds, he'd exchanged coins to lighten the load.

"Look, look." Joey smiled like a big kid. "All in one day I came out with fifteen bronze coins and one hundred seventy-nine coppers. I started with one hundred coppers, too."

"That's wonderful, dear," Emelia said in a pleasant but forced tone. Nate and Liam forced themselves to nod while beside her. They didn't look at his coins for long, paying more attention to their surroundings.

It was becoming dark out, and the jungle was teeming with dangerous life. Few adventurers would stay out in the dark. And if they did, they wouldn't move around during the night hours.

But Joey led the group with a can-do attitude. His cheer was through the roof. He hadn't realized how much he looted from New Zam City until he counted it all. He could've checked his profile, but it felt more fun doing it physically.

Yeah, sure, he'd probably left the city in chaos with a

major seat of power disturbed, but that wasn't his problem. If Domer cared to keep things in order, he could go back to New Zam City and correct things himself.

I wonder where he's at right now? The northern temples? Joey thought before shrugging. That was a concern for Future Joey.

For now, Joey bounced around in front of his group.

He did so quietly, of course.

He was excited, but he wasn't absolutely crazy. His group's safety came first. But beyond that, nothing could bring him down.

Except for the scared and downcast mood of his group. Joey slowed down and sighed, looking at his group of older folks while walking backward.

"You should drink a stamina potion each." Joey dug into his potion pouch and pulled out three.

He had a remaining one for himself. There were plenty more at his hideout.

"It's funny how there are no points to track or a bar for stamina," Joey said. "Nor is there one for health. I think the system lets that run a little more realistically. But the potions existing could mean there are hidden status numbers."

Liam and Nate nodded along, having nothing more to say. That was fine with Joey. He was trying to pull Emelia out of her sheltered mood to engage with him.

All it took was a little bait. She would bite. She couldn't help it.

"I've never played video games before," Emelia admitted. "It was Liam and Nate who helped me understand the gaming terms when we first met."

Joey tossed Emelia a potion as a reward for talking.

She caught it with her free hand and looked it over carefully. "These are expensive, you know? Over a bronze each in the lowest quality market. Sometimes more, depending on if the alchemist is running out. At the multiverse store, they're over four bronzes each."

Liam's and Nate's attention fell on the stamina potion. It was a solid glass bottle with a yellow liquid inside. A brown stopper plugged the top.

Joey gestured for Emelia to open it up and drink. She hesitated.

While the bottle distracted the steady ones, the rogue noticed a dangerous sound incoming fast. He dashed up and skewered a diving night bird with his tail spike. No headshot, but the beast landed hard on the side of the trail, blood leaking from its torso.

"Liam, shoot," Joey ordered, falling to the ground.

The man followed suit, landing an arrow on the bird's side before Joey touched down. Going for the kill, Joey activated his tail again and whipped the bird's head until it went splat.

[You've slain a Small Bird Nightwing lvl 47. Experience is reduced for having assistance.]

Joey checked his singularities.

Singularities: Dragon Pride (Superior), Slay The Dread Whale! (Great Quest/Part 1), High Moon Achievement List (Great Quest/0 Complete), New Zam City Quests (0/10 Complete).

By selecting the New Zam City Quests, a new prompt listing ten different quests appeared. There was one called

Night Time Danger. It requested the culling of nightwings.

Three would be fair. Joey figured killing twelve would be great.

"Can we find shelter?" Nate asked. "Please, Sir Joey?"

"Sir Joey?" The rogue blinked.

"Oh, no, did I offend you? Please don't burn me alive?" Nate looked like he was about to faint. He had too much spirit for that, though. "And don't hit me to death with your ghost tail!"

"Is it invisible now?" Liam asked. "I saw it while you thrashed that thing. Now it's gone."

"It's right behind him. Right there. It's looking at me." Nate pointed with his mace.

Emelia tapped her staff against a tree trunk to get everyone's attention. She exuded a serious demeanor, which made Joey worry.

The stamina potion remained unopened and unconsumed. She passed it back to him and looked into his eyes.

"We need a full explanation first. And some time to recollect ourselves. I promise we'll do our best not to slow you down. But we're not as strong as you." Emelia took a deep breath. "Please, Joey."

"Fine." He placed all the potions back into his pouch, feeling bothered. Everything was easier when he kept going from objective to objective. Emelia reminded him of Curi. Thinking of the curious kraken helped soothe Joey's mood.

I miss you, Curi. Joey sighed.

Instead of going away from danger, the rogue followed the direction of the greatest danger. He pointed up and looked at Liam.

The archer closed his eyes to listen. Then he drew an arrow and fired. Three nighthawks plunged from the dark branches with talons outstretched.

Shade Dragon Breath streamed out of Joey's mouth and coated their legs. The beasts flapped chaotically. Two of them fell down around the group.

Nate used his zone spell to keep one nighthawk from crashing into him. Emelia sliced the side of another with her conjured spearhead.

The third nighthawk flew away as the shady fire spread through the channels of its body. It fell from the darkening sky soon enough. Joey looked over and saw Liam had placed an arrow in each beast before they burned to death.

[You've slain a Small Bird Nightwing lvl 45. Experience is reduced for having assistance.]

[You've slain a Small Bird Nightwing lvl 48. Experience is reduced for having assistance.]

[You've slain a Small Bird Nightwing lvl 44. Experience is reduced for having assistance.]

"Good work, group," Joey complimented. "This thicket was their territory. I sensed it was the most dangerous spot here, so other beasts won't come near for a while. Wait here while I record the deaths with a crystal. I'll be back soon."

Ten minutes later, Joey returned from recording the nightwing kills with a quest crystal. He let the others know he was coming by walking normally. Their hushed whispers died down, which triggered Joey's anxiety.

He'd taken his time to think about how he would explain everything. He also talked himself into looking for signs of betrayal.

If he caught on to anything deceitful, he would kill them all. His greatness was more important than the group.

Resolved to do what was necessary, Joey found them sitting in a small circle with log seats and cut bushes stacked around them as a makeshift barrier. At the center was a glyph tile pulsating with a dull glow, offering low light.

Through gaps in the canopy, moons and swirling cosmic lights illuminated the night. The Zambwi Land Moon was the most dominant light in the sky above the jungle.

"I am a great adventurer," Joey said, pulling out a dagger to toss up and down.

He sat on the log that was left for him next to a boulder. He leaned back, like he was getting comfortable.

Beasts made their night cries to fill the heavy silence around their little camp circle. The older adults looked at Joey with wide eyes and leaned forward.

"I started east from here. Across multiple tides. No other human but me. All I had was a crate holding an Analyze skill book and a raft that kept me above water. I lost the crate."

Joey looked back at that moment fondly. It was hard to believe it was a little over a month ago. It felt like a lifetime. So much had happened. It was surprising that he found the words to describe it, continuing to speak.

"I've traded favors with a curious kraken, fought man-eating monsters all around the tides, dueled a relentless war princess for seven days straight, and escaped a devil with a promise to hurt and kill it. Then I came to your city and overturned it in one day, breaking the foundations of your strongest adventurer group."

He chuckled darkly to himself. "This is while I scouted you three and decided to take you from your city and bring you into the wilds at night. But as you can see, the night is nothing to me. It's safe to say I'm not much of a human."

Joey continued to flip the knife around. He thought about how he walked into New Zam City with the equivalent of one bronze coin and came out with nearly seventeen bronze coins. All it took was one day.

So, he had to repeat himself. "I am a great adventurer."

***

There was a long stretch of silence. The older adults needed time to absorb what Joey had told them. It was interesting for Joey to watch their facial expressions.

Yes, he was searching for potential betrayal. Then he could murder them quickly if need be.

But he was more interested in the way they reacted. He could see them cross referencing everything they'd seen from him with what they knew as steady ones.

It took a while for Liam and Nate to catch up with Emelia. The elderly woman was compiling her questions in her head, no doubt.

Joey could see her preparing to fire them out. He braced himself, catching his knife and sitting up.

"First, I want to give you a thank you for telling us this," Emelia said. "I imagine there is much at stake for you as a great adventurer. I'm going to start off by saying I am not interested in [#7]. I will not betray you for it. Please see I'm being earnest about this."

"Hey, what about us?" Nate asked.

"You need to say that to him yourself. And make sure you're being earnest." Emelia looked from Nate to the knife in Joey's hand. "Or else."

Nate gulped. "I won't betray you. I promise, I promise, oh, please believe me, I promise."

Everyone waited on Liam. He was contemplating something before he said, "What if I kill another great adventurer?"

Joey blinked. Out of all the responses, he liked that one the most. "If they die to you, then that'll be a shame on them. But let me talk to them first. I can use all the great ones I can get."

"Alright, well, I'm not interested in taking you out for the [#7]. I mean, dude, you're way too scary for me to fight. I'm pretty sure you have eyes on the back of your head."

Joey flashed him a toothy smile without giving much else away. Their answers satisfied him.

He tossed the knife around with more flair. That seemed to put them at ease, even if only a little.

"Okay, so is it fair to say one of the key differences between great ones and steady ones is our starting point?" Emelia asked.

"Yes. Great ones also get more options for overpowered magic. There's not many of us, as you might've figured, but just one of us is worth dozens to thousands of steady ones."

Joey caught the knife and frowned. There was more to being a great adventurer than the exact worth. It took him time to think about his next words.

"It's not about raw fighting power, I think," Joey said. "It's the potential to make a difference that could affect many people while having incredible abilities. The war princess I've fought for seven days straight is a ruler of an entire city, plus multiple territories, plus different subgroups of denizens. She's the most powerful great one in our beginner challenge."

Liam's eyes flashed with interest. "What's she like?"

"Not now," Emelia hissed.

"But I want to know, too," Nate said. "She sounds awesome."

Joey grinned, happy to talk big about the war princess.

"She is awesome! She's crazy strong. And relentless. Like, uber relentless. She's kind of a tyrant, so everyone's scared of her since she's tough on her subjects." Joey chuckled, as if that was a joking matter.

"But I figured she has to be that way," he added. "She's seventeen and was born here. Half human, too. She doesn't seem like much. She's so short, she makes me feel tall. And while we have our differences, whereas she needs to relax more, I admire how she carries so much responsibility and can have a huge effect on everything around her. Part of being here is to help her out, since she's helped me out."

"Uh, huh." Liam nodded. "That's it, right? Just two young great ones – an eighteen-year-old and a seventeen-year-old – helping each other out. Being great. Having huge effects on all the little people under them while they do great things for each other. That's it, I suppose."

Joey's greedy dragon side flared inside him. It took him a few seconds to suppress it. Before he could answer, Liam lifted his hands.

"It's alright. You don't have to say anything." He gave Joey a wink. "She's a princess, dude, so I'll understand if you keep it on the down low."

Nate laughed.

Emelia palmed her face and muttered angry Spanish. Joey didn't bother to translate.

"She sounds like a tough girl," Nate said. "You think you can handle her?"

Joey grinned. "I'll find a way. If I have to, I'll burn her alive."

The mood dropped fast. The others gawked at him as if he'd become a monster.

He blinked at them in confusion. "We're great ones. We'll probably fight seriously one day. She has more advantages than me. But I think I'm so unique and dangerous I can make things difficult. Then again, I only know one of her spells. I don't know the other five."

Joey rubbed his chin. "I should probably ask if she'll reveal them to me. She might not. But who knows? I'll figure something out to beat her even if she has all the advantages."

Joey tilted his head to the side. "Hopefully, Multiverse Z has a way to give great ones some slack. I don't want to end her greatness. Or I wouldn't be able to burn her alive with a smile."

The group didn't talk for a while as they soaked in Joey's words. He gave them time since the difference between him and them was stark.

Joey was also aware that he was different. *Am I a psychopath or a sociopath?*

He was unsure, but at least he acknowledged his mind frame working differently. At least he was sitting down and taking the time to speak to the steady ones.

"What happens when you die?" Emelia asked softly.

"My greatness ends," Joey said. "Please, understand that I would prefer to burn you all to death so you'll never try to cross me than to let that happen. Honestly, being frank with you and letting you get close is scarier than facing death in front of a bunch of enemies. Eventually, I'll have to let my guard down around you. I'll absolutely hate for that to be my downfall."

Joey sighed and fiddled with his dagger with less joy. "Please, don't backstab me and end my greatness. I don't want to go back to what I was before."

"I won't. I promise, I won't." Emelia looked at the men. They all nodded rapidly, making the same promises.

Joey sensed they understood the danger of what he was doing.

There were more questions, and Joey was more forthcoming about certain things. He didn't tell them his exact path, but he explained he had four spells. He could fight efficiently with his skills alone, which they had witnessed.

This segued into how the mind stat was important for essence control. Emelia, Liam, and Nate looked with wide-eyed wonder as Joey explained some of his processes of improving his skills to a deadly degree. Then he shifted the conversation to a prospect that had him interested.

"It is possible to push your spells until they're as powerful than mine," Joey said. "All of them are basic, right?"

They nodded.

"If you control them until they feel like they're level one, and then use them repeatedly against something challenging, you can level them up past the limit. But you need stat points in your mind. I'm guessing Liam has his points in body, and Nate in spirit?"

The men nodded shamefully.

"How did you know I kept my even?" Emelia asked.

"I've watched you as much as you've watched me," Joey said. "Now, I think that's all the explanation needed. I'm going to count tonight and the march tomorrow as freebies. We're going to link up with my battle maid and figure out what training to incorporate in between completing quests. I need to train each of my skills more, anyway, and see if I can embed them deeper without magic."

"If that's the case, then I'm calling last watch," Nate said, ready to sleep.

"Battlemaid?" Liam asked.

"How do you embed skills without magic?" Emelia blurted out, hungry for more information.

Joey sighed. "Everyone, be like Nate. Go to bed, I'll keep watch." His tone was final.

The next day, they crossed through the jungle with little issue. Because of Joey using Meditative Stasis and Danger Sense together last night, the entire group was more active since they had a solid night of rest.

Beasts died in droves, some that were part of their quests, others that weren't. Joey didn't always have to jump in first. The group took advantage of his presence and their new levels by leading with confidence.

They could take more risks and earn more awards since Joey had their backs. When they tired out and needed to meditate, Joey guarded and killed, allowing them to feel safe, too.

Unfortunately, Joey hit Level 44. But that was okay. Emelia reached Level 36. Liam reached Level 36. And Nate wasn't far behind while at Level 35.

"This is amazing. How are we gaining so many levels so fast?" Nate asked.

"We can take risks, dude," Liam answered.

"We have a dragon watching over us," Emelia said, nodding up at Joey perched in the tree canopy.

The mage froze when she saw he wasn't alone. A big, athletic, orange-skinned woman dressed in a two-piece jungle outfit sat in the branches with the rogue.

She had webbed skin between her fingers and toes. And she looked both alien and beautiful with long and dark blue hair.

But she was also strangely horrible to be around.

She emitted a scary air around her. Every sound she made was a little grating. She would seem like a monster if she wasn't a denizen.

Mollysea sniffed long and hard. "Mm. New trainees." She smiled like a monster. "How delicious. Thank you for bringing me such delights, Master Eclipse."

"Of course." Joey smiled down at the steady ones. "Do not worry. We will be gentle with you. So when you feel pain and fear, just know what we do is out of love."

32. DUDE, YOU'RE BUILT DIFFERENT

To Joey's shock, Mollysea started everything off by sitting with the steady ones in a circle. Then she had a simple chat with them as if they were normal people.

They were now back in their hideout. It was a cave Joey had cleared of giant centipede beasts. The centipedes hadn't been very strong – mostly in the low 30s – but he had to kill them all with Assassin Grappling dial down to Level 1.

It had been one of the most horrible experiences Joey suffered. So he felt bewildered to see Mollysea handle the steady ones with open care. While using the cave she cruelly tossed Joey into days ago.

In the meantime, she told him to run off and use his Dominator skill at Level 1 against some nearby baboons creeping in. She would take care of the steady ones henceforth.

This became the norm as their days in the wilds went by. Joey built up Danger Sense, Dominator, and Glyphlock Hitman quickly through pure grit and effort and painful moments. He figured he'd get more time with his group once those skills were up in the teens. But Mollysea was prepared for that.

She turned his attention to all of his existing skills, starting from the top. She wanted them close to Level 20, which was harder to achieve even with essence control.

What of the quests?

Mollysea would oversee them as she trained the bad habits out of the steady ones and integrated new habits and some skills. Joey had no need to worry about them anymore.

"Focus on yourself, Master Eclipse," Mollysea said, turning him away when he wanted to check up on his group. "You're different from them. Your path requires you to do things only you can do."

Joey understood what Mollysea was saying. He still sulked as he walked away, feeling like he'd given control of his group to his battle maid.

Or was it 'battlemaid?'

Yes, the former specialist knew what she was doing more than him. He'd never trained people before. He had no idea if he had the patience or technical know-how.

Yet, Joey still wondered. *Are we really that different from each other that I can't pass on what I know to them? There's nothing about me that's any different other than our starting points and our spell selections. I mean, Dragon Pride has a specific purpose. Heck! Their spells will be stronger than mine if they train them up properly. Once they reach my level, get their spell levels up, put to balance their stats, they'll have some advantages.*

Joey was certain of this. But his certainty wavered over time. Especially when he checked on the steady ones' progress.

Nate had Heal as one of his spells. He could risk taking damage for trades that would pay him off big-time. His spell for enhancing his next mace strike would blow apart a target, especially when defending someone else. But the guy didn't take advantage of that as much as he could.

Emelia could make it rain magic volleys and bombard a room-sized area hard. It did take a lot of essence. But if she endured the freezing channels, the bombardment would maximize her firepower.

But she would cut her magic volleys short when Joey felt she should go for more to annihilate her target area. She couldn't get past the discomfort of her channels freezing.

Between Liam's explosive arrow spell and his rapidfire spell, he'd get more damage-per-second with the latter. But the rapidfire spell burned up his stamina while freezing up his channels. He'd shown some toughness, enduring the double exhaustion. But he kept failing to push a little further to achieve more damage that Joey believed he could.

Ammunition wasn't an issue either. Mollysea helped Liam get a skill for arrow crafting in the wilds. He could haul around lots of arrows in a basket-style quiver and spend them as needed. But he had to take breaks from the hot and cold exhaustion when using his rapid fire spell.

Each time Joey felt certain the steady ones could push a little more, they stopped short. It was not a horrible sin. They were making progress that would put them way above other steady adventurers at their levels.

But Joey felt irked by their lack of drive. They took longer breaks more frequently. They rested more than they meditated. They ate more than necessary. They joked more than they should. They weren't devoting most, if not everything to training or killing or progressing.

It felt like they kept taking shortcuts.

It felt like they kept stopping short of...

"Greatness," Joey muttered to himself.

Seven days had gone by. It was the seventh night when Joey found himself standing on a tall jungle tree. His gaze was heavy while looking up, glaring into the watercolor cosmos and shifting moons.

A presence shifted closer to his back. Tail activated, he whipped it lightly and felt Mollysea's hand grab the tail. Instead of dismissing it, he used the tail to pull her to his side on a sturdy branch hundreds of feet off the ground.

After dismissing his tail, Joey glanced at the war siren towering at his side. She seemed way happier than him, glowing with enthusiasm from nurturing her new trainees.

She still had a nervous tic with the necklaces, caressing the four he'd given her. She was touching them more than usual as he watched her.

"You haven't asked for them back," she said.

"You belong to me, right? So they're already where I want them," Joey replied.

Mollysea nodded. She looked at the sky with him. "I wonder what it's like to ascend."

"Denizens can't?"

"I'm not sure. Most likely not." Mollysea swayed her head around. "Not without help or interference."

"Want to come with me when I ascend to the next realm?"

She smiled. "I would like that. It's either that or death for me. At this point, I don't mind either. I've survived for too long, and most of the war sirens I grew up with are gone." She sighed and looked down. "And I'm a deserter."

Joey studied her for some time, deciding not to say anything. He was a little angry at her downer mood.

She was part of his ... hoard ... so to lose her was a price he wasn't willing to pay. Instead of speaking about that, he looked down where he heard laughter from the mouth of the cave. His mood darkened.

"Is this good enough?" Joey pointed down. "Can't we push them a little more?"

Mollysea chuckled, which would disturb most people other than Joey. The steady ones had learned to endure the deserter's anti-charm pretty well, but it was not easy for them.

Joey waited for her response, so he was a little surprised when she tapped his chest.

"You're becoming like the War Princess," she accused, which was all she really needed to say to win the conversation.

Oh, that hurts. That hurts a lot.

Joey gawked at her. He tried and failed to overturn her words. It wasn't too long ago he tried to convince the War Princess she needed to relax more.

He also remembered vividly how everyone ran from her like she was a monster. She was really a tyrant, even if she was the most necessary evil to exist.

Thankfully, Mollysea continued to speak on her point to help soothe the ache Joey felt.

"I've met my fair share of adventurers, steady and great. It's usually the magic that separates the steady ones and the great ones, at first. But then you see the truly great ones invest everything into their greatness and separate themselves even more."

Mollysea chuckled. "Where others would let stamina tire them, the great ones kept pushing. Where others would get too cold from the freeze, the great ones kept pushing. Where others gave up against impossible odds, the great ones pushed the odds in their favor."

"Is it a difference of the person, then?" Joey asked. "Even with all the stats and the magic?"

Mollysea held up her index finger and thumb. There was an inch of space between them.

"I hear there are hidden numbers in the system. Numbers dictated by a person's inner drive. Or the soul. I don't know if that's true. Everyone speculates. But see here how small the space is between my thumb and finger. That can be the difference that leads to someone starting steady or being great. Or the difference between a seeker rising high and evolving their role, or getting stuck as a seeker until they face death."

"Why can't they push to cover that gap?" Joey waved down at the cave.

"That gap is the hardest gap ever." Mollysea shook her head. "It can be torture, you know? And you just can't expect everyone to cover that gap. Or you'll end up breaking them. Just like the princess."

"She's broken trainees before?"

"When she was younger and less experienced, yes."

Joey nodded stiffly. "Oh, crap. I would've done that, wouldn't I?"

Mollysea's smile was both kind and painful. "You're a great one, Master Eclipse. We'll need you to go harder and faster than others. You must cover that gap nobody else can cover. But please understand, not everyone can do what you can. Barely a few can, really. All we can do is help in our own way, okay?"

"Thanks for telling me this, Battlemaid."

Mollysea nodded before climbing down alone. After some time with his thoughts, Joey climbed down and entered the cave.

The laughter and conversation died down as if the older adults were scared children. Joey grabbed a coconut filled with sweet juice and pulp mixed together and sat against his pack.

"I'm here to take a break with you guys," Joey announced.

Liam and Nate cheered.

Emelia clapped.

Mollysea sat in the corner, playing with the necklaces.

***

"In the blue corner! We have three steady adventurers who are growing into something fierce. They aren't who you'll think of as heroes, but they're trying their best. Everyone, please welcome Negator Nate, Loose-fingers Liam, and Eminent Emelia! Let's go wild for them, people!"

Joey turned to the crowd of harmless monkey beasts watching from the trees. One threw a half-eaten fruit as others let out monkey chirps and cries.

It was a good showing on their ninth day out from New Zam City, so Joey felt extra cheerful. The steady ones looked a little nervous, however, but that was to be expected. They were going up against the champ.

"And in the red corner! My goodness, gracious, it's the people's champ! We all know him. We all love him. We'll never want to fight him since he has four answers for every problem. People, you know what to do. Give the rumbling, tumbling, awesome fighter Al Bruce Crabton his standing ovation!"

The Level 51 semblance crashed out into the open,

looking pale white and ethereal under the noon moon. Most monkeys fled from its appearance, raising a bunch of hoopla and screeches.

Al Bruce Crabton treated the noises as cheers, raising all four mighty pincers into the air while clicking them loudly. The semblance turned left and right while scuttling about to do a showy dance. Then Al Bruce Crabton looked down at his three opponents and thrust all his pincers at them.

"Uh, oh! It looks like Al Bruce Crabton is ready to maul and pummel his challengers!"

"Uh, Joey, maybe this isn't a good idea," Nate said.

Joey glanced over at Mollysea sitting in the shade. She gestured for him to continue.

The rogue smiled with all teeth. "Let the carnage begin!"

Obviously, Joey had worked things out with Al Bruce Crabton beforehand to ensure the semblance wouldn't go crazy. Summoning his semblance gave Joey good practice of learning to communicate verbally and nonverbally. Strong and simple mental commands worked on semblances, too.

At any moment, Joey was prepared to say and think 'stop' if things went out of hand. But to his growing joy, the steady adventurers showed that might not be necessary.

Liam shot an explosive arrow at ABC's face, forcing him to block. His pincers endured the damage, but ABC lost the opportunity to charge in first.

Nate dropped the zone spell to block off the semblance's legs. Emelia whirled her staff rapidly from side to side, hurling volleys after volleys of magic bolts upward.

ABC tried to ram forward, slowed by the walls and another explosive shot to the face. Then, with admirable coordination, Nate dropped his spell and let ABC move forward.

Unfortunately for the semblance, Emelia's magic bombardment targeted the spot he moved into. Harsh concussive blasts rained down from overhead, battering ABC hard, making the semblance buckle a little. Through the chaos, Liam fired explosive arrows at ABC's legs, attacking from below while Emelia attacked from above.

That would've spelled doom for a lesser monster, but ABC roared and pushed forward, anyway. It used all its pincers to block up top while charging into the group to strike with its sharp legs.

Emelia and Liam were stationary while hurling consistent attacks. The line between success and defeat could only be crossed by one person.

Nate rushed forward, charging his mace with magic that grew stronger while in defense of his comrades. The cleric jumped into the air, using every ounce of his new body stats, and swung a hammering blow. ABC lowered a pincer to block, absorbing the hit but not without sacrifice.

The semblance lost his momentum and stumbled back. More magic volleys blasted down. Explosive arrows chipped at his legs.

Nate fell into the middle of the attacks, catching the edges of friendly fire. But he actively healed himself while rushing out from under ABC and toward safety.

"Stop," Mollysea said.

Everyone ceased fire. Emelia went ahead and vanquished the last magic blasts before they collided with ABC's head.

Nate collapsed next to his team. Liam used his bow to support himself, looking a little exhausted. Emelia pretended her channels weren't chilly for her.

And ABC looked almost dead, his tough shell suffering breaks as ghost blood turned into mist before fading. The semblance collapsed into a seat on his lower body, and let out tired hissy noises. He looked over with one eye at Joey.

The rogue walked up and examined all the damage ABC soaked, which was pretty incredible. Joey remembered how long it took him to kill ABC, and he'd needed tricks to do it.

The steady ones had blocked ABC off from getting started. Then they had worked together to rain down a hard torrent of attacks that could've killed him if it went on longer.

Then again, as I am now, I can probably kill a similar hull crusher bruiser all by myself.

It was hard to gauge if the steady ones were doing well or if Joey was too much of a monster to use as a comparison. He glanced over at his group and saw them meditating while standing and staying observant.

They were recovering quickly so they could prepare to fight again. He approved.

I get it now. I can't expect them to go above and beyond in every fight. But I can ask them to give me consistent results. And that can make a big difference. By knowing what they can consistently do, I can implement that better with my great efforts.

All it really takes is making them better than the average, so it's even more shocking when we smash through rows of adversaries.

Now all Joey needed to do was expand this idea from three steady adventurers to hundreds of them. He also needed to find other great adventurers.

"You did well, everyone," Joey said. "And thanks, Al Bruce Crabton. I owe you some time getting into fights and beefing you up."

ABC hissed in agreement. It had waited for a long while to come out. It deserved time to fight and get stronger. For that reason, Joey had changed the experience options to fully award ABC for his actions.

"Let's give Al Bruce Crabton time to heal," Joey said.

The self regen wouldn't work while the semblance was stored away. It needed to stay out and heal, locking away 20% of Joey's essence.

But that was no problem for the rogue. He'd become more efficient with his essence lately.

"In the meantime, we can brainstorm our group's name," Joey offered.

[Multiverse Adventurer: Basic Human: Archer lvl 41.]

[Multiverse Adventurer: Basic Human: Mage lvl 40.]

[Multiverse Adventurer: Basic Human: Cleric lvl 40.]

"Way ahead of you, dude." Liam flashed his Hollywood surfer smile.

"Oh, no," Joey said, sighing. "Please, nothing silly."

The older adults smiled at each other. The men pushed Emelia forward, and the mage stood straight in front of Joey.

"Would the Renegades suffice?" Emelia asked.

Hm? That has me interested. Joey summoned his clones to check with them.

"Alright, you know what? I won't even lie. I think Renegades can work!" one clone said.

"We were thinking of the name shadow company. But that's fine. Let shadow be our thing. Shadow gang is the special ops of the Renegades," another clone said.

"I like it. Renegades. That's going to be the word that makes our haters hate even more."

"Let the hate flow! Renegades will always grow!"

Joey chuckled before dismissing his silly clones. "Well, it looks like Renegades is our name. Now onto the next business. We've done great work for ten quests. We won't get paid for that until we deliver the crystals to the guild."

The singularity [**New Zam City Quests (10/10 Complete*)**] would only go away after checking with the quest giver. And the entire group had to be there to receive their awards.

"But therein lies the problem." Joey sighed. "We might face resistance, which is no surprise. More importantly, I need to do something big to get more attention for the Renegades and make us grow bigger. It has to be something crazy. And I need your help to figure out what I can do."

"Oh, I don't know if I like the sound of this," Nate said.

Liam hummed. "What about those books? Maybe messing with Domer's operation in the northern temples might help."

"That's not big enough," Emelia said, looking into Joey's eyes. "I've picked up on it here and there that you need to gather more of us. And gather more great ones. This is to help the princess with something, right?"

"It's on the achievement list. [**#4 – Slay the Dread Whale!**]," Joey explained. "I need hundreds of adventurers. And more great ones than just me. And we need to get to Level 75 in a couple of months."

Emelia pursed her lips, her mind turning. Everyone looked at her because she'd shown intelligence that was more inherent than her stats. Joey always believed she was the one to look out for the most, and he hoped she could show why he'd believed that.

"Getting to Level 75 can wait. Making a successful recruitment drive comes first. And when you want to get everyone's attention," Emelia said, "you need to get the attention of the denizens. And if you want to get the denizens' attention right away, then you'll have to use what nobody else has. Your greatness."

"Hm," Joey hummed as inspiration struck him. A smile grew across his face. "It might be time to go see the guild manager. And do something … great."

"Uh oh," Liam said. "Looks like we're in for another banger."

"What happened to the simple days of having a dodge tank and being safe?" Nate groaned.

"Do I get to be involved?" Mollysea asked, interest piqued.

"Everyone's getting involved," Joey said. "You, too, Al Bruce Crabton."

The semblance raised its pincers and clacked in celebration.

Joey rubbed his hands together like a nefarious villain. He was Level 46 now, and most of his skills were Level 19 or 18.

He was going to need all of his powerful magic and the help of the Renegades for his next great stunt. Total domination of New Zam City and beyond.

33. THE ROGUE IN WHITE AND RED

Randall had some debt he'd owed to the thugs running the Main Zam Gambling Den. It was annoying being a Level 26 warrior while owing favors to a gang of commoner thugs.

But the thugs worked for Domer's People, and that group had power all over New Zam City. *Until some damn kid turned their operation upside down and embarrassed them all.*

Randall chuckled while standing on the market corner in Big Gate Zam. It was morning time. Today's gatherers had already left through the big gate. Out of all the commoners, Randall figured those guys had it the hardest.

But they only worked every other day and had living expenses, food, and all the basics covered while earning extra coppers. Commoners had it better in Multiverse Z compared to being a normal person surviving in the old world.

I should've picked being a commoner, Randall thought. *Simple work. Good pay. Yeah, you gotta put your life in someone else's hands. But at least you don't have to go kill and die for a living.*

Randall had died a couple of times already.

The big crystal ball in the middle of the market turned on. Randall and other adventurers on the 'advanced street team' looked up along with the early risers filling the market.

It was too early for the cute elf babe to hop on. Randall hoped to see her, anyway, but something worse came up.

Flashing red lights and a siren alarm.

The words [**Immunity Clause Activated!**] crawled across the red projection. Then the words Randall feared most came up next: [**400 from Domer's People versus 4 from the Renegades. Everyone beware of the city-wide pvp action and find your nearest shelter or multiverse denizen for protection!**]

"We're actually doing this? Holy cow, man, it's about to go down!" shouted a Level 27 archer on the advanced street team.

"We're definitely going to win. There's four hundred of us," said a female warrior, Level 22. She looked ratty and desperate while clutching her chipped sword. Other desperate adventurers agreed with her.

"Three hundred of those numbers are commoners, idiots," Randall grunted, keeping his voice low.

He didn't want Anthony to hear him. The top thug was ready to go ballistic after his humbling by the renegade kid. *And speak of the devil. There goes Anthony now.*

Anthony marched through the chaos of commoners running for shelter. Behind him were fifty thugs shoving people out of their way.

From every street, more men working for Anthony showed up, distinguishing themselves by bullying everyone else to create space. They weren't thugs yet. They might get the role switch if they worked under Anthony long enough.

Becoming a thug gave commoners more power over others. They could threaten adventurers, even.

Randall imagined if these three hundred could succeed against the Renegades, the thuggish power bloc in New Zam City would grow out of control. It would get harder on everyone low on the totem pole.

And how can the thugs fail? The advanced street team had fifty adventurers with them. Not the best adventurers. But this combined arms would certainly put the Renegades in their place.

The Renegades couldn't kill commoners, after all. And the fifty adventurers would rain down enough magic to kill someone in the Level 50s.

"Renegades!" Anthony roared, red in the face.

The market cleared of innocent people faster. Randall stood among the three hundred commoners and fifty adventurers. The commoners had clubs, shivs, tools, and just about anything they could grab to hurt someone.

They're acting so brave because it's against the rules to ... wait, wait, hold on.

Randall blinked. *Doesn't immunity mean no rules?*

He looked at the crystal ball and gawked at the **[Immunity Clause Activated!]** message scrolling by. He looked around at everyone as they focused on a lone person walking up from the big gate.

Randall felt a horrible feeling creeping up his spine. He wanted to shout and warn everyone. But he saw nobody was paying attention to the word 'immunity' other than him.

Maybe I'm the crazy one. Maybe I should just keep quiet.

Figuring he was wrong, Randall observed the loner.

Randall had to admit ... something about this kid was ... intimidating.

The kid was by himself and wearing mostly white. His boots, weapon harnesses, and belt were brown. It gave him a pristine mercenary look.

The big smile on the kid's face gave a vibe that everything was going the way he wanted. The three-fifty in his way were no problem.

[Multiverse Adventurer: Basic Human: Rogue lvl 46.]

"He's only Level 46," muttered an adventurer.

"That's higher than any of us, though," said another adventurer.

"But we have three-fifty, bro. He can't beat all of us," a third adventurer chimed in.

"So, why is he walking toward us and smiling?" Randall asked, mostly for himself. The other adventurers and some nearby commoners heard him. They all grew more nervous.

"My, my, my, is this all for me?" asked the rogue in white. "Wow, I feel so special. And, hey! I remember you. You're that bald guy I pimp slapped to sleep!"

Anthony looked like he was going to explode. "The name's Anthony! And we have it all, brat! We got three hundred men ready to beat you down! And fifty adventurers who'll back that up. You can't get past all of us!"

"Ah, you know what? You got a point. All these guys are a little too much for even me." The renegade's smile became scarier. It felt domineering. "But something tells me you guys are ill-informed. Did they tell you what happened to the last five people I killed?"

"It doesn't matter! Hunters! Archers! Prepare to shoot!"

Anthony said.

Two things happened at once. The three-fifty prepared to fire their first volley at the renegade. The renegade shot forward like a bullet, faster than anyone else could react.

Inky lines of darkness traced the ground where he'd crossed. He became easier to track after he skidded to a stop in front of Anthony.

The top thug started to swing his club when, suddenly, a tail speared through his gut. From out of nowhere.

Everyone stopped what they were doing and stared. Nobody jumped in to help as the tail lifted the screaming man up like a victim in the Alien movies.

Blood splattered down on the floor next to the rogue. Some of the blood fell on his white bodysuit.

"I burned the last five. Alive," the rogue said with a voice that nearly had Randall – a warrior – piss himself.

Then things became scarier when the rogue took a deep breath.

And still, nobody did a thing. They were frozen in shock just like Randall.

So everyone watched with morbid curiosity and sheer surprise as the rogue breathed fire.

Dark fire.

He coated Anthony's entire body in evil flames. He burned the man alive while holding him up like a shish kabob.

Three hundred and forty-nine people stood and watched a man scream to death. Then the dark flames faded and left a blackened skeleton that crumbled off the end of the dark tail.

The tail winked out of sight. The rogue in white beamed

the widest smile a kid could have.

Everything was silent. Randall had nearly forgotten to breathe. Then a brave soul said the thing that was on everyone's mind.

"You just broke a rule," another thug said. "The overseers are going to end you."

The rogue in white turned left. He turned right. He looked up and down. Hell, he even looked behind him.

There were no overseers.

"Oh, ha ha ha! I just figured it out." The rogue in white combed his fingers through his short dreadlocks. "It's the immunity clause that's happening now, right? So, well, it looks like I can kill commoners with no problems. Within reason, of course."

The tail flickered into view. The sounds of a loud whip crack and wet crunch spread over the market. The thug who had spoken lost his head in an explosion of gore.

Some brain bits fell on others next to the headless corpse. A few droplets added more red to the rogue in white.

Finally, the realization started hitting them all. Immunity gave them the right to fight anywhere in the city. It allowed them to die just the same.

And commoners didn't get free revival services. Only adventurers.

Almost everyone screamed as the rogue jogged into the crowd. He whipped his monster tail around, exploding heads left and right.

Blood, brains, and skull fragments rained in a constant spray. He carved a gradual line of death through the commoners.

"You want to be a thug! Fine then! You can die a thug!" The rogue in white and red shouted.

Randall ran away. So did the other adventurers of the advanced street team.

It made little sense. They could revive in the hall in five days. They should fight the lone rogue.

But Randall couldn't convince himself to fight the maniac. The rogue in white and red was too dominant, too scary, too horrid. The rogue had no mercy.

Randall could still envision Anthony's crazed screaming. The way his body had been held up and burned to death in front of everyone would haunt Randall forever. But that was a small part of what the renegade had done.

He did it! He did it all by himself! He beat three hundred and fifty people!

Randall couldn't believe it. How could an adventurer do such a thing?

He'd heard the rumors about him having magic flintlocks and cloning powers. But he hadn't heard of anything like the tail and the dark flames. Nobody should have powers like that.

Nobody ... unless ...

Randall stopped in a random alley. "He's a great adventurer." Randall felt like he was onto something big. "Holy shit! He has to be a great adventurer."

"Do you think we should let the guy go or keep him quiet?" a timid male voice asked.

"Eh, it might be too early for the greatness to spread. What do you think, Emelia?" asked another voice who sounded like a surfer bro.

Randall slowly turned until he faced three adventurers who looked rough but determined. He knew the descriptions of the Renegades and immediately recognized them.

"I won't say anything!" Randall shouted. "Just let me go!"

The old latina looked at him coldly. "No. Can't take any chances. We have a great one relying on us."

Randall tried to protect himself with a spell. But an arrow flew over the latina's shoulder fast. Everything went black for Randall.

***

"Sir, he broke all three-fifty of them. I counted thirty dead among the commoners. All thugs," a female rogue said with fear in her voice. "I switched with my colleague to report this. Last I checked, the renegade rogue was walking from Big Gate Zam to Main Zam. He's making a straight line to the adventurer guild. He's simply walking. In the open. While dressed in white from his body suit and red from all the—"

"I've heard enough," Joshua muttered, rubbing his brow.

Joshua couldn't believe Domer had sent him down to New Zam City to fix things. Now he was the man in charge of a huge mess.

Joshua was a Level 56 cleric. He'd been doing well grinding his levels against temple monsters. But the issue with the renegades needed someone from Domer's inner circle to go down and correct.

There were twenty of them in the Level 50s who came down with Joshua. They pulled together the core people here and raised their numbers to fifty that were reliable enough to fight.

Joshua had implemented the three-fifty as a measure

to slow down the Renegades. He figured the kid had a hero personality and wouldn't kill people weaker than him.

I was hoping for him to be dumb and not spot the issue with the immunity clause. He took full advantage like a monster and slaughtered our thugs. That's going to be a total bust for months to come. Maybe forever.

Joshua glanced at the personal crystal ball in the room. They picked a tall building near the adventurer guild as their temporary headquarters. He wondered if he should tell Domer to reconsider things and call this attack off.

But he remembered how adamant Domer had been. He wouldn't want to hear negative news. Only the results of good service.

At least everyone other than the scouting rogues was here. Joshua could give clear orders before rolling out to stop the renegades once and for all.

"Semblances and tamers, up front. Warriors follow and flank around. Archers and mages select your positions above the street and shoot at will. Clerics, with me." Joshua turned to the female rogue. "Level 46, right?"

"That's what I saw before I left," she said. "He won't level up from the thugs, of course. And with all of us level 45 and up, we might be able to overwhelm him. But we have to play this carefully. He's no steady adventurer. He's truly a great one. Just as we figured."

Is that what makes great ones great? Overwhelming power? Joshua grimaced. That kid needed to go down pronto or New Zam City might get taken away from Domer. That would hurt the group badly.

"He needs to be stopped. We cannot let a great one exist here," Joshua said.

"Silly, silly haters. Greatness is forever."

Joshua's heart nearly fell into his stomach. Everyone turned to the corner of the room. Semblances flashed into appearance, crowding the room even further. It was a big room, but it could barely contain forty-five adventurers and twenty semblances.

The rogue in white and red took the one corner that was unoccupied while near the open window. He was surrounded by all enemies. But his domineering smile was unnerving.

Joshua stared at the renegade in disbelief before recomposing himself. *What if this is a chance to change things around?*

"What do you want?" Joshua asked. "You're surrounded with no escape. We can cut a deal and end this."

"It's simple, haters," the rogue in white and red said. "The shadow gang's on the hunt for [#5]. And haters burn the best."

"Shoot him," Joshua ordered.

Arrows and magic bolts struck the rogue and destroyed him. Everyone stared, searching for a corpse. Something in the back of Joshua's head screamed at him.

He yelled, "Get out!"

Too late.

A dark hell rose from the floor. Shadow flames covered the entire room and caught everyone. All Joshua could recall was absolute pain and crazy screaming.

He rushed out the nearest window, falling five stories before hitting a fruit vendor stall underneath. He pushed his healing spell to help him, but the dark heat kept eating him from the inside.

Cleanse! Use cleanse!

Joshua ran his healing and cleanse spells together, and to his fortune, they were working. But the pain was so much, and his channels were freezing up. He endured as best he could.

The only reason he was still alive was because of his tough body as a cleric. But at the same time, it continued his torment of being burned from the inside out.

Finally, the dark flames died. Joshua remained alive, if barely. But his channels were frozen solid and ravaged. He lost a lot of his EP.

Someone was screaming, and it took Joshua a second to realize it was him. He stopped screaming and coughed blood. He couldn't move. He could hear, though. There was only silence.

Then he heard footsteps. Slow and easy-going. They were the most horrible and domineering footsteps Joshua had ever heard.

"I feel like a greedy pig," the rogue in white and red said. "I ate up so many adventurers. And semblances! All at once. But all my group got were scraps. They took out your rogues for me, clearing the area. Then I came straight to you guys."

He stopped and bent into a crouch. "Thanks, by the way. You're the first person to resist my fire. I figured clerics would be a weakness for me. And Domer's the strongest cleric, huh? Yeah, that's going to be an interesting fight."

Joshua tried to talk, but all that came out was raspy nonsense. He tried to move, but everything hurt so much.

"Alright, alright. I'll help send you off. But here's a word of advice you should consider when you revive later." A blade's edge pressed against Joshua's neck. "My name is Joey Eclipse. I have a few screws loose, but that's what makes me a great adventurer."

The blade sliced Joshua's neck and ended his torment. Everything went dark.

***

Joey sighed, feeling cold from the huge expense he'd paid for a shadow gang dragon breath. He'd added his own breath to catch every adventurer and semblance in the room.

He'd figured attacking from the floor below would take Domer's people longer to recognize than attacking from above. He'd guessed right and won big.

His system messages were stacked heavy in the corner of his vision, waiting for him to look through them. He could feel himself growing stronger and stronger.

But he also felt a little weary. He'd pushed himself harder than ever.

The fight hadn't been his hardest physically. But the mentality he'd used was the bloodiest and most savage.

I might've gone overboard on the thugs because of ... well ... I don't want them to think they are invincible. People should think twice about trying to prey on others when you lack true power.

"Are you okay, dear?" Emelia asked, appearing from around the corner. His group looked at him with concern.

Joey thought about his answer. "I found a new side of myself. But maybe it isn't new. Maybe it's been there the whole time, ready to unleash its power and enjoy it. But ... I don't think I want to use that side of me often."

He looked down at all the blood coating his white bodysuit. "I'm sorry if I scare you guys. I'm sorry I'm a monster."

Surprisingly, it was Nate who came forward and placed

a hand on Joey's shoulder. "Listen here. You are scary beyond belief. But I don't think you're a bad person. Or a bad monster. I can't understand what it takes to be great, but I think you're the best one to do it."

Nate pulled his hand away and slowly rubbed the blood off on a wall. "So, um, let's try to find the bright side. And calm down a little before the next ridiculous and violent event."

Joey nodded slowly before finding the pep talk from Nate a little funny. "Dammit, out of all people, it just got to be Nate."

Joey shook his head before laughing a little. "Come on, Renegades. Let's meet the big man."

The Renegades walked in peace all the way to the guild. Barely anyone was on the street even though the pvp action had ended and regular rules were reinstated.

Adventurers who appeared on the road ran away as soon as they saw Joey's blood speckled form. Overseers watched from the rooftops or alleyways, always silent and distant.

The Renegades walked to the guild's entrance and separated from there. As long as he was in the room, Joey was sure he'd get his quest results.

Emelia, Liam, and Nate went to the quest giver. And Joey stopped in front of the management office and looked the guild manager in the eye.

"I'm gonna check my messages real quick – for myself and on the crystal ball – and then I'll come in."

"No need to go anywhere, actually. Come on inside. I have personal crystal balls that have the fastest connections you can find in the lesser realms." The guild manager had a suave and deep voice. It was smooth and filled with hearty cheer. "Bring your friends along. I can deliver your quest results myself."

Joey blinked in surprise before beaming a bright smile. "Sweet."

He called his group back, and they walked into the great management office. Joey led the way.

The doorway flashed gold around him. It didn't flash for the others, but they weren't barred from entering.

They were in a group with a great adventurer.

Nate and Liam looked like kids entering their first candy store. Emelia held herself with professional grace, but her eyes shone with glee.

People watching the great office ran out of the guild. They were going to spread the news and make Joey's status official.

A great adventurer was fully public in New Zam City, and everything was going to change big time.

34. A MOMENT OF REFLECTION

Joey was puking his guts out in the great management restroom.

The office for great adventurers had everything at the most luxurious level. The countertops for the sinks were marble, with silver engravings swirling around. The mirror looked heavy and expensive.

Joey stared at his bloody reflection while it was framed by big and bold designs on the edges. Then he bowed his head and dry heaved into the sink some more.

He should have used the toilet. But the sinks were the closest to the door when he'd entered.

He had the faucets running to help drain down the mess and cover the noise of his puking. To his fortune, the sinks had magic. The mess washed away easily.

Joey stared at the running water, leaning on the countertops while in a mental fog. His own thoughts came out slow.

I killed thirty men. I ended them forever.

That was heavy to take in. Once things became more stable and safe inside the great management office, Joey had reflected.

The horror of what he'd become struck him. So here he was, dealing with it, trying to figure out how to go forward.

It was hard.

It was really, really hard.

He was more conscious of himself as a person than he wished. He'd never considered himself an upright person. He was more of a desperate survivor than anything else.

But he'd rarely hurt other people before Multiverse Z. Then after thirty days of being a rogue of the multiverse, he'd showed up to a land with other humans and started orchestrating their murders left and right.

It all felt like a game.

But the thugs dying forever had been a lot to take in for Joey.

"Did Anthony deserve what I did?" Joey asked himself. "Or maybe that's just how it is."

He'd made an example of Anthony for a reason. He'd slaughtered the thugs for a reason. It was all supposed to be rational.

Letting the commoners abuse their protective status felt like a hole that needed plugging. And Domer was behind it all.

Joey was ready to fight Domer on everything, from the bottom to the top. Not for a righteous cause. But because Joey wanted to achieve, grow, and further his greatness. And Domer felt like a worthy challenge.

"But if I'm really a monster, I shouldn't feel anything,"

Joey said. "Am I being soft right now? Should I even reflect on this?"

"It's a good thing to reflect! It shows you're more thoughtful of your actions than a mere beast," said a deep and suave voice.

Joey jumped from the sink counter. His movements felt lethargic while his mind was still catching up with him.

He had a kunai in hand, but he didn't feel ready to fight. If the guild manager had been an enemy, Joey might've died.

The epic elf raised his hands in peace. "Calm down, calm down. You've been through a lot, Joey boy."

"You got in here without me noticing." Joey pointed his knife at the manager.

"Can you blame me? I'm so excited to have you here. You've been teasing me for too long, Joey! Way too long!" The manager spread his arms wide and let out a big and booming laugh.

Joey glowered at him, his mood dimming. He was still in a bad funk from the thug massacre. The manager just felt way too cheery.

"I should've made you wait longer," Joey said.

"Oh, that would have driven me up the walls. I might've chased you down by then."

"I would run. I'll get on a boat and sail the tides."

"Joey boy! Don't be that way!" The guild manager was tall for an elf. And he was built like a weightlifter. Everything about him was loud and proud. "You know we had to meet up sooner or later. Something tells me you're going to make things very interesting. Very, very interesting."

Joey huffed, feeling drained. It wasn't the guild

manager's fault. The guy had been nothing but helpful and cheery.

He'd been waiting for a great adventurer to show up for a while. But Joey needed time to recollect himself.

"Give me an hour. Please."

"Alright, sorry, I'm just so darn excited. But I'll give you an hour or two or even three. I'll entertain your steady ones in the meantime, okay? Once you're ready, we'll go over your quest results and then talk shop from there."

The guild manager moved for the door.

"Wait." Joey straightened. "Your name."

"Oh! Pardon me. Where are my manners?" The guild manager bowed. "I am Finnuili Finnroris of the Frivolous Forest Realm! But everyone calls me Finn."

"Alright, Finn. We'll talk soon."

Finn beamed a great smile before exiting the restroom. Joey watched the door closed before finding a cool wall and sitting against it.

He thought about using Mediative Stasis, but decided not to. He ignored Stress Management. He didn't quite stew in his bad feelings. He just let himself sit and rest until the words he wanted to say came up.

"I am doing the best I can for myself," Joey said. "Harsh. Domineering. Horrible. But also fearless, determined, and brave. There are lots of negatives. But there are positives, too. It's like Nate said, right? I'm not a bad person. Or a bad monster."

Joey tilted his head as he looked at things logically. "And I was up against hundreds of people that wanted to end me while not knowing their full rights."

Joey nodded. "Could I have talked to them?" He shook his head. "Nah. Multiverse Z is a place where might makes right. Little talk. All action. Or at least that's what I've seen so far."

He looked at his hands before glancing at his swaying tail. "I'll cross lines. I'll show my enemies I'm not afraid. And I'll fight almost anyone. But in the end, it's not for no reason. Selfish, sure. But I can live with that."

Joey let the silence fall into place again. But this time, he felt way better. He hadn't known if the self-talk would work. But he'd done it before.

This was how he'd kept going before Multiverse Z. Even now, with all the power he had, looking back at the times before Multiverse Z made Joey feel a little emotional.

He'd been so powerless back then. With little hope. He'd been a living zombie, clinging to unlife. No wonder he was willing to push himself hard with this new opportunity for greatness.

I don't want to go back. I don't want to become anything less than great. I will fight tooth and nail before I fall.

Anthony and his thugs reminded Joey of the times before reaching Multiverse Z. They were like everyone who'd preyed on Joey when he was a weak and defenseless guy.

I wonder if the princess has her moments where she's tripping on her power. Then again, she's probably used to having all that power where it becomes the norm.

Joey was still getting used to his power. In the grand scheme of things, he hadn't been doing this for long.

For a moment, he almost imagined himself slowing down a bit to smell the roses. But then he shook his head.

He could slow down when he was dead. They could grow

a rose bush over his grave at that point.

He had a devil to torment and kill.

He had the Dread Whale to slay.

He had a relentless war princess to defeat in a proper duel.

There were achievements, his Level 100 ascension, and more powers waiting for him.

"Let's go, Joey," said the rogue of the multiverse. "Let's go."

He used the wall to get back to his feet. He swayed slightly, feeling a little woozy. All that reflecting had done a number on him. But after a few steps, he felt better and recomposed.

Joey revisited the sink and washed the blood off his face and hair. He washed out his mouth with water.

The bodysuit would clean itself once fed essence, which was one of its enchantments. In fact, since he was here, Joey gave himself another look over. He used Analyze on his superior quality gifts.

[War Prince Bodysuit – Charmer (Superior): This charm version is enchanted to be showy while enhancing the wearer's mental manipulations of others, especially an audience. It can resist lower quality attacks decently. It will clean and repair itself when given essence.]

[War Prince Boots (Superior): Your steps with these boots will find superior footing even on slippery or horrible terrain. Constricting binds of lower quality will slip off your boots. Use essence to activate the water walking enchantment.]

[War Prince Item Holder Harness (Superior): The

harness, belts, scabbards, and all that's connected are enchanted to refuse the stealing of the wearer's items. The enchantments help slide items back where they belong and keep them there. They will also repair small damages on weapons when given essence.]

[War Prince Short Swords (Superior): This pair of swords come at different sizes but share similar enchantments. They are made to weather harsh conditions of similar quality or lower. Enhance the duration of alchemy coatings with essence.]

[War Prince Kunais (Superior): These four knives have multiple uses. Weighted for both throwing and knife fighting. Can be used to dig, embed, hook onto an edge, and more. Extend a magic aura from each kunai with essence, granting farther reach and cutting length.]

Joey grinned at himself in the mirror. He was still having trouble believing Princess Maylolee would load him up with so much high-quality gear.

And they're all tied to being a war prince. What is that supposed to mean?

Joey had asked his battlemaid about it. Her response: "You're her equal, Master Eclipse."

The rogue felt honored and more. He also felt bothered by how Maylolee would go all out for him even when they could become future rivals.

One could say she was using him to free herself from her throne before tossing him aside. But Joey wondered if Maylolee respected him a lot and wanted to help.

She's been the only great one for a while. This is her way of connecting with someone else who truly understands her.

Joey readjusted the pistol holsters on his belt – the only

basic holders. Thankfully, the magic on the entire harness included the pistols. The magic guns were still a weak-link for not having superior holsters, but they weren't easy to remove without Joey's say so.

He nodded at himself as he used his essence to clean the white bodysuit. He had no need for the blood now.

Word of his greatness and his deeds would spread. His Dominator skill and charmer suit would find it easier to manipulate the masses.

Thankfully, the charm ability was passive. Superior quality stuff required superior essence costs when going active, which was around 10 EP a second.

It was an atrocious expense to activate any of this gear. But the enchantments worked quickly and effectively. His bodysuit became clean and pristine again.

I wonder what alchemy coatings I should use on the swords. Joey tilted his head to the side. *Would that be important against certain monsters that have specific weaknesses?*

That might be something worth considering in the next realm. Having a way to coat weapons with different alchemical effects was a fun magical concept, too.

The ninja knives were already useful, but having the ability to extend a magic edge could catch enemies by surprise. His Slick Knife Tricks would become a greater terror.

His boots were perfect for when Joey and the Renegades turned their attention off land. And he had the other bodysuits with their special enchantments to try out, [**War Prince Bodysuit – Hunter**] and [**War Prince Bodysuit – Assassin**].

"Darn it," Joey said to the restroom mirror. "I'm not sure if it's the princess who owes me, or if it's me who still owes the princess."

The dragon in him was unsure now. But that was fine with the rogue. He could use all the help he could get for his next stunt. It would be the craziest one yet.

But first things first, his system messages. Then the crystal ball correspondence.

35. MONSTROUS AND POPULAR

Joey exited the restroom and entered a shining hallway. Bright lights. Shiny marble flooring. The paintings on the walls looked expensive.

They were all portraits of different people with different magical themes. Joey looked at one with a renaissance woman surrounded by golden birds and a whirlwind of gold feathers.

"A great one?" Joey asked aloud. "We're all wildly different, aren't we?"

Joey felt more excitement to find other greats like him and Princess Maylolee. They could be anywhere around the beginner challenge area. He needed to reach as many as he could.

"If they come here and hear of me, I wonder if my deeds will draw them in or scare them away," Joey said, looking at his system messages. "Hopefully, it'll draw them."

[You've slain thirty Basic Human Thugs ranging from lvl 19 to lvl 30!]

There it is. No experience for slaying weaklings. But I can put this behind me and move forward. Joey nodded to himself and moved onto the next.

[You've slain twenty Semblances ranging from lvl 44 to lvl 56! Experience awarded!]

[You've slain forty-four Basic Humans ranging from lvl 45 to lvl 54! Experience awarded!]

[You've slain a Basic Human Cleric lvl 55! Experience awarded!]

"Thanks for compiling all of this for an easy read, System," Joey said before moving onto his gains.

[You've leveled up Shade Dragon Rogue from 46 to 51!]

[You've raised your mind from 130 to 140!]

[You've raised your body from 130 to 140!]

[You've raised your spirit from 133 to 138!]

[You've raised your free points from 0 to 15!]

Joey felt the initial temptation to dump free points into spirit. He held off because there was another system message waiting for him. A trade.

[Congrats! You have the opportunity to trade the Stress Management Skill for the Monstrous Momentum Skill!]

Joey froze, feeling anxious over the possible loss of Stress Management. He'd leaned on it a lot. But for the system to ask for a trade like this meant Monstrous Momentum was a good skill.

He reread over the old skill.

[Stress Management (Basic): Instead of letting stressors dictate your emotions, placate them as best you can. This will not eliminate all stress, but help mitigate it. *Best way to deal with stress is to stuff it down a hole and hope it never blows. Ever since I started doing that, I've been the most sane man who can claim to be sane!*]

Joey slowly swayed his head from side to side. "This is another test. If I give up Stress Management, then I'll have to grapple with my emotions for sure. Would that stop me?"

This had Joey wondering if he could master his emotions without the Stress Management skill. He had Meditative Stasis he could lean on, which cleared his mind better than Stress Management.

Maybe I have all I need to temper my mind, especially when I can move forward after what I've done today.

Joey slowly nodded to himself before checking the new skill.

[**Monstrous Momentum (Basic): You don't know how to stop. Especially when killing and scaring your enemies. Keep up this brutal momentum and see your endurance raised little by little passively.** *I didn't think one man could make a difference against an army. It ain't possible, I said. Then I watched him butcher them. And he wouldn't stop until he was all out of essence. That was enough to win the battle.*]

Joey wondered if this would have an effect on his essence supply. Then he reasoned it wouldn't. That would break the system's careful parameters.

Instead, he figured this would affect the conditions that slowed him the most: physical endurance and magical endurance.

It could count toward health, too, can't it? Having more endurance means you can take a few more hits. If so, this would synergize with Roll with the Hits.

[**Roll With The Hits (Basic): The attacks are coming. And you can't avoid them all. Endure what you can. Lessen**

the damages with deceptive movements. *I could've sworn I was hitting this guy with everything I have. But then my sword arm gets tired, and he attacks like he's never been hit!*]

If these two skills could synergize, Monstrous Momentum would go from an incredible skill to absolutely needed. And it was passive and without EP cost, which was rare.

It would make sense to receive something like Monstrous Momentum only after accomplishing big feats.

No wonder he needed to trade a skill to get this one.

Was this a sign the system wanted him to become more of a monster?

"I have to focus my stats in a different direction now," Joey said. "Temporarily."

[Congrats! You've traded the Stress Management Skill for the Monstrous Momentum Skill!]

[You've raised your mind from 140 to 150!]

[You've raised your spirit from 138 to 143!]

I have a lot of tricks from my skills, spells, and items. And I have a group who'll revolve around me. I need to leverage my focused mind to use everything as best I can.

Joey felt his decisions so far had been good ones. The other stats could catch up later. Body might lag behind for a little while, but his skills would help in that area.

He could feel his mind readjusting the most, becoming tingly with the changes. His focus sharpened. He was able to sense more around him and keep track of what he could do if a fight broke out.

Satisfied by this, Joey raised a fist to celebrate himself. He'd crossed the halfway point to Level 100.

Leveling up would become harder now. The challenges at the level 50s and beyond would become tougher, too.

But he was now at the level where he could hunt down hull crusher bruisers like they were mere grunts. And better yet, he was not far from completing a few achievements.

[#5 – Slay 100 steady adventurers above your level! 87/100.]

Thirteen more to go. I bet Domer and his best guys could satisfy this. Or random adventurers who get in my way.

Joey wore a feral smile before looking back at the portraits.

"What type of great one were you?" Joey asked the renaissance woman of gold birds and feathers. Her portrait didn't reply. "Were you savage? Petty? Super duper good? I wouldn't know what to think if I'm an outlier for even great ones."

Still no response, but that was fine. Joey let out a happy sigh before moving down the hall.

Laughter and excited voices sounded from the hallway down to his right. The guild's manager's office also worked as a personal lobby area where people could look inside from the wider guild lobby.

Joey wondered how many adventurers were camping outside and looking in with wonder and envy. Thankfully, the crystal ball section was in a private room in the opposite direction. He found a seat in front of the pink and purple glassy ball and accessed his account.

A message was waiting for him in his inbox. It was from Princess Maylolee. Feeling thrilled and anxious, Joey opened the message.

A humongous wall of text popped up. It was easily five times as big as the message he'd sent Maylolee. And it was written in a very dry, factual, nearly militant account of her views, day-by-day activities, and opinions of Joey's statements and questions.

She even had neatly indented subsections referring to the deeper parts of her thoughts. It was the work of an academic genius, and most people would've grown bored to death trying to read it.

Strangely, Joey found it entertaining.

"She's one-hundred percent being herself, huh?" He pulled up another chair to prop his feet on, readjusted his weapons, and got comfy.

He read it all. He imagined everything Maylolee was telling him.

Parts of it were fun, and parts of it were brutal. She even admitted to making mistakes all the time. She cost trainees their time when they needed to recover longer from her drills.

She admitted to her faults a lot, but she also spoke of some fun accomplishments – she killed another five floorwalkers. She liked culling them for fun. She could swim and fight at the bottom of the tides just fine, too, which was crazy to think about since she would need magic to endure the water pressure.

The meat from floorwalkers was given out across the city. The bones were being fashioned into new crafting projects and structures. She added some giant teeth to her throne.

Why?

She figured looking more ferocious was an efficient reason to decorate her throne while fighting boredom.

She also spoke about their short time together having felt like a dream that went too fast. She wanted more training sessions with Joey.

She even admitted to feeling regretful over refusing his offer to have a day off. She would make it up to him by asking him to accompany her to the best places.

"I do not have the words. What do you say to a princess who asks you out? Let me check my calendar?" Joey shook his head as he took his time to think of a reply.

He wasn't going to go for something uber long. But he was going to be himself as always, which was the important part. He wrote about his latest experiences and his opinions on her most interesting talking points.

Now and then, Joey would save the draft of his message and go back to rereading Maylolee's words. It was fun rediscovering things he glossed over earlier.

He especially liked her complimenting his actions to invade and take over New Zam City. She forgave the deaths. And she was happy he could grow so fast and deadly while finding exploits that worked for him.

Apparently, magic guns were nothing new. They were simply unreliable for most others. She even had some of her own.

Nice! Magic gun duels are a thing. Joey chuckled as he kept writing and editing until he finally sent his reply off.

The rogue sighed and enjoyed the peace and quiet. It was nice. Especially after reading and replying to the princess's message.

It didn't feel like she was trying to manipulate him. She was brutally earnest. Maybe even a little more eager than she was willing to admit.

All the help she was giving him was both for her benefit and for his.

"Well, whoever owes who will be accounted for eventually," Joey said. "We're definitely on the same page. In fact, I've never been able to vibe with someone so well before. Even when we're completely different people from completely different universes. I guess that's Multiverse Z for you."

Joey exited the room, a lazy smile on his face. He entered the main office area and looked at the exit.

Hundreds of adventurers crowded the big lobby area outside the great office, staring in. He turned away from them and smiled at his Renegades having coffee and snacks with the guild manager.

"And look who it is! The man of the hour!" Finn cheered. "Come on down here, Joey. Let's get your quest results out of the way and have some real fun."

36. A REQUEST TO KILL A VILLAIN

"Does that taste any good?" Joey asked, pointing at the platter of snacks on the manager's desk.

Nate looked up, his cheeks bulging like a middle-aged chipmunk. The man's stuffed face was probably a trustworthy sign. And the cut sandwiches, cookies, chocolate bars, and other snacks smelled good.

"I guess I'll indulge a little," Joey said.

"Indulge a little, my butt. Have at it, dude." Liam tossed some snacks on a plate and set it in front of the middle chair. Finn was already pouring coffee into a cup for Joey. The rogue sat in the middle of his group, directly opposite of the guild manager.

Joey chewed on a sandwich and enjoyed the taste. The bread, cheese, and cut meat were good. He didn't mind it being cold, either.

Chasing it with coffee was nice. Now that stress management was gone, Joey sampled each snack slowly and with purpose. He figured enjoying simple pleasures in between the action would become more worthwhile for him.

"You're looking good, Joey," Finn said. "I forgot to compliment your style. That's impressive superior quality gear. Tailored by the infamous war princess, I imagine."

"You can see?" Joey asked. So far, Analyze didn't work on other people's gear unless he touched the items.

"My unique role allows me to see a lot of things. And I am pretty high up there in level. But don't worry, I won't go digging too deep into your affairs with an infamous princess."

"Good thing you don't," Liam quipped. "Joey makes it sound like a nice night out for them is murdering each other."

Finn blinked a few times before erupting in cheer. "Isn't that the best way to judge another great one you admire? Good! Good! You young ones know how to get straight to the point."

"I can't say if I'm young compared to you," Emelia said. "But I do like to move things along, even as a steady one. I'm thrilled to hear about the results."

"Sure, let's get to it!"

Finn waved his hand. Ten quests with results appeared one after the other in front of Joey. They scrolled down as they evaluated and gave verdicts.

[**Congrats! You've accomplished a New Zam City Quest: Watch the Horns! (Difficulty: Level 45)!** *Adventurers, we've been having issues with jungle buffalos attacking our gatherers near water areas. Please be aware of their horn magic. It lets them shoot beams from their horns. Killing five as a group would be fair.*

Conducting quest results evaluation!

Did you do poorly? No.

Did you do well? No.

Did you do great? ... ... Yes!]

No experience for Joey. He was too high leveled now. But the group had gained a lot from killing twenty of those buffaloes. Nate had tanked a good amount of damage from those beams and practiced pushing through pain while healing himself.

The Night Time Danger quest came up as a Level 46 quest. They had killed fifteen of them, which led to great results. Liam had honed his night time shooting skills from that quest. Emelia had gotten better at dodging dive attacks while casting spells.

Joey nodded despite the lack of gains for himself. That was fine. All he wanted to see were great results with each quest evaluation.

He hadn't been there for some of them, honestly. Mollysea had overseen most of the group's activities, while Joey stayed focused on his personal training. He had participated in the last quest since it was the hardest on the list.

[Congrats! You've accomplished a New Zam City Quest: **Rumble on the Foothills! (Difficulty: Level 55)**! *Adventurers, the killer gorillas are leaving the foothills and attacking low level adventurers. Please be aware of their punching magic, extreme toughness, and healing abilities. Killing one of them would be fair.*

Conducting quest results evaluation!

Did you do poorly? No.

Did you do well? No.

Did you do great? ... ... Yes!

For accomplishing great results on a quest four levels above you, double bonus experience is awarded!]

Joey waved off the last quest evaluation, satisfied with all the results. The last one was the most deserving.

They'd killed five of those gorillas, and Joey had handled two of them by himself. *Those were some tough gorillas.*

The more important part was the achievement.

[#1 – Get 10 great results on quests! 11/10.]

The hidden quest for beating the princess counted toward my score. Joey still wanted to do ten at New Zam City just in case. And it did wonders for his group.

"So many levels!" Nate shouted.

"It was ten or so days ago when we were just hitting Level 30," Liam said in amazement. "Look at us now."

Emelia had nothing to say. But she did have a smile on her face while staring at open space – she was moving around her free points, most likely.

Joey used Analyze to see his group's progress.

[Multiverse Adventurer: Basic Human: Archer lvl 46.]

[Multiverse Adventurer: Basic Human: Cleric lvl 46.]

[Multiverse Adventurer: Basic Human: Mage lvl 46.]

Nice! I didn't get much from the quests, but it worked wonders for them. That was fair, in Joey's opinion. He'd gained a lot from slaughtering Domer's People.

He could see his steady ones were brimming with new power. They were more confident of themselves because of their introduction to war siren training and tactics. And they had the levels and stats to back it up. *My renegades are becoming more dangerous.*

And they were becoming richer.

Joey froze when he saw four coins that shone silver. There was one in front of each group member.

"Ay dios mío!" Emelia shouted. *Oh, my god!* That was a very appropriate thing to say in Spanish. In front of them was a huge fortune for a beginner challenge in a lesser realm.

"Is that for us?" Nate pointed with a shaky finger at the silver coins.

Finn's eyes gleamed with humor. "Want me to take them back?"

"No!" the entire group shouted, seizing their coins.

[Congrats! You've looted 1 Tidal Moon Silver Coin!]

"Does everyone get this if they get ten great quest results?" Joey asked.

"This is more than usual. Since I'm the guild manager, I can be flexible about the range."

"I've noticed," Emelia said, glancing from the coin in her hand to Joey. "Everything you touch is going to turn to death and gold, child."

"I do like to kill and loot." Joey shrugged like it was the most normal thing to say. "And I'm eighteen."

Liam nearly fell out of his chair as he barked with wild laughter. He held up his silver coin like it was the lotto ticket. "The secret to success is finding a shady teenager who kills and loots!"

"I'm going to the gnome inn. Damn it all if it's five bronzes a night! I want the gnomish luxury!" Nate held his silver coin like it was the most precious thing ever.

Joey chuckled. One silver coin was one hundred bronze coins. That sort of fortune in a place like New Zam City was major. Yet, the guild manager seemed to have spares lying around.

Another silver coin appeared in front of Joey. The rogue looked from the coin to the guild manager, eyebrow raised.

Finn waggled his eyebrows. "Oh, come now. Can't you guess what that's for? We've literally put your greatness at risk. Twice!"

One silver coin for two city-wide pvp battles, with my group being outnumbered. The rest of the group watched as Joey became two silver coins richer than minutes prior.

Joey wondered if he should ask for more, but decided against it. He needed all the goodwill in the realm for what he wanted next.

"Is there anything else that comes from completing an achievement?" Emelia asked.

"The High Moon Achievement List is an all-or-nothing list. In fact, you're only getting the silver coins since the quests are tied with the guild. Everything else is up to you to achieve before ascension."

"To be honest with you, [#5] is kind of hard," Liam said. "It's great we're Level 46, but the higher we level, the harder it becomes to find steady ones higher than us."

"Tell the Tidal Moon Lord that." Finn spread his hands. "He came up with the list. Though, he can be a bit prickly when it comes to criticism. He doesn't take it well."

"Isn't he what we can consider ... a god?" Emelia asked.

"He's divine, that's for sure." Finn waved a hand as if it was no big deal. "Depending on what Joey has for me, we might even get to bug him a little. It's always fun annoying Realm Lords and Ladies. Unless they try to smite you. I had this one Realm Lady who really didn't like me. Fun times back in the Caravan Necropolis Realm."

Joey whistled as the group eyed Finn with open shock. The guild manager clearly knew a lot regarding the makeup of Multiverse Z. Was that because he was two realms higher?

[Multiverse Denizen: Epic Elf: Guild Manager lvl ???]

"Alright, I'll dig. What's your level?" Liam asked.

"Ha! I'm easy, but not that easy!" Finn grinned. "Now, let's get to the main course. Oh! I'm so excited!"

The epic elf rubbed his hands together and leveled his gaze at Joey. The rogue could feel everyone looking at him now.

The first step is always the hardest. Joey's dragon greed flared inside of him. He suppressed it because he needed to flip the script.

He had to go into battle … against his own group. And he needed total victory.

Joey put aside his pride and fell to a knee.

"What is he doing?" Nate asked the others.

"Joey, stop!" Liam shouted.

Emelia sighed.

"Emelia, Liam, Nate. I need your help." Joey looked up at the older adults with trembling eyes. "I need your silver coins. Please. It will help with the next part."

"You are too much." Emelia gave up her coin.

"Bro, come on?" Liam winced as he looked into Joey's eyes. "You can't go from being scary to being sweet. That's just not how … oh, don't you give me that look. No! No, no, no. Ugh. Fine." Liam gave up his coin.

Nate sobbed like a big baby, babbling over the loss of the gnomish inn stay. It looked like he was being physically hurt as he handed over his silver coin. Liam had to give the man a brotherly hug.

"Thanks, guys!" Joey hopped back into his seat with a broad smile. His group looked at him like he'd grown devil horns.

[Congrats! You've looted 3 Tidal Moon Silver Coins!]

"Wow." Finn laughed. "Now that's how you play people for suckers!"

"Oh, I'm just getting started." Joey looked back at the crowded lobby.

"They can't hear what's inside," Finn said. "And I've set the barrier to cloud their vision. To them, we look like blobs."

"Good." Joey unattached a pouch from his belt and set it down on the desk. It clacked loudly. Then he spread out the silver coins. "Five silver coins. Sixty-five bronze coins. This is my offer."

"Normally, Joey boy, people would be informed of what's being requested before you give out the coins." The guild manager sat back with a coffee mug. He took a slow sip. "But I like your style. It interests me. Keep going."

"I need a job done, Finn. It's a big job." Joey spoke roughly, as if he was a crime boss. Since he was asking for something crazy, he might as well act crazy. "I need someone to have their number punched. But that someone isn't going to make things easy."

Finn leaned forward. He was clearly captivated. "Well, you see, Joey boy, the guild is pretty good at putting out requests and finding some willing hands." Finn glanced at the amount on the table. "There are going to be a lot of willing hands."

"I get that, Finn, I get that. But I need the guild to put something up, too. I need more on the table. And it needs to reach out to every adventurer in the beginner challenge area."

"Every adventurer?"

"That's what I said, Finn. You keeping up?"

The epic guild manager's eyes opened wide, mouth agape. As if the basic rogue had slapped him.

"I'm glad we have snacks," Liam said to Nate. "This is like a good movie."

Nate was too busy staring at the coins on the table to respond. Emelia was deeply focused on the conversation between Joey and Finn. Granted, her background came from business.

Finn placed his mug down. "Okay, now you've gone from having my interest to exceeding my expectations. Who is it that you want murdered that badly? Domer? You sure you can't handle that yourself? Or is this you trying to motivate everyone to go after the Dread Whale? That could work, but you might get people rushing that quest when they're not ready for it."

Joey shook his head. "Come on, Finn! Come on! I thought you were on my level!"

"I'm only a guild manager! You're killing me, Joey. Who is it? What is it? Let me know! Help me so I can help you!"

Joey slapped his hands down on the desk and leaned forward. He had a dark expression on his face. Everyone was leaning on the edge of their seats, waiting for him to give a name for the hit job.

"This person is not even a person. He's a creature. A monster. We need him eliminated. We have to put up as many coins as we can for this job. And it needs to be done within … twenty days. We'll give the adventurers that long. Or the coins are going to the inhuman, psychotic, twisted, vile, fiendish villain who may grow unstoppable if he succeeds."

Finn could barely speak, his hands clenched together. "Who is he?"

"Who else can he be?" The rogue smirked. "Other than me, Joey Eclipse."

There was no better bait, after all. If Joey wanted to gather as much attention from all the best adventurers, he would have to use himself and hope the guild backed it up with a ridiculous monetary reward.

37. THE SLAUGHTER AT THE GUILD

Finn spent the next half an hour rolling across the floor, roaring with laughter. The elf had tears in his eyes. It became a little dangerous when he slapped down and shook the entire office with his epic power.

Once the guild manager calmed down, he added fifteen silver coins to the pile – raising it to twenty. Nate was turning pale from all the fortune on the desk.

Finn took the bronze coins as a 'small' fee for the guild's services. Nobody was really paying attention to that other than Emelia.

Finn also helped Joey iron out some details the rogue hadn't thought about. For one, Finn suggested changing the quest to a capture or kill model.

Capture Joey Eclipse for twenty silver coins.

Or kill and provide proof for ten silver coins.

He also suggested Joey's group couldn't claim anything if Joey didn't win the twenty-day quest. This helped the group steer clear of potential betrayal.

As ugly as that sounded, Emelia agreed to the added measure. Joey had kept this idea to himself, so his group was blindsided along with the guild manager. And twenty silver coins was a lot of money in this realm.

With the details ironed out, a magic contract was signed by Joey and the guild manager using their essence. Part of the contract included some nifty things provided to the Renegades.

The group received time to shower and rest on cots in the management office. Then Finn gave the steady ones upgrades to their gear. The stuff was still basic quality, but at the higher end.

A new bow for Liam. Nate had a round shield to go with a new mace. And Emelia received a new staff. They all gained light but durable leathers with a chest plate each.

They took the night and morning off before Finn prepared a teleportation ritual. Emelia, Liam, and Nate would go into the jungle and get staged.

Joey waved his group farewell and promised to see them later. They flashed away in a burst of light that reminded Joey of how nifty magic could be.

Then the rogue lounged around and chatted with the guild manager, learning a little more about the state of the beginner challenge area across New Zam City and all the major adventurer hubs. This generation moved faster compared to the last, apparently.

There were great ones making themselves known in other hubs, too, which was exciting for Joey to hear. While New Zam City wasn't the largest, it was the most important hub for its location near the eastern tides and the challenges there.

Finn was the Head Guild Manager, so all the other managers answered to him. Learning all of this gave Joey an appreciation of the broad scale of this operation. It was a lot to take in when considering the initiation of a bunch of new humans to Multiverse Z.

There were some things Finn wasn't willing to talk about. He avoided questions about devils and dungeons, for example. He also denied answering specific system questions and what was happening up top.

He'd spoken of the Tidal Moon Lord like the guy in charge of the realm was no big deal. So Joey assumed there were more powerful beings in control of everything.

He was certainly onto something when Finn diverted the questions about the true rulers of Multiverse Z. Joey wondered who could be at the top of it all and how powerful could they be.

Other than that, the two went over music from Earth, going from classic rock and hip hop to notable selections from the 2000s. They did not agree on which songs would work better for the start of the event. But they did agree to play music in the lobby area to set the mood leading up to the event.

The hunt for Joey would not start until sunset this evening. But the guild was already prepping the denizens at every adventurer hub city and town all around the challenge area.

A constant stream of messages popped up on Finn's crystal ball. The multiverse denizens were excited. They were passing that excitement onto their adventurers without giving away the exact details. They promised all adventurers a big announcement at sunset.

"Joey," Finn called while smoking a cigar, "this will be the greatest event I'll witness at your level. I'm putting that out there because I've been around for a few thousand years and seen quite a bit. Even if you fail, this will be noteworthy."

"And if I succeed?" Joey asked, sitting across from the guild manager at his desk. They'd been playing cards, and the guild manager kept winning.

As Finn pondered on Joey's question, another song filled with hype and badass lyrics played in the background.

The lobby was filled with excited adventurers. The atmosphere was amped up higher than ever. It was electric. And it could all lead to the end of Joey Eclipse as a great adventurer.

"I'm not sure," Finn said, blowing smoke rings. "Again, something like this has never happened at your level. From my experience, that is."

"Hm. You know, it's interesting how this whole initiation to Multiverse Z is so game-like but dangerous," Joey said. "It offers new chances. New opportunities. But it doesn't offer the best to everyone. The system seems to be selective. But I can't say if that's right or wrong."

Joey leaned back in his chair. "But I will say this. This all makes me think the creators or the people in charge want to see the best spectacles from the best prospects. We're gladiators in a multiverse-wide coliseum. I can see why most people would dislike that. Especially when we have no idea what happened to our original world. What of the kids and all that? Or the elderly? Or the families?"

Joey leaned forward, looking deep into Finn's eyes. "It looks like the initiates here are people with little back home. Still, that'll raise concerns for some people. But for other people, for people like me, this is pretty ... amazing."

Finn kept smoking his cigar, saying nothing.

"Anyway, I'm only trying to get the attention of the best steady and great adventurers," Joey continued. "And this is the best way I can imagine doing it. Greed and greatness. All or nothing."

"And people like you are the reason why I left home," Finn said. "There's nobody like you back there."

"The Frivolous Forest Realm sounds nice," Joey said.

"It certainly is! I would've been a wood carver like my father, and my father's father, and the whole generational line before me. But I wanted more than that. So here I am, with you, Joey, ready to see you wow the masses and go out in a blaze of glory."

Joey smiled, knowing he had to wrestle with his own anxiety without a skill's help. He was missing stress management already.

But he knew deep down once the action started, he wouldn't worry anymore. He would simply put out his best performance.

"I can't fail," Joey said, placing the cards down. There was an old grandfather clock against the wall. Sunset was soon. "You hear me, Finn. I cannot fail."

The guild manager nodded slowly. "The odds are against you with something like this. And the guild is inclined to give adventurers as much help as they'll need."

Joey gave the guild manager a wild grin. "So it's me against everyone you got in the beginner challenge area, huh?"

The rogue snorted. "I don't know about those odds you're talking about. From what I can see, I'm the favorite."

Finn roared with laughter, holding nothing back.

Joey could appreciate how the guild manager lived

his Multiverse Z existence to the max. The multiverse was probably filled with madmen and crazy women and horrible monsters who existed for the sake of being true to themselves.

I can roll with some parts of it. And other parts require some killing and looting.

Joey looked at the clock again. It was almost time. He gave the guild manager a nod. Finn returned a two-finger salute as he continued to smoke his cigar.

A new song filled with hype and atmosphere played from the crystal speakers around the guild. Joey paid attention and noticed a change in the lyrics compared to the version he remembered from his universe.

That slight change was almost bewildering. It gave the impression that Joey was part of a vast network of universes with countless earth copies.

What if there's nothing happening with my world? Joey thought. *What if there's so many worlds, it's easy to pick up people with little to nothing to lose and give them a welcoming to Multiverse Z? And our worlds are all so similar that it doesn't seem like nothing is adrift?*

That also meant Joey wasn't alone with living his best life in Multiverse Z. After all, there were adventurers openly talking about slaying him for achievement [#7]. Regardless of what happened to the families, children, and those with closer connections, the initiates of the Tidal Moon Realm were more inclined to do things for themselves.

Joey walked closer to the exit. He observed the different faces trying to examine him through the nearly one-way veil.

"Is that him?" said a female archer.

"The whole city is getting turned upside down because of this guy," said a male warrior with a large axe. "I wonder if he's doing this on purpose."

"What is he, some sort of mastermind?" asked a cleric with a flail and a shield. "I'll believe it if he is. He has to be a genius to destroy Domer's People. Twice!"

"Look. I'm not saying any of us can do it by ourselves. But if we work together, maybe one of us can get the [#7]. There's bound to be something amazing if you slay a great adventurer."

"Have you not heard of what he'd done to people?"

"Well, now we know. He's got no more tricks. We can take him, I bet."

No more tricks, Joey thought.

It was funny to hear that. In a sense, they had a strong point. He was out of his biggest tricks. So what came next would answer the greatest question on Joey's mind.

Do I always need tricks to win?

A new song played from the crystal speakers, the volume raised to the max. The bass was so hard the air shook near the speakers.

The big crystal ball in the guild lobby came to life. It projected a red screen with a message in bold white letters.

[Great Quest! Great Quest!

Capture and deliver Great Adventurer Joey Eclipse, the Unstoppable Renegade, for 20 Silver Coins!

Kill Great Adventurer Joey Eclipse, the Unstoppable Renegade, and provide solid proof for 10 Silver Coins!

Be warned! Joey Eclipse has the immunity clause activated. But actions against him are given immunity, as well!]

There was a split second of stillness while the music was

pounding loudly. All the adventurers in the lobby were trying to comprehend what this all meant.

Nobody other than Joey and the denizens had seen silver coins before. So it might take them an extra split-second to use their heads and convert silver to bronze.

Then they might take the time to convert that to coppers, the usual coinage the adventurers dealt with here.

In that span of time, Joey drew a single sword and summoned eleven clones armed with the same sword copy. The expense of 440 EP felt light compared to all the times he'd summoned a bunch of clones.

Joey and the shadow gang paired up into battle buddies and launched from the great office. The expense paid off quickly.

Twenty-two adventurers fell dead. Blood sprayed everywhere. All in one second.

Joey's would-be hunters started to catch on at that point.

The slaughter was just beginning. He'd managed to kill three adventurers who were over his level: a Level 52 mage, a Level 53 archer, and a Level 54 warrior. Everyone else was weaker than him, but there were at least a thousand in the lobby.

No problem.

Joey and his shadow gang tore through the adventurers with viciousness and focused intent. Their blades flashed. Blood rained. Heads and limbs rolled across the marble floor. Footing became slippery for most adventurers. Some fell over in surprise while lying in the blood puddles of their group members.

Not everyone was a target. But Joey and the gang chopped and hacked through most adventurers who got in their way.

The shadow gang maneuvered with perfect synchrony, going low and high. They weaved from side to side. They worked together to target the adventurers without tough bodies. They avoided moving in straight lines, zigging and zagging constantly.

By placing confused and panicked adventurers between each other, the shadow gang avoided retaliation. Everyone erupted into random violence and friendly fire.

Heavy sword chops. Explosive magic bolts. Rapid fire arrows. Semblances with claws extended and teeth bare.

Everything flew out in attack, but barely anything got close to Joey and his clones. The adventurers were either targeting random rogues or the strangers next to them while lost in complete chaos.

Things worked out in Joey's favor for a good while longer than he hoped. Then clones started falling left and right, signaling it was time to take his exit pronto.

He beheaded an enemy rogue with a swipe of his sword. He vaulted over a tackle from a tamer. His shadow buddy followed up just the same.

Joey and his shadow rolled across the floor under magic attacks. Then the duo rose into a sliding knee and sliced through a warrior from both sides, chopping the man in half.

Joey's shadow buddy mirrored his movements. They carved a way to the exit. They used straight physical skills with no magic.

This was the reason Joey worked hard to embed the physical aspect of his skills. His clones picked up on the physical aspects and could accomplish a lot without the magic.

This saved Joey big on EP against lesser adventurers. But

Joey knew he could only get away with so much.

After all, he was up against a thousand adventurers. He knew he would get tested.

Volleys of magic explosions erupted near the entrance. Joey left his shadow buddy behind. The explosions destroyed his buddy.

He dashed through the bombardment. He barely avoided serious damage and got knocked out of the air.

Joey fell into a hard tumble down the root-based staircase. He grunted as he rolled to a stop, silently thanking the war princess for the superior quality of his bodysuit. None of his clones made it out with him.

Joey got up on his feet and kept running.

"Get him! Get him!" roared an adventurer from the exit. "That's Joey Eclipse! That's twenty silver coins!"

There were adventurers standing around the square. The distance between Joey and the rest of the city seemed farther than ever. And there was too much space.

"Shadow gang!" Joey shouted, summoning nine clones. Each one had two Dark Dash spells, an expense of 400 EP. Now Joey was starting to feel the chill, but he gritted his teeth and endured.

A volley of arrows, magic bolts, and sword crescent waves flew in. Flying semblances dove down. Various containment zones slammed into place. Enemy rogues chased like hunters from behind.

Joey and his shadow gang dashed and weaved like daredevils through the closing net of magic and greed.

He flipped between arrow shots and explosive bolts. He side-stepped zones, rolled past sword crescents, and used diving semblances as launch pads. The shadow gang did their best to follow, but they fell one by one until Joey was alone again.

A wall of adventurers blocked off the exit from the courtyard.

A female warrior screamed, "Twenty silver coins!" Her eyes flashed with so much greed it was nearly more than Joey's. Her fellow adventurers raised their weapons and magic.

Joey dashed straight at them and revealed his tail. He avoided an overhead cut for his shoulder and beheaded the female warrior.

His tail whipped and cracked the heads of her nearest group members. He dove through the hole in their line.

A magic bomb erupted where he'd escaped from.

The adventurers exploded themselves, but the shockwave struck Joey hard in the back and sent him flying through a vegetable vendor. Wooden beams snapped. A tarp fell. Lots of produce squashed under him, mixing juices with all the blood coating him.

His bones felt rattled. His back pulsed with pain. Joey spat blood from the cut inside his cheek and forced himself to stand back on his feet. He kept running.

"Twenty silver coins!" screamed another crazed adventurer. "Come back, come back, Joey Eclipse! You are my twenty silver coins!"

Hearing something like that should scare most people. Joey couldn't help but laugh. He was already hurting and feeling chilly.

It hadn't crossed five minutes since this started. He had twenty days of this brutal game. But this was his path to greatness.

All or nothing.

38. THE HUNT FOR JOEY ECLIPSE

Joey realized quickly he had lines he wouldn't cross. He avoided areas with heavy commoner traffic. They were running amok to get to safety right now, but they were not that fast.

Mixing with them would make his escape from the city easier. But that felt wrong to the rogue – most commoners were innocent people trying to live their new existence in Multiverse Z.

He didn't want them involved in his crazy stunts.

Strangely, Joey felt very relieved by this even with all the trouble he was in. It was nice knowing he wasn't truly an evil villain.

He was merely playing a role. But having those lines he wouldn't cross meant he'd struggle and bleed more.

Hence Joey's current situation involving ninja-like fights across empty rooftops and plank bridges. Arrows flew by his head as he dodged ranged attacks and diving rogues slashing down at him.

He avoided them and the flying semblances of man-sized hawks, hornets, and the bats that used sonic attacks to stun their targets – he grappled and tossed rogues at the bats, letting them crash into each other and block the sonic attacks.

From nearby rooftops, mages hopped and flipped around while aiming their staffs and shooting bolts at him. They kept up because of their obvious imbalance in stats – these hunters favored their body a lot. Also, there were more than just stats for Joey to deal with.

Some mages pole vaulted with their staffs and used a magic blast at the end that sent them flying over large gaps between buildings. Some rogues had skills helping them chase and move faster while trying to assassinate or capture a target.

Tamers followed while pumped up for the chase because of their hunting affinity. And they could ride on top of their semblances that moved even faster than most humans.

"Joey Eclipse!" shouted a tamer on the street. He was riding on the back of a shadowstalker. "I swear I'll lend you a silver coin if you come with me! It's twenty on the line, man! Twenty silvers!"

"Come and earn it!" Joey tossed down the head of a slain rogue.

He jumped off a plank bridge and dove through a window of an office-like structure.

A flying semblance crashed into the wall near the window – it was a split second too slow from reaching him. His hand sifted through his pouches before activating and tossing a glyph tile.

The tile flashed and turned into a liquid orb.

The water bolt crashed into the rogue diving through the window behind Joey. The adventurer flew back out the same window.

Joey slowed down as he exited the business room and prowled through the halls. He wasn't far from the big gate, but he needed to catch his breath and regulate his physical and magical stamina.

Obviously, his would-be hunters wouldn't wait outside for long. Joey put away his sword and drew a single kunai.

In the next few moments, the hallway filled with rogues dressed in dark clothing.

He was the only one in white – the blood cleaned off.

"You guys know you aren't as strong as me," Joey said with a domineering smile. "But there are more of you than me. So, do you feel like you're good enough?"

[If you can get past us, you need to teach us your moves,] a female rogue said in an Asian language. [Let us see how great you are, Joey Eclipse.]

The rogues attacked at once with their short swords. The ones that had his back moved the fastest, their Backstab spell guiding them for the kill shot.

Joey's tail battled the backstabbers from behind, slicing and whipping. He dove ahead and knocked aside sword strikes with his knife and grappled with his enemies.

He gutted a rogue. He grabbed the head of another and shoved her face into a sword thrust meant for him. He grabbed another rogue by the neck – stabbed his friend in the eye – and slammed the grabbed rogue against the railings of the staircase Joey led them into.

Rogues attacked and met the vicious resistance of an unstoppable renegade, their bodies getting torn and mangled before being tossed over the railings. They fell down the chute and hit the bottom dead. Other rogues rolled down the stairs like sacks filled with potatoes.

Joey stopped his violent staircase descent when tamers and warriors crashed into the staircase from the first floor and started climbing up. He took the third floor, his tail slapping aside attackers from behind while he dragged a rogue by her hair and threw her forward into a magic bolt shot through a window.

Her body exploded like a bloody balloon filled with sausages.

He took the door to his right, stabbed an ambusher up the jaw with his kunai, and threw the corpse behind him to slow down pursuers. Then Joey dove out another window. There were adventurers waiting outside, aiming their weapons and magic upward.

"Face the champ!" Joey yelled, summoning his semblance. "Al Bruce Crabton!"

ABC slammed down on the adventurers and their semblances with a reckoning. The Level 51 hull crusher bruiser swung his massive pincers around adventurers and split them in halves. He caught a leaping shadowstalker and beheaded the feline with a quick snip. He kicked out his legs, smashing aside a cleric and stabbing through a warrior's unarmored torso.

In the meantime, Joey landed on top of his semblance as it fought and created space for them. Joey clenched his jaw, enduring the essence freeze while he gripped ABC's eyestalks like reins. They were his lifelines at this point.

"Go, Al Bruce Crabton, go!" he urged on, and his semblance listened.

ABC slapped aside bolts with his pincers and crashed into the main road leading to the big gate. He surprised the adventurers waiting there, none of them having seen a hull crusher before, let alone a bruiser.

ABC plowed through obstacles like a runaway train, punching out his pincers and reveling in the chaos. Adventurers got snapped in half, trampled, or smacked out of the way.

But those were the adventurers on the ground. The archers and mages on the walls were free to attack with little retaliation.

Joey activated all the barrier tiles he had.

Multiple bubble-like barriers layered over him. They soaked damage and broke as they endured a pounding from multiple angles.

The barriers helped ABC focus on what was in front of him instead of covering up from the top. But there weren't enough barriers for them to pass the gate and make the climb out of the basin slope without getting blasted from the rear.

Joey had to cover their tail.

Together, Joey and ABC crashed out of the big gate. The last barrier covering their heads popped. Archers and mages moved from one side of the wall to the other and aimed down at the duo.

A six second Shade Dragon Breath streamed from Joey's mouth, splashing over the top of the wall and coating the nearest adventurers in dark flames. Men and women screamed like dying animals in torturous pain.

The attacks against Joey and ABC died down quickly. All the adventurers felt the horror and dominance of Joey's ruthless power.

"Molt drive, Al Bruce Crabton. This is our chance," Joey said through chattering teeth. His channels felt so cold, he struggled not to curl up and shut down.

He struggled with one hand to pop open potion bottles and gulp down all of their contents. Essence, stamina, and health went down the hatch, helping a lot.

Meanwhile, ABC listened to his master and shedded his heavy armor. Dented, pitted, cracked pieces of ABC's shell rained down quickly, leaving a trail behind him. Little by little, the hull crusher bruiser picked up speed. His ghost flesh showed as a pinkish white color, soft and vulnerable.

But he was lightweight now. Very lightweight for his size. ABC hissed in celebration of the freedom, scuttling forward faster than his size suggested. The basin top drew closer, but the volley of arrows raining down from behind moved even quicker.

Joey wrapped his tail around one of ABC's eyestalks and held out both swords. He parried arrows that felt less dangerous. He hurled out clones as body shields for arrows that felt more dangerous, exploding them midair. The ground around them soaked arrows and explosions, shaking ABC up while avoiding direct hits.

The unstoppable renegade covered their backs all the way to the top of the basin and out of view of the gate. Joey heard hundreds of adventurers scream in anger, forced to watch the renegade ride away on top of his rare semblance.

No matter. They would group up. Tamers and rogues would lead the way. They would chase and chase. But they would have to organize first, so Joey let himself fall back and relax as ABC scuttled at full speed down the path into the jungle.

"I can't believe it. Did I actually pull that off?" Joey asked, staring at the moons and watercolor cosmos of the night sky. "I guess I did have one big trick they had no idea about. My semblance. Nice job, Al Bruce Crabton."

The hull crusher bruiser raised his pink claws and hissed in celebration once more. Clearly, ABC was just as happy as Joey with the results. The semblance finally got to have some fun and go wild – and use Molt Drive.

Finn and the Renegades had doubted Joey's decision to start from the guild. The Head Guild Manager had suggested the rogue should get a head start in the jungle with his group. But Joey had denied each attempt to urge him into having an advantage.

It wasn't great enough for him.

Joey was convinced running and killing his way out of the guild and out of New Zam City was necessary. He also knew this was a great way to test and level up Monstrous Momentum on the fly. So he was more than glad his plan worked out.

I want to leave an impression on the adventurers of this port city. And this will reach the ones who'll come from the other adventurer hubs.

It hadn't been enough for Domer's People to feel Joey's greatness. Everyone needed to feel it or have a better idea of what they were facing. That would make the hunt for him all the better.

***

"I can't believe it," Finn said, staring at a projected screen hovering over his desk. A dozen squares of crystal ball recordings from the overseers showed on the screen. They played back Joey's great escape from New Zam City.

It was up to Finn to approve which parts would get shown on an emergency update with Zelva commentating. This would go to every adventurer hub in the beginner challenge area to add fervor to the great quest.

To Finn's surprise, most of the recordings were usable.

Joey had escaped New Zam City cleanly.

If other adventurers were in his position, great or not, Finn was certain they would've used the commoners as meat shields. It would've been a dark tactic, but a logical one.

There was more goodness in the kid's heart than it seemed. Or he was so arrogant he didn't want to sully his greatness with fodder.

"One way or the other, he showed me up. I really thought starting at the guild was dumb."

Finn leaned back in his seat, still feeling stunned. Bewildered, even. He'd never seen something like that from a beginner. Not even from the greats he'd managed.

Rumors had pointed toward the War Princess being one of the outliers in this beginner initiation. The Tidal Moon Lord favored her more than greatly, in fact.

She was a rarity among great ones. Most managers would be hard pressed finding the great rarities in hundreds of realms.

Finn handled her delicately with invitations for her to come to New Zam City. She'd refused so far, which was understandable. She was seventeen with rulership over an empire.

So it was quite the surprise to have Joey show up and strut around with more advanced skill than the usual young greats and wear gear that clearly came from the war sirens. Now Joey had shown he was one of those rare great ones as well.

To have two great ones who were rarities in the same realm was insane! Impossible. Inconceivable.

"I told you, Dad," Finn muttered. "I told you this job is worth it."

Finn approved all the recordings. He'd let the commentator team figure out the best angles and views. It wouldn't take them long.

Zelva was passionate about her work. While many in her position had stopped caring and phoned it in, the all-star commentator put her heart into each update, no matter what.

Finn loved working with people who cared in Multiverse Z. There were too many who stopped caring and became dull robots.

Finn got on the live chat with his guild managers. Right on time, he received a sample video from Zelva's lightning fast production crew.

He showed his subordinates. Every one was either stunned silent or shouting in excitement as the video displayed the best angles of the great escape.

In the end, Finn and all his managers approved. Zelva hit the major crystal ball network with the video and began commentating everywhere in the beginner challenge area.

"Ladies and gentlemen," Finn said softly, "this right here is something I've never seen in my experience as a denizen in service to the multiverse. This right here is special. We have a beginner who's putting everything on the line to provide us with a great show. Something we may never see again in thousands of years."

"What if he fails?" asked a subordinate manager from Goose Town.

"Then he shall fail grandly." Finn tapped his knuckles near his crystal ball. "But what if he succeeds? His aim is to gather the best adventurers, great and steady. This could lead to the completion of that troublesome quest."

"The Dread Whale," grunted a manager from Styx Alley.

The others made unhappy noises as well.

"Exactly. So, I'm going to be square with you. I'm asking for you to gamble. I have already put down fifteen myself. I know this is–"

All at once, Finn saw financial messages from his crystal ball reporting money transfers. A silver coin here. Three silver coins there. It all added up quite quickly. Finn felt fortunate. It was truly a pleasure to work with others who were passionate gamblers like him.

Finn barely looked at the results. He transferred them to his quest givers to update the network on the bounty. It would be a good experience for their roles. Most of them had never handled such a large amount before.

Zelva received the updated bounty on the fly. Like a true worker of her craft, she handled it with cheer and flexibility. She didn't say it right away – she was good at building up anticipation – but once she was sure she had her audience's attention she said it aloud.

Sixty-six silver coins to capture. Thirty-three to prove the kill.

Finn bit the top of his knuckles, a nervous habit he shouldn't show as the Head Guild Manager. But who could blame him? That money needed to go to Joey.

But the guild had to give all adventurers help to find the unstoppable renegade. It was almost a screwy position to be in.

Working at the grand level in Multiverse Z required some flexibility and honesty. Everyone knew how angry the rulers could get when corruption was found among the multiverse denizens.

A new message popped up. It was from the Tidal Moon Lord.

[TML: Have you finally lost your mind, Finn?]

The epic elf grinned. Ah, yes, the best stress reliever he could find.

[HGM: I don't know what you're talking about. I gave a new tailor a chance two days ago. I think they did a good job with my latest wardrobe.]

[TML: I should've listened to the Caravan Necropolis Lady. You are trouble.]

[HGM: And I'm handsome, too!]

[TML: This Joey child better succeed. If this entire event ends up in failure, consider yourself retired. And don't forget. You must help the adventurers find him. We must be honest. Or else.]

Finn didn't bother replying, feeling the pressure again. He'd gotten to his position because he gambled big and won. But he'd fallen from the loftiest heights because he'd gambled big and lost. If those silver coins went to the wrong adventurer, it could screw the economics and ruin the beginner challenge.

"All or nothing," Finn said.

***

While the guild manager walked a tightrope, Joey linked up with his group and his battlemaid. They began their great journey north. The Renegades had big plans to fulfill while getting chased by desperate adventurers from a port city being left in disarray.

But this simple point of view of Joey and the Renegades could not truly expand on the size of this great quest. The ridiculous bounty was spreading everywhere around the beginner challenge area, going further than Joey could conceive at the moment.

It certainly reached steady adventurers from cities and towns across the western tides. It reached great adventurers inside and outside of these hub areas. Since this event was so large, guild semblances of flying beasts flew out while gripping crystal balls.

These items projected the news loud and clear for many miles. Great adventurers staying out in the wilderness turned their attention to the Zambwi Land.

The bounty reached Aqua Star City as fast as it reached any adventurer hub. As a ruler, Princess Maylolee could keep updated on major adventurer events through her local crystal network.

She was reading reports from the agricultural arm – bored halfway to death – when her advisor ran into the banquet room, shouting for her attention. The advisor shoved a crystal ball into her face.

Maylolee watched the recording of the commentator elf and video clips of Joey fighting his way out of New Zam City. Then she saw the bounty, knowing right away this was a scheme by Joey.

Maylolee couldn't stop herself from smiling before bursting into giggles that felt awkward and broken. She couldn't remember the last time she'd laughed.

While the War Princess wished all the best to Joey Eclipse, there were other creatures that only wished for his downfall. The monster leaders had their ways of staying updated on adventurer news. Something like this wouldn't go unnoticed by them since an adventurer could get a big bounty for their lives at any time.

All that silver was dangerous in the hands of adventurers. Joey Eclipse needed to disappear, and preferably doing so as a meal for the Monster Leaders. Thus, orders spread among the two major monster groups.

Those orders caught the attention of the water nagas who'd work for anyone, even monsters. There was no doubt the nagas could double dip if they caught the attention of adventurers with enough coins. Thus, monsters and denizens turned their attention toward the Zambwi Land, hungering for Joey Eclipse's life and the fortune attached to it.

But that wasn't the worst thing to happen in the area. The worst thing was for a certain type of slave to catch news of this giant bounty. The slave was a former adventurer equipped with enough awareness and a position to track big updates on the adventurer network.

That slave, who dreaded the displeasure of his mistress, screamed at the news of the sixty-six silver coin bounty. Then the adventurer slave exited his outpost and ran straight to an enslaved war siren unit positioned nearby. They shrieked in dread when they saw the adventurer slave.

Their dreadful screams told each other what they needed to do. They would return together to the territory of their mistress. And tell her of the suspicious update.

The Dread Whale would soon know the name of Joey Eclipse.

While that was the worst consequence for the area, this view of the event would fail to give justice to how far Joey's name would reach. Nothing like this had happened in a beginner challenge area in a long time.

Thus, Joey had caught the attention of beings outside of the realms. And such beings should not be giving attention to an initiated human whatsoever.

Yet, these outer beings looked down at the realm, ready to bear witness. This made the Tidal Moon Lord feel very nervous. Now he had to be extra honest while under heavy supervision, just like Finn.

This was indeed an all-or-nothing event for everyone involved. And Joey was at the center of it, ignorant of the grand scope of his reach and how costly his failure could be.

TO BE CONTINUED

Please don't forget to leave a review!

Thanks for reading! And check out the links below for some extra goodies:

Follow The Author On Amazon - You'll get email updates on when the next books are coming out. You might even see what drops for my newest series. *Direct Link you can Copy & Paste:* https://www.amazon.com/stores/Hunter-Mythos/author/B0BHR8YPLS

Get the next book (Rogue Ascension Book 2) here - You can pre-order to ensure you get the book as soon as it comes out. Unless it's already out. Enjoy! *Direct Link you can Copy & Paste:* https://www.amazon.com/gp/product/B0CL1338FY

Mythos Pantheon Discord - Join and talk directly with the author, have fun, and hang out. You can also use this to get updates and announcements. *Direct Link you can Copy & Paste: https://discord.gg/Ru97qXEkac*

Hunter Mythos Patreon - You can get advanced chapters of the books I'm working on and see how they progress through the

updates. You can also join this just to help
support. Thanks a lot for your support! *Direct Link you can Copy
& Paste: http://patreon.com/user?u=76776966*

BOOKS BY THIS AUTHOR

Apocalypse Comedy (Gravity And Divinity System 1)

A jokester crashes the System. He angers the gods. And he becomes more powerful with every climactic battle. A weak to strong progression with Gravity Magic.

Apocalypse Command (Gravity And Divinity System 2)

A jokester gets serious and grows from strong to OP with Gravity Magic. But that's not enough. He takes control of the System. He gets command of the Champions.

Apocalypse Crusade (Gravity And Divinity System 3)

A jokester gets angry. He grows from OP to extremely OP with Gravity Magic. He needs more power to fight the System and the evil assassin leaders. He needs a crusade.

Apocalypse Conquest (Gravity And Divinity System 4)

The world is different. Survival is a fight. And the Commander of Champions thrives in this environment. His powers can only grow stronger from here.

Apocalypse Challenge (Gravity And Divinity System 5)

The biggest war the Earth has faced ended. It's time for Jay

Luckrun to lead the fight against the Dungeon Goblins and stop them from invading their universe.

Apocalypse Change (Gravity And Divinity System 6)

When your greatest enemies are the end bosses of the apocalypse, why not become the ultimate boss yourself?

The Magic Brawler 1

Urmatia needs heroes, and John the brawler is the man who answers the call. With fists up at the ready, he punches his way through monster waves and deadly challenges with his fists and magic.

ABOUT THE AUTHOR

Hunter Mythos

Raised out of the 305, Hunter Mythos takes his pet gator out on walks and spends his weekends getting into Kung Fu matches with someone's grandmother to get the best avocado from the stores. Outside of those accounts of being your everyday Florida Man, he likes to read, watch sitcoms, and spend his time writing into existence new universes.

AUTHOR SHOUT OUT

Battleforged: Survivor: A LitRPG Apocalypse Adventure - Book 1 by M.H. Johnson.

To do list for the post apocalypse:

1. Survive the orcs rampaging through your city.

2. Survive the pod trying to steal your mind.

3. Pull off the greatest heist of all time.

Eager for a fast-paced adventure with a survivor determined to get the best of everyone trying to kill him and make a fortune while doing so? Then give Battleforged: Survivor a read.

FACEBOOK GROUPS

Join these groups to discuss LitRPG with other fans!

GameLit Society: A place to talk to other GameLit readers.
https://www.facebook.com/groups/LitRPGsociety

LitRPG & GameLit Readers: It's growing!
https://www.facebook.com/groups/940262549853662

SuperLit Book Club: Superpowers and loads of fun.
https://www.facebook.com/groups/SuperLit

LitRPG Books: This one has a big following!
https://www.facebook.com/groups/litrpgs/

LitRPG Books: This is a different group. Still a good place.
https://www.facebook.com/groups/LitRPG.books

LitRPG Legends: LitRPG, Gamelit & Progression Fantasy.
https://www.facebook.com/groups/litrpglegends
Discord: https://discord.gg/YGtjN8r

LitRPG Legion: A place to discuss your favorite LitRPGs!
https://www.facebook.com/groups/litrpglegion

LITRPPG GROUP

LitRPG Group: To learn more about LitRPG, talk to authors including myself, and just have an awesome time, please join the LitRPG Group
https://www.facebook.com/groups/LitRPGGroup

Made in the USA
Columbia, SC
27 October 2024

45134518R00288